a novel by
Robert Flynn

TCU Press • Fort Worth, Texas

Other books by Robert Flynn

North to Yesterday
In the House of the Lord
The Sounds of Rescue, the Signs of Hope
Seasonal Rain
When I was Just Your Age, (with Susan Russell)
A Personal War in Vietnam
Wanderer Springs
The Last Klick
Living With the Hyenas
The Devils Tiger
Growing Up a Sullen Baptist

Library of Congress Cataloging in Publication Data

Flynn, Robert, 1932-
Tir-fast country: a novel / by Robert Flynn
p. cm.
ISBN 0-87565-244-1 (alk. paper)
1. Women ranchers--Fiction. 2. Grandmothers--Fiction. 3. Texas, West--Fiction.
4. Aged women--Fiction. 5. Ranch life--Fiction. 6. Young men--Fiction. I. Title

PS3556.L9 T54 2001
813'.54--dc21
2001023413

Jacket illustration/Deirdre Flynn Bass
Jacket and book design/Margie Adkins Graphic Design

For Jim McMullan, Best Texas Goat Roper

Tie-Fast Country

In cattle country there are two kinds of ropers—
dally ropers wrap the rope around the saddle horn after the
catch, holding the loose end in their hand so they can let it
go if something goes wrong. Tie-fast ropers
tie the rope hard to the saddle horn and plan on
hanging on to whatever is on the other end.
Texas was tie-fast country.

1

1910

Claris McCloud was a tie-fast man. He didn't dally because he had never tossed his rope on something he couldn't hang on to. Then one day he tied onto a mossy-horned bull that was wilder than a camp meeting prayer. The longhorn nearly jerked the saddle off his horse and his horse off its feet. Claris tried to cut the stumbling horse free of the rope, but the bull came back down the rope, ran under the horse's belly, and the horse blew Claris out of the saddle.

Claris threw the knife away before he hit the ground in a pile. In the moment it took to regain his senses and breath, he realized he was alive only because the bull had attacked his horse that was tangled in the rope. Claris slid along the ground until he found his knife, cut the rope, and lay still until the bull lost interest and trotted away. Claris cut the horse's throat to end its suffering and sat beside the shuddering horse to ponder his life.

He had been born on the Indian frontier, six years before the last Comanche raid. He remembered his father, Doss McCloud, leaving a loaded rifle and six-shooter for his mother before joining other men to trail marauding Indians. He left the rifle for her to use on Indians; the pistol was to use on her children and then herself. On that last raid, Claris and his father were at the house. His mother and sister, JackieLou, were in the open picking berries.

When he was seven Claris made a hand. When he was ten, barbed wire came to the plains. When he was twelve, Claris was shot at and his horse killed while he was cutting wire that fenced off a deep hole in Six Mile Draw. When he was fourteen, his father's horse tangled in broken wire, and his father, trying to free the horse before it cut itself to pieces, was kicked to death by the spooked horse. Claris was owner of a homestead, a brand, a remuda and a herd of cattle, and range boss of a handful of cow-boys scarcely older and tougher than he.

When he was twenty, there was a drought and die-off followed by a blizzard. Farmers pulled out; most of the land wouldn't support a farm. Claris bought their land with a milk cow or a couple of steers. They were glad to have something to leave with. Sometimes he gave them another steer to plant hay on the land before they left it and wintered his cattle on the hay.

When Claris was thirty, the value of Longhorns plummeted, and he had to give up buying land to buy blooded bulls to warm up the herd, paying top dollar for bulls and horses and bottom dollar for cowboys. He spent years ridding himself of Longhorns, selling their hides and tallow, and riding into scrapes like today. He was forty years old and without get. He needed a son.

Claris considered going to Fort Worth and marrying a whore. They had a work ethic and when you married one you knew what you were getting. If he could find one that had been a buffalo gal long enough to dream of rescue but not long enough to develop contempt for men, she would appreciate it and would work at making him a good wife, giving him sons to help with the ranch. The thing that stopped him was fear that some of his cowboys might know her. He didn't want them looking at her like a bronc they had broke. Bronc busters took a proprietary interest in horses they broke to the saddle, watching how they took the rein, how they rode.

Besides, a whore would be accustomed to a lot of sex. That would be all right for a while, but ten, twenty years down the road he might be less than she was used to. That was a worry he didn't have time for. He sure didn't have time to sit around the house keeping an eye on her. A widow would be grateful and accustomed to a husband's demands but perhaps too attached to another man's habit. He decided to seek a spinster and break her to bit and saddle and teach her a man's wont. A sheltered woman who wouldn't know or expect someone else's measure.

Sitting beside the twitching horse, Claris considered himself. He looked tall in boots and hat. Thin—because you didn't get fat on sourdough bullets and beans—but not drawn. His face was creased like a good hat. His eyes were clear, he had his front teeth, a trip to the barber would take care of his shaggy hair and moustache, and he had land, good horses, and blooded bulls. Danged, if he wasn't a rooster. A woman who couldn't make something of that didn't deserve to marry.

Claris tugged his saddle free of the horse, threw it on his shoulder and started to the house. While high-heeling it, he rounded up his chances and cut the shells. There were three spinsters in the county. Ploma was a shell, as old as he and no good for childbearing. Edna was good hearty stock, looked like she could bear healthy boys, and she was dragging her rope hoping some man would grab it. German family, overbearing, but he could put up with Emil, and he wouldn't have to see a lot of Irmagarde.

When he went to see Edna he almost asked her to marry him. She would never own any part of her father's land, he knew that. She was beefy plumb to her hocks, lumpy now and would get pillowy like her mother after a child or two, but he could abide that. The gristle in his jerky was the way she brayed when she laughed. Closest thing to a jackass he had ever heard. He chewed on that, telling himself he could abide it. He would be away from the house most of the time, and he sure as hell wouldn't try to make her laugh.

When they got to talking about how many boys he wanted, how he didn't have much time or place for privacy but the hands never used the outhouse anyway, everything he said sent her into spells of braying. He stood up, apologized, and told her he wanted to check another pasture. She started braying again, but now her eyes were big, panicky, like a cornered cow. Her father and brothers came outside to watch him leave, trying to decide whether or not they were obliged to beat him to calm her down.

That left Celestine, scant and quiet as a whisper in a windstorm. It annoyed him the way she tiptoed around, but he thought when he got her to his place where there was nothing to break, she would get over it. Claris had no time for courting.

4

She was available and was young enough to bear children. Her father owned an adjoining ranch, and there were no other heirs. Claris and Olin had done some hell-raising together when they were younger. Nothing to be ashamed of—getting drunk, fighting, spending the night in a whorehouse. Claris recounted his horses and cows, and Olin said it was time for Celestine to take the bit. It was a marriage made in the saddle.

When Claris told Celestine of his plans for children she stared at her lap, her face red as a Hereford's neck. When he asked her to marry him she didn't change her posture, and he had to ask her to repeat what she said. Still he wasn't sure. "Yes?" he asked, and she nodded. He knew then he should have thrown a wider loop, but he had asked, and he couldn't go back on his word, and she was the only heir to her father's land.

Celestine was twenty-three when she moved to Claris' bare-board, box-and-strip, two-room ranch house. One room for cooking and eating and one room for dressing and sleeping. For furniture he had a table and benches for the cowhands, a cookstove and a bed.

Celestine brought with her a wagon load of necessities: two ladder-back chairs—one for each of them as if he would be sitting in the house—her rocker, a hope chest filled with towels, embroidered linen, patchwork quilts, her trousseau, and a glass-door bookcase with her romance novels that inclined her to dally. She also brought a mirror and a good bed and mattress. Claris' bed had been a bedroll thrown over a frame strung with rawhide and he had used a bucket of water for a mirror.

Celestine cherished Claris for offering her a life as a wife and mother. She intended to please him, but there were no doors she could close, no shades she could draw before dressing for bed, and no closets or shelves for her to place her clothes, only nails driven into the wall to hang things on.

Wash-up was done on the porch where the cowboys gallantly waited so Celestine would have clean water and towel. Bathing was done in a galvanized tub in the bedroom where she crouched in a corner of the doorless, curtainless room after the cowboys had brought water for her to heat. The cowboys, who believed too much bathing wore away the scarf-skin and exposed the nerves, knew every time she took a bath.

Cooking and eating were done in the kitchen where she cooked for everyone. Metal pans were used for plates and a coffee can on the table held bent flatware. At roundup when there were extra hands, some had to eat with spoons or use their pocketknives because there were not enough utensils for everyone. When finished, the cowboys dropped their dishes in the wreck pan, her galvanized bathtub she had placed on the stove to heat water for washing dishes.

Celestine, who had always been shy around boys and frightened by loud noise, had to cook in front of the hungry hands who watched her as they ate. She was appalled at their gobbling and guzzling, grunting their pleasure and pointing when they wanted more. They rarely spoke and when they did it was to each other.

"I reckon I could eat them flapjacks fast as she can fry 'em," one cowboy said around a mouthful.

"Yeah, but for how long?" asked another.

"Till I starved to death, I reckon," said the first.

Their appetites were ravenous, animalistic. Her father had eaten with the hands, but Celestine and her mother waited until the cowboys returned to work, then ate quietly talking of church, sewing circle, and play parties.

Celestine's father offered to help Claris enlarge the house for the kids they would have so Claris bought a house from homesteaders who were leaving. He put it on runners, hitched it to a team of mules to lizard over to his place, and nailed it to his house, giving him five rooms in a string. At one end of the house was the room where the hands ate, at the other was a sitting room for Celestine, and in between were bedrooms for the kids Claris planned to have.

Celestine's skittishness kept her wire-eyed and unbred so Claris moved the cookstove into a separate room so she didn't have to cook in front of the hands. In the bedroom he curtained off a corner for her to bathe and dress. Claris and Olin built a porch outside the sitting room for Celestine's sewing machine where she could sew while watching the kids in the yard.

But there were no kids in the yard. Claris wondered if he should have married a calico queen, one who had been painted long enough she wanted out but not so long she couldn't quit. Celestine was as uncomplaining as a brood cow and as silent, but without result. Her mother came to see him. Celestine stared at her lap and colored up but didn't say anything while Genevieve laid out a woman's particulars. Claris colored at that—sounded to him like they wanted to be pets instead of hands. He said he needed sons now so that in ten, twelve years he'd have help and asked her to ride over the trail again.

"Some women aren't made to have children; I think Celestine may be one of them," Genevieve said. Hell of a time to tell him that. "I gave my husband a child because he demanded one, but I demanded that there not be another one, and I devoted my life to the one child God gave me." That confirmed the rumors Claris had heard in town—that when Celestine was born, Genevieve told Olin she had done churned her butter.

Men laughed about it sometimes; said what they would do. Send Genevieve back to her folks and the kid with her. Throw her down on the bed and teach her what a woman was for. Take her to church and let the preacher tell her a woman's duty. Buy her a dress and not let her leave the house until she showed appreciation. Slap her until she softened up like a woman was supposed to.

When Genevieve left, Celestine raised her eyes and looked at him. It was the look of a scared dog—don't kick me anymore. He went outside, jumped on a horse, and nearly rode it to death trying to pound the rage out of his head. He worked the horse up Comanche Peak and stood looking over rolling, rock-rimmed hills; the grassy valleys where his cattle grazed, the stands of oak, cedar and mesquite that housed deer, bobcats, and coyotes, the glittering ribbon of Six Mile Draw, the Bone Yard where his mother and father were buried. She married him. She took his bed. He expected an heir. What did she expect?

Claris didn't go to church—too far and no time. But when he could he read, and the only thing he had to read was the family Bible. The Bible seemed very real to him. He knew why David sang. He understood why Lot's wife looked back. He sensed how Isaac sported with Rebekah. When Sarah didn't give Abraham a son, he used a handmaiden. Sarah got pregnant and Abraham ended up with a brush baby.

On his horse or on his blanket under the stars he felt as close to God as any preacher, as any pope in Rome. Now he had a roof, a wife, and a busted cinch, and he was eating gravel while the gate closed.

He had never been unkind or unforgiving to Celestine. A woman without fortitude was like a man without courage, more to be pitied than shamed. He would no more divorce Celestine than he would cut his stake rope and leave the ranch. But what if he never had a son?

He walked the horse back to the barn, unsaddled, turned the horse loose, and faced the house. Either she was his wife or she was her mother's daughter, and she was going to have to choose. He led her away from the sewing machine where she was making him a shirt, took her to the bedroom, petted and played with her like a puppy, and stroked her like a favorite horse.

Celestine thrashed, scratched, cried out, and when he finished she could not look at him, ashamed of what she had felt, afraid of what she might become. For days she shied from him, and when next he took her, no amount of playing or stroking could move her beyond staunch acceptance.

When Celestine found she was pregnant she became tender. She teased him sometimes, calling him "Papa." But it was in the morning when he was saddled with a day's work in his head. Never at night when it would have mattered.

Even pregnant Celestine looked poorly. Claris bought a goat from a farmer who sold his crops in the field and headed for a big cotton pick. Genevieve moved with Celestine into the curtained room, milked the goat, made soups and puddings for Celestine, and cooked for Claris' hands. Olin had to hire a cook for his ranch. Claris put old horseshoes in a bucket of water, and every day he gave Celestine a sip to put iron in her blood.

When Celestine didn't get stronger, Genevieve took her to

her home. Claris didn't go with her because it was the best part of a day by wagon, and he had to go back to cooking for his hands. Celestine's baby, a girl, came hard. Genevieve planted the umbilical cord under a rose bush so the baby would have a rosy complexion. When Claris went in to see her, Celestine would not look at him. "Don't fret yourself," he comforted her. "We still have time for boys."

Celestine said she wasn't bound to go with him yet. Hell, he understood that. This time his father-in-law talked to him. "Celestine was raised by her mother," he said. "Genevieve kept her in the house reading, taught her the finer things—cooking, canning, sewing. She don't know much about animal matters, coming in season and all that. That was a shock to her. She's real proud of her daughter, wants to name her Clarista, after you. But, as for having boys, she might not be up to that."

What the hell was he supposed to do? He went back to his ranch alone. He rode over to his father-in-law's when he could, every week or so, to see his wife and daughter. Celestine was a long time coming home. When she did come home, Olin carried her inside, and Genevieve brought in a new but narrow bed. "She has to rest, get her strength back," she said, giving him a look that would give a fence post the flux. "I'll stay with her for a week or so, see that you have something to eat and clothes to wear. But you can't go back to treating her like she was a brood mare. You'll kill that poor girl."

Genevieve went home a month later, after hanging cedar branches in the house to freshen the air. Celestine stayed mostly in her room playing with Clarista. She cooked and washed and kept house, but when he was in it she was skulky as a coyote around a garbage pit, not wanting to leave but afraid to get close.

He wasn't going to have any sons. It took some doing but Claris settled his mind on that. Clarista was going to have to be the son he wanted. The first time he took her to see the cows, she laughed and clapped her hands, but it was the horses she loved. Claris put her in the saddle with him whenever he could.

Claris was riding on the Three Crosses looking for stray cattle when he saw a boy, a couple of years younger than Clarista, sitting on a pile of corn to keep the crows out of it. He was pug-nosed and ugly, but Claris would have traded a herd of cows for him, maybe even a pasture. Claris spurred his horse into a lope.

When Clarista was four, he found her eating dirt. "You'll get your craw full of this land soon enough," he said, wiping her mouth.

When Clarista was seven, she was running hot irons to the branding crew when a cow made a run at the backs of the men kneeling on the ground holding its bawling calf. Clarista ran in front of the cow to turn it back. Claris had one end of his rope around the hind feet of a steer and the other tied fast to the saddle. He put a wave in the rope, trying to roll the rope and shake the loop loose, but he wasn't fast enough to get between Clarista and the cow. Clarista stood her ground. The cow tossed its horns and turned away. Claris got off his horse, proud and scared at the same time. He could have lost his only heir. "Don't never get between a cow and its calf," he scolded her. He trimmed the brim of his Stetson so she could see out from under it and had Celestine sew cotton stuffing inside so it would sit on her head.

When Clarista was eight she carried food from the kitchen to the table where the hands ate. She did the cooking when Celestine was weak or dizzy. She ate with the hands, washed their

11

dishes, and ran to the corral to catch and saddle a horse and ride after the men who didn't wait for her.

When she was ten, Genevieve and Celestine explained that Clarista could lose her maiden pledge astride a saddle and the man she loved might leave her on her wedding night when he discovered she lacked the essential evidence. A fall on a horse could alter her insides so that she could never be a mother. Clarista wanted to be a wife and mother some day, but that day seemed a long lope and a wide loop away so she continued to ride with the hands. She had sooner sleep with a skunk than be useless.

When Clarista was twelve, Claris had gone from selling cattle by the head to beef by the pound. He had to pay sixty dollars for 500 pounds of hay. In a bad winter a cow could eat twenty to twenty-five pounds a day, but he got only thirty dollars for a beef. Congress had erected tariffs after the Great War to protect American business from foreign competition. Prices for everything Claris needed soared but cattle prices fell as other countries stopped importing beef in retaliation for the tariffs.

Claris had to give away an old mare because he couldn't sell her. He couldn't pay the note at the bank so the bank wrote a new loan and kept the two hundred dollars he had paid on the old loan. When he tried to borrow money to pay for extra hands during calving season a young clerk, Smiley Wooten, told him to postpone calving season.

During a drought Claris rode up on Clarista skinning a cow. When a cow died, she skinned it, and Claris sold the hide for sixteen cents a pound. Claris got off his horse to wave the flies from her face while she worked. "You got the land in you, haven't you, girl? I hope I can hang on to it long enough to leave it to you."

Clarista was fourteen when her Grandfather Olin took sick. She looked after his windmills and cows and passed his orders to his cowboys. When he died, Genevieve came to take care of Celestine and cook for Claris' hands. Claris and Clarista rode over to her grandfather's place. Claris opened the wire gap into his father-in-law's pasture but caught Clarista's horse's bridle before she passed through.

"This place belongs to your grandma now," Claris said. "Someday it'll belong to your ma and then to you—if you can hang on to it so your grandma don't feel she has to sell it. It's yours to run if you want it; I don't have time for it. It'll give you your life or it'll take it. Set your mind to that if you want it."

Clarista jumped off her horse and gave Claris a hug, the first hug he remembered since she was a child. Then she sprang on her horse, howled like a coyote, and raced into her future, fanning the horse with her hat.

Claris watched her ride—tall, confident, and full of sand. Mindful of what he had tied her to, he closed the gap behind her not entirely happy with what he had done. From that day, Clarista insisted on being called Rista and slapped a Running R brand on her calves.

2

1990

"**S**omething has to be done with your grandmother," a man said over the telephone. It was the telephone that rang only when there was a crisis at the TV station. "She's old and can't take care of herself."

"Who is this?" I signaled Shana to mute the TV.

"One of her neighbors. We're worried about her." Someone at the station thought there was an emergency and gave him this number. "She must be eighty. Living alone out there with that cowboy who is almost as old as she is. He came to town last week and wanted bandages; said a cow mashed her hand against the corral. What if she broke her hip? Got sick and couldn't get to the bathroom? Something has to be done."

I had been waiting for Rista to die; maybe this was as good. "Then do something," I said. The television screen ran the same ad back to back. I smiled at the gaffe by the other station. They would have to apologize to the ad agency, maybe give a make-good. "I don't even know her," I said.

"Rista is your responsibility. You're the only relative she has."

Her only heir. Mother had an abortion to preserve the inheritance for me. Rista sat on a million dollars worth of land, too mean to die quietly. Some cowboy was hanging on to talk her into leaving the ranch to him, but this was November, our most important rating season. Mine was going to be another life Rista interrupted.

"Okay," I said. "I'll do something about her." Put her in a nursing home, sell the ranch and get back to the TV station as fast as possible.

"Did you see that?" Shana said when I hung up, pointing out a rule violation that was obvious to everyone except those paid to flag such violations. Shana worked a variety of shifts—nights, weekends, holidays. On a rare Sunday afternoon together we sometimes watched football. I hooted at the announcers who spent more time watching themselves on monitors than they did the game. Shana studied the officiating. "The referee was look-ing right at it and didn't call it. Different rules for different folks." Shana contended there were two games—one as it was played on the field and the other as it was seen by the officials and reported by the media.

There were celebrity rules; everyone in the media knew that. Winners won. When a nobody won, it was national news whether it was in a stadium or the Supreme Court. "It's part of the game."

"Why don't we report that part of the game?"

I didn't argue football because Shana knew more about the rules than I did, but I was general manager of a TV station, and I did know the media. There was a success bias; we had few clients who were losers. Stories about losers were either howls or three hankies, but every reporter I knew dreamed of bleming a glamour face, scorching a fig-leaf story. "We try to report the news evenhandedly." This was a soap opera argument—it ran every day and if you missed a week you could pick it up where you left off.

"Name a friend who is a union leader or working class," she said. I negotiated contracts with unions; we weren't adversaries, but we weren't friends either. "Name a golfing buddy who isn't a CEO or director of an ad agency," she continued, unwilling to let me fade to black. "We are big business, and we want what other big businesses want."

Yeah, to make a profit, but I didn't say that because Shana believed business wanted more government subsidy and protection from consumers, less regulation and less competition from others. Shana sat in shorts and T-shirt, one knee propped under her chin, watching the game. We had hired consultants to choose her makeup and coloring, buy her clothes, cut her hair, critique how she read, and create her image. Like other reporters and anchors she was required to look the same in the grocery store as she did on the screen. She kept clothes at my condo to be herself.

"I have to go to Texas, put my grandmother away and sell her ranch," I said. I should take a writer and make a TV movie about her—a woman who killed two men and drove her daughter and grandson from her house. What would be the snapper? A nursing home? Too beige. Kill her for revenge? Too plaid.

"You've never mentioned a grandmother." Shana knew my grandfather had been murdered. "She wasn't at your mother's funeral."

"I didn't tell her."

"You didn't tell her that her daughter was dying?"

"It's complicated," I said. "Family ghosting."

"Can I go with you? I'd like to meet your grandmother."

"I'd better go alone." I didn't want her to know the kind of family I had.

17

"How long will you be gone?"

"No longer than necessary. I'll hire a lawyer there to handle the details. I'll leave after the staff meeting in the morning," I said. If Rista had moments of lucidity maybe she could tell me something about Mother. All I knew of her early years was that she hated Rista and Shad. I had her scrapbook—yellowed pages of newspaper stories of crimes, passions, glamour, but none of the stories seemed to be about her. I wondered if I should first go to Montana to see if Shad was my father.

"Maybe it's best that I not go," Shana said reluctantly. "We both need some time alone."

▲▼▲

Shana worked at the station rewriting the wire-service news, feeding paper and changing ribbons on the teletypes, answering the telephones and dumb questions, and listening to complaints. Carey asked her to attend a chili cookoff the station was covering. She took a bite of chili and dove into the pool to cool off. That film led our six o'clock news.

Sometimes there wasn't any weather news—day after day of the same highs and lows—but we had to fill the slot because we had sold it. Carey tried remotes with the weatherman in front of local backgrounds—the park, crowds lined up for a movie, Christmas decorations in yards and on houses. No viewer response. Carey put Shana in a bikini holding a parasol and thermometer for hot, a bikini and an umbrella for wet, a bikini and a fur stole for cold. We got a lot of viewer response, and men watched the monitors at the station when she was on the screen. Shana not only had a body made for bikinis, "she has a billboard face," Carey said.

Promotions made up a press kit of photographs of Shana with

a banner, "Our Reporters Make a Difference." Area newspapers used the banner with pictures of Shana in a bikini.

Shana came to see me, dressed the way Carey saw her—a too-tight white dress with big collars and purple flowers, too much makeup, oversized earrings, puffy blonde hair, and fake nails that looked like canoes when she turned her hand over. Even in the Daisy Mae costume Carey had put her in, she was beautiful—more Diana than Aphrodite. Athletic rather than sensuous, too tenacious to be delicate, too ardent to be soft, she had survived adolescence and education with her sense of self intact.

I thought she was Carey's latest squeeze trying to promote the relationship into fringe benefits. I told her Carey was her supervisor and could outline her duties and reminded her of the swimming pool stunt. "It was a prank. I didn't know they were going to use it on the air," she said.

"You knew they were taping you in a bikini. What did you think that would do to your image as a reporter?" Carey sent her to drive the remote truck and cover the opening of a new car sales lot by a major advertiser. He also sent Scottie, a run-and-shoot photographer able to cover the story if she failed. Scottie was brash, brilliant, and a lousy driver. "Just be pretty," Carey told her, "and speak clearly."

"I didn't know I was going to be a reporter," she said. "I thought I was a writer."

I asked Carey what he told Shana. He told her that viewers were loyal to one news program, regarded those anchors as friends, and that we had to grab their attention. He told her we had spent thousands for a new set, better sound, and lighting that was homier. We spent more thousands on consultants to tell us

19

what would hold the channel surfer. Viewers would catch a glimpse of her in a bikini and stay tuned a minute longer, maybe through the next commercial hoping for another glimpse of her, perhaps tune in tomorrow. "We want to exploit the changes we have made," Carey told her. "We need your help. The news team needs you."

"Did you promise her a job as a reporter?"

"She's got it all—charisma, chemistry. She makes magic happen."

"She has no experience," I pointed out.

"She has attitude. You've always said attitude is as important as experience. She has talent. She has the face."

Carey sent her to a trade show in Miami to interview fashion models. Designers recommended an exclusive restaurant. "Tell them Sergio and Yvonne sent you." "Surgeon Yvonne sent me," she said to the puzzled maitre'd. Newspaper columnists reported the gaffe. They also accused Shana of reporting the shift of focus from the bust line to the hip line by saying, "A woman who worries about the size of her bust has nothing to worry about."

"Shana Sullivan thought sunbathing was what people did when they didn't have water," wrote one columnist getting into the game. "When Shana Sullivan's family moved to town and she attended her first large school, she sat in the same seat all day, unable to understand why the other students got up and left every time the buzzer sounded."

One columnist wrote that Shana saw a driverless car rolling down the street, jumped inside, and pulled the brake. When she got out of the car she saw a man following it. "I stopped your car," she said. "I know," he said. "I was the one pushing it." Another wrote that a service station attendant said, "There's no oil on your dip stick." "Squirt some on it; I'm in a hurry," Shana said. Shana was a local celebrity and dumb-blonde joke, trapped in the image we had created for her.

"Put her in silk sweaters," I said, "designer jackets, graduated pearls, cut her hair straighter and shorter and closer to her natural color. But keep her in spike heels. For attitude even when you can't see them. And tell her to enterprise and break stories independent of the desk."

Shana interviewed a woman in jail for selling pirated videos. Her ex-husband wouldn't pay child support but sent the children videos; she sold them for food. If she told police she got the videos from him they'd both be in jail with no one to care for the children. If she didn't tell them, he would get custody because she had been arrested.

Carey told her the story was too heavy, too hard to follow, and wrong for her image and assigned her stories on a business that opened a bar for employees so they could discuss ideas and problems in a relaxed atmosphere and avoid rush-hour traffic; a man suing his girlfriend because she licked his ear, dislodging his hearing aid and causing him to lose it; and a man suing a booking agent because he asked for a stripper with a forty-inch chest, dressed in a teacher's costume who would strip before paddling the birthday boy with a ruler, one smack for each year of his life. Instead they send a 36-A stripper who did a regular strip.

"Is this what you hired me for?" Shana asked.

"Don't worry about news content," Carey told her. "We're after viewers. The numbers are everything."

"The numbers are more important than the news?"

"The numbers are the area code of God. The news is the hook-up."

Shana reported a school bus accident—minor, no injuries, but school bus accidents drew a big audience. She came to see me again. "That's not my story," she said.

Another ego who thought she was the story and her every word was sacred. I watched the story with her and was impressed. She could draw people out, get them to expose themselves in front of the camera. The driver talked about nightmares of children scattered across the highway.

I explained that on TV you wrote short. Anything was boring after two minutes without change; for local news the window was much smaller. That wasn't what upset her. She told the facts—the driver was not at fault; his worst nightmare was injuring children. The camera told the story—damage to the bus, frightened children. A high-angle shot of the driver made him look weak, and a close-up of his eyes flitting side to side as he described his nightmare made him look unreliable.

"We made him look bad to his family, employers, kids who ride his bus, people who don't even know him," she said.

I thought her concern was overboard and suggested we discuss it over a drink. In a quiet bar I explained that television succeeded at demonstrating but was less effective at explaining. "That's why we lead with a car wreck instead of a report on auto safety."

Shana said she wanted to report the truth. I scoffed at the conceit. Everyone had a different set of facts, and truth was complicated and elusive. "Truth takes time, something we don't have. Our stock-in-trade is images." Einstein, Kennedy, Nixon weren't complex on TV. Those who caught the eye of the camera had created an image for themselves, or we gave them one—the sexiest man in America, the fastest man alive, jet-setter, sex symbol, Tricky Dick, Ron Retard.

"Learn to tell a story," I told her. "Start with easy questions, off the wall questions to get the subject off guard, and then the killer questions. Get your message out there with the vehicle you have. Package it so it makes the point you want—not what the subject wants, but the story Carey sent you to get."

Shana was so gorgeous I forgot to take her seriously. She was so serious she became exasperated at my dismissal of her ideas. The meeting ended awkwardly. I thought she was Carey's girl-friend; she thought I was checking the station's merchandise.

In addition to reporting, Carey used Shana as a substitute news anchor for experience, then made her co-host of the morning show and weekend anchor. I made suggestions after each show—slow her delivery to the local verbal velocity, sit closer to the co-host to achieve a buddy effect, exchange smiles and glances for intimacy. In the morning people listened while getting the kids off to school. They didn't have time for pictures. In the evening they watched the pictures; the words hardly mattered. I talked to her about libel laws and advised her to learn the names of current celebrities.

"No one at the station has ever heard of this guy," she said.

"The network said he was a celebrity so he's a celebrity."

We argued news, journalistic ethics, had coffee, a drink, sometimes a meal, went to a game or a movie. Both of us chose not to call it dating. Both of us were wary—I that she would use me to advance her career; she that I would use my position to get her in bed.

During the May sweeps the morning show featured prostitutes, and Shana's report on the evening news was about homosexual trysting spots.

"Are you proud of that show?" Shana asked.

"I'm proud it gave us parity with the other station during that slot."

"Why did we lead with my report on homosexual trysts?"

"Because it's exciting, it's controversial."

"It's trash."

"Trash sells. Trash captures a big audience."

"It's okay to teach kids that trash is important?"

"News is what the public will watch in big numbers."

"That's pandering. We condescend to whatever will boost ratings."

"This is a business. Making money is our business. News is—"

"I know, news is the hook-up."

The newspapers ridiculed Shana and her report. A talk radio program called her a heroine for exposing homosexuals and their agenda of seducing America's youth. To improve her image promotions released stories to the area newspapers that Shana was a Phi Beta Kappa who had majored in English and spent a year in law school, that she did volunteer work with children, had traveled to Mexico with a church group, and that her hobbies were reading and writing. The newspapers highlighted her bikini days in weather reporting. A columnist doing a humorous piece on "Most Memorable Stupidities of the Year" included Shana saying, "He's a good driver," about a school bus driver standing in front of a wrecked bus.

Shana said she had to find another job. I told her she had to learn to take criticism. "It's not the criticism," she said. "They were right."

I knew that other stations had asked her for a resumé and demo tape and assumed she wanted to move to lose her image. I told her we were going to make her co-anchor until Bob's contract ran out. "Viewers want attractive people with warm smiles, friendly dispositions. Bob is wonky."

"I don't want to replace Bob. What will he do?"

"What do you want?"

She looked at me, looked away, then looked at me again. "I'm falling in love with you, and I can't do that and work at the station."

"I'm falling for you too, but—" Shana was a bachelor's dream and nightmare—beautiful, sexy, smart. We were a low one hundred station, and she was headed for a top ten. I was thirty-eight years old and considered myself damn lucky to have gotten as far as I had. There was no way I could keep up with her, and talent had no room for sentimentality.

"Don't you see how impossible this is?" she said.

For a long run, yes, but for now—"Shana, I'll talk to Carey. I'll tell him that as far as you are concerned, the chain of command stops at his desk. That I don't want to know about his decisions. Give it a chance."

Shana thought the separation caused by my trip to Texas would give each of us time to decide what we wanted. I was determined not to be gone that long.

▲▼▲

I hadn't taken a vacation since I became station manager—the owners considered conventions my vacations. The only fire-plug at a dog show, my pager or my telephone rang constantly. When I wasn't placating clients, listening to viewer complaints, soothing talent egos, putting out personnel fires, being the bad guy, and selling, I spoke to the Rotary, the Lions, the Chamber of Commerce. A great day for me was going to bed at night knowing there were no major screwups. I took only two days when Mother died, but I told the owners Rista was a "family emergency," and I promised to stay in contact with the station.

We were a small TV station in a small market in Florida. The other station was owned by a mega corporation that could buy the best programming for their own use or to keep us from using it. It had been designed as a TV station and had superior space, electrical power, air conditioning, and equipment. It had parking spaces for all its employees.

Our station began as a one-camera, one-studio operation, at one end of a radio station, plugging into the coaxial line for eight hours of network broadcasting. Television took over the building that had been expanded to provide more studio space, more insulation, more power, but the building was outdated and inefficient. At every meeting with the owners, the sales manager, chief engineer, and I pleaded for a new building with up-to-date equipment. None of the owners lived in the state; none watched the station; none cared that we were affiliated with the weakest network in the market area; their only interest was low expenses and high sales. A good book, good numbers in the sweeps, meant high expenses.

When I came to the station as program director my first act was to stop televising high school football games. The station had no telescopic lenses, no cameramen who could track to follow the ball, and viewers who cared about the game were at the game. We made more money running a network show and taking a share of the national advertising outlay.

I substituted local wrestling for football. Andy Smith, the

announcer, became a minor talent doing interviews with the wrestlers. I put him in a clown suit and started an afternoon kiddie show with Andy the Clown between western movies. We brought kids into the studio, showed them on camera so their parents would watch, and raised the advertising rates on the time slots.

When I was promoted to station manager, the owners' only commandment was that I "grow the station and the market." I dumped Andy the Clown; the network kid shows were better. I replaced Will Morgan with Carey Kirkham and novelty news. Will was an ink journalist, liked hard news, and every month we lost market share to the other station that did splash and crash, girls and gore, blood and bikini stories. Carey had superb teasing skills, giving enough information to hook viewers but not enough to predict the outcome. He was not so good at stacking stories that flowed and sometimes was too hip for the room.

Some at the station saw me as a boy wonder, an instant topper, but I had spent most of my thirty-eight years studying TV, and since my first hire I had spent every waking hour working for the station whether I was at the station or not—selling, looking for new sources of revenue, new approaches in promotion, stories that would grab viewers.

Then one of the owners sold out to Jerry Maxwell, a businessman who made a fortune selling an improved wheelchair and tapping into Medicare. "God gave me the money," he said, "and God tells me how to spend it." God wanted "wholesome, family entertainment"—meaning cheap reruns of off-network shows—and "patriotic movies"—meaning any film shot during World War II. God did not want "inclusive programming that promoted a gay, black, liberal agenda."

27

God also wanted pre-employment drug testing and a station that disparaged public education and praised free enterprise. Jerry had owned a religious TV station and was happy with "the return on my nickel," but wanted to affect a wider audience. Now I had three owners who wanted profit and one owner who wanted profit and what God wanted. And Jerry did watch the station.

▲▼▲

My weekly session with the heads of sales, program, news, business, promotion, traffic, and chief engineer resembled a turf battle over internal control and policies. We met in my office so I could manage the environment and keep the discussion from bogging down in personal gripes.

The engineer gave us good quality control of on-air and transmitter operations, but he wanted the latest bells and whistles, and no one could predict where the new technologies were going. Business chanted "cost awareness" and wanted the other station to test high-definition TV at their cost. "We've always been about people first," I said, "We need to be technologically current, but having and keeping the right staff is vital."

The other station had professional football on Sunday afternoon; we countered with made-fors and theatricals. We had used the cheap ones; the other station bought the good ones; Jerry opposed the ones that were edgy and out there. Sales wanted no musicals, costumers, or black-and-whites. Sales wanted low-budget, high-action martial combat movies slanted for children because of the fourth-quarter toy sales. Program wanted movies aimed at women who didn't watch football but would watch movies about a woman who beat the odds despite her lover's lack of faith. Sales gave the research numbers on the targeted demographic.

The other station advertised news-weather-sports on billboards. We had the best promotion director in the market area, able to create news images about our hard-hitting, first-on-the-scene newsroom and promoting our top story of the day, but we couldn't match the billboards, and sales complained that trading TV time for newspaper space was time they were not permitted to sell.

The other-station envy was followed by complaints over vacation plans. The station operated twenty-four hours a day, 365 days a year; we didn't want people on vacation during the November, February, May, or July sweeps so everyone wanted vacation at the same time.

An ad agency hadn't paid an invoice; there was a discrepancy between the time slot the agency bought and when the spot was shown. Our sales manager was a detail man, good at managing the inventory, able to sell outside the box, but didn't interface well. "Get me a copy of the log," I said.

Business complained that there were too many make-goods. Traffic said they were because of product conflict, program pre-emptions, and a commercial no longer in use had mistakenly been run. Business said news was over budget due to more location shots, and sales wanted more credit extension to major clients to boost sales morale. I'd have to call each client.

Sales wanted giveaways to boost viewership during the sweeps and wanted them on Sunday afternoons when our numbers were down. News wanted them during news-weather-sports because the giveaways might allow them for the first time to beat the other station. I gave the nod to sales because the director and five salesmen produced the revenue. All other employees were cost items.

Sales wanted to cut rates to attract clients from the other station. Business said that would weaken sales rates in the future. "Maintain the integrity of our rate position," I said, "but if the other station is not providing equitable rates, point it out to the client."

Advertisers complained that news was anti-business because, after a story about a prominent businessman sent to jail for white-collar crime, Bob Blaine had turned to the weather guy and said, "A good thing too."

▲▼▲

My secretary was waiting when they left. She had explained that I had a family emergency, but Jerry wanted me to call him. "It's urgent," she said with lifted brows. I told her to ask Bob to come to the office.

Jerry was exercised about a sitcom in which a man shared an apartment with two women who thought he was homosexual. I asked if Jerry had seen the church service we carried on the Sunday God spot. Jerry had and Jerry did not approve of the church or of their service that he found to be "hollow."

Mister Opportunity imposed himself in the door until I hung up. Bob was called Mister Opportunity because he never missed an opportunity to promote himself. When Bob overheard it, he thought they said, "Missed her opportunity." When Bob shared the camera with sports or weather, he complained that he wasn't properly framed. He leaned forward to focus attention on himself; he seemed to puff himself up to look bigger, more intent so that it was hard not to watch him.

Consultants told us we needed warm-fuzzy and that Bob, forty-five and Churchillian, was Nadaville. Styles had changed. Viewers wanted glib tongues, pretty faces, riveting visuals.

Viewers wanted to be insiders, to hear the banter, enjoy the inside jokes. Consultants encouraged ad-libs to make Bob seem chummy. They wanted a next-door-neighbor image for Bob. "Someone who could grow tomatoes."

During one happy-talk episode Bob disparaged a movie. His comment was followed by an ad for the movie. "Sit down," I said. Bob imposed his regal self on a chair. "I told Carey to structure ad-libbing. Now I'm telling you—clear all ad-libs with Carey before you go on the air."

"I don't want to sound scripted," Bob said.

"Chatter. Pleasant noise. No content, no comment, no complaints."

"Did Shana say something?" Bob asked, spelling the line.

I stared to let some of the gas out of him before I spoke. "The advertisers complained. If you have anything to say about Shana, say it to Carey." Bob opened his mouth then thought better of it.

▲▼▲

After the meeting Shana drove me to the airport and I bought a ticket to Billings. "I thought you were going to Texas," she said.

"There's a man in Montana who may be my father." When I was a kid I dreamed of Shad Carter riding up on his horse, telling everyone he was my father, and carrying me away. If he was my father he was the only male member of my family Rista hadn't shot. I could use his advice.

Shana put her hands on my face. "Chance," she said. She couldn't imagine not knowing who her father was. "Does he know you're coming?"

"I thought I would open cold," I said. The most revealing

interviews were spontaneous, before the subject had time to prepare a face or put a story together.

3
1918

Clarista loved horses before she ever saw one. Her father brought them to her crib when he rode to her grandfather's house to see her. Every time he picked her up she breathed the richness of their smell, felt the prick and sting of their hair on his shirt sleeves. Her first ride was in her father's arms when he brought her home.

Claris kept an old, wind-broke gelding at the house for Celestine. Celestine did not like animals, their smells, their noises, the messes they made. Clarista played at Smoky's feet, rode his leg when he walked to the next mouthful of grass. She tried to climb Smoky's leg and one day led Smoky to the corral, climbed on the top rail, and jumped on his back.

Clarista was six when the Great War ended, but the biggest event in her life was that her father gave her Henry, an old roper with sprung knees. Although Celestine wanted her indoors, Clarista carried water from the windmill to the garden to water the beans, okra, and tomatoes. She fed the hogs and hens, picked up the eggs and killed the roosters that fed the cowboys. She twisted cottontails out of prairie dog holes with barbed wire and skinned them for her mother to cook. The hands were partial to squirrel and dumplings. It was usually prairie dog and dumplings. Some days she found lamb's quarters and picked a mess of greens for supper.

When she was eight Claris let her ride green-broke horses in exchange for additional chores. Clarista picked up scattered heads of maize for feed, fed the dogies—learning to moo like a cow so the frightened calves would come to her—chased the milk cow into the pen, tied off the calf, and milked. She strained the milk through a cedar bough inserted in a funnel to catch hair, clots, and bits of dirt. When the milk cow went dry she helped kill and butcher it and took a hindquarter to the Three Crosses to be repaid when they slaughtered.

When the sow got out and ate two hens, Clarista tried to drive it back into its pen. Unable to do so, she slipped a water bucket over the sow's head. The sow tried to back out of the bucket, and Clarista guided it into its pen.

Whenever possible Clarista worked green-broke horses, finding newborn foals and calves, riding into a new morning, riding through fields of bluebonnets, Indian paintbrush, Mexican hat, wild verbena, wine cup, Texas frog fruit. She wore her father's old boots, packing them with socks to make them fit. She stuffed her hair into an old Stetson with a cut-down brim, a felt hat because it was easier to keep on in a wind and didn't spook a horse when brush dragged across it. She kept her ropes in lard buckets to keep them pliable and never took her spurs off her boots. She roped her mother's goat so many times it turned and ran to the horse as soon as it felt a rope around its neck and waited to be turned loose.

Clarista went to school when she could, first at the Three Crosses where Sue Caldwell taught her own brood on the porch unless it was so cold they had to meet inside. There wasn't always heat inside, but it was out of the wind. Later she rode to the free school in Red Rock, fifteen miles on horseback. In the winter Clarista took a horse that had night eyes and was steady because it was dark when she left home and dark when she returned. When the weather was bad she had to spend the night with the teacher, Oma Dodd.

At the Red Rock school she got in trouble because she wouldn't take off her spurs. She didn't have fancy straps with buckles; she tied her spurs on with rawhide, and she tied them fast. She would have to cut her leathers to remove the spurs, and she wouldn't be able be put them back on until she got more leather. Miss Dodd switched her three times before giving up and letting Clarista wear her spurs.

Miss Dodd didn't permit girls to wear pants so Clarista carried a smock in her lunch sack—a flour sack tied to the saddle. When she got to school, she rolled up her pants legs and slipped the smock over her head. The smock didn't get dirty so she wore it all week. Once, when standing at the front of the room to recite, her pants leg unrolled and the other children giggled at the worn thing they saw hanging beneath her smock.

Clarista didn't have any friends in school. Already it was clear she was a throwback, towering over the girls and some of the boys in her class. She was going to be taller than both her parents. She didn't pack much meat on her bones, but she was strong as four strands of barbed wire. When Puggy Caldwell was a weaner he sometimes rode to school with her. He wore his sister's hand-me-down shoes and then only to school. At home, he and his brothers went barefoot unless there was snow on the ground. At night they lay on the floor with their feet in the air and their mother took a needle and picked out the stickers and splinters.

35

When older boys made fun of Puggy's shoes, Clarista pikered them to fight her. When Puggy was the only one in school who didn't get a valentine, Clarista gave him the one she got. Lucinda Gillin made a valentine for everyone of red construction paper trimmed with white lace with a poem printed on it but didn't expect Puggy to be at school.

Clarista wished she had given Puggy the valentine she had made by cutting the tail off her red flannel gown and sewing it over an old shingle she had whittled into a heart. Stoddard Keating got a valentine from everyone in the school and loudly counted them, picking out his favorites, until Clarista grabbed them and threw them on the ground.

When Anita Barnes, who sat in front of Clarista, said she smelled bad, Clarista took a pin out of the torn shirt under her smock, caught it in the hem of Anita's dress and pinned it to her sailor collar. Anita went to the black board, her drawers showing, and everyone except Lucinda Gillin and Miss Dodd laughed.

Clarista challenged the boys to horseback races after school and won until they stopped racing with her. She also beat them at marbles and mumblety-peg until they stopped playing with her. She was sent home for fighting with Stoddard. She rode a straight-colored black gelding to school, and he said it was fiddle headed.

Because her father received money only when calves were marketed, he hired her out to other ranches when he could spare her. She missed school during fall and spring roundup, wrangling the horse herd day and night, rustling wood and water, and in her spare time practicing roping. It was the only way she could get out of being a wrangler.

She worked for owners who didn't know what they were

doing and yelled at her because their own hands would quit at such treatment. They paid her two bits a day, half what they paid boys her age, and told her to help with dinner while the other hands sat in the shade. When the call came to put a boy on a horse to run an errand or carry a message, she knew they meant her.

When Clarista was twelve there was a blizzard. She wanted to be with her father and the hands who fed and checked the cattle, looking for the old, the weak, and the young. Her mother was sick and Claris told Clarista to care for her. When it started snowing again and Clarista knew the hands were going to be out all night, she overturned the long table the hands ate on, wrapped her mother in quilts and put her on it, hitched a horse to the table legs, mounted the horse, and dragged her mother over the snow to her grandfather's house. Leaving Celestine in Genevieve's care, she rode back to the ranch, boiled coffee, fried biscuits and bacon, and rode off to look for her father and the scattered hands.

Her feet and hands were numb from the cold, her stirrups slick with ice. She was returning to the house, huddled in the saddle against the snow, when she went to sleep and rode under a tree limb. Clarista was knocked to the ground; the horse kept going, head up and high-stepping to avoid the trailing reins. When she recovered her breath, Clarista got up, put her hat on and followed the horse's tracks until they were obliterated by the blowing snow. She knew the wind was from the north, but also that she might walk past the house in the darkness, walk until she dropped in exhaustion and froze to death. Biting her lip to keep from crying, she fell to her hands and knees to rest.

Clarista's faith was homespun, like that of her father. She didn't blame God for the snow; she chose to be out in it. She didn't blame God for putting a tree in her path. She was glad they had the tree, and she shouldn't have tucked her chin into her jacket, tied her bandana over her ears, pulled her hat on tight and gone to sleep. She didn't ask forgiveness for things that God should be able to understand, and she didn't ask God to give her things she could get on her own. But if she were going to live, she needed God's help, and she needed it now. As she prayed, she realized her hand rested on a wagon rut. On her knees, feeling for the rut with her hands, she made her way to the house.

When Claris returned home at mid-day he found a pot of coffee and a pot of beans working on the stove, the fire almost burned out, and Clarista curled on the floor between the wood-box and the stove. He picked her up and carried her to bed before collapsing on his own bed in his clothes.

Her mother never forgave her, and her father chided her for risking her life riding around at night in freezing weather, but the look on her father's and the cowboys' faces when she gave them biscuit sandwiches and coffee was reward enough. She was one of them, and they were proud to have her riding with them.

When Clarista was thirteen, her first period came while she and Puggy Caldwell held cattle after branding so the cows and calves could mother up. The blood ran down her leg and into her boot. When she got off her horse, a startled Puggy saw her stained jeans and asked what was wrong with her. "You're supposed to be watching the cattle," she snapped. She cut the tail off her shirt and folded it into a pad.

When her mother asked what happened to her shirt, she said, "I needed it to sit on." Celestine made a satchel out of a sugar sack for her to tie onto her saddle and filled it with rags. The satchel was too dainty for Clarista, and she was never happy with it until it was stained with saddle oil and horse lather. At night Clarista rinsed the rags in coal oil.

Although her mother couldn't look at her, Genevieve explained the shameful things that happened to a woman, the weakness, the bleeding, the nesting urge, enduring a man, bearing children. Clarista was confused; if a woman's lot was so difficult, shouldn't women be stronger? She saw cows deliver calves and had few illusions about the travail of birth, but she also saw cows lick, nuzzle, and nurse their newborn with what could only be affection, even in a cow.

She saw bulls mounting cows, forcing the cow's hindquarters down, had seen the urgent, vicious thrusting. It had frightened her at first, that impulsive, violent need. She saw that only open heifers tried to escape the bull's lunges, and that if a cow couldn't take a bull it was hamburger. Clarista knew it wasn't love, but it was life and that animal passion stirred her. She determined that when her time came she would spit and say howdy, unlike her mother who feared the need of it and her grandmother who disapproved the indelicacy.

When Clarista was fourteen Olin died and Claris gave her charge of Olin's ranch. Her father oversaw things and his cowboys helped with roundup and branding, calving and windmill repair, but she was jefe and they called her Rista. She told her cowboys their chores, checked their work, fired those who didn't take orders from a girl, and hired Shell Castleberry to cook.

Shell, who was so stove-up he could no longer ride, said, "I can't do nothing but fry and wash dishes."

"Can you pick figs, fry fritters, and boil coffee? You're hired."

▲▼▲

The day Claris gave Rista charge of her own ranch, Celestine set her face for sundown. Genevieve moved into Claris' house and did the cooking, washing, and cleaning. Rista sat with Celestine through long nights of vague pains and apprehensions, rubbing her with a hot flat iron wrapped in flannel and giving her draughts of rock candy and rock camphor dissolved in rye whiskey. No matter how long she was up with her mother at night, Rista was in the saddle at daybreak. She rode as long as there was light to see, carrying cornbread or biscuits in a greasy sack to last her until supper.

One day when chasing steers, her horse stepped in a hole and bowed a tendon. Rista unsaddled, pried off the shoe, and tied the horse in the creek in water over its knees. When she failed to return for supper, Celestine cried that Rista was lying in the pasture with a broken back and begged Claris to look for her. Claris said if Rista was injured her horse would have returned with an empty saddle and that it was useless to search for her before daylight. Celestine wailed that he always put things off, that he had promised her shelves and closets the day they married. "You are the most impatient woman I have ever known," Claris said.

The next day, Paco brought her a horse, and Rista rode home, put cornbread and fried meat in a sack, and grabbed a blanket. She was going to stay with the horse. Claris told her to leave it in the creek for three days, burn chicken feathers to smoke the swell, then re-shoe the foot shortening the toe and leaving the quarters long, and to rub a Spanish fly blister into the skin. He also told her not to get any of the blister in the haired area of her hand or arm. Celestine was driven to despair by Rista's antics with Claris' nod. Genevieve sighed, shook her head and cut, hemmed, and patched Olin's clothes so that Rista would not look indecent in the saddle. Rista rolled up the pants legs and carried fence staples in the roll.

Rista and Puggy Caldwell worked on a windmill while the cows bawled and hooked each other, half-crazed by thirst. Puggy cut a deep gash in his scalp. Puggy was a button, two years younger than she. Going to the doctor was a day's work, leaving the thirsty cows was shameful, and they were miles from head-quarters. Rista pulled Puggy's scalp together and tied his hair across the gash to hold it closed. Then she wrapped his head with her bandana, which was cleaner than his. He pulled his hat tight over the bandana, they got the windmill running, and returned to the house after the others finished supper. Celestine was horri-fied by the blood-stained dressing and Claris offered to look at the wound, but Puggy proudly refused. His scalp healed with a neat scar.

Rista found a lop-horned cow that had waded into Dead Man's Tank to escape the heel flies and had bogged. It was a job for one man on a horse to pull the cow free, one on a shovel to dig its legs out of the mud. There was no shovel, and no one to help her. She was riding a jerk-away piebald, but she tightened the latigos on her saddle and dropped a rope over the cow's horns. She put a handful of rocks in her shirt pocket, pulled off her boots to avoid bogging herself, rolled up her britches legs as far as she could, waded into the mire, dug out the cow's front legs with her hands, then its back legs while working her legs up and down to avoid bogging herself, threw rocks at the horse to back it up while tailing the cow up and pushing her from the rear.

When she got the cow out of the mud, the cow's legs were so shaky it collapsed. Rista stood panting herself, then tried to get the rope off the cow's horns. The cow shook its horns, got to its feet, and tried to hook her. Rista ran for the jerk-away horse and tried to get in the saddle, but the horse jerked its head and side-stepped.

The cow fell again. Rista worked the rope off its horns, coiled it, settled her horse, then pulled at the cow's tail until she persuaded it to stand. Again the cow turned on her, but without the rope to worry about, Rista got the horse between her and the cow. When the cow fell again she pushed the cow's head over, sticking one horn into the ground to give her time to mount or throw sand in its eyes if it attacked. The cow lay so still Rista tailed it up again. This time the cow shook its horns but stood panting and trembling and Rista backed slowly to the horse, caught it, reset her saddle and tightened the cinch before swinging onto the horse. She waited to be certain the cow was all right before riding away.

She rode home, proud of her mud-caked trousers, dirty face, and stained shirt. Rista's appearance sent Celestine into such a sinking spell that not even Genevieve's soups and puddings could part her lips. One day Celestine asked Rista to move her to a bed in another room so that Genevieve wouldn't see her dead on rumpled sheets.

Rista changed the sheets on her own bed, carried her mother into her bedroom and laid her down. "I gave Claris everything he wanted," Celestine said. "I gave you twice." She asked Rista to take the lamp out of the room.

Rista was fifteen when her mother died. Celestine had surrendered to illness so seeing her surrender to death was like seeing a bronc from the saddle rather than from the ground—more painful but no scarier. Rista was never lonely outdoors, but when she came in to eat or sleep, she missed her mother, missed carrying her a cup of soup, a cold cloth, riding to the root doctor for herbs and brewing them into a tea, missed sitting by her bed and reading to her from English novels of society and romance.

Celestine was buried in the graveyard on the ranch. Claris didn't go to funerals. He sat on his horse on a little knoll and watched, wishing to grieve alone. Claris didn't miss the comfort she gave him for she gave little comfort. He didn't miss talking to her because they rarely talked. He missed seeing her in her rocking chair, although her wan and spiritless look drove him to exasperation. He missed her slipping through the house as though afraid someone would notice her presence, even though such self-erasure depressed him. He missed the concern for her that kept a corner of his mind distracted from the work that needed to be done.

When she was sixteen, Rista found a heifer unable to bear her first calf. The calf had died and swelled inside the womb. Rista was alone with no one to help. Claris was laid up by a horse that stepped in a prairie dog hole. The only way to save the heifer was to cut off the calf's head.

Rista took the knife her father had given her, worked her hands into the heifer's womb, her fingers groping for sight, careful not to cut the heifer or herself. Each time the heifer had a contraction it mashed her hand against the pelvic bone, but her fingers found eye sockets, ears. She worked her hands to the neck, cut through gristle, found the joints, and cut between the neck bones because she couldn't cut through bone. When she cut the throat, fluids and gasses escaped, sickening her.

She wanted to quit; she wanted to ride away more than anything except being a cowboy. Crying and throwing up, she tugged the calf's head free, surprised at how heavy it was. She had to cut off one of the calf's shoulders before the heifer could deliver. She tried to get the heifer up, twisting its tail and pushing, slapping it with a rope, holding its nostrils closed to force it to stand.

She was unable to get the heifer to stand and knew that it would slowly die while birds pecked out its eyes and coyotes ate the calf and then started on the soft parts of the heifer. Her arms filthy with slime, she cut the heifer's throat and sat and cried as it died. But she knew she had found her life's work. She had looked under herself and saw that all she had was all she needed.

I used the flight and the layover in Denver to call clients about credit extensions, contract discrepancies and unpaid invoices. In Billings I rented a car, found a motel, and called Shana. I wanted to be on the road early the next morning for the drive to Wolf Creek. It wouldn't take fifteen minutes for Shad Carter to call me "bastard," but it might take most of the day for him to call me "son."

Because of the time difference, Shana was in bed but not asleep. "Did we have a good line-up tonight?" I asked.

"I think we got a strong lead-in from the Monday pic slot. It had good carry-over for a telepic."

"What's wrong?"

"I had a story—a couple of Christian teachers who took their children out of the best schools in the city and moved to a poor neighborhood with poor schools because they think they can make a difference there. Instead Carey went with a story about an image of Jesus that appeared in the rust of a screen door."

Better visuals, easier to comprehend, and it didn't make you feel uncomfortable watching TV while other people tried to do something noble but probably foolish too. TV informed, but it also had to entertain. A dog show would lead before an explanation of the national debt on any station.

"If you have Jesus in your heart, why would you need him or even want him in a rusty door?" asked Shana.

Shana called it "dumbing down," but we had to turn Jesus into an easy-to-understand memorable moment to a large group of people who cared more about gee whiz than Jesus.

"It scares me that we are creating a nation of people who are ignorant about the world," Shana said. "What scares me even more is that they think they know. All they have are attitudes and biases, and that makes very dangerous citizens."

"I'll talk to—no, I can't."

"No, you can't," Shana said. "I shouldn't have said anything to you. I just don't have anyone else. I can't say anything to Carey or Bob or anyone at the station. They all know we're seeing each other."

"Anything else you need to tell me? I promise not to hear it," I said.

She sighed. "Not a complaint, I'm asking advice. Carey says I need more community involvement. I teach a Sunday school class, sing in the choir, do volunteer work through the church."

"That's low profile with a small group. You need to be in the celebrity softball game, caddy for Brad McConnell when he's in town—"

"Who is Brad McConnell?"

"Shana, that's a name people want to know about."

"Is he a current celebrity or a current legend?" When I didn't answer, she said, "We criticize the schools because kids don't know history. What do you think they are going to remember when they are grandparents? Natural disasters, celebrity criminals, coddled athletes."

Shana enlarged twenty-second news segments to ethical and

philosophical tantrums. "They are going to remember that they became police because of cop shows, doctors and nurses because of doc shows, that they learned history and geography through time travel."

"And learned it wrong, plus six versions of the 'true story' of Al Capone, and a dozen of Jesse James, and at least three of JFK," Shana said with a laugh. "Have you seen your father yet?"

"Tomorrow. And he may not be my father."

"I love you. Call me tomorrow and tell me how the meeting went."

Shana's father was a church musician who wrote commercial ditties to support his family. Her only childhood pet was a rooster, which she entered in a contest at the county fair. As part of the judging, she turned her rooster upside down to show its tail feathers, and in her excitement, squeezed the rooster's crop and it strangled. Shana burst into tears, but the rooster won first place. For the award ceremony she had to hold her dead pet, propping up its head, and smile for the cameras.

When Shana was fourteen her father was murdered by a six-teen-year-old boy who stole his car. The boy told the police that he stole the car and shot her father when he resisted. His lawyer said that her father tried to rape the boy who killed him in self-defense and fled in the car. The media reported that the boy was found guilty but did not report that it was because the jury did not believe the lawyer's story of the attempted rape—the story most often told by the media.

After her father's death, Shana's mother worked as a waitress, and Shana helped her after school and on Saturdays. She did not date in high school. Her grades earned her a scholarship to college, and she worked in the college radio station for extra money. She had no serious boyfriends in college but was pursued by graduate students and professors.

She enrolled in law school but dropped out after the first year because "the law is on the side with the biggest bankroll." She sold ads for a television station. That sometimes meant dinner or drinks with clients and getting them to say yes while she was saying no. She and a client were forced into a car at gunpoint in a restaurant parking lot and taken to a remote area where they were ordered to undress. When the gunman was distracted by Shana's nakedness, the client wrestled with him, and she ran into the darkness. The client was shot but not killed, and the mugger fired shots at her before escaping in the car. Shana ran until she found a service station. With only her head visible, she called until the attendant came outside. "Ladies is on the other side," he told her.

"Throw me the key and call the police," she said. When she emerged, covered by a police-provided blanket, she found photographers waiting. In the first newspaper and TV reports, she and the client were naked in a remote area where the mugger found them. The stories were never entirely corrected.

I understood Shana's exasperation with the media, but television was the father that took me fishing, camping, that took me around the world, told me how to be a man, how to be a father, what girls were like, and how I should treat them. Television was the father that comforted me when I was lonely, that made me laugh when I was sad, that made me cry when things became too real. Television was the best teacher I ever had.

▲▼▲

The November wind was cold as I walked up the short

driveway to the log house near Wolf Creek in the tree-bare coulee part of Montana where Shad Carter managed a ranch. A TV antenna angled from the roof, and that gave me comfort. Mother said Rista thought the telephone had ruined the country, but Shad was a member of the global village. "I'm Chance Carter," I told the man who answered the door in boots, jeans, and western shirt. "My mother was Cassie Carter."

Shad showed neither interest nor surprise. "Come in," he said, shaking my hand. "This is my wife, Lena. Lena, this is Cassie's boy." He turned to me. "She knows about your mother."

Lena looked like someone's grandmother, soft, round faced, gentle. I couldn't imagine Rista looking like that. "We have two boys and a girl," Lena said, "and four grandchildren. How many children do you have?"

"I've never married," I said. Before Shana there was Eloise who headed a public relations firm. We were secure in ourselves, financially stable, emotionally matched, sexually attracted. We watched TV together; she talked about children, the house she wanted to build, the neighborhood with the best schools. She had set the alarm on her biological clock, but there was nothing in my mother's or grandmother's life to recommend children. They seemed to give and take pain in equal amounts.

"You're still young enough to have kids," Lena said. Lena gave Shad a look. "Well, I guess you two want to be alone."

Shad sat in a recliner and waved a hand at the couch with fake wagon wheel legs. I sat and Shad and I looked at each other. I don't know what I was looking for. Kinship? Resemblance? He was shorter than I expected, and his nearly hairless head seemed oversized, giving him a bulldog look.

"Let me say right out I don't think you're mine," Shad said.

49

"I never have. When your mother came to see me in jail, I said, 'It's not mine, is it?' She said, 'It could be.' I couldn't live like that. One day you looking like my side of the family, the next day hers, the next day his. I couldn't abide seeing you do something that reminded me of that son of a bitch. He was your father. When she named you Chance, I knew for sure."

Mother said she had prayed for a chance, and when I was born she knew I was the answer to that prayer. "Mother died," I said. "Cancer."

"I'm sorry. I never should have married your mother. We were young. I was a virgin. I thought she was too. There was no way I could do that to a woman and not marry her if she wanted me to."

"I got a call that something had to be done about Rista," I said. Shad volunteered nothing. "Some people say she killed two men."

"I don't know nothing about your grandfather, Odis. I do know that she wasn't the only one who had reason to kill him. I don't know who killed your daddy. I know I didn't."

"You left the state when he was killed."

"I didn't stop for no kisses. They thought I was watering at night, but I just wanted to get away from a mess like that. It's not complicated to know that a horse that isn't trained proper and worked regular is going to make a mistake that is going to hurt you and maybe him too. I wanted to ride away from that mess and start out with a whole new string." Shad looked at his boots then at me. His face was lined by the sun and wind, but his eyes were calm. "You walk through a cow lot, and you're going to smell like cow shit. You may want to remember your mother the way you knew her. Do what you can for Rista and stand clear of that other stuff."

"Did you try to contact my mother? Ask about me?"

"Your mother was riding the wrong pasture. No matter what she roped it wouldn't be right. Some of it could be my fault, but it's no good thinking about it now, and I don't need the hurt. I don't want to be drawn back into thinking about things that don't grow and bear fruit."

"Did you know Rusty McGinty? When I was little I thought he was my father."

"Then he was."

"He left when I was ten." A long time before he left he let me know I wasn't his son. "Shad is his father; why can't he pay for his damn shoes?"

Mother explained. "Shad was that damn cowboy I was married to when you were born. Rusty thinks Shad should send you money, but Rusty wants to be your father." Rusty had a hard time showing it, and when Rusty left, Shad was no longer "that damn cowboy" but my daddy and I was supposed to hate Rista for what she had tried to do to him. "Your grandmother almost sent your father to the electric chair," Mother said.

"You cull heifers by looking at their mamas," Shad said. "I figured being Rista's daughter, your mama was going to be special. She was a fence walker. What you come for I can't give you. I didn't leave nothing in Texas. That's the way I decided it, and that's the way I want it to be."

"There are tests that can tell for sure. I'd like to know," I said.

"Make up your mind the way I did. I'm not going to have no tests."

"People used to say I looked a lot like you."

51

Shad crossed his arms, leaned back, and examined me. "You look like your ma and her mother. The kind of rangy that don't fatten out. You got your ma and Odis' eyes, not studying the pasture you're in but the one you wish you were in and walking the fence. I never saw Rista look like that. My daughter can't ride in her shadow. My boys either. I wanted to. Maybe your ma wanted to. Odis. But every time you rode out with her you were made aware that you were a little less than you thought yourself to be. Don't count on leaving her feeling as good as you did when you rode in."

I stood. I had gotten all Shad was going to give.

"Where do you live anyway?" he asked, getting to his feet.

I was a geographical bastard; one expressway looked the same as another. "I manage a TV station in Florida." People were usually impressed by that, but I had misjudged Shad. The television was for his grandkids when they visited. To him television meant cartoons, car wrecks, and crime. "I oversee the big picture," I explained. I wanted him to wish I were his son.

"Your grandma don't fit in the big picture. She don't fit in any picture at all. She takes up the whole frame."

Lena offered coffee, but I declined. There was nothing for us to talk about, and I didn't want to play the groveling bastard hoping to be warmed by a man's smile. I envied their uncomplicated lives of shared coffee, shared work, shared cares, but I would have fled it as my mother had. On television the pictures changed, promising something better.

▲▼▲

It's a long way from Montana to Texas, across prairie states that I had been taught to disdain just as I had been taught to scorn Rista. Rusty used to say, "Nothing is close when you have

52

to cross Oklahoma to get there." I used the flight to call Shana and the station. I told Shana that Shad Carter wasn't coming to rescue me. "Damn cowboy," I said.

"I'm in love with a bastard?" Shana said in mock surprise. I asked how the morning show went. "A story about a woman with ninety-nine cats, a man on trial for rape who lost his moral compass five years ago when a girlfriend said he was bald, a new movie, the star of a new TV series, tape of an explosion in India, an earthquake in South America, flooding in Oregon, and a thirty-five-car pile-up on the autobahn. Meaningless horror punctuated by meaningless glamour. That's what we teach children. Other lives have no meaning and no purpose except our amusement."

I promised to call her when I got to Rista's ranch. When I called the station, sales said there was a flow problem because a family show—"half of the audience is on oxygen"—was followed by a program closer to the back seat that couldn't get an audience and was hard to sell. I told him to talk to program and get back to me.

Carey said the new videotape editor lost speed when he gave attention to detail and lost detail when he speeded up. Bob's happy talk was great and got a laugh from the cameramen. No one remembered what Bob said but it was funny. "Perfect," I said.

Promotions wanted news to do brief presentations to visitors to the station. Carey wanted Shana to do the presentations to enhance her image. He also wanted a plastic surgeon to enlarge her upper lip to give her a pouty look. "Talk to Shana," I said.

▲▼▲

Texas had more trees, more hills, more dead animals beside the road than I had expected. From Dallas I drove on the interstate past towns marked only by signs and wide fields devoid of humans or habitations. Cars whipped past as though everyone was trying to pass everyone else. I turned off the interstate on to state roads with the same speeding motorists until they abruptly braked at city limits where tractors, pickups, and traffic lights determined progress, and teenagers believed you wanted to hear their music in addition to that on your car radio.

The drive gave me time to decide that I didn't want Shad for a father. I didn't want Rista for a grandmother either, but she was the only living link to my heritage and probably too senile to tell me what my mother was like before I was born or who my father was.

If Rista knew that I had come to put her away and sell her ranch she would probably shoot me on sight. If she were as senile as I hoped, she might not remember me. If I couldn't slide Rista off her land without a fight, I intended to restrict the fighting to the courtroom and get back to the condo I shared with the big-screen TV, back to the world I controlled.

I stopped in Claypool, the county seat, to hire a lawyer. The town looked run-down and tired. Two stores on the square were vacant; another sold used goods advertised as antiques. The lawyer was smooth as a model's underwear with a bald head, sly eyes that could read a contract however you wanted it read, tiny mouse's teeth that chewed holes in the law. "I can get you a buyer," he assured me. "All you got to do is get Rista to sign a power of attorney letting you or me handle her affairs."

That was the nut. "She may be senile. She may refuse to see me. Shoot me on sight." I made it a joke, but he would remember.

"If you swear to a judge that she is a danger to herself or others you can have her held for observation. Since you're an outsider local rules will require someone known locally."

"Whoever called me said she was a danger to herself. Do you know who that might be?" The lawyer didn't know but said Pug Caldwell who worked for her might be a corroborating witness. Yeah, and he would probably want a piece of the ranch for his testimony.

"Do you know him?" I asked.

"Only by reputation. Someone told Rista he was in jail and it took two lawmen to arrest him. She said if it took only two it wasn't Pug."

At a service station I asked directions to the ranch and was told to watch for a rusted pickup door. "Does it have her name on it?"

"Used to be purple but I don't think you can see it any more. Why do you go there?" the attendant blurted. He was Hispanic and looked like a sun-dried Jesus without the beard. His rising inflection indicated questions. "Some doctors and lawyers bought that ranch across the fence from hers? The O-Bar? They don't do nothing but have parties and shoot deer. They don't keep up the fence or nothing. She called them on my telephone; she don't have a telephone. She said a bunch of their cows was in her pasture. She said for them to bring a truck because she shot three of them."

"Where can I get a mobile phone?"

He shrugged. "Fort Worth, maybe? You going out there? You couldn't call nobody from out there."

"I'm her grandson," I said. "I've come to do something with her."

He gaped at me. "Man, you know how she is. I asked if she been serviced and she wanted to shoot me. She said, 'Not by you, sonny boy.'"

Before I left the service station I called my secretary to tell her I didn't have a telephone and it might be a couple of days before I could call again. Jerry had complained about laxative ads and female hygiene products that he found offensive. I asked her to call business and sales and get the numbers. Then I called Jerry and told him about the revenue those ads created. "It's your nickel." Jerry wanted sales to try to replace those ads and said we should think about reducing staff in broadcast operations and engineering for greater earnings.

I called sales and told them to replace one or two of the ads, something I could tell Jerry. I'd ignore the threat to reduce staff until the other owners said something. A major client had seen an effect on network TV and wanted the same look in his ad. Production said we didn't have the equipment to produce the effect. "Ask them how that will that sell their product," I said.

I called Shana to explain that Rista didn't have a telephone and it might be a couple of days before I could get one. "Rista hates telephones."

"How does she know you're coming?"

"She doesn't know I'm coming. It's going to be a big surprise for both of us."

▲ ▼ ▲

Mother always talked about how far it was to town, but on the good state highway it took half an hour from Claypool to the turnoff to Rista's ranch. It wasn't until I entered the ranch that I began to understand distance as I bumped over the caliche road the oil company had laid when Mother was a baby. I turned off the main road the oil trucks used onto a rutted, weedy track marked "Private Road: Keep Out." Furrows had been plowed across the road.

I slowed the car to a crawl and bumped along until I found boulders blocking the way. I left the car and walked down the overgrown tracks through dry grass, brittle weeds, and oak trees. Hanging from the trees were coyotes in various stages of decomposition. Along a fence, rattlesnakes hung belly up to the sun. It had been freezing in Montana. Although the shadows were long, walking beneath the Texas sun was hot, and I threw my coat over my shoulder and stopped to enjoy the shade of a passing cloud.

The ranch looked deserted. Bleak, I thought. This is what bleak means. The house, barn, and outbuildings were bare of paint and weathered gray, the barn in better shape than the house. A tangle of old, upright planking stood beside the barn, inviting a fire. An ancient tractor, something mounted on a trailer, barrels, rolls and balls of wire rusted on the ground. Nothing seemed familiar or inviting. It smelled like a petting zoo. I started toward the house that lacked a yard or shade tree.

"That's far enough. You can turn around right there and go back to whatever hole you come from." The voice was husky but firm, a voice accustomed to yelling at animals and people.

"It's me. Chance," I said without turning, involuntarily raising my hands. I intended to call her Grandmother but that line would have to be dubbed. "I'm Cassie's son."

5

1928

With Claris laid up from a fall when his horse stepped in a prairie dog hole, Rista took charge of roundup, branding and driving steers to the railroad shipping trap in Claypool. When she could, she worked on other ranches earning a dollar a day for herself, fifty cents for her horse. When she returned to school the next year, the other students laughed at her because she had never heard of the St. Valentine's Day Massacre.

Rista soaked Claris' feet in hot water when his nose bled, rubbed him with rattlesnake oil, massaged his joints with cattle bones and gave him draughts of vinegar and honey, but he didn't get better. The cowboys made demands of her they had never made of Claris. The doghouse was a one-room, box-and-strip house with no window, nails for their gear, and a stove in the middle for heat if they cut wood or picked up cow chips. Rista put tarpaper over the inside walls, added a table and chairs, bought mattresses, and had the hands build bunks. The cowboys, who had been sleeping in bedrolls on straw over the floor, were so grateful they called it the bunkhouse. She put a chuck box on the wagon so Genevieve could drive to the pasture and cook dinner at noon.

Still hands quit because she could not pay them until only Pug and Paco were left. She hired farmers to plow firebreaks around the pastures, paying them with a cow to milk and a calf to feed out and butcher. She leased land to farmers who wanted to grow hi-gear for hay because it thrived on scant rainfall. They paid for the lease with a third of the hay for winter feeding.

One farmer charged money on her account in Red Rock and then moved, leaving a crop that was worth less than what he had charged. Rista had never played with guns any more than she had played with saddles, but when she went in search of him she placed a pistol in her belt the same way she placed a saddle on her horse. The farmer claimed he didn't have the money. "Papa is laid up and can't work, and I'll die before I lose his land," she said. "And I'll kill you before I kill myself." He paid.

When Rista was eighteen her father, who had never recovered from his injuries, died. When Paco and Pug finished digging the grave, they came to the house and put Claris' body in the kitchen so they could sit with it that night to keep a cat from jumping over it. There were no cats on the ranch, but they kept vigil playing their guitars and quietly singing. Genevieve told Rista she must wash and roll her hair for the funeral. Rista washed her hair in water from the rain barrel, and sat with Paco and Pug, listening to them play while it dried.

Genevieve and Rista prepared breakfast that they ate in Claris' presence. They put him in the wagon, carried him to the Bone Yard, their horses following the wagon, and buried him.

After the burial, Pug and Paco returned to their duties. Genevieve and Rista sat beside the grave for a while, but when they returned to the house, despite Genevieve's pleas, Rista saddled a horse and rode off also. She rode to her grandfather's ranch that her father had given her charge of, telling her that it would give her life or take it. Now she had charge of both ranches without her father to advise her and only two cowboys to help.

She entered the house where her mother was born and slowly walked through the rooms. Some of the furniture remained as there was no room for it in Claris' house. Some of it had been taken by cowboys when they left; some had been borrowed by neighbors. She had no use for it and no place. She found an old broom, swept the house clean of mouse droppings, dead crickets, wasps, and sand and closed the door. "The thing to do is do," her father always said. She would sell the house to pay some of the debt on the ranch.

▲▼▲

At eighteen, Rista was heir to a lot of desirable land. A rider brought an invitation to a play party at the J-B Connected. Most women Rista's age were married or engaged, and she needed a husband and children to help with the ranch. She had little time for attending parties, but her father's death added urgency. She wasn't going to find a husband in the bunkhouse. Pug was too young, Paco too old.

Rista determined to go to the play party although she had no party clothes, and Celestine had bought no party clothes after she married Claris. "When you die can I have your clothes?" she asked Genevieve.

"May I," her grandmother corrected. "Yes, and that may be a long time so let's pick out what you like right now." Genevieve picked out three dresses and fitted them although Rista thought they fit well enough. "Men like a small waist," Genevieve said. "You've got a small waist. Women have to take advantage of their assets."

Rista dipped water from the rain barrel, washed and combed most of the tangles out of her hair, and Genevieve trimmed the ends, sighing that Rista would have the shortest hair at the party.

To wear her hair from under her hat was to risk having it jerked out if it caught on a limb.

Rista hung a dress on the clothesline until the dew fell to dampen it for ironing. She had never had anything worth ironing and ruined one of the dresses learning how. It was the dress she liked the least. She carefully ironed the dress she liked second best—a white linen "lingerie" dress with lace ruffles around the stand-up collar, the shoulders, and the full-length hem—rolled it in her slicker and tied it to the saddle along with Genevieve's high-button boots with pointed toes and French heels.

Although it had a cold jaw and might give her trouble at the river, Rista rode the grulla because the bluish-gray color set off her dress. She crossed the river without trouble, took off her work clothes, waded into the river—dipping herself and splashing her face—put on clean knitted underwear and rode to the party. Rufus Brown had cut down a large tree, hitched a mule team to it, and dragged it through the weeds and brush to make a road to his house. She stopped under a tree near the house, tied her horse, hung her hat over the horn, and puffed up her hair. She tied her boots across the saddle, slipped on her dress and high-button boots, and was ready for the party, wet but clean.

Nobody saw the horse she had ridden to set off her dress. She stood for a moment in the darkness, tugging at the dress, trying to get it to feel right, certain that it was too tight in some places and too loose in others. She wished she had a mirror to check her dress, her hair, at least her face.

She walked slowly and unsteadily to the house in the button boots. Rufus Brown sat in a chair in the yard; the furniture had been moved outside to make room for the party. He chewed tobacco and watched the players as though trying to cipher what was going on. Rista thought he was troubling over his nephew Levi, who had been shot by his wife ten years earlier. Rufus had never married and had no friends but Levi.

The party had been going on most of the day. The boys had played follow the leader, blind man's bluff and ante over with a rock wrapped in a heavy sock while the girls made sorghum taffy. Together the boys and girls had played forfeit, drop the handkerchief, and fine or superfine.

Rista had arrived during an interlude for punch and conversation. When she entered, she saw the other girls stop and look at each other in mock amazement. "That dress must be ten years old." "She's wearing boots." Most of them wore pumps, skirts and blouses or chemises of various lengths, and their short hair was marcelled in waves or curled in kinky spirals. In their glad rags, they looked too fine to speak to. She was as out of place as a cow in the kitchen. She smoothed the unfamiliar dress and tried to pretend she belonged.

Coy Banister had worked for her once, and she believed he was sweet on her. At some point she had stopped growing, although she was still as tall as he. "Are the screwflies bad on your place?" she asked. Coy started to answer, but Anita Barnes wafted by in a cloud of talcum powder, and he lost his train of thought. The girls ignored her, but she plunged ahead like a bull in a briar patch. "Yesterday I had to shoot and skin out a calf that was eaten up with screwworms." One of the girls gave her a look that would put the lid on a mason jar. Rista smiled and tried to pretend interest in things they talked about. "Who is Judge Crater?" she asked. "What is coquette?" The girls looked at one another and rolled their eyes.

Anita got fainty and had Coy bring her punch to revive her.

Rista thought it was because of the screwworms, but Anita said that it was mating season and her body was telling her to have a baby. Coy dropped his rope on her three months later.

Rista knew only one other boy—Stoddard Keating, son of the newspaper owner. Stoddard had been the smartest student and the best dresser in school. He was now as tall as she. The cowboys looked like they had been scrubbed with the same brush they used on their low-necked clothes. Stoddard was a college student, impeccably dressed in a red choke strap, gray sack suit with a matching vest and paint shoes, and as self-assured as the cowboys were shy. Rista stared at his soft, white hands and clean fingernails. His face seemed never to have been roughened by the sun or bruised by the wind, nor had his dark, silky hair been crushed by a hat.

When they began to play clap in, clap out, Rista tried to join the puncture ladies who sat in the corners puncturing reputations, but the other girls insisted she play. The girls sat in a circle with the boys in another room. One by one the girls sent for the boy they wanted to sit next to them. The boy had to guess who sent for him and sit by that girl. If he sat by the wrong girl the other girls clapped the blushing boy out of the room. Although cowboys continued to arrive, there were more girls than boys, leaving some girls red faced and rejected.

Rista panicked when she realized she would be second to send for a boy. Anita, who insisted Rista sit close, sent for Coy who correctly sat beside her. Rista begged to be excused, but the other girls refused. She was certain that the handsome, sophisticated Stoddard was the favorite of many of the girls. He would never guess she had said his name; he hardly knew her. He would sit by someone else, the other girls would laugh at her presumption, and he would hate her for his embarrassment.

When his name was called, Stoddard came into the room. Unlike Coy, he slowly surveyed the circle while the girls blushed and tittered or averted their eyes. She could not look at him, and her face burned so she was sure her hair was red. She heard his footsteps come near and then he sat beside her. She was so grateful she could have hugged him. She could feel the glare from the other girls, but from the corner of her eye she saw him smile at her. "You gave me an ugly valentine," he said. "I don't blame you for hating me." Was that what he thought of her valentine?

During another game it was the boy's turn to choose the girl, only this time the couple walked around the house and everyone watched to see how much time they took and whether the girl blushed when they returned. Rista was certain no boy would call her name, and when Stoddard did she worried what she would talk about. Her worry wasn't necessary; Stoddard did all the talking. He complimented her courage in wearing an old-fashioned dress.

"They think good taste is more important than good sense," he said. She regretted not having good taste and wasn't certain she had good sense, but she was pleased he admired her. "They think they know something about fashion, but they would be laughed at in Austin where folks know what's fashionable in New York and Paris." Rista promised herself never to go to Austin where she would be laughed at.

"You remind me of a sculpture I saw of Dawn," he said. "Fresh. Rising. Just beginning to come alive. I'd have come courting if your father didn't lynch anyone who tried. A lot of other fellows would have too."

His words shocked and confused her. A young man had come to the ranch two or three times to ride with her. She thought he was sweet on her, but Claris thought he was looking over their stock, and they were short on the cow count. Claris threw a rope over the man's head, looped it over a limb and dragged him half out of his saddle. Claris told him to make long tracks because if he saw him again, he'd hang him. The next day Claris went looking for him, but his horse stepped in a prairie-dog hole. No one saw the young man again, and they lost no more cows.

"My father wouldn't lynch anyone," she said.

"Your father wouldn't run a horse through a prairie dog town unless he was trying to rope something real important."

She had warted herself over that. She had pleasured in the man's company while putting miles on a green-broke horse. Was he a cow thief? Was she responsible for her father's death?

Stoddard asked if he could see her home. She was so surprised she blurted, "I have to cross the river."

"I know how to ride and how to swim," he said.

After the party everyone watched as Stoddard escorted her outside—the girls jealous, the boys noticing her for the first time. Stoddard borrowed a horse because he had come to the party with friends in a wagon. The country was too rough for a car or even a buggy. Rista led her horse to where he saddled his. "That's a little far back, isn't it?" she asked, moving the saddle up on the withers and tightening the cinch. They rode together while he talked of college and his plans. His father wanted him to learn the newspaper trade and take over the paper.

"That sounds important," she said, marveling that she knew someone who could publish a newspaper.

"A paper is a mobile billboard," he said. "When I'm home I sell ads. If I sell a lot of ads, Dad has to find news to carry it— who was born, died, got married, club meetings, church meetings. That's why stories about Floyd Collins or Judge Crater are important. You can expand them to fit the space left over after the ads. You can keep it going for days. Police find new evidence; police are baffled. Have you read Zane Grey?"

She hadn't read anything outside of school except a medical remedy book and the fool books she read to her mother.

"I want to be a writer like him. I want to write about the lives of people here."

Rista was excited. Stoddard would write about Nonie Othart who died outside the hotel and whether she was part Indian. Her father, Leon, cowboyed until he got a little squat of his own, the Lazy L. He and his wife tried to build up a little spread, but he barely had enough beef for a barbecue. One day he found a neighbor on his land with a small fire, branding a calf with a cinch ring. Nearby was one of Leon's cows. Leon shot the neighbor as a rustler. When the dead man fell over the calf, Leon saw the man was branding the calf for him, a neighborly thing to do. Leon was trying to hang on to the few calves he had, and the law understood that but advised him to move on before folks decided to do something themselves. His wife went back to her folks. He came to Red Rock and tried to start over, but folks shunned him, except for an Indian woman.

"Do you think Doc Evans was a real doctor?"

"Who?"

"Doc Evans." Red Rock didn't have a doctor so the pharmacist, Doc Evans, prescribed medicines, set bones, and delivered babies. A raccoon got between the wall and sheetrock in his office, had a litter, and died. The birth softened the sheetrock, and the baby raccoons' feet scratched through the wall. Doc Evans saw little hands reaching out to him. It scared him so he ran out into the street. Folks who went to the Aginers Church said that proved he was an abortionist and churched him.

Stoddard shrugged. "This county has history and your father and grandfather are part of it. So is my father. You and I are part of it, too."

She had never been part of something important, and she loved Stoddard for including her. "Do you know what happened to Dave Verstuft after he shot another boy in the cemetery?" Wes Verstuft, a Quarter-Circle J cowboy, got drunk and tried to start a conversation with a drummer. When the man ignored him, Wes pulled a pistol. The drummer ran into the street and Wes shot at him. Sheriff Grover took the pistol, locked Wes up until he was sober and fined him for being drunk. Grover said Wes was just trying to scare the man, and anyway, he missed.

Wes' younger brother, Dave, bragged about how brave he was and another kid dared him to go to the graveyard at midnight. Dave did but took Wes' pistol with him. The other kid jumped from behind a tombstone to scare him and Dave shot him. Grover arrested Dave. Grover knew if the other boy's folks killed Dave, Wes would try to kill them, and he'd have a feud on his hands. The boy's folks stood outside the jail and demanded Grover turn Dave over to them. Grover opened the door, said, "Clear out or I'm going to arrest all of you," and that was the end of it. Dave, who was thirteen, escaped the jail and was never seen again.

Stoddard wasn't interested in that story; he wanted to write about Dan Beasley who killed Clint Houston in a gunfight. Dan and his brother Roy were kids on the O-Bar. They fought constantly, and Dan, the younger, stabbed Roy with a knife. Roy survived but Dan was sent to live with a family in Red Rock so they wouldn't kill each other. They fought at their father's funeral, and it took the sheriff and two deputies to separate them. They were both at a dance at the Slash 6 when Roy got in a fight with Clinton Houston, the tick inspector.

Clinton was so small he carried buckshot in his pockets so he didn't fly out of the saddle. He was so careful he carried a list to check off. If he checked a brand that wasn't on the list, he wrote it down so he could scratch it off. Roy accused him of being careless in his inspection, Clinton said something about O-Bar cattle, the fight spilled outside, Clinton pulled a knife, and Roy ran. Roy tripped and fell, and Clinton bent down and cut Roy's throat while he was on his hands and knees.

Dan came outside, saw his brother, and picked up a single-tree. Clinton ran for the brush. Everybody came outside and after a while they heard Clinton screaming and blows like hitting something hollow. They heard Clinton dying and begging for his life. Dan came back with blood all over him and rode to the O-Bar. The sheriff refused to go after him. Grover was appointed sheriff, rode to the O-Bar, told Dan if he came to town he would kill him, and rode back to town.

"The only person Dan ever killed, he killed with a single-tree," Rista said but Stoddard ignored her.

"I want to write about how Doss and Claris McCloud fought off a Comanche raid and then chased the Indians back to the reservation, not stopping to bury Claris' mother and sister."

Stoddard had confused two separate incidents. Her grandfather and others had followed Indians after a raid and killed five of them in their sleep. During another raid her grandmother and aunt had been killed. In that raid, the last in the county, Claris told her they didn't know the Indians were there until they heard his mother screaming with a lance through her. Doss gave Claris a pistol, put him on a horse, and sent him to warn the neighbors. Doss thought the Indians had kidnapped his daughter. He buried his wife in the graveyard someone else had started. The neighbors buried JackieLou. When she had been in the ground long enough to dig up, Doss and Claris couldn't find her grave, and the neighbors had gone back to Tennessee. Rista explained the separate incidents.

"Doss McCloud was the greatest Indian fighter and the toughest man in the county. He rounded up every unbranded cow in two counties, drove them to Kansas, came back with a saddlebag full of money and bought land, running off anyone who didn't want to sell."

Rista wanted to snort that her grandfather never owned a saddlebag, nor her father, nor she either. If they needed to pack something they packed it in a gunny sack. "Grandfather bought land from homesteaders who couldn't make a living." Stoddard's father and his newspaper had drawn farmers to the county, promising them cheap, fertile farm land and a healthy climate. "You can grow anything here you can grow any where else except Negroes. We don't have any, and we don't want any," he wrote.

"I want to write about the fence-cutting wars," Stoddard said, "and how your father, younger than Billy the Kid, shot it out with fence cutters to keep them from stampeding your grandfather's cattle."

It was her father who cut the wire because it fenced off the deep holes in Six Mile Draw. Eventually he was able to buy the land and fence it himself. Why did Stoddard fancify their stories?

"When Doss McCloud died, the other ranchers tried to run Claris off his land. Especially Dan Beasley and his bunch of outlaws. Claris rode over there alone although he was just a kid. He told Beasley that if another fence was cut or if he found an O-Bar stray in his pasture, he would kill Beasley. And Dan Beasley ducked down in his boots. In front of his hired guns. What a story that will make."

Her father told her that the Big Rock fence was cut, his cattle got out, and he believed some of his calves had been branded by the O-Bar. Claris knew that if he and his hands rode to the O-Bar there would be trouble, but if Beasley buffaloed him others would try, and he could hang up his saddle. He led his hands to the O-Bar, leaving them under cover in rifle range of the house. Dan Beasley was alone. "Get off my ranch or I'll turn the dogs on you," he said. "You ain't big enough to pack a gun."

"My men are ready to shoot anyone looking for trouble," Claris said.

"I don't see nobody," Dan said, his eyes flitting over the horizon.

"You won't hear the bullet either. If it happens again, I won't ride up to your front door to talk," Claris said.

He turned and rode away and his hands joined him eager to know what happened. "We won't have any more trouble from the O-Bar," Claris said. The hands wanted to go to Red Rock and celebrate. "If you do, pack your bedroll," Claris said. They grumbled but he had their respect.

"Stoddard," Rista began, "O-Bar cows always seemed to have twins, and the cowboys were a hard winter bunch, but they weren't outlaws."

"Your father didn't tell you the whole story because you're a girl. I'm going to make Claris McCloud a hero. If he had killed Dan Beasley, he'd be a bigger hero than Billy the Kid."

"Billy the Kid was no hero, and my father was no killer." She would have said more, but they had reached the river.

Rista told Stoddard to ride ahead and she would catch up. He refused, citing the danger of crossing the river. When she insisted, he thought she had a call of nature and volunteered to ride down the river and wait for her. When he was out of sight, she undressed, put on her work clothes, and joined him. When he saw she had changed clothes, he told her that the other girls changed at the party host's house.

She felt so stupid she was certain he would never ride with her again. He didn't notice how well she handled the grulla in the river and kept his horse from drifting downstream. Instead, he told her he liked her better in clothes fit for a girl.

When they reached the ranch house and she unsaddled her horse and turned it loose, he asked if he could take her to a dance. When she told him she didn't know how to dance he said he was particularly pleased because he wanted to teach her. Then he took her hand and kissed it.

Rista watched him ride away when there was so much she wanted to ask him. She had never had a beau before; was he her beau? How was she supposed to act? Play like she was an unweaned heifer? Or a branded cow? Did he really believe her father could have been a murderer like Billy the Kid? That her grandfather had left his wife and child unburied to chase

Indians? Or did he cut a shine to stand tall on the skyline like an Aginer at a revival?

Stoddard was lovably boy-like when he talked about all he was going to do. He seemed so needy, like he needed a friend, and she wanted to be his friend, to brush the hair out of his eyes. She admired him for wanting to be more than his father, but she was troubled that he saw her father as a buscadero rather than a laborer in the Lord's vineyard.

Genevieve had been awakened by the horses and lighted a lamp when Rista went inside. "How was the party? Did you meet anyone?" she asked, propped on her pillows.

"Coy Bannister was there, but Anita Barnes cabbaged on to him."

"Did she shake her fanger at him? A man may not know it, but when a woman shakes a fanger at him she has her bonnet set for him. Did I hear two horses?"

"Stoddard Keating escorted me home."

"Rista, you have a beau! Did he say you were pretty?"

"He said I had good sense. He said I looked like Dawn."

"He paid you a compliment. That means he thinks you're special."

But did he think she was pretty? "He asked me to a dance."

"Rista, he's serious. Come sit beside me."

Rista unrolled her dress, shook out the folds, and hung it on a nail.

"Put it on a hanger, dear. There's one on the rope." Claris had nailed a rope across the corner to hang clothes on.

Genevieve had lived a gentle life in a land ruled by men and horses. She was innocent to the custom of horses but wise to the fashion of men. "Rista, this is your first prospect, and you must make the most of it. Do you like this . . . Stoddard?"

"He is so handsome. His hair is curried like he never wears a hat, and he dresses like he's advertising a college. He wants to be a writer."

"That's not necessarily bad," Genevieve said to Rista's relief. "We'll catch him. Give your old granny time to think how."

Rista scarcely slept that night and pondered Dawn all the next day. What did he mean? She had always been taller and firmer than other girls her age and she favored her mother who was said to be beautiful, but Rista had never before attracted the attention of a man, except for one who was after their cattle. And Puggy. She felt like his big sister. She put castor oil on her eyelashes to make them longer and posed like Dawn in Celestine's mirror—fresh, rising, alive.

Two days later she noticed a scarf tied to a fence post. Pinned to the scarf was a poem addressed to her about "the pensive economy of your smile." She intended to keep the poem forever and to wear the scarf to the dance.

The day Stoddard was to take her to a dance a grass fire broke out on the Three Crosses. Pug and Paco were working different pastures, but she knew when they saw the smoke they would race to the fire. By the time she reached the fire, a neighbor had killed a cow and split it open with an axe. She tied the carcass to her saddle and dragged it along the front edge of the fire to smother it. It was after dark when the fire died out. The women and children had gathered near a dirt tank for safety. They gave the men big hugs for putting out the fire, especially Pug, but looked at her in embarrassment. Her face was smudged, and her eyebrows and lashes and the hair that escaped her hat were singed.

She rode back to the ranch wondering who Stoddard danced with and if he missed her. When she got home she found him in the sitting room talking to her grandmother about the books he was going to write of daring and danger and the life he was going to lead in exciting places. Genevieve showed him her shroud that she had made and kept in a chest.

"I came to take you to the dance. Since you weren't here I couldn't go without you," he said.

She loved him for that. She apologized for causing him to miss the dance. He smiled, mentioned the lateness of the hour and said he should leave. Although she didn't feel like Dawn, she walked him outside. She was so grateful to him for coming and so ashamed of her scorched hair, fire-blackened face and smelly clothes that she permitted him to kiss her.

The next morning she found a bouquet of wilted wildflowers tied to her saddle along with a poem. "I want the world to know my gain and share my joy and sport with me through fields of pain and daring. And thus to end alive. Together." She hugged the poem to her breast wanting to share his joy, his pain and daring. But he made no mention of her, only of the world.

She pressed the flowers in the family Bible and placed the poem on top of the first one. She didn't dare write him a poem, but she whispered her love on the wind. She didn't care if he couldn't ride a packhorse.

6
Tuesday, 1990

"Chance? Is it you, Chance? It took you long enough to get here."

When I turned I knew that whoever said Rista couldn't take care of herself didn't know Rista very well. Her sun-mottled face was crushed leather, her mouth sunken as though teeth were missing, and stiff white hair poked from under her hat. The years had battered her, but she looked mean enough to wrestle alligators.

"Where's Cassie?" she asked, her thumbs clenched in her belt loops.

"Mother is dead."

"Cassie's dead? Why didn't someone tell me?"

"She didn't want to see you."

Her faded eyes glinted. "If you come to blame me for what happened to your mother, you can save your spit."

A big ugly cowboy came around the barn with a shotgun. The sun had burned wrinkles and maybe cancers into his long red face. He had a short nose, a rough mouth, and his lower jaw seemed out of line as though something didn't suit him. His eyes beneath spiky eyebrows were a pale gray that had seen everything. "Look what blew in with the tumbleweeds," Pug said and threw an arm around my shoulder. "Boy, are we glad to see you. We're fixing to feed, and I got to where I can hardly load."

"Pug's been here so long he's like one of the horses," Rista said. "I can't ship him to the glue factory so I keep him around. Give us a hand. You ain't too pretty to help."

There was something familiar about Pug—a childhood memory? I looked at a man so limited in imagination he spent his whole life in the same place and repressed a shudder. "I left my car down the road with my clothes in it. Maybe I should put it some place safe."

"It's safe. There ain't a banker in thirty miles," Rista said.

I followed them to the barn where they loaded bags of cattle feed into a battered pickup. I grabbed a bag and tugged. "You got to get your weight under it," Rista said. "You're slow as a cow with sore teats. I want to get done before dark." Both she and Pug moved the sacks faster than I did. "Pack them on your shoulder. It's easier."

"I'm not dressed for this kind of work," I said. The bags stained my white shirt and dusted my slacks. I had thrown my coat in the pickup.

"My heart fell when I saw you dressed like a drug dealer," Rista said. "You're not a banker are you?"

"No," I said, renewing my struggle with the bags.

"Throw some feed to that rider steer," she said, gesturing at a pen, "and let's go."

The pens consisted of old cross ties sunk into the ground for posts with a jumble of rotting planks, many of them split, all of them faded and worn, nailed into the posts. While I fed the steer, Pug leaned the shotgun inside the feed bin. "Where you got feed you got rats, and rattlesnakes gravitating to the rats," he said.

The three of us got in the pickup with me on the outside so I could open the wire gates or "gaps" as they called them. After the third gap, Pug started honking, driving slowly, then stopped and honked some more. We waited for the cows to gather around us, Pug and Rista checking them.

"Cancer eye," Pug said, pointing at one of the cows.

"Better market her while we can."

I tugged the bags to the tailgate of the truck where Rista sat scattering feed as Pug slowly drove. I climbed back in the cab ready to rest only to discover that we had two pastures to go. Rista and Pug had fed the others. I reached up to steady myself and grabbed one of two rifles in a rack over the seat. "I hope it's not loaded," I said.

"Every gun we got is loaded," Rista said. "Only thing more useless than a gun that don't shoot is a cow that don't breed, a horse that don't ride, a man that don't work."

"Why do you need guns out here? Except for rats and rattlesnakes?"

"Wild hogs, coyotes, rabid skunks," Rista said.

"Halloween, kids come out to torment us or scare themselves," Pug said. "We never bothered about Halloween until teenagers got cars."

"Poachers," Rista said. "They think isolated ranches are easy pickings. They come out here at night and spotlight deer for their horns."

I was surprised no poachers were hanging with the coyotes. "Have you shot anyone?" I asked. I almost said, besides my grandfather.

Both Rista and Pug got stiff. "I almost shot Pug once. I was working a horse and had a pistol because I saw a rattlesnake in the corral. I'd raised Jug, halter broke him. I didn't expect any trouble, and he wasn't any when I saddled him. When I got in the saddle, he squealed, went bald headed, took me to church and made a Christian of me. I lost a stirrup, landed hard, looked up and here he came, snorting and kicking like he didn't intend to stop. I pawed around on the ground until I found the pistol and shot him. Fell right on top of me. I couldn't get him off me, and I couldn't get out from under him because I was against the corral. I knew Pug was working in the horse trap so I emptied the pistol in the air so he'd know something was wrong. I hollered until my throat gave out. After a while he came in, went to the house, came out, and was fixing to drive off when he saw a horse down in the corral. Then he saw me laying under it. 'Is Jug okay?' he asked. 'Get the damn horse off me,' I told him. He hooked a come-along to the snubbing post and dragged the horse to where I could get out from under it. 'Didn't you hear me shooting?' I asked. 'I figured you was just fooling around.' 'Why did you come to the house?' 'I needed you to help me.' I said, 'Pug, it's a damn good thing I'm out of bullets.'"

"I got in the truck and drove off. I don't remember what I did, but I didn't come back until after dark," Pug said.

That sounded like more than an employer-employee relationship, and it sounded like a warning. Did she know why I had come?

"I didn't break nothing but I loosened some hinges that was already flapping," Rista said. "That was the last horse we trained. Too short handed, and me and Pug have broken all the bones we care to break. That's all we know, horses and cows. We had goats once. The government wanted mohair and guaranteed the price so I had to do like everyone else and get hair goats.

They're smarter than sheep and they look kind of dainty with that hair hanging down like a skirt, but there's no pride in goats. One old cowboy came looking for work, took a look at them goats and said, 'I don't know nothing about sheep.' I said, 'I know. Them are goats.'"

"Too dainty for my taste," Pug said. "I don't know that you can ever say that a goat is yours. It belongs to whoever has a fence around it at the moment. But a cow or horse you know it by sight, and people have been killed for claiming the wrong one."

An awkward silence passed through the truck, and I wondered if Pug was telling me not to claim the cows and horses or not to claim anything.

It got cold when the sun went down, and I put on my coat and shivered. When I got out to open and close a gap, I snagged the coat on barbed wire. "Put your shoulder in it," Rista yelled as I struggled to close the gap and slip the wire loop over the free post.

When we got back to the house Rista told me to peel potatoes and onions. She and Pug worked side by side, she frying steak, potatoes, and onions, he putting tin plates and assorted silverware on the table. There was no discernible rank. He drove, she bossed; he advised, she listened. I didn't know how couples acted when they had been together for fifty years, but it might be the way Pug and Rista went about their chores. They meshed like co-anchors, taking and yielding without strain, seemingly without thought. I was the outsider.

"I hope you weren't expecting a salad because there isn't one," Rista said. "Pug, open a can of that red cabbage. We need something green for supper. And get down that jar of algerita jelly. That's the last jar so if you want any more somebody is going to have to pick the berries. Eat up, Chance," she said, turning to Pug. "Don't he look wormy to you?"

▲▼▲

After supper, Pug drove me to my car. I tried to warm up with the car heater as I followed Pug back the unmarked trail to the house that was as square and plain as a cardboard box. Mother called it a box-and-strip house—one-by-twelve boards vertically with one-by-four boards nailed over cracks between the one by twelves. Mother said the only insulation was tarpaper with newspapers tacked over it. When she was a girl she read the papers on the wall—stories of Ingrid Bergman, Gary Cooper, Bess Myerson, the Texas City disaster, Danny Kaye, Judy Holliday, the Kinsey report, the DAR turning away a Negro singer, the Brink's robbery, the samba, Loretta Young, the assassination of Mohandas Gandhi.

Pug parked outside the house and went to the bunkhouse as if by habit. Did he and Rista live separately or was this for my benefit? I parked beside Rista's truck and went into her house.

It was colder in the house than it was outside although the walls had been covered with fiberboard and painted. I doubted the house was solid enough to move to Claypool to sell. It smelled like a man's house—worn clothes, old boots, sweated leather, grease, fried meat, molding potatoes, rotting apples. There was no hint of perfume, powder, or scented soaps.

Rista called to me from the sitting room. "It's warm in here. I poured you a cup of coffee," she said.

I stood for a moment in front of the electric heater before sitting in a worn ladder-back chair. Rista held her cup in her hands as though warming them. Linoleum showed at the corners of the room but had been worn through in places, and I could see scars in the wood flooring. "Odis did that when he rode a horse through here," Rista said. I looked at her; she had put on glasses. Odis rode a horse in the house? She was auditioning for a nursing home.

Except for the beds, all her furniture seemed to be in that room, dominated by a writing desk and a glass-door bookcase. I looked at the books inside—an old family Bible, a few school-books, an out-of-date family medical book, faded English romance novels. I opened the case and took out a biography of Helen Keller for children.

"That was your mother's book. Helen Keller was her hero." She seemed a strange hero for Mother. "She said it was because Helen lived in a dark world. The romances belonged to my mother, the Bible to my father. The medical book is mine. I was the only doctor the hands knew."

On one side of the bookcase was a rifle, on the other a shot-gun. On the desk and bookcase were an ancient radio, a revolver, a child's spurs, rattlesnake rattles and a lead-backed brush and hand mirror that must have been a wedding present. The pistol might bring a hundred, $25 tops for the rest. I picked up the rattles.

"First rattlesnake I ever killed," Rista said, rousing herself. She had been slumped in a rocker, hands curled in her lap, her face drawn, unable to hide her age and the work she had done that day. Her ears were paper thin. "My mother, your great-grandmother, was going to pick up eggs and came across the snake and couldn't move. I yelled at her to back up. The thing to do is do, but she acted like she was paralyzed. I got the shotgun although I had never shot it and killed the snake. The shotgun knocked me down. Mother fainted. I dragged her to the house

83

and picked up the eggs. The job was mine until Mother died. When I had to do the cooking, I told the hands if they wanted eggs for breakfast they had to find the eggs. I wasn't no hen wrangler."

She picked at scabs on her hands that were gnarled and crusty. "I skinned the rattlesnake so Papa could make me a hat-band." She pronounced it Poppa. "Even when they're dead, skinned and gutted a snake will wiggle and try to coil. Mother wouldn't cook it so I cut away the white meat down its back, battered and fried it. The hands were partial to it."

"Are there a lot of rattlesnakes?"

"Bankers put more people in the cemetery than rattlesnakes. People are always afraid of the wrong thing. Cassie was like that."

"Mother was afraid of rattlesnakes?"

"She was afraid she would miss something. Life is work and it was all around her but Cassie wanted to find it someplace else. That was Odis' fault. Many a time chickens and eggs stood between us and starvation. No cowboy wants to pick up eggs or milk cows, but I did it. When there was more milk than we could use I curdled it and fed it to the hogs. If I sent Cassie to bring in the milk cow she'd come back with a steer. Couldn't cook beans that didn't rattle on your plate. Thought she was too good to fork a horse, that it would give her a big bottom. After Odis died she had to make a hand and she did. She could do a good job with something that didn't matter, but she couldn't find her life in it."

Mother didn't have a career; she had jobs. Ranching was Rista's life, her family. I don't know if Mother ever found her life. If she looked for it in love, she didn't. Men were slow to accept their own children; providing for someone else's kid was viewed as both heroic and moronic.

"I never was around babies except you and your mother, but I bathed you and taught you to play cowboy. When you weren't playing cowboy you were wearing out the steering wheel on the truck. Sometimes I hoped Cassie wouldn't have more kids because I wouldn't know them. I don't think Cassie liked kids. She loved you, I saw that, but I don't think she dreamed of a house full of kids."

If it hadn't been for me would Mother have had a happy life with Rusty, singing and laughing in the hammer lane? Riding the road the way Rista rode the range, her embrace bigger, her grasp lighter? "Do you have any pictures of Mother?"

Rista got a worn album from a chest of drawers. She had to move furniture before she could open the drawer. The cheap black pages of the album crumbled at her touch, the yellowing photographs falling like leaves. There were only a few—a studio photograph taken from the side with Odis looking down at the camera, his arms crossed with a pistol in one hand; a wedding picture of Odis with his arm around Rista as his proudest possession, Mother standing on a chair with Odis standing behind her, his arms around her waist, his chin on her shoulder; school pictures with Mother in a cloud of children, Mother and Shad with Shad holding a horse. There were no Christmas or birthday photographs. Mother said they didn't celebrate much—a boot full of hard candy and a present Christmas morning, a cake on birthdays. No parties, ever.

I looked at the picture of Mother and Shad. Mother looked thin even then, incredibly young, smiling with effort. Shad stood proudly between his wife and his horse. "I went to see Shad," I said. She waited for me to describe my reception; I waited for her to tell me if Shad was my father.

"Shad was a good man," she said, "but he never made anyone laugh."

I stared at Rista; was she senile or did she tell me something I didn't understand? "Who is this?" I asked about a pretty woman who wasn't Rista but from her dress appeared to be from the same era.

"That's Lucinda Gillin, Judge Gillin's daughter. That was taken when she was judged Best Hatted Lady. I wanted to look like that." She took the album. "Your mother was pretty from the day she was born. I didn't have a lot of time for babies, but I loved your mother. The older she got the more I loved her and the less I liked her."

Mother was tall and trim, an expert with makeup and exercise. Men said she could be a movie star and she loved to hear it. Maybe she could have been an actress; she played roles, different roles for different men. Some lived with us for a time—some called me "son" before proving themselves inadequate or finding better accommodations.

One man I called Mr. Mister because I wasn't permitted to know his name. For one man, Mother became religious, and I had to go to Sunday school so that when he met me I wouldn't act dumb when he asked if I had been slain in the spirit, washed in the blood. I learned many vocabularies—low boy, reefer, hammer lane and lot lizard; pumper, nozzle man, lay a line, med-assist; slap fest, volume hag, flat fee and getting ganked; cash flow and critical balance; lesson plans, resource room and Ritalin; interrogatory, arraignment, mag court; stock the vault, stick the tank, do a drop—before I left home and learned board fade, camera chain, and damping control.

Eventually, Mother's face took on a hard shine—first from the smoking, drinking, the effort of being beautiful in order to be loved, and then from the chemotherapy. "Mother had lung cancer."

"Did she smoke?"

Cigarettes were a craving she could satisfy. "Rusty smoked; she smoked with him." Rusty McGinty had been a soldier, truck driver, oil-field troubleshooter and after Mother left with him, a truck driver again. Rusty talked about the places he had been— Big D, Mile High, A-Town, Twin Cities, Shaky City, Alamo City, Motor City, Windy City, OKC, the Big Apple, Mormon Town, Opry Town, Tinsel Town, Gay Bay, Graceland, Mardi Gras. He had seen it all from the cab of a truck, and he wanted to show it to Mother—greasy truck stops, greasy cafes, a lifetime of high-way get-away, sleeping in a different town every night, eating in a different restaurant every meal. That appealed to Mother. Riding the road with the whole country in her embrace.

Then Mother had to stop in one place so I could go to school. Rusty didn't want to stop, except for a few hours to sleep, eat, load, or refuel, and wherever he was there were women for whom a few hours was enough.

"I begged Cassie not to take you and run off with Rusty," Rista said.

Mother adored her father. She said that after Rista killed Odis, she spent the rest of her life looking for a man to give her the same love and attention.

"Your mother was like a filly," Rista said. "She wanted to run from one side of the pasture to the other. She wanted to see everything, to spook at butterflies and rear, pitch, kick for no reason except the joy of it. I was glad when she married Shad because I thought she would be safe. And she was. Safe as a dead calf. Shad was hobbles on a blooded mare."

I put hobbles on her. Whenever they fought, Rusty said, "We'd be all right if I didn't have to take care of someone else's damn kid."

"Tell me about Cassie's death."

"They put her on chemotherapy, but she didn't like the person she was becoming." That was all I intended to give.

"Damn cigarettes," she said. "And cars. That's what kills people. Stoddard was happy to advertise them. Courted them, did favors to get their dollars. But that fool Claypool newspaper said beef killed people, and folks should grow more carrots. How many carrots do you think I can grow on this place? Oh, you could turn parts of this ranch into farms for a year or two, folks have done it, and then they freeze out, or wash out, or blow away, and they move on. I can show you places on this ranch where farmers ruined the land for longer than I've been alive. I'm trying to save the land, the wildlife, cows. How many deer do you think there would be if this was a carrot farm? Or jackrabbits? How many cows do you think there would be if there were no profit in them? A handful in zoos."

The loss of tobacco advertising had been a blow to the station. I started to tell Rista what I could do with that tobacco money but thought better of it. There was no reason to tell her of the exposé of the beef industry that the station had carried. The charge had been overly broad, some shots faked, the promotion sensationalized, but the network sold the story.

Rista sank back into her chair, apparently exhausted by her

fit of anger. For a moment she looked frail. "When she was little and she did something wrong, I called her full name, Cassie Rae. She thought Rae was a bad word so when she got mad at me she said, 'Mamma Rae.'" She tried to smile but failed. "Why didn't someone tell me she was dying?" She looked at me as though "someone" were my name. "I would have come."

"She didn't want you to come." I had asked Mother if she was sure. She said, "If I see her I might forgive her."

Rista and I stared at each other for a moment. Then I looked away trying not to feel sorry for her.

"I'd like her to be buried here. With her family."

"She's happy where she is." Mother hated the ranch. Her revenge would come when I sold it, graves and all.

"Cassie dreamed of the stars and was blind to the grass."

I looked out the curtainless window into the darkness. There wasn't even a light from the barn. I tried to imagine being sick and dying in this place. "Don't you wish you were closer to a doctor?" I asked.

"Doctor told me not to ride horses, lift anything heavy, or do anything strenuous. I said, 'Okay, doc, you run my ranch and I'll sit here in your office and tell folks what to do.' He refused to see me after that. Said I was non-compliant because I wouldn't follow his instructions. Besides, Medicare won't pay him the kind of money Smiley and those lawyers do."

"But you're so far from anything," I tried again.

"When my grandpa came to this country, my grandma kept wanting to turn back. One day when Grandpa had ridden ahead, Grandma turned the wagon and headed back to Alabama. Grandpa caught up with her, told her he would drop the reins on the horse's neck and if it was God's will the horse would go back

89

to Alabama. He pointed the horse toward Alabama and dropped the reins, and the horse turned and started for this place. What he didn't tell her was that Six Mile Draw was over the next hill, and the horse had already smelled the water."

"Wasn't your grandmother killed by Indians?"

"She and Aunt Jack. Grandpa wanted to bury Aunt Jack beside her mother but couldn't find her grave. He looked for it the rest of his life. So did my father. So have I. Maybe you can help me find it."

I didn't plan to be around long enough to look for a grave. "Did your father ever say how he felt about 'God's will' bringing his mother and sister here to die?"

"Papa said if Grandpa's horse had gone back to Alabama he'd have come here and gotten this place on his own. I'd of helped him. Some folks think he was a hard man but you have to be tough when you work with wild horses and cattle. You have to be patient with them but honest. You have to think the way they do and act on instinct. Papa always said, 'The thing to do is do. Don't just sit thinking about it.' He did what he had to do."

Rista talked for a long time about her father and what he thought he had to do, stories Mother never heard or else forgot. I needed a gray scale; Hitler probably thought he did what he had to do.

"I don't remember Papa ever saying he loved me or me ever needing him to," Rista said. "I've always been suspicious of folks who talk about how much they love you. Usually that's what it is, talk."

I wondered who she referred to. I doubted Mother ever talked about how much she loved Rista.

"You learn to work being cold and being hungry and being

90

wet and dirty and tired out. You learn when to rein, when to pat, and when to spur. You learn you have to ride your own horse. Nobody is going to break your bronc for you. You tame it or you turn it into an outlaw."

I wasn't sure whether she was talking about Mother's failure to control her life or whether Rista meant that she turned Mother into an outlaw, or both.

Rista led me through one bedroom and into another. There was no hallway. "This is your old bedroom. It's nice having you home, Chance." She gave me a tight hug that I didn't return, then left.

It didn't feel like home, and it was cold. There were no closets. I hung my suit and shirts on the broomstick across a corner of the bedroom and left the rest of the clothes in the suitcase. On the bed was a stuffed pink bunny with a neck elongated perhaps by being carried by a child. I picked it up and smelled it. It smelled old, musty with a faint trace of . . . I smelled it again . . . coffee? I wondered if it had been Mother's toy when she was a girl or if it had been mine. I looked around for a place to put it. The only choice was the bed or the suitcase. I put in on the suitcase.

I looked at my watch. Nine o'clock. What was happening at the station? What was happening in the world? I tiptoed through the darkened house, closing doors before searching for lights. Despite the age of the house some of the rooms were bare and seem to have been scarcely used. I looked for a television but found none. I slipped into the sitting room and turned on the radio to get the news. The radio didn't work. At the station I had my finger on the world's pulse. Here, I was in a world as dark as Helen Keller's. I didn't even know what the weather was like.

I returned to the bedroom, undressed quickly, turned off the light, huddled in the cold bed and listened to the unfamiliar noises—the old walls creaking, the wind whispering around the house, the steady pump of the windmill, the movement of horses in the corral, the yip and wail of coyotes. It took me a long time to go to sleep—I was listening for something—and when I did sleep someone banged on the door and flipped on the overhead light. "Breakfast is ready," Rista said.

I had no stomach for breakfast although Pug seemed to think it was special. Fried eggs, fried sausage, fried bread, and fried pancakes. With coffee strong enough to fuse metal. Pug saw me wince when I tasted it.

"It'll slip the hair off a dog," he said. "I wish we had company every day. Long time since I seen splatter dabs." When he smiled I saw he was missing a few teeth.

"Eat it up because we got work to do," Rista said. "Chance, I need you to saddle a couple of horses."

"I don't know how to saddle a horse."

"Pug will show you. Pug brought a jacket and some jeans for you to wear. You'll slide right out of the saddle in them silk pants."

I picked up the shirt, fingering the snaps.

"You don't want to work in something you can't get out of in a hurry," Pug said.

"This hat and these boots belonged to your grandfather. See if they'll fit. Get out of them bow-tie shoes."

I stepped into another room and slipped on the jeans and work shirt, hat and boots in the cold. Rista talked through the closed door. "I buried Odis in the only suit he had. Your mother wanted me to bury his good Stetson, boots, and spurs with him, but I saved them for you." When I walked back into the kitchen Pug looked at me and then nodded at Rista.

"Good to see you looking like somebody," she said. "Not one of them weasel slicks. These are your grandfather's spurs. I think you outgrowed yours." They were ornate silver spurs. "These were Odis' courting spurs with jinglebobs so you could hear him coming."

"I can't ride."

"Can't never could. Don't worry about riding. You always end up on the ground, one way or another."

I balked at the spurs. "I don't want to hurt the horse."

"I don't allow anybody to hurt my horses," she said, turning on me, her eyes glinting, her hands on her hips. "My cows either. Do you think a wheat farmer abuses his wheat? Do you imagine an apple grower abuses his apple trees? I care as much for my cows as city folks do for their dogs, more than they do for their cats. I treat them better too, respect them for what they are. I don't keep them in the house or make them look like dolls instead of dogs. I hate to see people cage cats or paint a dog's nails. It humiliates them. They're intended for better than that." She stood waiting for me to challenge her. I tried to look disinterested.

"I always kept good horses to get good hands. But you can't get hands anymore, just kids who want to rodeo, and they want to work their own horses. I'm down to six horses, and we have to haul them around to get the work done. They don't get rode enough to work well. The spurs are to keep his attention."

I followed Pug to the corral, buttoning the jacket against the morning chill. "I'm going to put you on this whey belly," he said. "Sugar is old and tired so you're going to have to work to

93

keep him going. I'll saddle Two-Bits for Rista. That's about what he would bring for dog food. He was bit by a rattlesnake. I punctured the bite with Spanish dagger to drain it, smoked it with chicken feathers, and treated it with salt and coal oil, but he still limps. Rista won't like it but Two-Bits'll keep her from running off and leaving you."

Pug showed me how to bridle and saddle the horse. "You got the belly band twisted," he said shouldering me aside. "That'll gall the horse." He finished the job, caught the saddle horn in one hand and gave it a shake. "He hasn't been ridden for a while. Let him soak for a minute in case he has a notion to pitch." He tied a sling hoe to Rista's saddle. "Maybe you never used one of these, but I expect you to do most of the work. She won't wait for you to ask."

▲▼▲

I shivered in the predawn chill, and I was glad I had put on the too-tight boots because I didn't know what I was standing in. There was a light in the east, but I could barely see the ground when Rista stepped up on the water trough and then into the saddle and Pug let us out of the corral. The horses were cold too—they left in a trot. I held on, my hat and shoulders flopping, my backside bouncing off the saddle until the horses slowed to a brisk walk. By then the sun was up, and I was feeling better. The day was beautiful, I hadn't fallen off the horse and there was something exhilarating about being in the saddle.

"You should have seen the wildflowers when they were in bloom," Rista said.

Most of my attention was on the horse but I saw tufts of dry grass and dead weeds. Wildflowers bloomed for two days; the rest of the time they looked like weeds. I wondered if Rista had ever bloomed.

"You ride like a sack," Rista said. "Stop choking the saddle horn."

Rista looked wedded to the horse, but Shad had led me to expect trick riding, like standing on her saddle. "Was my mother a good rider?"

"She was good at riding the pickup. There was a school party or game she had to go to almost every night."

"I bet you were a good rider."

"I took a spill right over there," Rista said. "Old Bucket. Good roper but had a bucket head. I was chasing a steer and just as I was ready to smear a rope on it, Bucket broke in half. I lost a stirrup, landed crossways on his neck, bounced across the saddle a couple of times and when I came down on his rump, he swallowed his head and came undone. I don't know whether he kicked me or I landed on a rock. I was unconscious for a while and saw double the rest of the day so it was hard to rope. I had a knot on my head that would make a preacher proud.

"I didn't get thrown much when I was a girl. Horses fell with me a few times, but I was limber enough to bounce. I used to say I'd ride as long as I could slap leather on a horse, but now I let Pug saddle for me. Then I said, I'd ride as long as I could get on a horse. I sometimes cheat a little and climb up on the water trough to step across the horse. But I can still sit a saddle better than you can. You ride like a sack."

Saddles are heavier than they look in the movies, and harder. Before long my shoulders ached from the bouncing, my trousers had wrinkled against the saddle and the wrinkles rubbed blisters on my seat. It was a relief to get off the horse to open a gap, but my knees were shaky.

"What are those sticks in the ground?" I asked, pointing under the trees where shrubs seemed to have died into square stumps.

"That's where we didn't find Aunt Jack. We break up old sucker rods from the wells, sharpen one end and drive it into the ground every place we don't find her so we don't keep digging in the same place."

"You could miss it by a foot. How do you ever expect to find her?"

"We'll find her. She'll wait until we do."

Rista stopped and dismounted. I crawled off the horse that seemed to have grown taller, stretched my legs, and took a few steps. Although I didn't recognize it at first I stood in a small cemetery. If the graves had been marked the markers were gone.

Rista untied the sling hoe. "You a golfer? Practice your golf swing," she said, demonstrating how to cut the weeds just above the ground. "The cows do most of the work, but we have to cut what they don't eat."

"If this is a cemetery why don't you fence it?" I asked, swinging the hoe to loosen the tightness in my shoulders.

"I figure they enjoy hearing horses or cows cropping the grass around them. These four graves were here when my father bought this place. Pa figured from the size of the graves that it was a man and woman and two children. Probably killed by Indians and buried where they died. Those were the first graves.

"That grave you're standing on was Healey Wilhite, kid from back east who wanted to be a cowboy. He saw some Indians and ran and his horse fell, broke its neck and landed on Healey. The

Indians were peaceful, but Healey had read stories about them torturing people and cut his wrists. He was running from an imaginary danger but a danger he had a right to believe in since books and magazines made it real. He cut his own wrists, but I always thought Stoddard was like the folks that killed him."

"You mean the Indians?"

"No, fool," she said sharply. She pointed at another low mound of earth. "This cowboy lived in Rattlesnake Canyon on his lonesome. Ride in there except dead of winter and you can hear rattlesnakes sing. Horses hated it but Longhorns never seemed to be bothered. Neither was the old man. Said he had been bitten until he was immune. Pa took him coffee, beans, flour, salt and pepper, matches, lard, and a gallon of molasses now and then. He loved molasses. He roped and branded them old outlaw Longhorns. Pa found him dead among the graves like he came here to be buried, put his bandana over his face, and buried him in his bedroll. I never saw him but from time to time I saw outlaws he had branded. Some of them may still be back in the canyon. Odis was going to sell them for dog food but gave it up."

"What was the cowboy's name?"

"He didn't have a local name. We called him Tujay because he rode in on a horse branded with two Js. Papa figured he was on the dodge, but I think he just liked being by himself. Seems like there used to be a lot of loners soured on folks. Batch-a-liar folks called them, no use to anybody. But Tujay was a good hand. If you can't be of some use you're just taking up space, and it's too crowded already."

There were more loners today, but now they joined the militia or planned bombings and assassinations or died and left fortunes to cats. We covered a lot of those stories. I took off my jacket and leaned on the hoe to catch my breath. At my feet was what looked like a green mole with thick spines growing from it.

"Horse crippler," Rista said, kicking at the flat-base cactus with the toe of her boot. "This was Shell Castleberry. All boogered up when I knew him, couldn't ride anymore. Wasn't much of a cook. He cut his own firewood, but he'd get lost looking for deadwood. We fenced off twenty acres for him and when he cleaned that up, another twenty acres. He couldn't read or write and rarely went to town. Someone found a piece of music without words and told him it was writing, and he entertained himself for days trying to figure what kind of language it was. Mother sewed a zipper in a coat I had, and he had never seen one before. He'd sit out in the sun and watch me zip and unzip like it was a birth or a death, only better.

"This was Rufus Brown, Levi's uncle. His ranch was stolen by Smiley Wooten and a movie star. He just sat staring at the corral, wondering where he was. Smiley took everything but his reputation."

"He hung around the ranch until he died?"

"Ranches don't have retirement policies, but I've never known one to turn away an old cowboy."

She made it sound generous, but I noticed she gave him no headstone, just an unfenced spot under the grass.

"We called this old cowboy Bamanitious. He rode to the O-Bar with my father. I never saw him without a chaw of tobacco, and you could hardly understand him talking around it. When he died Papa was going to put his name on a tombstone and asked Knock if he knew how to spell it. Knock said, 'When he come here you asked what he went by and he said, 'by my initials.'

Papa thought he said 'Bamanitious.' After that Papa didn't feel like putting up a tombstone for anyone."

I knew the name of every employee, and I required department heads to know every member of their department by first name.

"Paco was like a father to me, especially after my father died. He was the best cowhand I ever knew."

But he was a Mexican. "You don't even know his last name."

She looked at me like she was deciding whether I was worth hanging with the coyotes. "Paco never voted, never paid taxes. I don't think he was legal. But there was more loyalty in his Mexican heart than most people have in their whole family."

I didn't say anything, but I knew she was talking about Mother, and maybe me. She led me to five graves.

"Mother was cautious about everything, tiptoeing to her grave like she was afraid of disturbing something. Papa sat his horse on that knoll and watched her funeral. You cry for a lot of reasons. What might have been is one of them." She shrugged. "Papa didn't go to anyone's funeral. He said, 'If you go to their funeral they sure as hell won't come to yours.'"

If he watched from that knoll he sat a high horse because the knoll was covered with brush.

"This is my husband, Odis Wyler, your grandfather. This is Papa's grave, your great-grandfather, Claris McCloud. His father's and mother's graves. I don't think they would have wanted to be pinned down to one place with a gravestone. This whole ranch is their grave."

"How do people know who is in what grave?"

"Everyone who needs to know knows."

99

7

1931

Despite the hard times, or maybe because of them, there were frequent get-togethers. Genevieve encouraged Rista to attend them. She dared not die and leave Rista alone. She had kept Celestine pure, waiting for some refined man to value her treasure; Claris' courtship had been a surprise to both her and Celestine. The same could happen to Rista if she could not win Stoddard's heart.

She insisted that Rista go to a singing and box dinner to save the Three Crosses. Rista had been up all night with a colicky horse. She drenched him with mineral oil and walked him to keep him from going down and rolling. By daylight, the horse was better, but Rista was exhausted. Nevertheless, she trimmed her hair and wrapped it in the scarf Stoddard had given her, hoping to look fresh. Genevieve fried two chickens, stuffed eggs, baked fresh biscuits and a three-layer cake for her to sell. Pug made her a box from scrap lumber. He wanted to go with her but a horse had stuck a hoof in his hip pocket, and he was out of the saddle for a couple of days. He offered to buy her dinner, but she couldn't let him buy food when board was part of his pay and the box dinner was to save his mother's ranch.

Rista wiped her saddle and bridle with egg white to restore their luster, then ran the horses into the corral to choose one to ride. She knew she should ride a green-broke horse to take the kinks out of it, but she picked the coyote dun, although it ran into the bit, because it was so pretty. Genevieve placed a clean cup towel over the top of the box, and Rista carried it in her arms, afraid to rest it on the saddle for fear the cake would slide and smear the icing.

She kept a tight rein on the dun so her dinner wasn't bounced around, but she wanted to push on the reins in her eagerness to see Stoddard. He would be waiting to spy her dinner and make the highest bid, and she would shake her finger at him for spending so much. When she got off her horse at the Three Crosses a man looked at her so intently that she stopped and stood uncertainly for a moment. "Good looking horse, ma'am," he said, tipping his hat. His spurs tinkled when he walked.

She walked to the clapboard house without paint or screens. It wasn't until she reached the porch that she realized the other dinners were in fancy boxes with pretty bows. She knew then it was the box that had caught the man's eye, not her horse. She was so embarrassed she would have ridden home had Stoddard not seen her. He and everyone else had turned to look at her wooden box covered with an old cup towel. Thank goodness for the cup towel or the flies would have carried her dinner away. The preacher took her box and added it to the others on the porch where it looked like a Longhorn in a herd of Angus. She looked at Stoddard to tell him he didn't have to bid on her box, but he had turned away.

She went to the outhouse to change into Genevieve's frock with trumpet sleeves that was too big and too short, and pumps with high tongue and buckle. She wiggled and fussed with her clothes, stomped the jumped-up shoes and almost changed back into jeans, shirt, and boots. Instead, she stayed as long as she could stand the stifling, smelly place.

When she emerged, she tried to appear rising and coming alive. Pug's mother and sister asked why he hadn't come. She was ashamed to tell them Pug had made her box. She saw Stoddard and they talked of coming dances and parties and whether or not he would be home from college. She hoped he wouldn't bid on her box because she would die of embarrassment, but if he bid on the ugly thing she would love him forever. He seemed not to notice that she wore his scarf although she smoothed it with her hand.

She asked about the man with the cold eyes and jinglebob spurs. "That's Odis Wyler, the deputy that cleaned up Claypool." Claypool was a rough railroad town that ranchers shunned except to ship cattle. The railroad bypassed Red Rock, because of quicksand in the river, they said. Then a steam engine caused a grass fire that ruined a Quarter Circle J pasture. Red Rock had been subdued by a cowboy preacher, Brother Bob, and farmers and ranchers elected it county seat rather than Claypool, which was named after a railroad executive who had never even been to Texas.

Rista remembered those unnerving blue eyes, the oft-broken nose, the sly smile that hovered on the edge of insolence. She couldn't imagine Odis backing down to anyone, but Stoddard seemed amused by town-tamer Odis Wyler. Stoddard didn't invite her to any of the dances they talked about. Dawn didn't have arms hanging out of her dress like an orangutan in a vest. Lucinda wore a wide white hat with a pink ribbon and white long-sleeve dress with a matching pink cinch strap.

When the bidding began Stoddard bid on the prettiest box,

which belonged to Lucinda Gillin. Rista was dark, earthy. She knew life as beauty and ugliness, pleasure and pain. Lucinda's fair cheeks had never been burned by sun or shame, her clear blue eyes never darkened by anger or fear, her heart never stained by jealousy and doubt. She was small enough to ride double.

Watching the boxes sell—some quickly, some slowly—was torture. Frank LeGrand, old but still looking for a wife, bid on every box. Rista vowed if he bid on hers she would marry him even if he made her drink tea, but she feared no one would bid on her dinner and she would have to claim the hideous thing in front of everyone, jump on her horse, and ride home in disgrace. What would she tell Genevieve?

Bravely the preacher offered her box for bidding. The silence seemed to last forever. Even the preacher got nervous. Then she heard a bid at three dollars. There was no other bid, but it was almost as much as Lucinda's dinner and gratefully she watched to see who claimed it. Odis was scarcely older than Stoddard and lacked his confidence but made up for it with authority.

"I've been wanting to meet you," he said when she opened the box for him, ashamed of its ugliness and proud that it brought three dollars.

"You didn't have to pay three dollars," she said without shaking a finger as she spread a blanket under an oak tree for them to sit on.

"I would have paid more," he said, waving at the flies that stuck to them like money on a politician. "You're the prettiest girl in the county."

Rista looked at him in astonishment. She had never been pretty before and wondered how she should act. Was she supposed to play like she was Lucinda? Lucinda was rapt while

Stoddard talked, probably about her beauty. "Do I remind you of Dawn?" she asked.

"Dawn who?"

"Rising dawn."

"You make me think of a woman who could tear a man's heart out and make him glad for the chance. You'd look good in a storm cellar."

What did that mean? While Rista pondered how she was supposed to look, Odis talked about his work. After prohibition, Smiley Wooten organized a club in Claypool and put in slot machines, women, and liquor. "I put Smiley out of business in Claypool. Didn't hurt him none at the bank, though. They didn't know he was involved."

Odis walked into the back rooms of barbershops and fraternal lodges, and when he found gambling he took the cards, dice, and money and told outsiders to clear out or go to jail. Townsfolk didn't let him catch them again. He stopped cockfighting and dogfighting and wouldn't permit a carnival to come to town because people didn't have money to spare. He cuffed drunks to a ladder and let them sober up rather than take them to the jail in Red Rock. After the oil boom in the next county, Odis met the trains and ordered whores back on; they weren't stopping in his town. Rista stole glances at him while he talked, unable and unwilling to meet those eyes, and wondered how he knew which were whores.

Odis worked mostly at night so he slept late. She laughed at that. She was in the saddle before sunrise and looked forward to the shorter days of winter when she had time to catch up with the bookwork for the ranch, oil and mend the saddles and tack, restock her remedies, and repair the house. "Come day, go day,

God send Sunday," the cowboys said, but mostly Sunday was a workday. "The work is heavier in the winter, having to feed the cattle."

"That's too heavy for a woman," he said.

"I got a shirttail outfit. Two cowboys and they don't like being pitchfork gladiators."

"I don't have much time for partying, and the ones I've gone to you haven't. But I guess I'm going to have to make time," Odis said.

She wondered at that, but neither he nor Stoddard asked her to a dance or party. When she left, she made a running mount, wheeled the horse around, and reared him to wave goodbye. Stoddard was talking to Lucinda who looked like she was ready to give down her milk. He never even noticed her horse.

Genevieve waited for her. "Did Stoddard buy your box dinner?" she asked.

"Odis Wyler did, and he put on his sideboards. He said your chicken was throat-tickling good, and he used the cake to swab it with." She did not mention the box looked like a prickly pear in a bed of daisies.

"Isn't he that deputy over in Claypool?"

"You know how when one of them brammer bulls turns and looks at you, you just sit your saddle until they start thinking about something else? That's the way he looked at me. And I sat light." She had been excited by his attention and disappointed that he had thanked her for the dinner and left her to throw the ugly box behind the corral.

"Do you think he has snake blood?"

Smiley Wooten had snake blood, so cold he had to sidle up

106

to a dead coyote. "He's used to living alone. He said I'd look good in a storm cellar."

"Did he ask you to a dance?"

"No." Maybe she didn't act pretty. Maybe she didn't play like she liked him enough. When he bought her dinner, she thought she had two beaus; now she had none.

"Men don't know who or what they want until you tell them," Genevieve said. "They think working and drinking and whoring is all there is. I met your grandfather at a dance and I said, 'Mr. Olin, when you get over the calico fever you may call on me.' And he did."

▲▼▲

Two weeks later Odis rode up at dusk and asked if he could escort Rista to the dance at the Slash Six. She hurriedly bathed and dressed while Genevieve served Odis coffee and inquired about his prospects. As Rista and Odis were leaving, Stoddard appeared as jaunty as ever. "I'm here to take you to the dance," he said.

"She's riding with me," Odis said.

"That's up to the lady to decide."

"She's done decided," Odis said, getting off his horse to fight.

Rista was flattered at having two men courting her and more excited than she wanted to admit that one of them was ready to fight for her, but she insisted that they all ride together. Stoddard was on an ugly cow-hocked, hammer-headed bay, and she rode between the two men and had to be alert to prevent Odis, the better rider, from cutting Stoddard out. Stoddard shifted from side to side in the saddle, giving his borrowed horse a sore back. Odis grumbled that Stoddard was trying to breed when he wasn't big enough to suck.

It was a slow ride with Odis sulky, Stoddard expansive, and Rista trying to look fresh in a storm cellar. Stoddard said whores came to Claypool pretending to sell magazines. Cowboys and railroad men visited their house posing as subscribers. Odis courted one of the women until he discovered her trade. The Red Rock newspaper headlined the story, "Deputy Falls For Police Gazette," which the women sold. Odis believed the story damaged his reputation and his chances of being sheriff. When Stoddard said Odis' authority appealed to low women, Odis jumped off the horse and tried to fight Stoddard.

Rista kept the two men separated but felt less pretty for it. She wondered what Lucinda would do—ride serenely away and ignore men's business? Although Stoddard had offered to teach her to dance, she stumbled through the first dance with Odis. She didn't know if it was proper, but it was prudent.

She danced with both men, dreading the last song because with Stoddard's graceful leading she became less awkward and because she didn't know what would happen when the party ended. Stoddard went outside for a smile from the fruit jar. Odis followed him, knocked him down from behind and kicked him where he was the biggest. He would have stomped Stoddard if others hadn't intervened. Stoddard dusted himself off and went inside. Odis drank from the jar.

After the dance both men rode home with her, Odis brooding and Stoddard gossiping about the people at the dance. Lucinda Gillin, he said, had a rod up her corset. Lucinda was smart in school and refined in public. A favorite among the young people, she recited "Curfew Must Not Ring Tonight" at play parties. She had once spent an hour showing Stoddard her family album—this is Uncle Bob when he got married, Aunt Hettie when she got married, Mom and Dad when they got married. "I felt like it was an invitation to be part of her family," Stoddard said.

"She has a good family," Rista said, secretly afraid that Stoddard wanted to be part of it. Lucinda, daughter of the county judge, lived in Red Rock and could pass by the newspaper office or Stoddard's home as many times as she wished. What chance did Rista have?

"One of the dullest in the state," Stoddard agreed. "If I'm going to be a writer I can't be trapped in a dull family life."

Odis snorted at such a noble sentiment. Rista was impressed by Stoddard's seriousness and saddened by it. Neither she nor her family was worthy of such an ambitious beau. Then her thoughts brightened. She could tell him stories while they worked side by side, he admiring her roping skill. At night while she cooked supper, he could write about Day McVicar, hanged for shooting Bill Bennet. Day's brother Dink was shot trying to deliver a message for Tim Tingle who hanged himself. Didn't that beat a snake on stilts? Day had two lawyers at his trial, but he looked so guilty they thought the best thing they could do for him was sit shoulder to shoulder so the jury couldn't see him.

Bill's family was given seats in front of the gallows. Day, who was a teenager, cried when he apologized to the family. When they put the noose around Day's neck, Bill's sister, Vada, screamed and ran down the street. After Day was hanged, Bill's father asked for the rope and put it noose and all over his fireplace. Folks said when her father died Vada put the noose in the hope chest she was preparing when Day was hanged but Rista remembered it over the mantle. Vada must have looked at it so long she was used to it. Rista hoped that Stoddard could rescue Vada from the shame of burning her child in the fireplace. While

109

Stoddard saved Vada's reputation and that of Doc Evans and Frank LeGrand, she would bring him coffee and brush his hair out of his eyes.

While Rista dreamed of a life with Stoddard, Odis schemed of a moment alone with him. It was dawn when they returned to the ranchhouse. Rista invited Odis in for breakfast to give Stoddard time to escape pursuit.

The next morning she found that Stoddard had left a poem under a rock on the porch. "Why is the moon your friend? Is it because you are the brightest reflection of its rays? Is that why it moves the tide and sends wavelets to lick your toes? I think it must be because it finds its form in the sliver of your smile. Only in your laughter is it full of love, and it rises in the night on the brightness of your joy."

Rista woke me before daylight as she had the previous day. I was stiff from the horseback ride the day before and had resolved to tell Rista I wasn't riding. At breakfast Pug said he wanted me to check the pastures with him from the truck. Rista stopped me before I followed Pug to the barn. "Don't get crossways with Pug. He's been in more fights than he has whorehouses."

That Pug, like the Pug who required more than two deputies to jail, was a memory of this morning's Pug. His knees were stiff, his fierce eyes clouded. I needed this Pug to assist me in putting Rista in a safe place.

"Watch out for the headache rack," Pug said as we loaded bags of range cubes into his truck. The headache rack was metal pipe welded across the back of the truck. On the rack were posthole diggers, chains, fence stretchers, shovel, hammer, and other tools. On the front of the truck was a winch for getting out of bogs, stretching fence and pulling posts and windmill pipe. Over the seat was a rack holding two rifles and a coiled rope.

"Throw some hay to that steer in the sick pen while I load the horse." I was relieved that Pug saddled and loaded only one horse into the trailer. "That's a rider steer," he said, closing the tailgate on the trailer. "The other steers rode it until they crippled it. We're feeding it out until we can sell it."

I had to force the door of the old truck. The seat was plywood over bare springs; an old saddle blanket was upholstery. I smiled at the thought that this was my inheritance. Even in the semi-darkness Pug must have seen the smile. "It runs good," he said. It failed to start. With the flat of his hand, Pug scraped something off the hood before raising it and fiddled with the engine for a few minutes before trying again.

"Why don't you get a new one?" I asked as we bounced over ranch roads that would have tested a jeep. The truck lurched, the horse trailer rattled and bucked. The heater didn't work.

"Me and Rista are hanging on, hoping for oil lease money. We could use one man to do nothing but fight brush."

He and Rista. And they were just hanging on? Was he trying to con me? I had written TV commercials. "How much is this land worth?"

"If you had to buy it, it'd cost $200 an acre, more than that if you broke it up into smaller plots. If you had to make a living on it, you couldn't pay $50 an acre and come out ahead. Folks retire and will pay hundreds for a few acres where you can breathe the air, drink the water, see deer, hear coyotes. The only people who get rich off land like this is developers, and they don't produce nothing, just trash."

We came to a fence and he stopped. "I drive, you get the gaps," he said. Opening the gaps meant brushing something brown off at least one post, forcing two posts together until the wire loop could be tugged from around the loose post, pulling the gap open until Pug had driven through it and then forcing

112

the loop back over the post. "What is that brown stuff that's on everything?" I asked.

"Coon shit," Pug said. "They get on everything. One time me and Rista saw that Russian Sputnik and I said, 'How high do you think that thang is?' Rista said, 'I don't know but I bet it's got coon shit on it.'"

After the second gap I understood why Pug wanted me along. I wondered whether he or Rista drove when the two worked together.

"We call this the Bone Yard," Pug said, tapping the horn softly as we passed the graves I had cleaned the day before. "Rise and shine, Paco," he yelled.

"You name the pastures?" I asked with amusement.

"If Rista says to work Borracho Creek or Fort Hoggard, I know where she means, and if the truck broke down and I had to hoof it, she'd know where to come looking."

If the horse in the trailer was a spare tire I knew who would be walking and who would be riding. Pug stopped near a tree. "I used to argue with my bowels," he said, tearing a sheet from an old newspaper. "Nowadays the conversation is pretty short."

We checked the grass, water and cattle in Six Mile Draw— the draw was dry, The Burn, although no traces remained of the prairie fire that had given the pasture its name, and Comanche Peak. "They would pay Rista to put a telephone relay antenna up there, and you and she could use mobile phones to communicate," I said.

Pug looked at me with the contempt he reserved for pedestrians. "You sound like a suitcase rancher."

The land was rolling with little valleys surrounded by rocky ridges and studded with trees, sometimes clumps of trees that

113

Pug called "mottes." The oak trees held their leaves although it was late fall; the mesquites were spidery shadows, the cedars bushed out and dusty. Deer stared at us, then wheeled and disappeared in the shadows of the mottes. A flock of wild turkeys crossed a grassy valley that had a raw red scar that Pug called a wash.

"This is my favorite time of year," Pug said. "Not real hot, not real cold, the grasses cured, game more active. Deer were damn near extinct before the government started the screwfly program. Now we got more than we can feed. You can't round them up to sell so you have to kill them selectively, or nature will cull them by starvation or disease. Every drought or hard winter fawns and old bucks die. I hate to see that. You can shoot one if you want."

"No thanks."

"When a deer or cow dies, that's a waste. Someone ought to get some good out of it. I shoot a couple of deer a year. That's all me and Rista can eat. I shoot one for day help if they want it. We've tried leasing the place to hunters a time or two. There's money in it, but they leave gaps open, dump trash, get in the way, act like it was their property, get crossways with the neighbors. We used to have neighbors. Now we got the telephone company and the lawyers."

At each stop Pug honked until the cows came, then scattered range cubes, walking through the cows. "You got to watch what cows eat. Hard chips are due to dehydration or poor-quality diet," he said, kicking one. "When they're soft, the protein content is good. Cows squirt in the spring, but it's not diarrhea. See that brockled cow? A bloater. You got to watch her, especially after a rain or heavy dew on spring grass."

114

He pointed at another. "Hooves are growing crooked on her left rear foot. If she starts limping we'll market her." He replaced some salt licks, unloaded the horse, roped and treated a cow with a lacerated udder. "Feeding is a steady job," he said. "Every day or two in the winter, and if you're sick or it's sleeting or you'd like to sleep late because it's Christmas, too bad."

As we bounced and rattled our way across the pasture, Pug spat tobacco out the window giving himself a sideways sideburn. "Studying the cows is as important as feeding them," he said. "A cow with a full udder lost her calf. You want to keep an eye on her, but it may not be her fault. You see a cow bawling and looking nervous, sign of trouble with her calf. See that long calf, that yearling there? Good stock. That cow off to herself didn't come up for feed. If she's not better the next time we check, we'll market her. That one is a fence walker. If there's a hole in a fence, she'll find it. That bull is standing in the shade every time I see him. He better show some action or he's bologna. Rista won't buy a fat bull. She wants bulls that walk to water, rustle feed and chase down reluctant cows."

There were no cattle in Two Dollar Flat, only large round bales of hay. "Ordinarily we take the hay to the cows, but if the weather's real bad, snow on the ground, we'll move the cows in here for a couple of days. The man who homesteaded this place sold it for two dollars and pulled out with his crops in the field. We lease it to farmers to raise hay for us."

Two Dollar Flat had sold before Pug was born, but there was no masking the contempt in his voice at a quitter who left his crops in the field. He nursed that resentment to the next wire gap.

"We call this the Big Rock pasture. Your great-grandfather, Claris, found a big rock all by itself. He pulled it up with a team

115

of mules and found a well underneath with good water in it. It could have been buffalo hunters that dug it, but it's not likely buffalo hunters would take the time. He figured it must have been the family buried in the Bone Yard. You can still find charred wood, broken glass, and rusted tin around here. Indians must have burned the house. We put a windmill over the well."

He spoke of this family with admiration although they sold their lives for the land and left nothing but four graves on someone else's property. The ground around the trough was wet. "Need to replace the leathers," he said. He pulled a wooden cover off one corner of the trough, took apart a valve, cut a gasket from an old inner tube in the back of the truck and put the valve back together. He tested it, pushing the float down with his hand, eyed it critically, then got in the truck and drove away.

"That's the cow with cancer eye," Pug said, stopping the truck. "Stay in the truck until I rope her."

He unloaded the horse, roped the cow, and dragged it to the trailer, then threw the rope over a ball welded to the top of the trailer and pulled the cow into the trailer with the horse. He tied the cow up close, and the horse jumped in the trailer with it. "What does a poor man throw away that a rich man puts in his pocket?" Pug asked, putting a thumb to his nose and blowing before getting in the truck. I thought we would start back to the house, but there were other pastures to check, other cattle to feed.

Pug stopped the truck and got out a metal can with water. He put a dipper in the water, rinsed out the dust, and handed it to me. "We used to spread a bandana over a mudhole and use it as a strainer to drink through. Probably why we had boils. Treated them with a chaw of tobacco and sat off-center in the saddle."

He put a wad of tobacco in his mouth, bulging his cheek and making a white spot on his red face. He took off his hat and rubbed a scar on top of his head. "Your grandmother was the only doctor us cowboys knew. If we blistered or burned she treated us with canned tomatoes or a poultice made of grated raw potatoes. When we had rope burns or sores on our hands she burned them out with powdered alum. Many a night she sat up putting poultices of axle grease, turpentine, and red peppers on our chests. One time a thorn went through my boot, and my foot swelled to where I couldn't get my boot off. Rista put my foot in a bucket of coal oil until I could get the boot off, then drew the thorn with salt pork. When Paco's horse ran him into a wasp nest, Rista bathed him in coal oil and put tobacco juice on the stings. I did the chewing. One time she had us drinking olive oil to prevent appendicitis and when we had a stomach ache she gave us castor oil. We never admitted to being that sick, but she suspected it sometimes and made us take bile beans anyway.

"I been struck by lightning, run over by a cow, hooked by a bull, dragged by a horse, tangled in a rope and hung to a horse, but Paco was a hand when cowboys were cowboys. He was so hard twist he could draw a blood blister on a saddle. One time we were working Borracho Creek and it was freezing. We wrapped gunny sacks around our boots to keep our feet warm. Paco had piles so bad I told him to go back to the bunkhouse and put castor oil on them, but he broke ice on the creek and rubbed the ice over his piles until he could sit a horse."

Pug stopped the truck near some trees. "Grab the grub pile," he said. Rista had prepared our lunch, although Pug called it

117

dinner. "The wind's shifted," he said. The sun was warm, but the wind was out of the north and cold, and I was hot with the jacket on and cold with it off. Pug took off his coat but wore a padded vest. We had steak sandwiches—fried steak, mustard, and bread—with hot coffee while Pug told me about Fort Hoggard.

Some soldiers saw what they thought were Comanches and forted up in the trees. It turned out to be Doss McCloud and his cowboys rounding up cattle. The cowboys named it after the lieutenant who mistook them for Indians. "We need to move some cows in here," Pug said.

"Did you know Stoddard Keating?" I asked while trying to chew the tough steak. "What was he like?"

"Educated beyond his learning. Sniffed around like a dog at a horse show, not wanting to be part but hoping to find something he could use. I tried to fight him, but he was above it. When you've never had to fight for something, never had to get on a horse you knew you couldn't stay on, never had to rope and load a bull or climb a windmill in a wind with no one around to help you if something went wrong, it gives you funny notions. A man like that thinks things outside himself are important because he's never been inside himself."

Pug examined me, his once fierce eyes like a camera, taking everything and giving nothing. "Stoddard was going to dab his twine on the truth. The wind floated his loop."

Pug put the paper remains of his sandwich in the cooler, fiddled with the carburetor, got the truck running again, and we continued. "That's Rattlesnake Canyon," he said, pointing at a rocky canyon filled with brush. "I don't know the last time we were in there. Since Rista couldn't pay us, Paco and me asked a favor—that Rattlesnake Canyon be left as a tribute to Knock, Bamanitious, and them other cowboys. Rista promised as long as she was alive there'd be something wild on this place. She made us fence it so none of her fancy cows got in there. Hell, they're barn cows. I don't think you could drive them in there."

Was he staking a claim to Rattlesnake Canyon, or was he asking me to honor Rista's pledge after she died and left the place to me? Did she still owe him back pay?

"I wish I had lived back when Claris was young, when they spent more time in the saddle than on the ground and more time in bedrolls than in the bunkhouse. They worked with real cows. Heat and insects don't bother Longhorns. They survive screwworms—stand in water to drown the larvae and keep out the flies, lick the worms out of a calf's navel—winter without feeding, and no calving problems. The more you breed for size, the more calving problems you have. Now buyers want steers that never walked to water but stood in a feed lot all day. I don't believe it's good for people, and I know it's not good for cattle. That's what marketing does. Turns everything to plastic. Even the damn trucks are half plastic."

"Is anyone ever happy with the time of their life?"

"Claris was. He lived through Indian raids, cattle drives, open range. Paco could remember when there was only one fence around the whole place. We keep cutting it into smaller pastures so we can work it from a truck, and every time we put up a fence Rista has to borrow money to do it. We don't breed and train our own horses anymore, we nursemaid cows, we have to hire day help. They want to go home to the TV at night.

"We used to drive the remuda to a pasture, round up, brand, mark, and castrate the calves then move to another pasture.

Cooked over a mesquite fire, slept in a bedroll, bathed in a cattle trough. A good hand was not only good with a horse, he was good with a rope. Now we run calves into the corral and use a squeeze chute so me and Rista can handle them.

"Horses were brutes in them days. We didn't break horses until they were four or five years old. They'd buck, but we worked them steady, wore out two horses a day, and they got over it. Nowadays, they've gentled the spirit out of them until you think they're dead but won't lay down."

"What changed everything?"

"The screwfly eradication program. Before that, we had to ride out every day during the summer and check the stock. If a horse got a break in the skin or an eartick got full and dropped off a cow, screwflies laid eggs in the opening and the larvae ate the animal alive. We had to ride out every day looking for cows with screwworms. Horses would come to the corral like they knew you were their only chance. One year they were so bad a cowboy on the O-Bar got them in the back of his head.

"Then the oil companies put in caliche roads, and we started trailering horses to the pasture, going back to the bunkhouse at night. When I was a kid we didn't breed cows, they just accumulated. We didn't dehorn, vaccinate, spray. We burned them and booted them. Horses and cows were tough, and cowboys were tougher."

If he thought ranching was tough he should be station manager during a telethon—live all day, local poster child, national feed, then local broadcasting, a nightmare of timing and juggling. "You don't like the way Rista runs the place?"

"Your grandmother has seen a lot of changes, just like me. She deals with them better. Says this is a business not a museum.

You buy a horse for $800, he's worth $800 when you get him home. Maybe $900. Same with a cow. You buy a car, you buy a shirt, the minute you pay for it, it's worth less than when you picked it up. When we give up, only the rich will eat beef. The corporate ranchers, feed lot operators, packagers, and politicians will control the price."

Again there was the suggestion that they were partners, perhaps more. "You've known Rista a long time."

"My dad had more kids than he could feed. I worked roundup for Claris when I was ten, moved into the bunkhouse when I was twelve."

"You must have known Odis pretty well."

"Odis got caught in his own loop. There was a time when sheriffs, Rangers set the law and enforced it. He should have been born back then. He could have been as famous as Ben Thompson, Wyatt Earp, King Fisher."

"Maybe Rista was born too late, too."

"Whatever Rista did, she had a reason for."

"Reason enough to kill someone?"

Pug's look wasn't angry or defensive. It was open but unreadable, the look of a man who had no doubts. A man who could have ridden with Ben Thompson or King Fisher. Mother said some people thought he was the one who shot Odis, and maybe Stoddard, but did it for Rista.

"You don't know a damn thing about Rista," he said. "When her daddy died, the O-Bar thought they could cold blaze her. It kept us busy rounding up strays before they range branded them. That was a summer-name outfit. Dan Beasley, the only one that went by the name he was born with, killed a man with a single-tree. An O-Bar bull got in with some of our heifers. Rista drove it

121

back to the O-Bar with a whip. Drove it up in the yard where it collapsed and died. They kept their fences up after that."

We fed the cattle in the West Fork pasture, and Pug stopped once to replace the wooden cover and straighten the float in a water trough. "Cows break that off and we got real trouble," he said. "That'll drain the tank."

When we returned to the house I realized what had seemed a tangle of wooden fences was a collection of varying sized pens connected by lanes down which cattle could be driven. I could see there was a design to the chaos, but I didn't know what it was.

Pug turned the cow into the sick pen with the rider steer for the night, then unloaded and unsaddled the horse and, ducking under buckets, fed the horse in a copper tub. Pug said they fed in copper tubs and used copper bits to keep mares from going into heat. "We don't have mares anymore. We used to put water in the hanging buckets. The reflection looked like spider webs and kept flies away. Now we use fly spray."

Pug put the saddle and bridle in a dark, dusty room that looked like a museum. Chaps, quirts, spurs, saddles, horsehair bridles, clamps, forceps, files, blades, shears, nose tongs, hot shots, and nippers hung on the wall. Cracked, high-back saddles hung from the ceiling or were tipped on their horns on the floor. Pug noticed my attention. "Doss had reins cut from the back of a dead Indian," he said.

"What happened to them?"

"Wore out. Had some folks out here once that wanted to buy it, but Claris or Rista threw it away. Breaking a rein is like losing your steering wheel and brakes at the same time." He closed the door on the tack room.

"Have you thought what you'd do when Rista is no longer able to run this place?"

"I plan to be buried in the Bone Yard. I think I earned that."

That's all you earned, I thought. "Pug, Rista is old and tired. It's too hard for her living out here. She needs to be some place where people look after her, see that she eats right, takes her medicine—"

"When she's ready to go I won't stand in the gate."

Again, Pug sounded more like a husband than an employee. "I want to move her into a place like that. I could use your help."

"Before we go to the house, let's get something straight," Pug said. He was brusque, like a doctor or a late-night store clerk. "I work for your grandma, and as long as I ride for the brand, I fight for the brand. I don't give a shit how smart you are."

I looked into those faded gray eyes, and I knew Pug would do whatever it took to please Rista. I would have to take care of her myself.

▲▼▲

"Hopping John," Pug said when we reached the table. He grabbed the ladle in the pot and spooned a gray mess of peas, rice, and meat on his plate. I took a smaller helping.

"And Jeff Davis pie," Rista said proudly. "I can do more than fry meat when I have time."

"Feud pie," Pug said. Rista looked at him, and he turned his attention to his food. I would discover later that after the Pug-Dalhart fight, Rista made Jeff Davis pie to patch things up. Rista and Pug ate without looking at each other.

"Do you think there are Longhorns in Rattlesnake Canyon?" I asked Rista.

Pug looked at me me so sharply I almost flinched. Was that a forbidden subject or did Pug think I called him a liar?

"Pug likes to think so. He wants them Longhorns to stampede out of the canyon and run them muleys back to Washington."

"But you don't think so?"

"I think it's a muley world."

Pug dropped his plate, fork, and coffee cup in the sink and went to the bunkhouse without a word. We had each used one plate and one fork for soup, salad, entrée, and dessert.

I told Rista that Pug said she was barely able to keep the ranch going. "Cow and calf operation like we got is just a slow way to go broke," Rista said. "You always got too many cows or not enough. If you're not selling, you're buying. If Pug asked me for what I owe him in back wages, I'd have to sell this place to pay him. Rattlesnake Canyon is kind of a pledge."

"What do you owe him?"

"About a hundred thousand."

Dollars? I wondered what else she owed. "But the land is worth more than that?"

"Oh, I can always get a loan on the land. The value of the land keeps going up. That's about all that's kept me afloat. That and the oil leases. With help from Papa, my grandpa and the oil companies, I made a pretty good rancher. One time before the oil leases, I couldn't pay what I owed, and Smiley Wooten made me sign a rental contract. I rented the ranch from the bank. That way the bank got first call on any income before I paid the hands or fed the cows."

Rista didn't want to talk about the ranch; she wanted to know about me. I told her what I wanted her to know—that I graduated from high school and went to college while working

124

part-time for a television station. After college I sold ads for the station, wrote ads, did some reporting until in a live interview about Yeats and Keats I fell into "Yeets" and "Kates." I worked my way into production where I cut ads for the spots I sold. I moved to a smaller station as production manager, made friends of the station's clients, and parlayed that into station manager.

I didn't tell her my only friends were clients with whom I needed to maintain a long-term relationship. I didn't tell her that I had few friends in high school and was considered a "mama's boy" because I tried to please her. That meant not calling teachers dirty names out of class or being insolent in class, not hanging out at convenience stores where items were pilfered and other customers harassed, not smoking or drinking or fighting.

I wasn't big but I was tall and the football coach thought I might make an end. I got into one game, caught a pass over the middle, was hit by a linebacker and dislocated my shoulder. It hurt when I dislocated it, it hurt when the coach popped it back in place, but what hurt most was seeing my mother on the field. "Are you all right, Chance?" she asked in front of the coaches, the players, the officials, the fans, the band. I knew then my playing days were over.

I didn't tell Rista of the nights I spent alone with the TV because Mother was out with a boyfriend, or the nights I spent in my room with the TV because some man visited Mother. Television was my imaginary playmate, my secret garden, my Eden, my promised land.

Every magazine Mother read said I needed a father, and she tried to find one for me. It was hard for me to understand that Mother needed more than me, that she needed a man's attention, a man's company, a man's touch. She found men who could please her and make her life more secure, but they also had to be good fathers. She slyly introduced me to them to see how they reacted. I felt like the family ghost, the shameful secret dragged from the closet, and I was angry at myself for being embarrassed, angry with Mother for embarrassing me. I never made a good impression, leaving Mother in tears, disappointed that the man had failed the test, angry with me for sabotaging her plans.

"Leave me out of it," I yelled at her. "Do what you want to do and leave me out of it."

"If I tell them I have a son, they will pretend they like you, and they will deceive me and maybe themselves and they'll turn out to be like Rusty. I have to see how they react when they see you."

If they could bear me they could bear anything? Mother fled to her room to escape in tears. I went to my room to escape in television.

Every dream I had was shaped by television. Every attitude, every reaction, every ambition derived from a favorite TV show. I wanted to work at a television station the way a priest wanted to work at the Vatican—to be at the heart and center of what I loved, where souls found rest, and bargains, and information.

"Rista, if you had a satellite dish you could get television out here." I had never been so confined.

"I don't want television out here. Take a horse that's bigger and stronger than you are, that can kill you if you're careless, train it to respond like you're dancing, and you'll find out entertainment isn't something someone does for you. It's being close to the land and the wind and feeling the rain. Sitting on the top rail of the corral and talking about how you're going to hang on to the place another year, or whether a horse or a cow is worth a man's life, or whether it's okay to steal slowly and legally because you own the bank or the store. How do you think you'd compete with Six Mile Draw when it used to run all the time?"

We'd win every time. And we'd goose the news during rating season. "Raging fire threatens city; that story after this announcement." Not telling until after the commercials that the fire was in another country.

"You know how I cleared prairie dogs out of the pasture? I'd lie on the ground and wave a foot until they stood up to look and then I'd shoot one. The others'd duck back in their holes and in a few minutes they'd stand up for another look. That's how television is. No matter how many lives are ruined the other folks have to keep looking to see if anything worthwhile ever comes on."

"The world saw a man walk on the moon." The back of my knee itched, and I turned my attention to that as she raved on.

"In school you learn that Will Rogers was a cowboy and Audie Murphy was a hero, but news people substitute phonies like John Wayne who never worked cows and Ronald Reagan who never fought a war. They weren't even real. They were inventions for folks who don't want to know what it takes for a cow to need a bull or for a man to shoot a horse or for a woman to put up with a man who thinks he's better than she is."

I didn't know who the man was who thought he was better than Rista, but I was sure he was dead. Mother feared Rista's genes. When I was fourteen, she prepared a celebration— steaks, baked potatoes, imported beer—for a man who didn't want children. Before she cut the cake, she told him she was no longer pregnant and waited for his proposal. He said she misunderstood. It wasn't a handshake—she aborted, he proposed—it was more like a feeler. "You bastard," she said and stabbed him in the arm with the cake knife. She might have stabbed him in the heart if he hadn't thrown up his arm. After he left she hugged me and swore she would never do that to me. Never.

I was as confused by Mother as I was by the scene at the table. She would never abort me? I didn't know then the genes she and I carried. Even now I couldn't imagine killing anyone, not even when news led with the city council meeting and production punched up a segment on pigs with slop streaming down their jowls. We killed lights and props, not people.

"I don't know what happened to Cassie after she left here."

Mother said she made bad choices because she didn't understand men, but I think she knew too much of their rough appeal and rougher hands, hard heads and soft minds, tender egos and Teflon hearts, the ease with which they turned a pat into a punch. She knew that when the heat was on them they believed in eternal love and when their lust was sated, their thoughts turned to something new. Patting or punching, loving or leaving they thought they were better than she.

"Have you ever been in love?" Rista asked. "Loving someone so much that you can give up everything for them, except the one thing you know you can't live without."

I loved Shana, but I couldn't match her march to the top, and I couldn't be her shadow carrying her makeup bag.

"Your mother didn't have anything she couldn't give up for love." Rista sat in a rocking chair in the cramped sitting room like a queen on her throne. Was that what she couldn't give up for love? "You know that rider steer we have to feed every day? It got some smell on it, I reckon. The other steers rode it until they crippled it."

Was she reading the wrong cue cards or was that supposed to make sense?

"Did Cassie talk to you about me?" she asked.

No segue, no transition. If I could get her to talk that way before a judge, I could be home by the weekend. "I know everything, Rista." It was a bluff, but I wanted her to know my posture. If her expression changed I didn't see it.

"Did she say anything before she died?"

"Not about you." Mother waved me close, tried to smile and gave me a kiss. Although it was hard for her to talk, she gasped, "My Chance," her last words.

"Did she look pretty?" Rista asked.

She couldn't force herself to say, "in her coffin." Mother was buried in a steel gray casket she had selected with bouquets of forget-me-nots painted on the sides. She bought a pink suit with a white scarf for the occasion, and I had Shana's hairdresser do her thin hair. I bought a corsage of white carnations and baby's breath and a casket spray of seventy-five pink carnations. Her hands were clasped with her left hand on top. Mother wanted a ring, a thin gold band with a tiny diamond, buried with her.

Shana presided over a kind of wake at the station. We had pizza, barbecue, pasta, sandwiches, fried chicken, potato salad, cake, cookies, ice cream, and lime-pineapple Jell-O that everyone avoided. No one said much about her because no one knew her, except Shana who knew her only when she was dying. We ate and drank, told jokes and tried to pretend we were acknowledging a passage. I said Mother named me Chance because I was the best chance she had.

"Chance of what?" Bob Blaine asked. I couldn't think of an answer and everyone else seemed embarrassed, but Shana said, "Her best chance for someone to love her." That ended the party for me. I escaped to my office and not even Shana dared follow. I watched the monitor, unwilling to be alone with my thoughts. I hated Rista for what she had done to my mother. Mother had never forgiven her and neither would I.

"Is there anything you can tell me, Chance?"

In those last days when she was dying, Mother told me things she didn't want Rista to know. That Odis took her to play with children while he played with their mother. The children hated him and turned their anger on her. She didn't want to go with him, but even more she didn't want to disappoint him. That she had forced Shad to marry her, that Rusty refused to marry her, that sometimes at night she had cried for her mother, that Stoddard had never stopped loving Rista.

I turned my attention to the itch behind my knee. "I think I have a tick," I said. "What should I do?"

"Look for more," she said and went to bed.

9

1932

The country was broke, the land blistered in a drought, cattle were worthless. Rista, Pug, and Paco drove cows to the railroad trap at Claypool. There were no buyers. With no roads on the ranch, no trucks to carry the cattle, they had to be driven home. Some cattle were so poor they fell and had to be tailed up until they could no longer stand. Rista took the knife her father had given her, cut their throats and took their hides and tried to remember the times she had seen them sleek and shining after a rain.

The drought was broken by the worst blizzard in years. Rista and her hands were in the saddle day and night breaking trails through drifts so the cows could get to water, breaking ice on the tanks so they could drink, driving cows to hay. Some cattle froze, especially the young and old. Others lived but their feet froze. Those that had more than one foot frozen were shot, gutted, and hung from a windmill, before the coyotes got them. Those that could move were driven to hay. The others were fed whenever possible. Some of them survived with a stump for one leg and still bred, calved, and suckled their young.

The beeves hanging from windmills were loaded onto the wagon. Rista kept two calves for use on the ranch although the meat was of poor quality because the calves had been drawn by the cold and without food or water. The others she took to town to give to the churches to distribute, stopping first to leave one at the orphanage run by Vada Bennet. Vada insisted that she come inside to thaw out. Rista drank tea in front of the fireplace where Vada was supposed to have burned her baby, beneath the noose that hanged Day McVicar. Vada, who had never married, cooed to a baby whose mother had died. Older children played at her feet.

Spring brought grass and good weather but no money. Fences were repaired with old wire, the barn went without paint, Rista cut the tops off her boots to fill holes in the bottoms. There was no money for coal oil except for medicinal purposes so Genevieve went back to cooking on the wood stove. Rista and Genevieve had stretched the blanket as far as it would go and were eating water cooked with beans. Pug called it three-bean soup because it wasn't much more than that.

One day Rista rode alone, checking a mare to see if she was any good with cows before breeding her. A boy jumped from behind a tree and tried to grab her horse, but she pulled her knife and he backed off. "I'm sorry, ma'am," he said. "I didn't mean to scare you, but I need a horse real bad. I robbed a bank, and they're looking for me."

She recognized the boy as one of Pete Laumbach's dogies. Pete was a trapper, and everything about him—his clothes, house, wife, kids—smelled of skunk. When he died his widow moved the children into a deserted farmhouse to escape the stench. "What did you do with the money?" Rista asked.

"Give it to my maw." He began to cry.

"Did you hurt anyone? Can you ride bareback? Turn the

mare loose when you can, and she'll come home." She packed her saddle until Paco found her.

▲▼▲

Pug complained of scorpions in the bunkhouse. "Hell, I got scorpions in the main house. When you get done stomping the ones you got, come give me a hand," she said.

Paco and Pug got lice off the cattle, and there was an infestation in the bunkhouse. Rista had the cowboys lay their bedding in ant beds so ants would kill the lice, doused the bedsprings with coal oil, and set them on fire. She had them throw their clothes out the door so Genevieve could put them in a pot of boiling water. While they bathed in the horse trough with lye soap, Rista burned sulfur in the bunkhouse to fumigate it. They killed lice on the horses with coal oil, and when the hair came off, they rubbed the horses with tallow until the hair grew back.

One of Pug's sisters died giving birth, and the baby died soon after. Folks said they had starved to death because they could see the mother's teeth shining through the clenched jaws and count the baby's ribs through the worn sheet it was wrapped in. Until she got pregnant she had been a chili queen, turning her mother's shelly cows into chili, selling it door to door, and meeting the trains in Claypool. Her husband didn't have enough money to bury her and the child, so Rista and Paco dug a grave while Pug made a box. They buried the two together, the baby's skeletal head on its mother's breast, and neighbors took up a collection so the man and his surviving children could leave.

Rista spied blood and entrails where a calf had been butchered. She carried a six-shooter rolled in a gunny sack for cattle too sick or crippled to live. She unwrapped the gun and followed the trail. She found a woman and children squatted around a fire where chunks of flesh cooked, grabbing and eating the half-raw meat, burning their hands. The thief was Bob Hanks' son. Rista knew the cow thief would have sold the family Bible, with all its history, for a pinch of salt. She watched him watching his hungry wife and kids filling their bellies, walked back to her horse, and quietly rode away. After that she branded early, made certain that she and the hands didn't all leave the ranch when she had beef hanging in the barn, and wondered how long she could hang on.

Stoddard was in Austin attending college. Rista went to dances and parties alone or rode with Odis. One day she found a poem tied to a horse's mane with a ribbon. The poem was about a man who couldn't see his sweetheart so he stroked the horse that had carried her. Stoddard had come to see her, but she had been working on a windmill.

Burt Brownfield, Jr., one of Stoddard's friends, appeared at her door and waited with Genevieve until Rista returned to the house. Stoddard's father was ill, and Stoddard had come home to publish the newspaper. He had been too busy to see her, but there was going to be a picture show and a movie star was going to be there. As publisher of the paper Stoddard had been invited to the after-show party and wanted to take her.

"Stoddard has made arrangements for you to spend the night with Lucinda Gillin's family," Brownfield explained.

Rista had more anxiety about what she would wear in Lucinda's house than what she would wear to the party. The only nights she had spent away from home had been at her grandfather's deserted ranchhouse or in a bedroll in the pasture. What would she wear to bed? To breakfast?

Rista packed her fresh clothes in a flour sack and rode a

spiritless lady-broke bay to Judge Gillin's house because the horse was well mannered and wouldn't fight the judge's mare. She missed the parade where the movie star, with Stoddard beside her, rode a buggy down Wagonseller Road followed by suited townspeople on saddled draft horses. Only Smiley Wooten was absent from the mounted posse.

Rista bathed—her first time in a bath tub—washed her hair and changed into her party clothes. Because Stoddard liked it, she wore the lingerie dress she had worn at the play party. Lucinda helped her with her hair and loaned her a red sash to make the dress more festive.

When Stoddard came to walk her to the picture show, Lucinda hugged Rista and wished her a good time. Stoddard was the most eligible bachelor in the county, handsome, heir to his father's newspaper, and he had been to college. Yet, Lucinda wasn't jealous that Stoddard asked Rista to the party after Lucinda refused because it seemed superficial. Rista didn't want to make Lucinda jealous, but she wanted her to care.

Hams hung from the marquee to be given away as door prizes, and the bright lights attracted black crickets that clung to trousers and skirts and crunched under foot. Young boys, paid as ushers, swept them in piles in the street. Inside, the buttered popcorn smelled to Rista a little like roasted cricket. Fans stirred the warm air and sweat soaked Rista's dress as Stoddard introduced her to friends before seating her.

Rista fiddle-footed through the movie. The cowboys couldn't ride, neither the saddles nor six-shooters were authentic, and the actors looked like an advertisement for a leather shop, wearing cow rigging like minstrel actors wore black-face—not to add character but ridicule. The movie cowboys

135

ran their horses everywhere they went, chased cows like they were trying to run the beef off them and spent most of their time in a town that seemed just over the hill from the ranch. The town was busier than Red Rock had ever been with wagons, riders, and townsfolk in a street free of horse manure and flies. The women were "dance hall girls" or decoration. The rancher's daughter rode sidesaddle, cried and wrung her hands while the cowboy hero fought off a mob to save her, and fainted when he was shot. A brave dance hall girl dressed the wound and saved his life. After the show the star who had played the rancher's daughter wobbled onto the stage with the support of Smiley Wooten and the theater manager and drunkenly told how she loved the West and was buying a three-acre ranch in California to raise horses.

It was a relief to Rista to escape into the night air and walk across the street to the courthouse. The second-floor courtroom, where the party was held, had large windows that had been opened, and a fresh breeze blew through them. Frank LeGrand, Wes Verstuft, and Julian Barnes, who had been painting their noses with tarantula juice, sat near the top of the stairs unable to go farther. None of them had seen the show; Wes and Julian said they knew all about cowboys they wanted to know. Frank came to the party to look for a widow who didn't fear poisoning.

Rista studied the crowd, wondering who had so little to do. Judge Gillin and Sheriff Grover bulged in wherever there were potential voters. Deputy Ralph Wilberg guarded the star while Odis guarded Claypool. Anita Barnes and Coy Bannister honeymooned at the movie. Burt Brownfield who ran the general mercantile came to see who wore mail-order clothing. Dale Rollins, who had stomped on the bar in the saloon, wanted to talk to the actress about a movie career. Birdie Kesey, who married Dexter Kesey and divorced him because of his hygiene and tobacco, brought her daughter who was feathered out like a dance-hall movie star.

As Rista made her way through the crowd, she heard Stoddard tell the movie star that he wanted her to meet a real cowgirl. "Her father fought Indians when he was six, and when he was fourteen he backed down Dan Beasley, a gunfighter that even the sheriff was afraid of. Dan knew it would be a cartridge-and-corpse occasion and crawled in front of his hands. Shortly before he died, her father lynched a rustler."

"Stoddard," Rista protested.

"Or ran him out of the country, nobody is sure," Stoddard said. "Claris was the only man in the county brave enough to keep a gunfighter who was so scary they called him—What did you call him? Abomin—"

"Bamanitious," Rista said and escaped to the ladies room by the stairs. The star staggered into the room to throw up, missed the toilet, and stained her lacy, pleated dress and cowboy boots that had her name set in red leather. Rista pointed out that her dress now matched the wallpaper in the bathroom. Two ladies came in, wiped vomit off the actress' dress, cleaned her boots, and washed the woman's face while Rista escaped her cursing.

When she returned to the courtroom she saw Smiley Wooten, the town banker, posing as though folks didn't know where he came from. Smiley was his mother's maiden name; he rarely smiled. When he did, his cheeks pulled his skin so tight it pointed his nose. Smiley was tall, thin, slick as a newborn calf, with barbered hair and New York suits although the bank couldn't pay its depositors. He studied people the way Paco

137

studied cattle and could spot weakness through a brick wall. He inspected Rista, gauging the curves beneath her dress. She had been sixteen when Smiley offered a bank loan in exchange for sex.

"I'll introduce you to the guest of honor," he said in a voice that had a smile pressed around it.

"I've already met her," Rista said, walking away. Smiley was as welcome around her as a skunk in the tack room. Stoddard wanted her to talk to the movie star. "I'd sooner eat supper with a coyote," she snapped. "She's no more a cowboy than I'm a stallion. What if someone believed the picture show was real?"

"Rista, no one cares about the real thing. That's what they're trying to escape. That's why they admire anyone who offers them diversion. I'm going to write about this party because everyone in the county wants to know about it. I'm going to interview the actress and send the story to newspapers all over the country because people want to know about her."

"Are you going to write that she is snot-slinging drunk, aired her paunch in the ladies room and cussed the women who cleaned her up?"

Stoddard took her hand between both of his. "Rista, radio is trying to run the newspaper out of business." A radio station ran "Swap Shop" from the Red Rock implement store where listeners could swap goods without charge. They broadcast music, drama, and news minutes after it happened. Teachers said pupils from homes with radios were better informed about current events. "How can I compete with that?" Stoddard asked. "I'm going to write about this party because radio can't mask her drunkenness."

"And you're going to."

"Rista, I'm trying to find a wider audience for the newspaper, increase subscriptions and advertising so I can sell the newspaper and write what I want."

For all his arrogance there was a runt-of-the-litter air about Stoddard that Rista found appealing. She brushed back the hair that fell over his eyes. Why would he write about a movie star when he could write about the war between the Aginers and the Anythings, Tim Tingle hanging himself because of Oma Dodd, Trudy Wooten shooting Levi Brown?

Stoddard brought her hand to his lips. "If you'll excuse me, I have an interview to do."

Rista watched Stoddard flattering and faunching to curry favor, then she walked to the newspaper office alone.

"I got what I wanted," Stoddard boasted when he rejoined Rista. "The story of her affair with Wallace Beery. It's the biggest story I've ever written." He was eager to be alone with his story.

Rista walked alone to Judge Gillin's house. Lucinda was in pajamas. Rista slipped into a shift that had belonged to her mother. "The party was what you said," she told Lucinda. "You were too savvy to go."

"If I support Stoddard in such things will he grow up?" Lucinda asked. She believed Stoddard had flunked out of college, was incapable of hard work, and played at being a writer. She could never marry someone so shallow.

Rista found it hard to sleep. Lucinda seemed to be what Stoddard built his loop for, but Rista and Stoddard were made of the same leather; they were trying to hang on to what their fathers had given them.

Rista woke early as usual and before Lucinda awoke, Rista studied her closets, her dresser drawers, the cosmetics on her dresser, trying to determine how she should look. On the dresser was a photograph of Lucinda the day she was selected "Best Hatted Lady." Rista had never worn a woman's hat. Quietly she took one of Lucinda's hats and examined herself in the mirror, striking poses as Dawn and coming alive. She could be what Stoddard wanted but to save him she had to be what he needed.

Lucinda woke, dressed, and showed Rista her cat that had kittens in a hen's nest. The hen thought they were hers and fought the cat for them. At breakfast, Rista asked if the eggs were from the hen that thought she had hatched kittens. Lucinda, who thought there were two kinds of eggs, those hens laid and those people ate, left the table, unable to eat something that came out of the end of a chicken. Rista knew then that Lucinda could not save Stoddard.

▲▼▲

Stoddard asked Rista to accompany him to the Harley Sadler show. This would be different from the movie, he promised. Harley was from Texas, a real actor, and his company went to church on Sunday. She wondered if Stoddard had asked Lucinda first.

Rista made a rare trip to town to buy a dress, telling Genevieve she had to go to the bank. She went by the newspaper office hoping Stoddard would help her pick a dress he liked, but he was busy on the telephone with a rumor that the kidnapper of the Lindbergh baby had been seen in Texas. He asked Rista to call Odis in Claypool and ask what information he had. Trains stopped in Claypool, and passengers carried the latest news. Rista had never used a telephone before. Stoddard asked the operator to place the call then thrust the telephone at her. "He'll listen to you," he said.

She was startled to hear Odis' voice over the wire, different yet recognizable. When she asked what he had heard about the Lindbergh kidnapper being in Texas she could sense his anger before he spoke. "I can't believe you listen to that bullshit," he said, hanging up the telephone.

Rista told Stoddard that Odis didn't believe the rumors and received the supercilious look he had perfected in college. She had appeared a fool to one man and had failed the other. She wished she had stayed on the ranch where she liked who she was.

She found no refuge at Brownfield's mercantile. She didn't know her size and when she asked to try on a dress, Burt Junior looked at her shirt and jeans and said she would have to wear something under the dress before he would let her put it on. He held a slip against her, said it was the right size, and she bought it. There were only two dresses that fit her, and one was a hideous cow teat pink. There was a new dry goods store, but Rista's courage was exhausted. When Burt Junior said she needed hose instead of cotton stockings and a garter belt to hold up the hose, she stood on her heels. She bought the bias cut, black chiffon with satin ruffles and a wide sash, and left the store hating the dress and herself for buying it. She had planned to buy shoes but couldn't bear to pull off her boots and dirty socks in front of Burt Junior who had worked in a store in Dallas.

She returned to the newspaper office where Stoddard and his lady assistant had their heads together over a desk. He seemed disappointed to see her. "I hoped you could look at this dress," she said.

Stoddard sighed, rolled his eyes at his assistant and said, "This is a newspaper office. Ask Burt Junior to look at your dress."

▲▼▲

The Harley Sadler show was in a big tent, but Stoddard had excellent seats, courtesy of the newspaper. Rista squirmed in the sticky black chiffon with satin ruffles. She stood out like a deacon at a whoop-up because most folks wore jeans, overalls, and gingham. Stoddard wore what he had worn to the office—gray flannel trousers, fried shirt, dark vest, and brown-and-white piebald shoes. Only Smiley Wooten wore a suit and tie. Smiley always looked like he had been ironed with too much starch. Rista wished Stoddard would say something about her good sense, but he seemed preoccupied. She didn't like her dress; why would he?

A warm breeze came through the rolled-up sides bearing the smell of sawdust and tarpaulin. Dale Rollins sat on the front row where he sat the whole week the show was in town. Rista overheard a woman who had sold two laying hens so she could see the show. Rista looked at her in wonder. The woman went to the Aginers church, too.

The show was "Rose of the Rio Grande." Harley played a cowboy but made it clear he wasn't a real cowboy; he made fun of himself pretending to be a cowboy. The acts were amusing and between acts Harley sold candy. Inside some wrappers were coupons for prizes. Stoddard bought several boxes and in one of them was a diamond ring. Stoddard slipped it on her finger. It was a thin gold band with a tiny diamond, but it was the first ring she had ever worn and she adored it. He said it was a "friendship" ring, but she knew that they were engaged. And it didn't matter if he won the ring because he published the newspaper. A man in a white tuxedo and woman in a pink evening gown danced to "Three O'Clock in the Morning." It was the loveliest

142

thing Rista had ever seen. She dreamed of dancing like that with Stoddard.

At a party in the tent after the show, Stoddard introduced her to Harley and his wife Billie. She liked them but when he introduced her to the couple who had danced, she asked if that was all they did. She couldn't imagine spending her life doing something so flighty. How did they feel at the end of the day? They studied her, wrinkling their noses at her dress the way Stoddard looked at dung beetles when she explained their usefulness aerating and fertilizing the soil.

Stoddard talked to the actresses about the kidnapping, giving them tidbits about Charles and Ann, the baby, police activities. He watched the actresses, fascinated by the way they talked, the way they walked and sat in their clothes, while they looked at her and whispered behind their hands. He studied their fine dresses, manicured nails, curled hair, painted faces and suggested ways Rista could be like them. Rista would never have hands that soft, nails that long. And their hair. Their faces. When would she have time for that? She couldn't even get the seams of her hose straight.

Even when he talked to her, Stoddard's mind was full of them. "You're as pretty as any of them," he said. "You could be that glamorous."

He thought she was pretty; couldn't he also see she was useful? "I don't have time to be glamorous," she admitted. Or money. For what she spent on the dress she could have bought a bridle and a new rope.

"Wouldn't you like to have that kind of attention? Everywhere you go people watching you, admiring you."

"That's the way we look at horses," she said. "Cows." She wanted to be the center of his attention, and for that attention she would provide him with home, love, and all the children he wanted.

"Harley could be governor. Everyone loves him, loves to be in his presence," Stoddard said. "He makes them forget their kids are hungry."

Stoddard was easy to listen to, saying terrible things in a voice that made them seem less terrible. He could talk Six Mile Draw into thinking it was the Brazos River. She loved to listen to him, but it was pretty noise, like leaves on a metal roof that sounded like rain but didn't grow anything.

▲▼▲

Rista told Genevieve of the doll-like women and the dancers who lived like water striders that skated on the horse trough. Genevieve said she had seen Dale Rollins dance when he was young. She wanted to hear nothing about the Lindbergh baby. "How can decent people talk of such things?"

When Rista showed her the ring Genevieve wanted to announce the engagement. Rista said no. She looked at the tiny band on her finger and swore she would never take it off. Stoddard could announce their engagement in the newspaper whenever he wished.

Over breakfast I listened to Rista and Pug discuss taking the cow to Claypool to sell to a packinghouse for bologna while the eye cancer was mild enough to pass inspection. If the cow couldn't pass inspection it would be sold for pet food at half its value.

Rista invited me along, but I would have gone even if I had to ride with the cow. I needed to call Shana. And the TV station; it could have gone off the air for all I knew.

The corral had a loading chute—an angled, walled, floored passageway up which the cow was driven into the trailer. The chute was supported on cut-off telephone poles, the side planks were broken and gapped, and the flooring looked too weak to support the cow's weight—old boards nailed over broken boards until the whole thing looked like a relic from the O.K. Corral.

Pug twisted the cow's tail and pushed from behind, and Rista yelled the cow into the trailer. Rista drove her pickup; Pug's truck had no license tags and never left the ranch. Rista's truck had factory upholstery, and the truck started easily and ran smoothly. She didn't trouble to remove the guns from the gunrack.

Rista leaned over the steering wheel and peered through the window like she didn't see well, and her hands on the steering wheel were jerky and erratic. Her spurs raked the floor of the truck.

"First time I went to Claypool I saw smoke from a train and I thought the town was on fire and was going to burn up before I got to see it. The last time, I was there for a wedding and I had to ask a woman directions to the church. When I didn't recognize the bride I knew I was at the wrong church." Rista went to the foyer to get her present to take to the right wedding. She was looking through the gifts when a man asked her to leave. "Don't ever ask directions of a woman wearing panty hose."

I wanted the man who asked her to leave to tell a judge how he found her pawing through the wedding presents.

We passed a horse farm with a colonial house, metal pens, pole fences, blooded horses—what I thought ranches looked like. "Hardy Rollins," Rista said as though I had asked. "His grandfather, Dale, ran away with the Harley Sadler show, came back to Claypool, sold insurance. Hardy said I couldn't afford his horses. They're for city folks—pleasure riding, barrel racing, calf roping, show competition."

At the edge of town was a lighted arena I mistook for a football field, but there were chutes at both ends and no grass. "Roping arena," Rista said. "I used to rope there until they cut me out. Place orginally belonged to Ike Davis. He and his wife, Subie, lived in a tent with a brush arbor. That's where Rose was born. She died a few days later, and Subie demanded a regular house. Then they had Cisco and he died of double pneumonia. Subie never got over that. It was like she put her faith in the house and Cisco died anyway. Then Smiley Wooten stole Ike's car and they drifted away."

The sales barn was down Trash Dump Road, across the railroad track, past a boarded-up depot. The infrequent trains didn't stop anymore. The sales barn was a metal building surrounded by metal pens that were a larger, rational version of Rista's pens. I waited in the truck to avoid the rich smell of manure while Rista went in the office. The sales barn would sell the cow, take a commission, and deposit the rest in her bank account.

Rista got in, backed up the trailer, unloaded the cow, and drove to a sprawling general store. Outside was a half-acre of flatbed, gooseneck, horse and stock trailers; metal loading chutes, squeeze chutes, push gates and fence panels, hunting blinds and deer feeders; stacks of fence posts, rolls of wire and a yard-full of barbecue grills, smokers, wheelbarrows. Inside, the store looked like the prop room for a horse opera—guns, spurs, knives, ropes, prods, stick and rocking horses, animal remedies, farm and ranch tools, curb bits, correction bits, snaffle bits. I priced a saddle; I could buy a computer for what it cost. While Rista shopped, I called Shana to tell her that I might be gone longer than I thought.

"Thank God you called. I wish you were here because I wanted to say this to your face." I leaned my head against the wall. While I was trying to put away a crazy woman and take her ranch Shana had gotten an offer from another station. "I don't want to be the woman I am on the screen."

I breathed relief. "Shana, Carey is going to change your image." I didn't tell her Carey wanted to give her a pouty look.

"I really wanted to discuss this in private. I don't want to work in television. I thought I did, but I don't."

People went into a profession thinking they could change lives to discover it was more like changing diapers. They became disillusioned, a little cynical. Some changed professions to become disillusioned again, some dropped out to save their souls

147

by quitting their minds, most stayed on the job waiting for Friday. "Shana, you have such presence on TV."

"Does it bother you that we condemn in others what we admire in ourselves? Rubbernecking—if you do it, you're a creep. If I do it I'm a professional and may get professional awards if the horror is awful enough. If you complain about some wrong, you're a whiner. If I do it, I'm a courageous reporter. I'm tired of pointing fingers at those who fail and never doing anything positive myself. Being a buzzard at disasters. We turn our viewers into voyeurs and then despise them for it."

"What happened?"

"I was supposed to spell out our editorial position on welfare reform by exposing a deadbeat mother who neglected her children. She lived in a homeless shelter with her three daughters, all of them in one room. She was hooked on drugs, and she needed men to get them. Some of the men didn't want her; they wanted the sixteen-year-old. Some wanted the fourteen-year-old. They're already hooking for their mother and probably hooked on drugs. The nine-year-old—that's the average age of a homeless person—sleeps on the floor because the bed is the only place that's hers, and she keeps her possessions there—a Snoopy T-shirt, her good shoes, and a dirty Cabbage Patch doll. Her dream was to have her own room with a window. Her fear was that her mother would do drugs and they'd be thrown out of the shelter and the children put in foster homes.

"Scottie framed the mother tight, showing a lot of skin, with lights behind her so she looked big and sinister. She saw herself on the screen above a bar, saw herself as I portrayed her, and stabbed a man who wanted the nine-year-old. He's in the hospital, she's in jail, the two youngest children are in a juvenile facility, the oldest is on the street somewhere."

Unlike the other station, Carey and I didn't do on-camera editorials, but our clients didn't like homeless people and that was our editorial policy. "Shana, it was going to happen no matter what you did."

"That's my point. Her story made a few people angry, a few people cry, got us some good numbers, sold whatever we were selling. It didn't do anything for her. We used her and her children."

"Our policy is not to pay for interviews."

"I'm not talking about paying her. I'm talking about doing something for her as well as for ourselves. It's more than a story about a mother neglecting her children. It's bigger. It's more complicated."

"We don't handle complicated very well," I admitted. "Our stock is images, but there have been images that have changed—"

"My images didn't. I showed a woman who despises herself as much as we despise her. Who uses her children to get what she wants, the way we used her to get what we want."

"I'll talk to business," I said. Business would forecast the expense of a documentary and the impact on staff and facilities, and the budget would say the story was over. I'd like more documentaries, investigative reporting, but to get the budget I had to have the numbers, and to get the numbers, I had to entertain the masses with circus and sell them bread. "The station can buy the kids some shoes, clothes—I'll do it."

"It's not money the younger children need. It's a parent, a stable environment, a room with a window. I can't foster her, because I'm not married."

"Put her on camera and you'll find dozens of foster parents," I said, not wanting to discuss marriage or parenthood.

"At Thanksgiving we do a story on one hungry family, and they get a truckload of groceries. At Christmas we pick one child who isn't going to be visited by Santa Claus, and he is swamped with toys. And everyone who watches the show can feel better, and so can our sponsors. Everyone except the hungry families and toyless kids who didn't get picked."

"You told the story. Maybe someone will put pressure on the mayor to do something."

"If I'm in front of a camera I want it to be for something I have done. I want to storm the barricades, not describe the barricades and collect a check. I'm too upset to talk about this over the telephone."

Off camera Shana was the aggressive, hard-hitting image we wanted on camera. "Shana." I stopped, not sure I knew who I was talking to. "I'm going to be here longer than I thought. Rista is . . . strong-willed. That cowboy is devoted to her. Please don't do anything until we can talk. I'm going nuts out there without a TV or telephone."

"I won't say anything at the station until you get back, but then I'm quitting. I don't know what I will do. Something with children."

"Shana, don't walk out on me," I said, desperate to touch her.

"I love you, Chance. I wish you were here. But I'm not going to be a TV personality. If that's what you want, I'm sorry."

Thousands of people dreamed of doing what she had a chance of doing, and she was rejecting it because her story didn't redeem the subject of the story? Shana had no idea of the future she was rejecting, the power she could have to

150

shape ideas, change opinions. I would talk to her, but I wasn't sure I knew her as well as I thought. Was she the innocent who wanted to report the truth? The perfectionist who wanted the camera to say what she said? The dedicated reporter who got the story she was sent to get? The detached professional we were creating? Or the temperamental talent she was becoming?

I called the station to check the numbers and problems. The numbers were better than expected for Shana's morning show. The other station was still trying to define their show's personality and shuffling the on-air team. Our numbers were down for the ten o'clock news. Our weatherman was a trained meteorologist who could explain the weather in layman's terms and had good forecasting skills but no personality. We would let him go when his contract ran out.

Sales said I needed to do more selling of the network spots. Program said Carey, who doubled as assignment editor, was generating too many second-page stories and not efficiently scheduling reporters and photographers. Carey said engineering gave faulty equipment to a crew doing a remote. Engineering said it was in good condition when news got it and mishandled it. Our equipment was old, the duty cycle demanding, and we didn't have room to store it properly. I promised to talk to the owners about upgrading the equipment.

I asked Carey about Shana's story on the homeless woman. "Terrific. We got a lot of calls, all positive, all wanting to do some-thing about the homeless."

Yeah, put them in jail, I thought. It was easy to punish, hard to help. But that was Shana's line.

"I killed a car wreck," Carey said. "Car turned over, gas tank exploded. The camera identified the car."

One of our major clients. News carried the network story of the car's alleged exploding gas tanks, but locally our clients didn't want to see their cars highlighted in wrecks.

Shana called it self-censorship. She had found a whistle-blower who had stories of utility price fixing, overcharging and kickbacks to regulators. It would cost dollars and hours to research, there would be no graphic images, utility companies had more money, more lawyers and more clout with politicians than we did. I wasn't convinced our viewers cared, other businesses would close access to us, and we'd lose advertising. When Will Morgan rated restaurants regarding sanitation and health standards, the restaurants switched advertising to the other station. I told the whistle-blower to talk to the newspaper. I told Shana it was business.

"Yeah, and we've convinced the public. Juries don't find corporations guilty of ethical violations, price fixing, pollution, false advertising, exploitation of those without economic or political power. It's business."

"I wanted to check with you, but I didn't know how," Carey said.

"It's okay," I said. Unless there was spectacular footage or someone had died in the wreck, I would have killed the story. I had vowed not to involve myself in decisions regarding Shana, but I took a chance. "Carey, have you thought about a follow-up on the woman Shana interviewed?"

"What's our take? Another 'found God in the jailhouse' story?"

Carey couldn't think of a way to help the homeless without preaching or repeating ourselves, and neither could I. I hung up the telephone and looked for Rista. I had to resolve her situation and the ranch and get back before Shana and the station spun out of control.

Rista found me. "When you come to town you know you're going to be cheated; you just don't know how much. Country folks try to make a living. Town folks try to make a profit and buy their living out of their profit."

I wasn't in the mood for cracker-barrel philosophy. She wanted me to weigh on the feed scales. "You don't pack enough muscle for that much weight." I wasn't overweight, but it doesn't require muscle to give orders and answer the telephone.

While we waited for her purchases to be loaded—two cinches, a dozen fence posts, five cases of oil, a ton of feed, parts for a windmill, fence staples, a roll of barbed wire, and a pair of jeans for me—Rista pointed out a teenager who had won top money as a rodeo rider but had never worked on a ranch. "When I was a girl you rode a horse until it settled down and figured out what you wanted it to do. Everytime I got one where it was a joy to ride, my father sold it."

As we left the store she handed me a pink concoction that looked like a round piece of plastic with something brown embedded in it. "Everytime I went to town you cried if I didn't buy you a peanut patty." I unwrapped the cellophane and took a bite. The candy was grainy and too sweet, and the peanuts were stale. I doubted I had ever cried for that.

We drove through the business part of town—mostly brick buildings, half of which boasted sales—past the church of the wrong wedding; a modern, out-of-place looking courthouse; a double-decker cafe where more people—three men in boots, jeans, and Resistols—stood outside than sat inside. Rista stopped at what pretended to be a supermarket, the truck and trailer taking half the parking lot. Rista said, "Lock your door. I don't want anyone stealing my guns."

We went inside the brightly lighted store that had few shoppers but was crowded with variety. I bought a newspaper and read the headlines while Rista filled her list. According to the newspaper, Republican congressmen wanted to shut down the government. Smaller headlines told of fires, floods, earthquakes, wars, and murders. Inside were stories about spying, a state teachers' meeting, a new weapon against cancer, a new weapon against missiles, a new health diet, a suspected tax increase, and the engagement of two movie stars.

Rista bought flour, meal, coffee, sugar, canned goods, bacon, eggs, molasses. "Pug likes this heavy molasses because it fries good. We used to butcher our own cows before Odis joined that food locker bunch. The first time I bought beef in a grocery store I was embarrassed worse than the time I went to buy a dress at Brownfield's and had to buy a slip before they would let me try it on. They call this beef," she said, shaking a plastic-wrapped steak at me. "It's not even red, and it's tenderized to where there's no pleasure in chewing it."

"Do you ever eat fish?"

"We're partial to fried catfish, but we don't have time to go fishing."

"Wouldn't you like time for fishing and things you like to do?"

"I'm doing the things I like to do. I don't like catching catfish; I just like eating them."

A woman started down the aisle, saw Rista, and turned and went the other way. "There was a meeting at a restaurant where they explained the rights of old folks," Rista said. "I went in and sat down at that woman's table. She was with a bunch of other folks, and they asked if I wanted to use the chair. I said, no, I wanted to join them. They were discussing someone who was homosexual, and I said, hell, if you been around bulls you know that some of them are attracted to their own sex, some of them don't care about sex, and some of them will breed anything that will stand still. It wasn't until they got up and left that I realized the meeting was upstairs. When I got up there, they wanted me to eat alfalfa. No wonder I can't afford it for my cows."

The check-out clerk treated her with a deference that angered her. "They think I'm losing my mind," she told me outside the store. "I got in the wrong truck one time. There was a woman sitting in it and she said, 'Take the truck, just let me go.' Hell, it looked just like mine."

Now I had three stories for the judge. "Do you ever go to town just to visit?" I asked as we drove out of Claypool.

"Folks don't have time to visit any more. I saw Marcella Lucas in town not long after her mate died. They wouldn't let her drive her car anymore so she drove the tractor to town. Marcella gave me a truckload of carrots for the horses once. I was going to express my condolences about her mate, but she had to be home in time to watch an interview on the news with a man who wrote a book about how to be who you are. How can you not be who you are?"

That book sold millions of copies and was still on the bestseller list, but it was hard to argue news with someone who didn't own a TV. We had the same amount of time to fill whether we reported World War III or a fire in a vacant lot. No one wanted to admit it, but a missing child could seem like a godsend during rating season.

We rode in silence until Rista turned off onto a dirt road, and we shook and rattled over the rutted, seldom-used road to Red Rock. She took a key hanging from the rearview mirror and handed it to me. "Get the gate," she said.

I unlocked the iron gate that held a sign warning "No Trespassing." "Are we supposed to be in here?" I asked, after locking the gate behind us.

"I own Red Rock," she said. "I never planned to own a town. I never planned on Odis killing it either."

11

1933

One night when Rista returned to the house she found supper uncooked and Genevieve dead in Celestine's rocker. She knelt beside the chair and put her head in Genevieve's lap. She was alone. She had no family left, no one to love her, no one to help her, no one to give her advice. For a while she cried; then she took a deep breath and stood up. Paco and Pug had to be fed. She filled their plates when they came in and explained she had to get the preacher. Pug insisted that he ride for the preacher, and Paco rode to notify the neighbors. Rista dressed Genevieve in her shroud and sat vigil in the kitchen, the ranch on her shoulders as heavy as a six-string saddle.

Odis came in the patrol car when he heard, bouncing across the pasture, following cow trails, driving down fence lines to find the gaps, dodging rocks, holes, and trees. He brought the preacher and I. P. Rainwater. I .P. brought a coffin, and Pug helped him put Genevieve in it, I. P. grumbling about embalming and proper burial. The neighbors gathered at the house and followed Rista and Genevieve in the wagon. The preacher said a few words, they sang a song and buried Genevieve in the Bone Yard.

The men spread a wagon sheet on the ground and the women placed in the wagon that had borne Genevieve the food they had brought—fried chicken, gun-wadding bread, spotted pup, spuds with the bark on, boiled eggs, beans boiled with salt pork, boiled custard, fluff-duff, cornmeal and jelly pies, and a butter cake. Everyone sat on the wagon sheet, ate beside Genevieve's grave, and said their condolences and goodbyes.

Rista returned the wagon to the barn, turned one horse loose, saddled the other and got a six-shooter from the house. She returned alone to the cemetery, sat on her horse, and emptied the gun into the ground while the horse pranced and shied. Then she returned to the house and yelled at Paco and Pug. "Get some shovels. We're going to find Aunt Jack."

▲▼▲

After Genevieve's death, Rista had little time for parties. Before daylight she started a fire in the stove, rolled out biscuits and put them in the oven, spat in the skillet to be sure it was hot enough, sharpened the kitchen knife on the stove pipe, sliced bacon and dropped it in the skillet, added in the eggs, and started a pot of beans working on the fire. She cooked in her chaps to be ready for work. Pug and Paco ate, nodded approval, and dropped their dishes in the soapy wreck pan where they remained until Rista returned at dark. When she could, she rode in ahead of them, added wood under the beans, and rolled out biscuits. While they baked, she gave the tin plates a quick swipe and reset them on the table.

After breakfast, she fried biscuits and bacon sandwiches to hold the men until supper while they brought in the horses from the horse trap and saddled. She hurried out to list their duties for the day, then jumped on her own horse. There was no time for the chuck wagon; she unbolted the chuck box from the wagon and nailed it to the wall for a kitchen cabinet.

During spring round-up and branding when she, the Slash Six, the O-Bar, and the Three Crosses threw in together to have enough hands to work each ranch, she threaded the testicles from castrated calves on baling wire and roasted them over the fire. "I like mine soaked in buttermilk, rolled in flour, and deep fried," a Slash 6 hand said. "Eat them or go hungry," she said. They ate them but she could tell Pug and Paco were embarrassed at the cut straw and molasses; the other ranches fed better.

Exhausted, at night she lay awake under the whether. Whether to borrow money and hold on to the steers hoping the price would go up or sell them at a loss. Whether to lease more land to farmers and give up two-thirds of the crop or hire the planting and cutting done and hope to sell the excess hay. Whether she could let the windmill repair go another day until she got the fence fixed.

She needed to dig a new pit and move the outhouse over it, put out salt blocks, burn pear for the cattle to eat, work the green horses, feed the dogie calves, and no one had checked the Borracho Creek pasture in days. Paco found clay and said he could build an adobe milk house to replace the cooling shed that was falling down, but that meant less time in the saddle.

He made a vat in the clay, added hay to it and she and Pug tromped it while Paco added water until he had the right consistency. They packed the adobe in blocks to cure, then stacked them to form a room, laid cedar poles across the top, then hay, and covered it with dirt. Rista was proud of it but behind in everything else. Pug's throat swelled until he couldn't swallow. She sat up at night putting poultices of coal oil, grease, turpentine, and red chiles on it. When he couldn't breathe she burst the membrane with a knife.

159

Most days there were dishes in the wreck pan, mice in the walls, pissants on the floor, grease on the stove. She had bought Genevieve a gasoline-powered washing machine and now wondered how Genevieve had kept up with the wash. She slept from bed to bed, a week in each, because she had no time for making beds or washing sheets. When all the sheets were dirty she washed them and remade all the beds.

When she had to go to the store or the bank she took dirty clothes to the laundry in Red Rock but that took all day, because she had to take the wagon to bring home the laundry and supplies. Before she died, Genevieve bought a bolt of print cloth and made sheets, pillow cases, underwear and some of Rista's shirts out of it. She even made Pug and Paco shirts out of it because Rista couldn't pay them enough to buy their own clothes.

Maybe that was why the other women looked at her strangely as she poked clothes through the wringer. Maybe it was because she had so many sheets to wash, like she was sleeping with some-one different every night. Or maybe it was because she washed clothes in her boots and spurs. She had straps with buckles for her spurs but didn't take them off because she'd have to put them back on. Besides, she liked hearing them jingle; it made the house seem less lonely.

Sleeping in different beds gave her a chance to grab a gun one night when someone broke into her house but came through the wrong window. She shot at but missed the man who fled when he heard her cock the pistol. Paco and Pug came at a run and made a quick search but found no one. After that she kept a horse staked out front to nicker or stomp around if someone prowled. A horse was better than a dog. One dog got rabies and she had to shoot it, another started killing chickens, and one chased cows but couldn't be trained to follow directions.

Stoddard invited Rista to the Christmas dance. She longed to see him, but she was feeding cattle and couldn't speed feeding because she had to call up the cows and wait for them to come. Lacking the money and nerve to buy another dress she aired the hated black chiffon in a shady spot so it wouldn't fade. She loaded the wagon with hay the night before to get an early start but the morning of the dance it was sleeting. She dressed standing on a chair to keep her feet off the cold floor. The water troughs were frozen over, and she had to break the ice.

When she got to the party, Stoddard was dancing with Lucinda. When he saw her he was angry because she was late. She explained that she had to feed the cows. "I could have been here on time if you had helped me."

"I have my own work," he said, astonished that she expected help. He whispered, "They think Bonnie and Clyde may be headed this way," but also asked her to dance.

There was a fiddle and a melodeon, and the dancers made the calico crack. "Swing to the corner like swinging on a gate," and Stoddard swung her as though she were light as a biscuit. "Left alamand, right to your partner and hand over hand. Promenade right." They promenaded arm in arm for all the world to see.

▲▼▲

Stoddard's father, a lunger, moved to New Mexico where the air was better, leaving the paper to Stoddard. Stoddard sent Rista a letter inviting her to another dance. The thing to do is to do, she told herself. The hard part was to choose the best among the possibilities. Claris had warned her of the slim pickings in Red

Rock County, but he didn't have time to look elsewhere and neither did she.

She couldn't run the ranch by herself. She required more of Pug and Paco than she had a right to, and some days Paco was so stiff only pride got him in the saddle. Paco had enough sand for a beach house. Stoddard would be a skim-milk cowboy, but he could come to the barn to welcome her when she rode in after a day's work, maybe bring dinner to them in the pasture, keep the books. And he could write about her father and the people of Red Rock. Stoddard was young, stupid, and full of advice, but there was a bottom that she could bring out of him if she had to twist his tail to do it.

Rista found it hard to talk to Stoddard without touching him, wanting to absorb him into herself. Stoddard was content to coyote around. She remembered what Genevieve had told her was a last resort. "If a woman is a good woman, and if she lies down for a man and he is a good man, he will be so ashamed of what he has done to her that he will marry her." There was more than one way to get a rope on a snuffy steer. They had been at the spit-and-whittle stage too long.

She rode to the dance on a sorrel mare that had no sense of direction and took a lot of patience to get along with. When she arrived, she took her party dress and shoes from the saddle, washed in the horse trough and changed in the barn before going to the house. Stoddard guarded the barn door while she changed.

She could feel his eyes watching through the crack of the door, and she thrilled with embarrassment and excitement. He liked to look at her. She dressed quickly lest he see something that displeased him. When she came out of the barn his eyes widened to swallow her. "My God, you're beautiful." She carried

162

that glow into the house with her, and everyone remarked on her sparkle.

Stoddard danced with her as much as he could, although others wanted to try their hand. There were no musicians; they danced to the music of a Victrola. Someone played a song called "Dardenella." Some people left because they thought the music scandalous. Rista thought the dance was too lovely, too exciting to end, and it was well after midnight when it did.

She thanked her hosts, said her goodbyes, and went to the barn to change into riding clothes. She heard the barn door open. Stoddard slipped inside and softly called her name. She didn't answer because she had removed her dress, but in the darkness Stoddard had eyes to see. He found her like a butterfly found nectar, his hands as soft as wings about her neck, her shoulders. His lips, quick as eels, found her mouth, her neck, her breast as he gently laid her down. Where she was dark, he was light, and where she was light, he was dark. The hay prickled her bare skin but she noticed that only afterward. She felt his weight, his heat upon her, his need mouthing her breasts, his member probing her thighs and when he filled her openness it was a welcome chastening. What she was most conscious of was the roughness of her hands on his back, her broken nails as she wrapped her arms around his neck to keep from falling into nothingness.

He helped her grope for her clothes, and when he had to strike a match to find them she feared more that they would catch the barn on fire than that they would be discovered.

Stoddard was mostly silent on the long ride back to the ranch. She wanted assurance of his love and her loveliness, but when he talked it was of the newspaper. He wanted to move the news-paper to Claypool. "Famous people come to Texas, and a lot of

163

them pass through Claypool on the train. If the newspaper were in Claypool I could interview them. Claypool should be county seat; it's the future but old codgers keep voting for Red Rock."

Rista was appalled. Red Rock was the history, the heart of the county. Claypool was a railroad upstart. If he moved the newspaper to Claypool when would she see him? Did he think of her at all?

Stoddard talked of the column he had added on personalities—George Arliss, Mary Pickford, Lionel Barrymore. He ran daily bulletins on the Lindbergh story, although he sometimes had to drive to Claypool and meet the train to discover what people said about the kidnapping in other places, and measures they took to protect their children.

"Stoddard, you'll scare people."

"People like being scared. It makes them feel important. They don't want to read about Okies or soup lines in Chicago or Japanese in Manchuria. They want to get their minds off their problems. Some actors arrange their lives by the stars so I've added a horoscope."

"How do they solve their problems if they never think about them?"

"The radio gives them music, laughs. I compete with radio for advertising so I give readers comics and astrology."

"When a woman and her baby starve to death there's a sickness in the country and it's not going to be solved by people who worry about the wrong things, like their children being kidnapped."

Stoddard put on the imperious look he affected when challenged. "The Lindbergh baby is worth a hundred babies who starve, a thousand."

"Is that what you want to write? Gossip about that child and his parents and who may have killed him?"

"Nobody would read what I want to write," he said bitterly.

"I loved your poems," she said.

"The poems and my stories were rejected by every magazine I could find. The story I wrote about that actress' affair with Wallace Beery was published all over the country."

Did the magazines not want to know about Tim Tingle who hanged himself because of Oma Dodd? Tim, a teacher, fell in love with Oma, a student, who was big-eyed with dimples. They exchanged glances in school and church and walked together a couple of times but never touched hands. Oma's father threatened to shoot Tim if Tim saw Oma again. Tim asked Dink McVicar to carry a message to Oma telling her that he was going to resign from the school and move away and that she was to live a good and happy life with no more thoughts of him. Oma's father heard Dink at the window, thought it was Tim, and shot him. Tim hanged himself. Oma went to teachers college, returned to Red Rock, and taught school until she died.

"Oh, maybe if I worked at it for ten years, lived like a hobo. . . ."

He could live on the ranch. She would cook his meals, wash his clothes, and he could write poems to her or to the world if he wished. "You don't have to have a lot of money—"

"I don't have any money. I trade ads for food and clothing. I have to wear what Brownfield wants to sell, a walking ad so that everybody can look just like me. Don't you think I want to choose my own clothes? I want to sell the paper and go to New York or Hollywood."

She wanted to scream. Why hadn't he told her he wanted to move to Claypool, to New York?

165

When they reached the ranch he wanted to come in, but she wouldn't let him. Pug and Paco were in the bunkhouse, and she didn't want them thinking of her as a woman. Stoddard rode away, as always leaving something hanging on the line.

There was so little time to sleep that she washed herself instead and began breakfast before waking the hands for the day's work. She would sleep that night, if she could. And before going to bed, she would put tallow on her hands to soften them. She spent the day training a green, fiddle-footed horse, putting miles on it while checking the cattle, the grass, the fences, the water, and thinking what she was going to do.

Every conversation with Stoddard required another one to make certain the last was understood. Was he going to New York to prove he could write? Or to meet folks he could write gossip about? Or because when she had given him everything he found it was not enough? What if she were pregnant? What if she weren't pregnant?

She wondered how she would face him when next she saw him. Would he view her with contempt? Pride? Ownership? She wondered if she would see him again. Three days later she received a poem from Stoddard. "Special flowers show their beauty after hours. Their petals unfolding at the touch of night, they bloom to the rising moon." Her face warmed although she wasn't sure why. She looked at the tiny band on her finger and swore she would never take it off.

The next Saturday he drove up in a Model A. He had to find a way across the ranch that had no roads, fix two flats and borrow a team to pull him across a creek. "If I'm going courting, I decided I'd better have a car. You can dress up for the dance and not have to change in the barn," he said with a smile. "Not that I mind." She was happy to see him but happier that he had bought a car. He wouldn't buy a car if he were going to New York. Maybe he wouldn't move the newspaper to Claypool.

When he invited her for a ride, Rista took a bath and put on clean clothes because she had never ridden in a car before, but Stoddard didn't drive far across the pasture before stopping in a grove of trees. "Rista, I've never known anyone like you," he said. He had summer breath—tea, lemon, and mint. "You are so . . . straightforward. The way you know what you want and go after it scares me." She let him make love to her although she wasn't sure she liked what he said.

It was dusk when they started back to the house and Stoddard got lost following the dim headlights. Rista had to get out of the car and ask him to turn out the lights to determine where they were. Stoddard spent the night in the bunkhouse because he couldn't find his way across the ranch in the darkness, and Rista wouldn't let him sleep in the house.

Before he left the next morning, Stoddard gave her a heart-shaped pincushion. She looked at the useless thing with dismay. What did he think she was going to do with that? Before taking her to the picture show he gave her an autograph album so she could get the signatures of important people he introduced her to. After the Harley Sadler show he gave her a dressing case with red plush interior and a brush, comb, and mirror so she could look more like the actresses he admired. Last Christmas he gave her The "Song of Hiawatha" that she thought silly, and for her last birthday he gave her a celluloid glove box when the only gloves she wore were working gloves that belonged with her chaps.

When she was eight her father gave her a .22 rifle for shooting

167

prairie dogs. For her twelfth birthday he gave her a knife for castrating and ear-marking calves, cleaning wounds, and cutting the rope if she dabbed her string on something she couldn't handle. He gave her chaps when she was thirteen, her own boots when she was fourteen, and her proudest gift, a Yoakum saddle, when she was eighteen.

While Claris was laid up from his fall, without her knowing it, he had ordered the saddle with a rolled cantle and double rigging, built for work and equipped with eagle-beak tapaderos. Rista had a small foot,and he feared her foot might slip through a stirrup and she would be dragged or kicked to death. The tapaderos also kept brush from wearing the toes off her boots. Claris died before the saddle arrived, but Rista never stepped into it that she didn't think of him.

When she looked at the pincushion, the autograph album, the dressing case, she wondered if Stoddard could abide her without his improvements. Stoddard was as worrisome as a leaning fence.

▲▼▲

She was riding the Fort Hoggard pasture, without a running creek and only a dirt tank for water, when she found a leak in the dam. If she lost the water she would have to move the cows or they would die. Paco and Pug were working in different pastures; she would have to do it herself. She rode to the barn and hitched horses to the fresno. Claris had kept mules because they were stronger than horses and more resistant to heat, flies, and disease. Rista got rid of them when a mule picked up a calf by its back and trotted around with it until the mauled thing died. Mules like that had to be worked all the time, and she didn't have the time.

She had caught and hitched horses to the scraper and was looking for a shovel when Stoddard drove up. "Put your party dress on and grab your autograph album. I'm going to take you to meet the governor," he said.

He wanted her to meet the governor, and she couldn't pay her poll tax. "I have a dam that's leaking," she said.

"Do it tomorrow," he said.

He had taken her to see Ma Ferguson campaign. Pa Ferguson walked through the crowd shaking hands, women shouted, "Me for Ma," and children collected donations in buckets. Pa had been impeached, and Ma was called a "slave wife" because she did what he told her. "I can't leave cows without water."

"You'll be sorry that you thought watering cows was more important than meeting the governor," he said. "I'm not going alone." Stoddard didn't like going anywhere alone. He got in his car and slammed the door. "I had a flat coming out here," he said before driving away.

Rista got the shovel and had started back to the dam when she saw Odis, his patrol car bumping across the pasture. Another interruption. "I saw a car in your pasture," he said.

"Stoddard wanted me to meet the governor."

"She and Pa sell pardons to criminals," Odis said in disapproval. He asked if she still employed Pug Caldwell. Pug had written a hot check.

The bank had foreclosed on the Three Crosses, and Pug's mother had been evicted. "I'll take care of it, but I don't have time now," Rista said. "If I lose my water I may lose some cows."

"Then I better give you a hand," he said, getting out of the car and jumping bareback on a harnessed horse.

They worked the rest of the day scraping up dirt and

169

rebuilding the dam. She wondered if she would have been able to do it by herself. Odis was a hard worker. She could use a hand like him.

When they were done, they lay back against the fresh packed earth and caught their breath. "I am much obliged," she said. It was hot, close cloudy, and the gnats and sweat bees were bad. The horses stamped and flicked their tails, their hides quivering from the flies. Rista broke off a branch of cedar to fan away the insects.

"We make a good team," Odis said. That caught her by surprise. She was so caught up in her dream of Stoddard that she hadn't considered Odis. She turned to appraise him and noticed how raw his hands were from the shovel and the handles of the scraper. He wasn't accustomed to using his hands, but he could ride and he wasn't afraid of work. Stoddard would be like an imaginary playmate. Always there and never of any use.

"Come to the house with me, and I'll put something on those hands and make you some supper."

"You've got a deal," he said. "I need to talk to Pug."

"I'll take it out of his wages and I'll talk to him," she said. She hadn't paid Pug or Paco full wages since Genevieve died, giving them IOUs instead, and Pug needed money for his mother who took in laundry in Red Rock after being evicted from her ranch.

She put tallow and honey on Odis' hands and wrapped them in strips she tore from an old but clean sheet. While she boiled rice and raisins for spotted pup he listened to what she would like to do with the ranch. She needed better horses; you could always get good cowboys if you kept good horses. She wanted to raise quarter horses, train them for ranch work and sell them for cash. The barn was falling down. She needed another windmill. More than anything she wanted to pay off the debts she had run up to keep the ranch going. And to keep Smiley Wooten's hands off her.

The cowboys came in, Pug shifty-eyed in front of Odis and looking ready to fight. Odis ignored him.

After the hands had eaten and gone to the bunkhouse, Odis helped with the dishes and they sat on the porch and listened to Paco and Pug sing. Claris wouldn't hire anyone who played a guitar; he considered them idle and worthless. A fiddle, mouth organ, even a banjo was okay but not a guitar. She had no such prejudices, and if a man was a good hand, she considered his singing and playing something to boot.

Odis took her hand. "I want to marry you," he said. When she didn't respond he continued. "Ask anyone in the county, I got a good name, no debts. I have saved almost a hundred dollars. Rista, I fell in love with you when I saw you ride up with dinner in a wooden box. I'm like that box, not much to look at but a full dinner inside."

Odis frightened her a little; he was so passionate. She still stood fast when he fixed her with those clear blue eyes, but if a woman could harness him, she would have a horse. And a hundred dollars was more money than anyone had except Smiley Wooten. Stoddard hadn't grown a spine but she could put a spike in him. Odis could help her save the ranch, but he would never write a poem to her. He wouldn't give her a pincushion or an autograph album either. She was pretty to Odis; to Stoddard, pretty was something she had to do.

If only she could wean Stoddard from sucking vanity's hind tit. "Why did you wait so long to bid on the ugly thing?" she asked.

"I wanted you to want my bid as much as I wanted you."

She asked for time to consider his offer. She offered him a bed in the bunkhouse, but he thought it might not look right and drove back to town, finding his own way.

▲▼▲

Before she answered Odis, Rista had to know if Stoddard thought they were engaged. It was several days before she could leave the ranch. She bathed, put on a clean shirt and jeans, and saddled a crockhead roan that needed work. It was dusk when she reached town, and the newspaper office was closed. She rode to the white frame house on Wagonseller Road. As a schoolgirl she had ridden by the house and dared Stoddard to come outside because he made Puggie cry. When she was older she had ridden by his house hoping to see him.

This was the first time she had been inside the house and, although she had left her hat on the saddle, she was aware of the smell of sweat and horse lather that clung to her. Stoddard was expansive. He had interviewed the governor. She told him she was originally opposed to women voting and believed that "if a woman's home demands her, that's where she would be."

He had also met Babe Didrickson who won two gold medals at the 1932 Olympics, and he danced with a former Miss America from Oklahoma. She had been eighteen at the time and weighed 118 pounds. Six years later, she could still wear the same gown and was considering a career in the movies. Rista didn't know how she was going to talk to him about serious matters.

Stoddard wanted to bathe her and although she was shy about her body, she agreed because she did not want him to think her soiled. After he bathed and dried her, Stoddard asked her to put on his shirts because he wanted to think of her every time he wore one of them. She was not as surprised by his request as she was by how many shirts he had and the size of his closets. After the last shirt, he unbuttoned it, picked her up and carried her to his bed. Rista tried to please him every way she knew.

Later as they lay entwined on his bed, she said, "Odis has asked me to marry him."

Stoddard took his face in her hands. "Rista, I want to marry you. As soon as I can turn the newspaper into something worth selling. Come to Austin with me next week. There's going to be a party with politicians, musicians, famous people. We'll have a whole week together."

She couldn't be gone for a week; she felt guilty taking the time to ride here. She had never been farther from home than Claypool. New York and Hollywood were beyond her imagination, and Austin frightened her; she had been embarrassed enough by fashion. "Stoddard, I can count every dime I have without putting my hand in my pocket. I broke my last dollar to buy plug tobacco for Paco and Pug." She took his hands in hers and clasped them at her breast. "There's not a deer or cottontail left in the county. I have to kill barren cows to feed my hands. I can't keep up with the work; I can't keep up with the debts. I need you."

"Are you asking me to be a cowboy?"

"I'm asking you to marry me. You can write what you want to write, help me in your spare time. I won't ask you to do something you can't do. I know you don't ride well."

"I suppose you think Odis rides better."

"You could oil and repair the tack, paint the house and barn, replace the hinges on the corral gate—when you're not writing."

"I can't live on a ranch. I have to be with people who make things happen, who talk about ideas, politics—"

"Picture shows. Horoscopes."

"You can go with me, Rista."

"Go to parties, meet sparklies, and talk about fashions?"

"Imagine being where everyone else wants to be, drinking fine wine, talking about art and music with people everyone else wants to know."

"You don't know them, Stoddard. You serenade them from the porch. They like the music but they don't care who plays the tune."

"I have famous friends. You didn't even get their autographs."

He wanted her to fold into his dream but she couldn't. She didn't want to gossip with fancy people. They needed an audience, and Stoddard needed someone to adulate. He needed a king or a pope, but he had neither so he made actors his kings and queens and politicians his popes. He would serve them, and they would let him kiss their rings.

"A lot of people think your father threw a long rope with a wide loop," he said. "He fenced off farmers, ran them off their land, bought it for nothing. Now you sit around hoarding that land and counting your cows. That's not living. It's not even attractive."

She wasn't Dawn anymore, but she was what he needed. How could she make him understand? She told him how she, a young girl, came across a heifer unable to give birth. She had to cut off the calf's head and one shoulder to deliver it.

"I can see how you felt," he said. "You saved the heifer's life."

"The heifer died."

He looked at her like she was singing Chinese in a choir of lawyers.

"I did everything the best cowboy could have done."

"But the cow died."

"But I did it. I did everything that could be done."

"But it didn't do any good," he said.

"Yes it did."

"What good did it do?"

She threw up her hands. It was like trying to talk to a balky horse that looked at her, eyes staring, ears twitching, and heard not a word. "What do you want me to do?" she asked.

"Sell the ranch if you can find a buyer. I know that's hard; I can't find one for the newspaper. But we'll sell the ranch and newspaper as soon as we can. Wouldn't you like to live some place exciting?"

"Wherever I went I'd take this place with me, and I'd want to come back as soon as I could. I'd never leave if I thought I couldn't come back."

"I want more for us than that. I want us to be at the center of things with people who do important things."

Rista didn't know how to corral that. "Stoddard, you can't have it all. Not all at once. Not all the time. But you can have me."

"I want you, Rista. More than anything. When things look right."

It was like trying to corner a jackrabbit in a barbed-wire fence. Rista got up, put on her shirt and jeans, and pulled on her boots. "I'm giving you back your ring," she said. "I'm breaking our engagement."

"We weren't engaged."

"I was," she said, tossing the ring on the bed beside him.

The ride to the ranch was the longest ride she had ever made, riding away from her dreams. Stoddard wasn't going to marry her. Certainly not in time to help her save the ranch. She had to make up her mind to that. There was no time for dreaming now. She had to make other plans.

▲▼▲

"Before I say yes, I have to know what your dreams are," Rista told Odis. They stood on the knoll overlooking the Bone Yard. Rista noticed brush was covering the knoll, but she had no time to clear it.

Odis had never told anyone about his dreams. He took off his hat, looked into it as though searching for an answer, and replaced it. "I'm not making much as a deputy, but I may get a raise next year. If I do a good job, if I look out for people, I can run for high sheriff some day."

Rista didn't believe he would ever be sheriff. He was too intense. They liked that in a deputy—he kept hustlers, gamblers, prostitutes under control—but no one wanted a sheriff who scared honest folks. "Do you think you could be elected high sheriff?" she asked.

"I have a chance if people forget that story in the paper." He glanced at her, ashamed of being outwitted by a whore. "I guess being high sheriff is the only dream I ever had. People look up to a sheriff. When you walk into a place they know who you are."

She was pleased that he had no plans for the ranch. "This ranch is my life. If you marry me it'll mean living here, pitching in like everyone else, doing some mean jobs and some fun jobs. I have to know, can you give up being sheriff?"

"If I own a ranch I don't need to be sheriff to be somebody," he said, turning and surveying the country that rolled away from him. "I can give it up for you," he said.

They were married on the ranch. Paco gave her away, and Pug was the best man. It was so hot Rista fanned herself with the fancy Bible Genevieve had given her. Odis moved his few possessions into her house. After the wedding he took off his show Stetson, his dress Justin boots, his silver spurs with jingle-bobs and put them in the small safe he had brought with him.

Rista knew he must have spent several months pay for them and the safe. "No one is going to steal them out here," she said.

"I got to have something private," Odis said.

12
Friday, 1990

Red Rock looked like half a dozen towns I had seen in Texas, except they were occupied and not owned by one person. The square was paved but potholed. In the center was a two-story red sandstone courthouse with a bell tower and a jail. On three sides of the square were red sandstone buildings. On the fourth side a fire had left only the sidewalk, broken foundations, and blackened rocks. The side streets were dirt; weeds grew in the street and between the buildings. The few houses that remained were ramshackle frames with broken windows and missing shingles. It looked like a set for *The Twilight Zone.*

"Teenagers came out here for parties," Rista said. "Roasted hot dogs in the buildings. Climbed the water tower and painted stuff." Still visible were football scores, hearts, initials, and above everything else, Dalhart. "What's Dalhart?" I asked.

"I don't know how he got that high," Rista said. "Pug wanted to take a ladder up there and paint over it but it was too dangerous. I put up the fence, me and Pug took turns spending the night here, shot at everyone who drove up to the gate to scare them off. Word got around. The land around the town is owned by the telephone company but I got an easement to the gate."

According to Rista, Red Rock had begun as a general store/post office/courthouse/saloon/brothel for local ranchers and drovers taking trail herds north. The town had grown as farmers moved into the area; the general store, saloon, and courthouse became separate buildings, and a livery stable, church and bank were built. The post office moved from the general store to the bank. If someone wanted to deposit money, folks had to wait for their mail until the money was in the safe. If someone wanted to borrow money, they had to wait while the mail was sorted.

The railroad bypassed Red Rock so the railroad could plat a new town and sell lots for homes and stores. They intended to make Claypool the county seat and built a holding trap to keep cattle until ranchers could ship them. Ranchers feared the railroad's money and political power, and Red Rock remained county seat until after World War II when urban voters outnumbered rural voters. Then a fire destroyed one side of the square including the saddle shop, hotel, newspaper office, and picture show. Claypool was voted county seat. The new state highway from Claypool to the next county seat bypassed Red Rock.

If I thought I was going to get an establishing shot, I was wrong. Rista gave me a close-up without continuity, bridges, or transition and with no snapper at the end. She pointed out what had once been two grocery stores, newspaper office, drugstore, hotel, blacksmith, carpenter shop, saddle and boot shop that sold coffins, barber shop with lawyers' offices upstairs, general merchandise and feed store, public windmill and water trough in front of the livery stable and wagon yard that later became a fence, hardware, and implement store; two churches, the school with a Masonic Lodge upstairs, and picture show that had once been a saloon. There were benches in front of the barbershop, livery stable, and blacksmith shop where men collected information about the weather, the government, and what everyone else was doing.

The hotel had two baths, one for gents, one for ladies. Upstairs was a gambling room where men drank, smoked cigars, and played cards, which Odis didn't allow in Claypool. A bell in front summoned diners when dinner and supper were ready. Diners ran to get to the table before the best portions were gone. The hotel sold a five-dollar meal ticket for four dollars to encourage customers to return. Rista had put that in one of her baggies.

"One of the good things about Red Rock was that you couldn't kill yourself by jumping off a building," she said, but Tim Tingle hanged himself in the hotel over Oma Dodd. Nonie Othart lived in the hotel until she ran out of money. One night she wrapped up in a blanket with a coal-oil lantern inside the blanket to keep from freezing, the blanket caught fire, and she burned to death on the town square. "She slept on the ground rather than become a whore, but no one went to her funeral because she was Indian."

Nonie said the Indian her father lived with wasn't her mother, but no one believed her. She refused to sleep in the house with an Indian, did washing and cooking for a living when she was fourteen, but no one would marry her and she ended up sleeping on the ground.

"Folks said Leon and the Indian found each other during an eclipse." Rista shrugged. "When Nonie died Leon disappeared. Folks thought his squaw killed him but couldn't prove it. Neither his people nor hers would accept her. Whenever she left the house, kids sneaked in to look at her squaw dresses and jewelry she kept in a trunk."

"What happened to her?"

"That was what I wanted Stoddard to find out, but he said it wasn't a story. Stoddard was like a mule, you had to back him into work."

It could be a story. Two outcasts. He comes to love her because of her devotion to him but their daughter denies her. He disappears, the town accuses her of foul play. The daughter acknowledges her mother to save her, sharing her condemnation. He returns in time to save them from a lynch mob, and the three, united, leave the unworthy town. They would need to make some gesture at the end to show their disdain for prejudice and small-minded people. Spit on the town sign, or take the lynch rope and throw it on the ground.

Rista had three bags for the square. Before she was born some boys tied cans to dogs' tails; the dogs ran down the street and under the feet of O-Bar cowboys. "They rode into town with their tails over the dashboard, shot at the dogs, folks ran for cover." One dog didn't come home, and his owner, Zay Clopton, thought the cowboys shot him.

Clopton, "scarred up like an old boot and nothing for a sober woman to look at," lived at the edge of town with no friend but his dog. He went to the saloon with a shotgun and asked who killed his dog. A cowboy came in behind him and took the shotgun away from him. Clopton went home, got a rifle, and came back. He shot into the ceiling and demanded to know who shot his dog. Before he could shoot again, someone knocked him down with a bottle and took the rifle. Clopton crawled outside, went home and came back with a pistol. This time he opened the door and started shooting. The bartender shot Clopton with his own shotgun.

"The dog was under the porch, and he came out and laid on Clopton and wouldn't let anyone come close. The barkeep shot the dog."

The second bag was about a carnival on the square when Rista was a teenager. The carnival had balloon ascensions. "Inez Allen rode in the balloon that was tied to a rope and went way up above the top of the courthouse. Folks said she didn't wear underwear. A high wind blew down her house and scattered her clothes everywhere and people could see she did wear underwear.

"She married Corky Hanz. Old fool wrote hail and cyclone insurance and bought and sold cattle. I bought a young bull from him once. Too young. I told him the bull was sucking my cows. Old fool said, 'What did you buy him for?' He was hard of hearing, too."

The carnival had the biggest bull anyone had seen and fifty dollars, more than a month's pay, for anyone who could ride it. Paco had never seen a Brahma before but neither had he seen anything he couldn't ride. He stuck on the bull's back, and then the bull jumped over the fence and ran out of town. Pug and a J-B Connected cowboy roped the bull head-and-heel and stretched it out. "Get off of him," Pug yelled. "I can't," Paco said. "My spurs are stuck in the belly band."

"San Jacinto Day, I think it was," Rista said. They threw hens from the top of the hotel and whoever caught them got to keep them. There was a parade with a band, Indians, the Odd Fellows had three wagons, one to show visiting the sick and burying the dead, one visiting widows, and the third educating their children. Some girls rode decorated bicycles. The Aginers were outraged; girls on bicycles were indecent. There was a fiddlers' contest, horse races, tobacco spitting contest, a display of home-canned fruits and vegetables, gambling games for stuffed animals, a merry-go-round, a phrenologist, guessing the amount of money in a fruit jar in the window of the mercantile, a whistler who whistled whatever tune was requested, a cowboy yodeler. "Folks had never heard yodeling; didn't know whether they were supposed to laugh or not. Then this man came on the stage, scratched, said, 'I just come from Claypool and I got fleas.' Well, they laughed at that."

A man climbed a high tower and jumped into a tub of water. Rista waited all day and then had to ride home before he jumped. "He did it, but I didn't find out for almost a week when a Slash 6 cowboy came by looking for stray cattle. Said it was a real hair lifter."

The third bag was about a bet Stoddard and Odis had, before Odis and Rista married, on whether Hoover or Roosevelt won the election. "They were like two dogs that met over a bone." Stoddard, who lost, had to push Odis around the square. Stoddard got a wheelbarrow that had concrete in the bottom that hurt to sit on, but a crowd had gathered and Odis was determined to make Stoddard look foolish. They started out with the crowd running beside them laughing and Odis yelling at Stoddard like he was a mule. Stoddard tired and ran the wheelbarrow into a mudhole in the street. The wheelbarrow tipped over—Odis said on purpose—and Odis fell in the mud. Odis pulled his pistol and would have hit Stoddard with it if Sheriff Grover hadn't stopped him. Grover made Stoddard apologize, but Odis wouldn't shake his hand. "I think pulling

184

his pistol and not shaking Stoddard's hand would have cost Odis ever being sheriff."

Levi Brown wanted everyone to think he was tough. When he got drunk he rode down the street shooting his pistol and yelling. Grover took Levi's pistol and fined him. Levi said it was worth it seeing townsfolk running and screaming. Levi had a ring on his finger that was too tight so he tried to shoot it off. He shot off the ring and most of his finger. Grover cut the rest of the finger off with a pocket knife and sent Levi back to the ranch.

"Clyde Eubank, a porch percher, got drunk and went to a dance in Rag Town." Rag Town was where blacks lived. When Clyde got rough with one of the girls and was asked to leave, he pulled a pistol and shot the man who asked him. Then someone shot Clyde. Levi Brown formed a posse and rode into Red Rock. They saw Izzie, the black man who cleaned the bank, shot him in the head, then rode off to Rag Town. The bullet glanced off Izzie's head and knocked him unconscious. He came to, staggered across the street, and hid in the back of the pool hall. When the mob got to Rag Town they found the blacks armed and waiting. They came back to Red Rock and asked what happened to Izzie. A kid named Smiley Wooten told them where he was, and they dragged him to a big oak by the cemetery and hanged him.

"Grover was looking for cold brands on the Slash 6. Someone was burning the hair on their calves so it looked like they had been branded, then stamping his own brand on them when the hair grew out. When he got back he arrested Levi and some of the others in the mob. They said they found Izzie in the hotel, where blacks were not allowed, hiding in the women's bathroom waiting to rape some white woman. Nothing was done to any of them."

185

"Why did Smiley Wooten tell them where the man was?"

"Some folks thought it was because Levi was Smiley's step-father, but he wasn't. Levi was seeing Trudy, but she wouldn't marry him until he broke his back. Smiley was running errands for a nickel, and I think he wanted Izzie's job. That's a story I wanted Stoddard to look into."

Levi broke his back when a horse pitched him, and he spent the rest of his life in a wheelchair. Trudy Wooten married him. "Folks said she married Levi because she could outrun him," Rista said. Her first husband beat her. "Trudy was four pounds short of a side show."

Levi ordered her around, and she jeered him and called him a cripple. Trudy went visiting one day. "Levi didn't want her visiting anybody because he couldn't get to the fishing hole without her to push him." Levi took the ashes from the fireplace and threw them around the house so she'd have no time for visiting. Trudy pushed him into a plowed field and left him there most of the night. When she brought him back to the house she put weed killer in his biscuits, just enough to make him sick. Levi got corn and a stick and threw the corn to her hens. When they got close enough he killed them with the stick.

Trudy shot Levi one day when he was coming from the barn. Her lawyer got her off with self-defense although Levi was in his wheelchair and had a bucket of milk in his lap. "Some folks thought Smiley did it, because Levi treated Smiley and Larry the same way he treated their mama. I've never made the mis-take of saying something good about Smiley."

Smiley, who replaced Izzie sweeping the bank, involved his brother Larry in the banking business. Ike Davis bought a repos-sessed car from the bank for thirty dollars and got all the papers on it. Smiley had Larry take the car while Ike was at work. Ike would've had to pay ten dollars to file suit and put up a sixty-dollar bond for the sheriff to take the car with a writ of sequestration and Ike didn't have it. "Ralph Wilberg was the new sheriff, and he followed the law. If Odis had been sheriff, he would have gone and gotten the car. Odis was short on law, long on right and wrong. Ike and his wife had lost their kids, and when Smiley and Larry took their car they left the country."

Rista pointed out the location of the saloon. There were fights and one shootout but no one was hit, although at one point at least three men were shooting. It wasn't a story Rista asked Stoddard to write. The city council met in the saloon because decent women wouldn't come inside. However, one lady did. When cowboys came to town, they threw Dale Rollins behind them on their horse and took him to the saloon where he danced on the bar to amuse them. His mother would have to go to the saloon to get him. Dale ran off to join the circus, and his mother brought him home. She let him join the Harley Sadler show after Harley promised Dale would go to Sunday school every Sunday.

"I went to the saloon once," Rista said. Claris kept tobacco for the hands and sold it to them at cost so they couldn't use that as an excuse to ride to town, get drunk, and be hardly fit to work the next day. Claris was rounding up and needed every hand, and Red Ikom had slipped off to town.

"I was eight or nine but Papa couldn't go after him and didn't trust one of the hands. I don't remember much about the saloon except men standing at the bar rubbing calluses on their elbows. Some of them played checkers with bottle caps. There were tables and straight-backed chairs and a pool table at the end. They had electric lights and an overhead fan. I reckon that's the

187

first fan I ever saw, probably the first one in town. The place stank of stogies, scamper juice, and elbow lather. That was the only time I wished I had one of them perfumed handkerchiefs ladies waved in their faces.

"When the shock of me being there wore off, the men started making wolf calls, but I shut all that out. I walked up to the bar where Red was, and it got quiet as everyone wanted to hear what I had to say. He was called Red because he had a red crease across his nose; folks said it was from pressing a shot glass to his face. I said, 'Red, you're riding back to the ranch with me and when you get there you damn well better be sober.' He got up and followed me outside and everyone cheered. The saloon wanted to hire me to deal cards as a special attraction.

"Grover told me not go into the saloon alone, to come get him," Rista said, "but Red woulda had a ring around his ass if I had gotten the law after him. So would the other men."

During prohibition the saloon was replaced by a movie theater. "They changed one kind of foolishness for another," Rista said. The theater was destroyed by the fire. The woman who owned the theater thought her husband was inside and when she tried to rescue him the marquee fell on her. It was a metal marquee and it fell over her and protected her from the fire.

"She stood up in the Aginers Church and testified how God saved her when the town burned, but she wouldn't speak to me for a long time."

"What was the Aginers Church?"

"I'm going to tell you," she said. "It's all in the baggies." Rista unlocked the courthouse door and led me inside. The building seemed solid but needed a cleaning. Old newspapers, photographs, letters, and Ziploc bags were attached to the wall.

"These are stories about things that happened here. I put them in baggies so rats wouldn't get them before folks found them."

If she thought someone was going to look for them she was clearly delusional.

"This is the story of how Judge Gillin lost the election. That was his office right there. The story that he sent a man to the pen for stealing a pie is a lie. It never happened. It was a fourteen-year-old cowboy and the judge said that's where he would end up if he kept up his ways."

In the office was a heavy walnut mantle with inlaid white tile with angels in it, a rolltop desk, a kitchen table, and shelves of law books. On election day his opponent read stories of horrific things that men did to women, children, and other men, and said that Judge Gillin kept those stories in his office. They were case stories from law books, but no one knew that until after the election.

"This was the sheriff's office. Odis always thought this could have been his office but folks liked Ralph Wilberg." In a Ziploc bag was a story that Wilberg saved a drowning man on election day when the man yelled, "Help, I haven't voted yet!"

"Odis was too much like Grover. Grover was good for his day, but the day had passed." When the drugstore was broken into, Grover thought he knew who did it but couldn't prove it. "He told the man to slope. The courtroom is upstairs," she said, pointing at the stairs. "What I remember most about it is the party we had there for a movie star, but there were some important trials."

The Hanks family had a Bible with marriage, birth, baptism, and death records going back to the American Revolution. Bob had the Bible, but it had been willed to his sister, Willowdean. Willowdean sued to get the Bible back. Bob gave her the Bible

Robert Flynn

but cut the family records out of it. Bob's lawyer argued that
the will said Bible and family records weren't inspired. Judge
Gillin agreed. Bob and Willowdean never spoke again and the
fight divided the town with the Anythings saying Bible meant
a book and the Aginers saying the Bible was only the words
written by God.

"I don't know what happened to the records. I saw Bob's son
once eating stolen beef. He didn't look like he had them. Grover
came out one time and said, 'Bob stole a horse and I got to arrest
him.' Papa said, 'Bob wouldn't steal a horse.' Grover said, 'It was
your horse.' Papa said, 'Hang the son of a bitch.' Grover arrested
Bob, but when Bob was sitting in jail awaiting trial Papa went
and got him out.

"This baggie is the story of Day McVicar, the only person
legally hanged in Red Rock. A lot of folks thought Vada Bennet
was pregnant by Day and that her brother threatened Day and
Day shot him."

"Did she have a child?"

"Some folks said she had a child and burned it in the fireplace, but I think the fight had nothing to do with Vada. Two
boys fighting about nothing. One shot, the other hanged. I would
have run screaming down the street myself."

She, who had killed two men, would run screaming down the
street?

"Izzie was lynched by Levi Brown and that mob, and one
morning they found a man decorating the same tree. No one
knew who he was, but everybody suspected he was a cattle thief.
Folks figured it was the O-Bar. They were tough but careless
with a branding iron themselves. I think it was the Quarter-
Circle J—they went out of business because of cattle losses.

190

That whole ranch is gone, sold to farmers who plowed it under until it won't grow anything any more. They use part of it for a feed lot, part of it is a suburb of Claypool. What does Claypool need a suburb for? All those ranches—the O-Bar, Three Crosses, Slash 6, Quarter Circle J, J-B Connected, they're all gone. Nothing left but little cowpen ranches. The Three Crosses and the O-Bar are still under fence but it's all show."

Red Rock had a hanging tree. Horse opera was dead but there were more revivals in television than in churches. "What happened to the tree?"

"Streets hate trees and streets have the right of way." Rista shook her head at the memory, the brim of her hat brushing the bag. "Smiley pointing out Izzie and taking his job is a story Stoddard could have written, but it was like trying to milk a bull. During the Lindbergh kidnapping scare some high-school girl got tired of her baby brother and took him outside and put him in the garbage can. Town spent three hours searching for him. Stoddard put that on the front page of his paper." She shook her head so hard she fluttered newspapers attached to the wall.

"I don't know whether it's safe to go up to the bell tower or not," Rista said. Cowboys went to the bell tower on Sunday morning to see which church the prettiest girls went to. "Lucinda was the bell mare of the remuda. She went to the Aginers Church, and the other fillies followed her like she was a wagonload of alfalfa." The corners of her mouth turned up like she was amused by the memory. "She wasn't a true Aginer. The Aginers occasionally did something good and as though embarrassed by it, did something mean to make up for it. They had all just got over being poor and they couldn't abide folks who couldn't do the same."

191

A young cowboy, "Brother Bob," got a mission to preach. He wasn't educated so he rode out to ranches, pitched in with the work, took a meal if one was offered, a place in the bunkhouse if there was room and in the barn if there wasn't. He sang and when the hands gathered around he'd have a service.

"Cowboys love to prank and hurrah, and one night someone put a snake in his bedroll," Rista said. "Brother Bob knew it wasn't a rattler so he caught the snake and said, 'Get thee behind me, Satan' and threw it out in the room. It was quiet for a while and then somebody lit a lantern and everyone got up and looked for the snake. No one wanted to sleep with it."

"Somebody put fresh manure in his boots and when he put them on the next morning, he said, 'First time my feet have been warm all night.' They loved him for that."

Ranchers began introducing him to their daughters. Sara Mayhue, whose father owned the Three Crosses, visited ranches wherever he worked. There was a camp meeting on the river. People camped out, sang, visited, and had services for a week. Between preaching and Bible classes the children played in the river, the women fixed covered-dish suppers, the men traded yarns.

Sara and Brother Bob were together every day. Everyone thought they would get married, but Brother Bob couldn't ask her to follow him from ranch to ranch. "Brother Bob never asked for money, but if you stuck a dime or two bits in his pocket so he could feed his horse and repair his tack, he'd thank you," Rista said.

Sara collected money for a church in Red Rock so they could get married. They built a church with him as preacher, but one man's saint is another man's fool. "Sara dressed him up and slicked down his hair, but she couldn't do anything about the way he was and he wasn't city."

The church couldn't support Brother Bob's family so he worked in Brownfield's mercantile. Brownfield, a deacon in the church, thought cowboys were degenerate, homesteaders were panhandlers, and he didn't give credit to anyone. Brother Bob didn't understand business and if a woman needed a needle or a man needed a lamp wick and couldn't pay, he'd give it to them on their word. Burt said Brother Bob believed hard-working people should give their money to people who didn't want to work. Brother Bob said Burt overcharged hard-working people who could least afford to pay, and that was wicked. Burt fired him.

The next Sunday, Burt went to sleep during the sermon, dropped his stiff-brimmed straw hat, and the hat rolled to the altar. Brother Bob said, "Burt, are you going to join your hat at the altar and repent of your greed or are you going to Hell?" Burt had the church fire Brother Bob.

They hired a new preacher who bought an organ for the church. Burt was opposed to the expense, and he and his followers put the organ in his store and locked the door. Those for the organ broke in, put it back in the church and prevented those against the organ from coming inside. Church members armed themselves. Burt and his followers said the preacher broke into his store. The preacher and his followers said Burt stole the organ from the church. Sheriff Grover had to separate the two groups until those against the organ started their own church. "They called it the True Believers Church, but everyone else called it the Aginers Church. The True Believers called the other church the Anythings, said they would tolerate anything. The Aginers

193

knew life was sunshine and cowshit, but like Stoddard they preferred pretty lies.

"Once they got their own church the Aginers turned against everything—horses in the street, boys making noise, celebrations, and anyone who wasn't in their church. Bridge parties—there wasn't but four people that knew how, and they belonged to the Anythings.

"They made being right better than doing right. Corky Hanz left the church because he said any damn fool knew keeping the Sabbath didn't apply to someone who had milk cows. They threw Doc Evans out of the church, said he was an abortionist. They built a big church because everyone in town was against something. Painted the inside with turkey feathers because somebody said that was the way cathedrals were painted. Had to wait until spring when they could get enough turkey feathers to do it, but they thought it was high britches. Judge Gillin thought he could appease them by belonging to their church, but when his opponent said he read dirty books, they turned against him sooner than they would have an atheist."

It was comforting to know that politics and politicians hadn't changed. Neither had churches and churchgoers. "Which church did you belong to?" I asked Rista, who didn't appear to be religious.

"I was a follower of Brother Bob, just like Papa."

Brother Bob held services at ranches again, but he had to ask for money for his wife and children, and that changed the way he looked at people and they looked at him. People attended camp meetings but believed town people had something better, and there was more recollecting than testifying. Brother Bob had to go farther and farther to find an audience, sleeping in bunkhouses and preaching wherever people listened. He drifted to New Mexico and died on a reservation.

"Folks said he and some Indian sheepherders sat around the fire and sang songs and told stories. I reckon he died happy." There was a memorial service in front of the courthouse because the two churches got in a row over which church he belonged to—he started the church the Anythings prayed in, but the Aginers said he was opposed to an organ in the church. The two preachers competed to see who could say the grandest things about him while Sara worried how to feed her hungry children. The Anything preacher said Brother Bob was like David who sang his simple shepherd songs. The Aginers preacher said he was like Jesus who had no home. When he described Jesus whipped, spat on, and condemned to death, Wes Verstuft, who didn't go to church but had a soft spot for underdogs, stood up and said, "Let's go rescue the son of a bitch."

"Wes was always the first to a dance and the last to ask for a dance," Rista said. "Sara took the kids back to the Three Crosses when Bob started drifting. She raised them on beans and beatitudes. One day at school I asked Pug why he didn't eat dinner. 'It's not my turn,' he said. Pug was too poor to wear raggedy clothes, but the patches on his pants had patches, and he had to wear his sisters' hand-me-down shoes. He was the only boy in school with shoes that buckled, a stepchild kind of kid. That's why he came to work for us."

"Brother Bob was Pug's father?"

"Who did you think he was?" Rista snorted. Sara cared for her ailing parents and taught her kids to read and write. The children tried to help as best they could, the girls marrying, the boys leaving home to find work as soon as they were able. The bank foreclosed on the ranch, Sue moved to Red Rock and took in laundry, and was buried in the Aginers Church, clinging to the same religion as Burt Brownfield and Smiley Wooten.

Some years later, on the eve of World War II, two men came into Brownfield's store and asked Burt Junior his name. When he told them, they pulled out pistols and shot him six times, with both of them shooting. Then they walked out and drove away. Because neither Burt nor his wife recognized the men, who apparently shot him because of his name, Sheriff Wilberg thought it was part of the church feud.

Pug's oldest brother was a suspect. He had left home at fourteen because his mother couldn't feed him. Pug rode double with him to the train track so he could hop a freight and Pug could return the horse. His mother couldn't spare a biscuit to send with him. He hugged Pug goodbye, and Pug never saw him again.

"Everyone wanted to see Burt Junior laid out with six bullet holes in him but I. P. did a good job. I. P. Rainwater was kind of an artist. His name was Ivan Percival, but he strutted around like a banty rooster so everyone called him I. P. to ruffle his feathers. One time I. P. shot a mess of quail out of season, put them in a suitcase and would have gotten away with it except a bird dog went on point when he passed by and Ralph Wilberg saw it."

After Red Rock burned and the county seat was moved to Claypool, both churches disbanded. The Aginers hung on the longest, still believing Claypool to be an evil town, although the evildoers were no longer roughnecks, prostitutes, and gamblers but widows, orphans, those who couldn't find jobs or were too sick to work.

"The Aginers and Anythings was always more about

196

allowance than it was about theology," Rista said. "The Aginers didn't allow organ music or dancing, but you could lie in the pursuit of business, and you could hate everybody else. The Anythings allowed music and dancing, and you could skin folks if you skinned everyone the same."

I sometimes watched the church service we carried on Sundays. The church advertised itself as a place for love and forgiveness, but all I heard was hate and retribution for those who offended the minister. Every Sunday afternoon, the station received angry calls from devout listeners who called the minister a liar, heretic, and hypocrite.

▲▼▲

Rista wanted me to see Judge Gillin's house. "It doesn't look like much now, but I thought it was the finest house I had ever seen. It was always painted and there were flowers around the house and in the window. It had a paling fence to keep out cows. Stoddard said he didn't know whether Lucinda was Bible-scarred or Bible-scared, but she wasn't either. She just wanted to please."

In high school Lucinda went for walks, walking backward, because she thought it made her backside more attractive. She rode sidesaddle to preserve her maidenhead. Once she rode up on a man sitting in a car. He said he was lost and asked if she could help him locate himself on the map. Lucinda got off her horse and as she looked inside the car the man exposed himself. Lucinda jumped back and startled the horse so that it backed away. Lucinda tried to mount but could not get close to the side-stepping horse, and the man had to get out of the car and help her remount while she avoided looking at him.

"At a dance I saw her studying the crowd. 'I wonder if that

man who displayed himself is from around here,' she said. 'How would you recognize him?' I asked and she burst into tears and went home."

Rista had envied Lucinda's long, silky hair. Rista had to keep hers short and under a hat or it would be full of dust and burrs or catch on a limb and pull her out of the saddle. One night Lucinda's hair was cut off without her or anyone in the house knowing it. After that she wore hats.

"Who do you think did it?" I asked.

"Somebody who envied her hair." Rista pointed out the school she attended as a girl.

"I didn't get to school very often and when I did I was put with younger kids and was bigger than everybody so that I looked dumb. One time Oma Dodd asked me to open my mouth. I thought she was trying to guess my age so I said, 'I'm ten.' She said, 'Then you're old enough to brush your teeth.' I used a brush made from a hackberry limb, dipped it in salt, and rinsed with coal oil and sulphur, but I wasn't going to say so in front of the whole class. Another time she said, 'Detroit. Tell me everything you know about Detroit.' Hell, I thought Detroit was an Indian."

Someone tied a dead skunk to the rope for the school bell. Everyone blamed Louis Laumback because his father was a professional trapper and Louis smelled of skunk. Rista sold Laumback hides—cows that had died, deer, coyotes, bobcats. Laumback wanted her to poison or trap animals rather than shoot them but she didn't have time for trapping and didn't like poisoning. Coyote poison on the O-Bar killed a dog belonging to a cowboy on the Slash 6. It led to a shooting but no one was killed.

"Who do you think tied a skunk to the rope?"

"Someone who didn't like school."

The same person who cut Lucinda's hair while she was asleep and probably did a lot of other things that would send her to a reformatory today. "Okay, I've seen Red Rock," I said.

"You haven't seen the graveyard," Rista said. "We called this Desolation Road. It's the road homesteaders took out of town after ruining their lives believing a newspaper lie. The road went right past the paper."

"People have to be accountable for their actions."

"They were accountable. They ruined their health, their children's health, lost everything, and started over hoping the next promises weren't lies. Why wasn't the paper accountable? Lies cost the paper nothing."

It cost the newspaper credibility. If readers don't believe your news, they may not believe your ads.

Rista stopped at a weedy crossroad. "That's Wagonseller Road, leads to the graveyard. That was Stoddard's house."

"You didn't sell it?" Some people moved their houses to Claypool. Rista bought and sold most of the others.

"No one wanted to buy it."

I could understand why no one wanted to buy Stoddard's house from her, but I wondered if she hung on to Stoddard's house the way she hung on to the ranch, to Red Rock, to a past in which Longhorns ruled the range and Mother was under her control.

We walked along the weedy street to the cemetery and stopped at an unmarked grave. "I forget whose grave this was, boy who delivered milk for his father, going door to door, collecting nickels and dimes, came home with pockets bulging with coins. One day he was killed and robbed for the coins, but the

199

murderer left a trail of nickels and dimes and was caught coming back and picking them up. He wasn't but sixteen himself. Everybody felt sorry for him because he had to steal to eat and he didn't mean to kill the boy but they gave him the chair anyway. Waited until he was eighteen to do it. Times were hard. Parents couldn't afford a marker so they covered his grave with funny papers because he was fond of them. They moved away after the funeral.

"That's Roy Beasley's grave. Dan wanted to be buried beside his brother, but folks wouldn't allow him in the cemetery," Rista said. "When he died Dan screamed, 'I'm looking into Hell, I'm looking into Hell!' That sent a bunch of folks to church. He was buried on the O-Bar. He's out there with that bunch of lawyers."

"I thought Clint Houston was a gunman who shot Roy Beasley. Then Dan called him out and shot him." I had read that in Mother's scrapbook.

Rista ignored me. "This is Oma Dodd's grave. We called her 'Oh my God,'" Rista said. "When boys got rowdy, she'd have us shout out words and she would alphabetize them faster than we could spell them. Folks stood in awe of her, but mostly because Tim Tingle hanged himself. She lived almost entirely without female companionship, but I remember a church dinner on the ground where she brought mashed potatoes that were so smooth I thought they were cream gravy and put them on my bread."

"She took her sweetheart's place and spent the rest of her life in the school where they had flirted," I said. That might make an after-school special, students discovering the roots of their teacher's devotion to the school.

"Folks wanted a male teacher, but cowboys ran them off

because there weren't many women in the county back then and the cowboys wanted some young girl fresh out of college. When they hired a woman she had to promise she wouldn't marry the first year. Most of them broke their promise or went someplace else after two or three months because they didn't like the pickings."

"Oma Dodd never married. She must have been devoted to his memory," I said.

"Some folks said the school was haunted, that they saw lamplight at night where she waited for Tim. Some said they heard her calling Tim's name at night, others said it was Tim calling Dink, trying to stop him from delivering the message that would take his life."

That might be a story. "Did you ever hear it?" I asked.

"Oma graded papers at night. That was the lamplight. She mopped the floors. That was the sighing. She washed the blackboard. That was the voice calling 'Tim.' Stories by boys trying to scare each other. Oma had suitors. She wasn't going to marry some cowboy and teach him to read and write only to have him tell her how to cinch her saddle. Smiley came by a few times, but she was as cold as a rattlesnake in the shade.

"When the weather was real bad, I had to spend the night with her. She graded papers while I mopped the floor and washed the blackboard. Then we went to her house, and she fixed supper while I read to her about Greeks and Persians. After supper I did the dishes, and she read to me."

"Did she ever talk about Tim Tingle?"

"She said she walked with him because cowboys tried to pick fights with him but wouldn't if she were there. He told her his father was a magician in a tent show and fell in love with his

201

mother when they visited her town. They got married and his father tried to do shows in the town, but without the three-piece band and the clown no one would come. One night his father had a dream about a lake of fire, and he was out in the middle of it. When he woke up he got religion and was baptized in the creek. Then the preacher sold him a gin that was supposed to be free of debt. There was a lien against it that his father couldn't pay, and he lost the gin and his religion and left town, and Tim never saw him again."

Rista led me past the grave. "When they retired Oma to get her out of the school, Lucinda asked her if she had ever been bedridden. She said, 'Oh yes, hundreds of times and twice in a buggy.' There ought to be a state marker—"

"Wait," I said. "Oma Dodd had a lot of lovers?"

"I don't think so. I think she didn't want to be taken for granted. There ought to be a state marker on Julian Barnes' grave."

Julian was captured by the Comanches when he was a baby and by the rangers when he was a teenager. The Indians had killed his parents so he was raised by Ty Collins and his wife who were childless. He hated them and the older he got the more he liked the Indians. If you asked how he was he'd say, "I'd rather been an Indian."

"I went to school with his daughter, Anita. She said I was a flirt because I looked men in the eye. Well, hell, when you give orders where are you supposed to look?"

Anita married Coy Banister. He gave up cowboying and became a bill poster, posting advertisements for medicine shows, minstrel shows, Arbuckle coffee, Dr Pepper, whatever he could paint or paste on a barn. Anita had five kids and died of heart failure. "Coy came to see me after she and Odis both died. Said he had never forgotten me. He was manager of a drug store. Brought me some candy. I'd rather had horse liniment."

"It must cost you a lot of money to keep this place," I said, looking at the crumbling town and cemetery enclosed by her fence.

"Anything you love is worth keeping," Rista said. "Even if it brings you pain."

I was surprised at that. She didn't keep Odis, or Stoddard, or my mother. Certainly not me.

"Wanting gives you pleasure. Getting brings regret that you don't want it as much any more. Keeping is hard work and responsibility. Old-time ranchers went into the business because they didn't want to do anything else. Folks like me can't afford to ranch anymore. Doctors, lawyers, movie stars are pricing the land out of reason, making me the richest poor woman in these parts. They're looking for a tax loophole and a playpen where they can party and play like they're cowboys. Their ranches have metal barns, pipe corrals, blooded horses. The work is done by wets that sleep in the barn, eat tortillas and beans, and send their wages to their families in Mexico. That bunch at the Three Crosses got one of their hands deported because he complained about his wages."

When I locked the gate to Red Rock behind me I asked Rista why she had brought me there. "This is your heritage," she said.

Pug was going to get the ranch, and I was going to get Red Rock? What would I do with it, turn it into an amusement park? Sell T-shirts and souvenirs in Brownfield's store? Turn one of the other buildings into a saloon, decorate it with guns and saddles, deer and moose horns and have dancing girls inside and fake shootouts outside? Turn the cemetery into a boot hill? I'd have to tweak Stoddard's story about the Beasley brothers, have them love the same girl. Then at the end Dan killed the man who killed his brother and saved the woman who loved him.

A stagecoach could take people to the cemetery and then back to town in a roundabout way with a holdup or Indian chase. Western movies and TV shows in the Aginers Church. A hanging tree, a mock trial, and a lynching. I could use the courthouse for offices and ticket sales. Leave the photographs and newspapers on the walls for ambience or tear them down. I couldn't think of any use for the contents of the Ziploc bags.

"I'm giving you these stories," Rista said.

What stories? Rista's problem was that she had never watched the soaps. "The stories have no point," I said.

"You watch television," she said, dismissing me.

After the wedding, Rista expected Odis to fit in. Instead, neither guest nor hand, he stood in the corner and smoked a cigarette while she, Paco, and Pug fed the few neighbors who came to the wedding. When the guests left, he took her to bed and blew out the lamps, but they didn't undress because they knew a chivaree was coming.

Odis kissed and fondled her, but she had a hard time staying awake. Then horns blew, cowbells rang, women beat on tin pans. Some cowboys grabbed Odis, took him to the corral, started a fire, put a branding iron in the coals, blindfolded Odis and told him they were going to slap Rista's brand on him. As the hot iron was pressed sizzling into a piece of raw meat, a branding iron that had been hidden in a bucket of ice was applied to his bare chest. Odis screamed and wet his pants.

When they let him go, Odis tried to fight, but they wrestled him to the ground and held him until he agreed to holster it. He didn't return to bed. He sat on the top rail of the corral listening to Paco, Pug, and the other cowboys coyoting around in the bunkhouse until the whiskey ran out. He vowed someday they would eat dirt. When he did go to bed, accustomed to staying up late, he was ready for a night of love.

Rista tried to oblige him, but Odis didn't have much of a feel for a woman. After making love to him she knew what a steer felt like when it was flanked, thrown down, and branded, but she was proud that she had taken his charge and gentled him, and when he slept with his head on her shoulder, she smoothed down his hair and kissed his forehead.

Odis clung to her when she tried to get out of bed the next morning. He wanted to lie around and make love all day, but she had a day's work ahead of her and for him, and had to fix breakfast for the hands so they could be in the saddle at first light. She had to twist his tail to get him out of bed—worse than a bull that had sulled. Paco and Pug had saucered and blown their coffee before he stumbled out on the porch to wash up.

They had been up late too and sported hangovers, but they had caught horses and saddled by the time he got to the corral and climbed on Paco's horse. Paco didn't say anything—they were all Rista's horses. Paco saddled another horse, and when they rode out, Odis, who was accustomed to leading, rode in front of them, even across their trail. Rista saw Paco and Pug exchange looks. She didn't want to embarrass Odis. She would tell him the unwritten rules when they were alone—catch and saddle your own horse, don't ride in front of Paco and Pug.

Mid-morning when Odis dozed in his saddle, the two came up behind him with a rope between them and slipped it up under his horse's tail. The horse blew its plug, ducking and dodging while Paco and Pug yelled, "Waltz with him, stay in the tree." Odis stuck and they looked at each other and nodded—he could ride. Rista smiled; it was going to be okay.

The next morning, Odis sauntered out after the horses were saddled and got on Pug's horse, wanting to try them all. Pug and

Paco had tied the horses to stake pins to allow them to graze outside the corral. In the darkness, they slipped the stake ropes off their horses and Rista's and took off in a gallop with Odis trying to catch up. His horse hit the end of the rope, flipped and Odis skidded across the grass. Pug rode up to him, spread his arms like an umpire and yelled, "Safe." Rista and Odis never talked about it, but Odis thought she had allowed the hands to belittle him.

That afternoon when Odis dozed, Pug and Paco led his horse under a low limb that knocked him out of the saddle. Odis got up ready to fight, but Paco and Pug played like he had gotten off to pick up his hat. Rista could have stopped the pranks, but practical jokes were the most fun Pug and Paco had, sometimes all the fun they had. She couldn't deny them that. And if she asked them to coddle Odis, their opinion of him would be what he thought it was.

One day when they drove wet stuff to the house to check the cows, one of the calves quit the bunch. Odis went after it, threw a cotton-patch loop that the calf ran through and into the open door of the house. Odis stayed with it, ducking under the doors and jumping the horse off the back porch, and she loved him for that. When they got the cows in the corral, Paco said, "I didn't know we was supposed to take them to supper first." Pug said, "I thought he was going to take a nap in the house instead of in the saddle." Odis glared at them but could think of nothing to say except orders. "Get back to the pasture where you belong." She thought less of him for that.

While telling Paco and Pug what needed to be done one morning, Rista told Odis to move cattle from one pasture to another in front of them. He was so angry that he ran the cattle the whole way, ginning the herd and spilling cows all over the pasture. Odis was good with a horse but he had no cow sense. He didn't learn by looking, and he didn't learn by listening, and if he had been a cowboy she would have had no use for him.

On the other hand, Odis hung screens on the doors and windows. Cattle drew flies. Celestine and Genevieve had complained, but Claris and Rista saw little need for screens because flies were active in daylight, while they were up before dawn and got back to the house after dark. Odis bought a farmhouse, had it moved to the ranch, and added it to the ranch house so that instead of being five rooms in a string, there were eight rooms in a square. Rista knocked out the wall between two front rooms so that she cooked in the presence of her hands.

Odis bought a metal tank, which he put beside the windmill, and ran a pipe to the house. Although she begrudged him using Paco and Pug to help him, she had running water in the kitchen. Odis turned one room into a bathroom with a hinged enameled steel sink and wooden counter that tipped up to reveal a zinc-lined bathtub. It was a frill she would have declined if he had told her, especially when she discovered Odis had charged the bathtub to her.

With Odis came clutter, and she had to spend more time picking up and rearranging. Rista used what was oldest—meat, butter, eggs—before it went bad. Odis wanted the freshest eggs and opened a box of baking soda to brush his teeth when there was still some in the old box. His clothes had no history. She still had the Stetson with the trimmed brim and rattlesnake band, her grandfather's jeans that were cut to her size, her father's boots that she stuffed with socks, the shirt with the cut-off tail, the jeans stained from wading into a tank after a bogged cow. She remembered where and how she got each garment and how many times she or Genevieve had patched it.

Some cows came down with cornstalk disease because Odis put them in a harvested corn field rather than carrying feed to them. The pithy stalks plugged their guts. Rista put Odis to riding the rough string. Odis could ride anything but a hay baler. Horses were considered broken after being saddled and ridden a dozen or so times but still bucked for a few months and had no cow sense. The more they were ridden the smarter they got. She packed him a meal so he could work a horse all day riding fences, checking the stock, water, and windmills.

One night Odis rode in, unsaddled, turned his horse loose, and came to supper. While he was eating he mentioned a fence that was down. Her gravy dried to a halt on its way to her biscuit as she stared at him. "Did you fix it?" Rista asked. Paco and Pug went walleyed, left their plates, caught horses, and saddled to round up the cattle that had found the breech. "You don't ever leave a fence without fixing it," Rista explained.

"I didn't have anything to fix it with, and I was late for supper."

"If you couldn't fix it you should have stayed with it to keep the cows from getting out. Someone would have found you. If you don't ride your own saddle Paco and Pug won't have any respect for you."

"They don't have any respect for me because you treat me like a damn hired hand. Stay in the house and let me tell them what to do."

Rista looked into those pale blue eyes and sat still. "Odis, Paco and Pug respect me because I'll do anything I tell them to do. You're doing a good job smoothing the humps out of the horses. I'll get you some fencing pliers and staples to carry with you. You can help me fix the windmill next time one breaks down so you'll know how to do that."

Odis went his own way, sometimes waiting in the house until they were gone, and she never gave him orders in front of the hands. He trained three horses to neck and knee rein, for roping and working cattle. Rista sold them. Odis wanted to keep them as his horses.

"They're not worth much until they're trained," she said. "A good horse will buy a lot of cow feed."

To Rista, living meant independence and a good name. To Odis, independence and a good name required money. Rista resented Odis' wanting things that weren't needed. Odis resented Rista controlling their money the way she controlled everything else.

On hot summer nights, after Rista sprinkled water on the sheets to cool them, Otis made love to her then sat on the porch to cool off, smoking and watching the night, sometimes watching the bunkhouse. He wanted people to step out of his way. He wanted to walk through a door and have everyone look at him with respect.

Odis worked the horses, but their progress was slow. Rista believed it was because he didn't want to see them sold. Paco found him napping under a tree, his horse gone. Odis limped home. He told Rista he had gotten off, his horse had spooked, and he was worn out from walking. Rista told him to find the horse. "He's got a $200 saddle on him." When he went to catch another horse, he found his horse in the corral. At supper, Paco and Pug kept their eyes on their plates, but he knew they laughed at him.

Odis hired a man he had caught gambling but had not arrested. Rista fired him. "I can't afford to pay the two we got," she said.

"Get rid of Paco. He's not going to be able to ride much longer."

"As long as I own this ranch Paco will have a place here," Rista said.

Odis gave up trying to persuade Rista and turned to Paco. "How long you been working here?" he asked Paco, who was plating horses with the nails in his mouth, the rasp in his hand and the shoe and hammer in his boot.

"You know Comanche Peak? When I come here that was an anthill."

"About time you moved along while you can still sit a saddle."

Paco had never gone anywhere he wasn't wanted. He brooded over it, then packed his gear. Pug went to Rista. Rista went to the bunkhouse.

"I'm too old. I can't work like a young man," Paco said.

"Hell, Paco, I don't need rodeo riders. I need somebody who can look at a hundred head of cows and know which are springing, which are missing, and which need to be culled. I need someone who can look over a pasture and tell me how many cattle it will graze. There aren't any young men who can do that. You can't go off and leave me; where's your loyalty?"

Paco stayed. Rista returned to the house. "Don't ever try to fire Paco or Pug," she told Odis.

"I don't like being nobody," Odis said, cold as a hair brand. "This is your ranch and there is no way it will ever be mine. I have to have something of my own."

"What do you want?" she asked, angry herself and afraid of what he might want.

211

Odis studied her, thinking of something that would show his worth that she couldn't refuse. "I want to shoot the Longhorns and sell them." The Longhorns in Rattlesnake Canyon avoided pens, ducked into the brush when riders appeared, and had to be roped out of the ravines at night when they came out to graze. Odis wanted to sell their hides and horns, and their meat for dog food. "They eat as much as a money cow," he said.

Rista knew they weren't worth much, but they belonged on the ranch like Paco, like the Bone Yard. "I can't spare Pug or Paco," she said.

It riled Odis that she thought he couldn't shoot and pack out the cattle without getting lost, snakebit or gored. He took food, water, the wagon, and a rifle to Rattlesnake Canyon but couldn't get the wagon into the canyon. He shot some cows and packed the meat, hide, and horns back to the wagon on horseback, his shirt in rags, his boots and saddle scarred by the brush, his horse crippled by thorns. By the time he had a wagonload the meat was spoiling. When he got to the railroad in Claypool he found no buyers for the meat and spent two days selling a few of the hides and horns. The meat and the unsold hides he fed to the coyotes and buzzards.

He came home without a tail feather left, but he had met Corky Hanz who wanted him to buy and sell cattle. Rista had been saving money for a registered bull. Odis was sure he could work a swap to get her the bull, but he needed her money to buy into the deal. He worked for a few months buying and selling cows and spent what he made on linoleum for the house. Rista put the bull out of her mind and took out a loan so that he could go in cahoots with a friend building and patenting an automatic cattle feeder. The feeder worked but it was too heavy to move around the pasture and too expensive for a rancher to afford.

Odis planted a crop of watermelons and hauled them to town. He parked the wagon under an oak tree at the corner of Wagonseller and Desolation roads but few people stopped to buy. Marcella Lucas drove a wagon up and down the streets and the woman who lived with her sold the melons door-to-door. It took three days for Odis to sell his melons. He returned to the ranch for more melons, counting on Rista to sell them door-to-door, but she said she couldn't leave the ranch.

He returned to the intersection and the first night someone burst all the melons. Odis sold the ruined melons for hog feed and stayed in town hoping to knock someone's ears down. Every time he jumped for the ring, bad luck sat on his shirttail. Odis vowed someday Rista would see him standing on the skyline. He never found who burst his melons and his story of where he was when the melons were destroyed was shy of feathers, but Rista didn't have time to backtrack him.

For Christmas, Odis gave Rista an expensive broach. "Where the hell am I going to wear this?" she asked. She was disappointed that he spent money they didn't have on trinkets. At least he didn't give her flowers. She could pick her own flowers, but they were prettier where they grew. What she wanted was a knife to replace the one her father gave her before she broke it or wore it out. Odis should know that but he never bothered.

"Wear it when we go some place," Odis said. "We haven't been anywhere since we got married."

"I don't have time for running around. That's why I got married."

Odis went snake-eyed. "I thought you got married because you loved me and needed me."

"I do love you," she said, "and I do need you." He had piped water to the house, put up screens, and laid linoleum, but she needed a young Paco. She had to lengthen his stake rope; giving up his badge to marry her had shortened his stride. At supper she gave him tea made of violet blossoms as a remedy for grouchiness, but he didn't like the taste.

▲▼▲

A black blizzard lifted sand high into the air and turned daylight into dark. The wind was freezing, the linoleum flapping, and thunder rolled. It took Odis almost an hour to find the house. He turned his horse loose to find shelter, lighted a lamp, and put it in the window for Rista. Pug and Paco had seen it coming and had raced their horses to the bunkhouse, leading the horses inside. They too put a lamp in the window. When wind-driven debris broke the window and blew out the lamp, they stuffed their hats in the holes to keep out the sand.

Rista couldn't see her horse's ears, but she tied her bandana over her face and gave the horse its head. The horse took her to the corral. She slid off, tied the horse to the corral, and, afraid of being lost, took the free end of the rope that was tied to the horn and, stretching it to its length, made a sweep around the horse to locate herself. She found the barn. She hand-walked the rope back to the horse, led it to the barn, and felt her way along the wall until she found the tack room. When she found the door she couldn't open it because the wind was too strong and the horse was side-stepping and jerking its head. She unsaddled the horse, pulled it down beside the barn, and curled up between the horse and the barn, pulling the saddle and blanket over her.

When he could see the bunkhouse, Odis ordered Pug and Paco to get their horses out of the bunkhouse and look for Rista. He discovered Rista covered in sand and led her to the house. Rista made a loop of horsehair and dug the dirt from her ears and nose. "Are you okay?" Odis asked, wiping the sand from her eyes and mouth with a wet cloth.

"Fry some eggs," she said. "I think I'm pregnant."

The wind broke windowpanes on one side of the house, and the floor and bedding were covered with sand. Odis helped her sweep up and shovel out the sand before going to town to buy window glass. He returned with the news that the roads had been closed, power lines were down, and one man, whose car had stuck in sand, had gotten lost trying to walk to shelter and had been suffocated by the dust.

The water at the house was muddy so Rista threw in ashes to clarify it. The Big Rock windmill had blown away. There was so much sand in the grass and hay that some of the horses and cattle got sick. Paco and Pug drenched the sick horses with mineral oil and roped and treated the sick cattle while Odis and Rista rebuilt the windmill. It was the first time they had worked closely together since they had repaired a dam leak. When the windmill was up and pumping water, Rista threw her arms around Odis. "I'm glad I married you," she said.

"Make me a boy," he said.

Odis welcomed Rista's pregnancy and begged her to stay off horses. She ran the ranch from the house as best she could, outlining the work that needed to be done, and letting Odis tell Paco and Pug. Sometimes she joined them at noon, her shirt over her too-tight jeans. She built a fire, rolled slabs of bacon in flour and fried it for chuck wagon chicken, using the scraps and drippings in gravy. At night she interrupted their supper of fried sausage and potatoes with blackstrap molasses for dessert by asking questions about range conditions, the cattle, the horses, and how much they had gotten done. She listened closely for signs that Odis had let things slide.

Odis jumped out of bed to be the first in the saddle each morning. When she had morning sickness, he cooked breakfast and prepared food for the noon meal. When the cowboys rode away leaving her nibbling soda crackers, Rista knew she never wanted to be pregnant again. She cut the front out of Odis' discarded jeans, cinched them with one of Genevieve's scarves, and prowled the barn and corral looking for something to do.

Late in her pregnancy Pug and Paco nailed a tall pole to the top of the barn and attached part of a sheet to it so that if Rista needed help when the men were away from the house, she could raise it as a signal. Rista was feeding calves in the sick pen when her water broke filling her boots and making it hard for her to walk. She hoisted the sheet to the top of the pole, waddled to the house and lay down on the floor. She had started labor when she heard Odis ride in. "Ride for Paco, then get away from the house," she yelled when he burst through the door. "I reckon I'm going to have a baby with my boots on." She had been midwife to many cows, she knew what needed to be done, and she knew she could do it.

14
Friday, 1990

I thought Red Rock was behind us when I locked the gate on it, but Rista had not finished her stories. Red Rock almost had a Confederate monument, but there was anger over taxes to pay for it. James Holloway, a Yankee who met Ila Mae Bruner when he was training for World War I and married her after the war, tore down the Confederate flag at a rally. That started a fight: Holloway was shot and two other men wounded.

"They found Ila Mae's high-school yearbook after she died. Everyone had written that they loved her, but the handwriting was all the same."

Ila Mae spent the rest of her life in Red Rock although she had few friends because she had married a Yankee. She considered marrying Frank LeGrand who had a round face and wore long sideburns to make it look thinner. Frank had a college of telegraphy, shorthand and bookkeeping in Tennessee, but he was found guilty of poisoning his wife. A professor convinced the governor she died of lead poisoning—the teakettle killed her. The governor pardoned him, but Frank lost his college and worked as a telegrapher for the railroad at Claypool. He asked Ila Mae Holloway if she would see him. "Ila Mae had a face that would fit a hackamore but was afraid she might marry him and she'd never be able to drink tea again."

217

Where was the beef? It might be a story if an ill second wife discovered her husband did time for murdering his first wife and then was pardoned because of science. Some present terror would have to be substituted for lead poisoning, and viruses were overdone.

Rista was two commercials deep into a story about Red Rock quarantined with a fever epidemic. Dexter Kesey was sick and Birdie Lowrance ran away from home to take care of him. Dexter, a sheepshearer who became a barber, promised to marry Birdie when he saved a hundred dollars. Six months later Birdie asked Dexter how much he had saved. $83.37. "That's close enough," she said. They were married just long enough to have a daughter. Birdie said if he spent as much on soap as he did on tobacco she wouldn't have stopped sleeping with him. Dexter said if she spent as much time washing clothes as she did gossiping over the clothesline he'd have something to put on when he took a bath. After the divorce Dexter remained as town barber, and they both attended the Aginers Church, but they never spoke. When their daughter, Frances, got married, Dexter wasn't invited and Birdie hired a chimpanzee dressed in a suit to stand in Dexter's place and shake hands at the reception.

"I don't know where Birdie found the chimpanzee. I asked Stoddard but he was chasing foolishness about some miraculous place where cripples walked, the blind saw, poor folks received fortunes. Of course it was in some far-off place out of reach of anybody who needed it. Those parts of Stoddard's paper were like chain letter promises."

A chimp in the receiving line might be a scene in a sitcom, but no more than that. A miracle would lead the local news although it might never make the network. Carey sent Shana to do a live remote on a statue that cried real tears. Shana said it was an obvious hoax. Carey said it was news and no editorializing. He sent her back three days later to interview those who had prayed for or received miracles before it was proven a hoax. The hoax was a story we didn't cover, and the newspaper mocked Shana as St. Breathless who turned fake tears into fake news.

Rista was telling some story about Pug crying when he shaved. "It was the first time after the smallpox, and he still had sores. His face bled so that the lather was pink. Paco said he looked like he was eating peppermint candy." I tuned her out in disgust.

▲▼▲

When we got back to the ranch, Pug had saddled and loaded three horses. "I'm short a cow in Borracho Creek. Also, I found three goats."

"That bunch of horse thieves on the Three Crosses brings legislators out here, provides them with expensive alcohol and cheap women and feeds them cabrito," Rista said. "The goats the legislators don't eat or shoot end up in our pasture."

"What do you do with them?"

"If they're young enough we eat them. If they're old we take them to town and sell them. You can't steal from that bunch. They steal from everybody in the state and pay legislators for the privilege."

We had a quick meal of sandwiches with each of us building his own. Then the three of us crowded into Pug's old pickup, with me on the outside again to open the gaps. We drove to Borracho Creek; Pug unloaded the horses and we mounted. "Chance, you stay within sight of the fence and holler loud enough for Pug to hear you. He's going to stay within sight or hearing of you, I'm going to do the same with Pug. Check the draws and brush; she could be lying down. And keep that jug-head moving."

Pug had saddled Little Foot for me. "He's peppier than Two-Bits but calm when he gets in trouble." I winced at the tightness in my groin when I threw a leg over the horse and the saddle pinched, but as I warmed up I got into Little Foot's rhythm, and we rocked along at a steady clip. I felt self-conscious about yelling but answered Pug's whoops with my own. When we got to a brushy draw, the horse turned into it like he knew what he was supposed to do, then jumped out of it and made up for lost time.

We had been riding an hour when Little Foot saw something. He flushed three goats out of the brush and tried to pen them against the fence. Pug came with a rope but they split up, dodged behind brush, and ran between us, before ducking through the fence and disappearing. Pug waved goodbye to them. I felt the same.

I rode over a ridge and saw Rista chasing a cow, the horse turning with it. Then Rista raised herself, threw a loop over the cow's head and her horse slid to a stop. When the cow hit the end of the rope, she turned on Rista and the horse side-stepped out of the way, staying clear of the rope. Pug dug his spurs into his horse and shook out a loop, racing to help Rista. It was almost a ballet, Rista and the horse avoiding the cow's charges and leading her toward the stock trailer. Tiring of the game, Rista threw the rope over the cow's back and cut the horse sharply, jerking the cow off her feet. The cow rose slowly and allowed herself to be led to the trailer. Pug fell in behind the cow to encourage it.

Rista threw the rope over the ball on top of the trailer and pulled the cow inside. I joined them, Pug snubbed the cow close, the horses jumped into the trailer, and we drove back to the house.

"Ran the goats through the fence," Pug said.

"The calf died," Rista said. "That'd make anyone crazy. I'll pen the cow a couple of days, see if she straightens out."

"You got some good work out of Aggie," Pug said.

"Working together like that . . . it's like making love, knowing any minute you might bloom or you might wreck. I don't ever want to give that up."

"You're getting too old to wreck," Pug said.

"I thought about that," Rista said.

"Both you guys could take life a little easier," I said, but they weren't talking to me.

"I saw a cow with a snaggle horn and one with cuts on her teats like she got in the barbed wire."

"Get the tallow and a saw and take Chance with you," Rista said. "While you're doing that I'll rustle up some supper."

Pug unloaded the horses, turned the cow into the sick pen, unsaddled the horses Rista and I had ridden and turned them out, then reloaded his horse. He checked to be sure there was a saw in his pickup and got a coffee can of tallow from the tack room. We drove back to the pasture, with me opening and closing the gaps, and located the snagglehorn. Pug unloaded his horse, roped the cow, led her to the truck, pulled her head tight against the trailer, and dismounted. "Bring me the saw," he said.

With me holding the cow's muzzle to keep her head steady, Pug sawed off the horn, smeared something black on it, then turned her loose. He coiled the rope, got on his horse, and went looking for the sore-teated cow while I followed with the truck.

221

Again he led the cow to the truck, tied her close to the trailer and treated her teats with tallow. Then he caught her by one ear and pulled something off. "Tick," he said. "Swole up so big I could read his brand."

It was after dark when we got back to the house, and I expected Rista to have prepared something special for supper. Instead there was a concoction of canned tomatoes, sugar, and the biscuits left over from breakfast. I thought Pug would complain but he called it "pooch," said it was just what he wanted, and, after eating, went to the bunkhouse. Rista didn't make coffee but went directly to bed.

I put on the hat and coat for warmth and sat on the porch thinking about Shana. The windmill creaked and rattled, and the wind sifted around the house. Occasionally I could hear horses moving about. I hungered for background music, human voices, flickering pictures. I wanted to know the ball scores, the weather over the eastern U.S., the top twenty CDs, the highest grossing movies, the Dow, the headlines.

I heard the flapping of wings, and an owl dropped out of the darkness to catch a cottontail, then turned its pale eyes on me. I wished for a camera; there was so much you could do with that scene if you had it on film. How could Shana not want to be part of the most powerful communications system in history? How could she not want to be seen by thousands of admirers? Her career wasn't in writing or reporting but as an attractive personality who displayed the world that viewers believed in.

Carey tried to create an image for her as a hard-hitting reporter, although I feared it would lead to offers from bigger stations. He assigned her a story for public education week. I warned her to keep it simple and short. "You're not a writer, you're a verbal and visual communicator." She went to two public schools, spoke to bright and articulate students and came back with a story that had no audience appeal and was the wrong image for her. I told her to go to a hangout where students met to smoke and talk tough. They whistled at her, made crude remarks, and with a boom box for background professed not to have heard of the Bill of Rights, the Ten Commandments, or James Madison, but they could name the members of Black Crowes.

We hyped the report, it captured a big audience, and the newspaper ran editorials and op-ed pieces about the failure of the public schools. Teachers responded that students spent more time in front of the TV than they did in front of a teacher, so why didn't we give as much time to the Bill of Rights as we did to this month's rock group? The newspaper printed one representative letter, and we told them we reported news not history. The news was that public education had failed.

Shana said the story was unfair, that there wasn't a teacher in the city who didn't contribute more than she did, that public schools were open to attack because they were public and that there was no one to defend them. Bob Blaine said "troubled-schools" the way some had once said "damnyankee," as though the words were inseparable.

I reminded her that when public education wasn't blamed for the decline of civilization, television was.

"We have the protection of the First Amendment," Shana said, "and we hit back. No one can afford to make an enemy of us. They need us to publicize their accomplishments or products. It's unfair. Those kids knew exactly what we wanted from them. You wouldn't have run the story if they had the same answers as the students from the first two schools. But the viewers saw them

223

as the failure of public education rather than the shallowness of popular culture."

"Your story got a lot of response."

"That's not the point," she said.

"That is the only point. This is the real world where numbers mean jobs. Without sponsors there won't be any television news. And if we don't do stories that attract viewers there won't be any sponsors." Every time we preempted entertainment for breaking news, we were overwhelmed with complaints.

The ratings war meant life or death to the station. During November and May sweeps the other station hyped stories to get a good book. We did the same. A shooting could become an "alleged gang war" if a reporter could find someone to allege it. Competition could hype a tropical disturbance into an imminent hurricane, but it also enforced restraint. We couldn't afford to lose credibility. Competition also limited programming. When a popular show was offered as an off-network rerun, the other station bought it with no intention of using it to prevent us from airing it.

Shana's idealism was so naive it was annoying. She had done too much volunteer work. Maybe we hadn't yet found the right image for her. Bob Blaine was a pompous Olympic god in a dark suit; maybe Shana should represent the sensitive, human side of the news. She left law school when she realized the rich bought justice the same way they bought news.

I would develop a new image for Shana, one that saw people as neighbors, not just news commodities. She wouldn't go as far in her profession, but I would have her longer. She could still be entertaining, but she wouldn't have as big a part in shaping the lives of future generations.

15
1935

Odis was currying the kinks out of a green horse and every hour or so he forced the horse up Comanche Peak to check for Rista's signal. When he saw it, he whooped and rode for the house; he was going to be a father and he was going to receive his son from Rista's womb. Rista wanted Paco with her, so he saddled a fresh horse, rode for Paco and then went looking for Pug. He told Pug to ride for the doctor, and he returned to the house.

Odis had no intention of riding away from Rista and his son. "No horse or cow is that important," he said. He bathed Rista's face, did what Paco told him, and took the baby from Paco's hands. It was the next day before the doctor came, but he found mother and baby okay.

When Odis saw his child for the first time, he forgot he had wanted a son. They named her Cassandra Rae after his mother and called her Cassie. Odis got out of bed in the morning, brought the baby to Rista for feeding, then fixed breakfast and was in the saddle by daylight. When he came home at dusk he went directly to Cassie to hold, change or bathe her while Rista set supper on the table. He was happier than he had ever been.

Rista tied an asafetida bag around the baby's neck to prevent six-month colic. When Rista got the weed and her breasts caked, she fried fritters, buttered one side and laid the warm fritters over her breasts to start the milk flowing. She longed to be outside and on a horse. It did no good for Odis or the hands to tell her that the fences were up, the creeks and windmills running. Her eyes hungered for the land, the grass, the trees. She wanted to hear cows cropping grass, horses nickering, to smell their salt. Odis kept Cassie while Rista rode around the ranch. When the rides got longer, Odis took Cassie to her mother for feeding.

Odis had not rotated the pastures as fast as Rista liked. Some hay had been stacked when it was wet and had ruined. Odis had sold some of her best cows and kept their heifers meaning the calf crop would be smaller. Rista was angry that Paco or Pug had not told him better. "He don't listen," Pug said.

"Both of you told him?"

"We told him," Paco said and looked directly at her. "We also told him about the ghost steer, just to wart him."

Years earlier a Longhorn eating mistletoe in Rattlesnake Canyon got its horns caught between tree limbs. It hung there, starved, dried out, and mummified. Paco found it, started a story about a ghost steer, then propped it up at first dark when some cowboy was returning to the bunkhouse or wagon. The cowboy shook out a loop, made a run at it, and just when he dabbed his string, Paco jerked out the props, and the steer disappeared. When the rider wheeled his horse and looked back, there it was just where he left it. Some ropers blew two or three loops before they caught on. The hair wore off the steer in places but that made it more ghostly. It was Paco's favorite hurrah, and he had pulled it at every roundup for years. Those who fell for it talked up the ghost steer at the next roundup, waiting for someone else to rope air.

"What happened?" Rista asked.

"First time he come back and asked about the steer," Paco said. "Second time he didn't say anything but watched us like we was dealing cards. The third time Odis didn't try to rope it, he shot it."

"We didn't even know he had taken a gun," Pug said.

"You're going to wart Odis too far some day," she said mashing the bulb of her nose against the palm of her hand to relieve her anger. Odis should have been able to cull hurrahs from advice.

"You don't sell proven cows and keep their heifers," Rista told Odis. "Heifers are dead weight until their calves hit the ground. Didn't Paco or Pug tell you that?"

"You put me in charge when you couldn't ride any more."

"It's your ranch too, Odis. But Paco's been cowboying longer than the two of us together. Pug grew up on this ranch."

"If I listened to everything they said I'd shed my skin like a snake."

"What happened to the money from the cows?"

Odis had bought clothes and toys for Cassie, shirts for himself, and as a surprise had ordered a kitchen safe to replace the chuck wagon box nailed to the wall. The safe had a flour bin with built-in sifter, shelves for dishes, drawers for towels and silverware, and a counter top that pulled out to make a table. He couldn't account for the rest of the money.

"Odis, I'm barely hanging on," Rista cried. "We can't sell money-making cows and buy things that don't produce an income. Our business is raising beef, and if that means working hay and wearing old clothes then we do it because it keeps us in the cow business."

227

Rista put Cassie on a bottle and put Odis to milking. He fed Cassie while Paco and Pug saddled and rode off with Rista. Because Cassie could not be left alone, Paco and Pug made a two-wheeled cart out of discarded parts, and Odis pulled Cassie in it while he worked around the barn and corrals. He harnessed the cart to a horse and worked the close pastures, sometimes all of them working together and playing with Cassie when they stopped for the noon meal. Rista tried to get Cassie to feel a horse's muzzle, to stroke its neck, but Cassie turned her head away. Rista tried to lead her around on a horse, but Cassie cried until her father took her.

Odis liked caring for Cassie, but he believed Paco and Pug regarded him as a churn twister because of it. At supper they and Rista talked about fences, windmills, waterholes, livestock and wildlife while he listened. After they went to the bunkhouse, he told Rista about Cassie crawling, pulling up, saying her first word. Rista held Cassie, begging her to repeat her tricks—to say "mama," to stand, to take her first step.

Odis limped with an ingrown toenail. While Rista cut a notch in the center of the nail, heated tallow in a spoon over the lamp and dropped the hot tallow on the nail, Odis said he wanted another child. Rista said no and refused him because he had no condoms. When Odis went to town for supplies and returned with condoms, she rode in early. Before they began supper, they put Cassie in her crib, gave her a cracker to chew on, and tumbled into bed, pulling at each other's clothes.

Afterward, Rista went over the bill he had charged at Arky Black's store, pointing out his extravagances—a toy for Cassie when she played with spoons and pans, a new razor for himself when his and Claris' old razors rusted on the porch. For her birthday Odis bought Rista a Monopoly set, and they sat up most of the night playing. Although both had to be up early he would not quit until he won.

Odis' older brother, Mackie, came to see Odis, who was at the house with Cassie. Mackie was losing his farm and the money he had paid on it. "That's out and out stealing," Odis said.

"It's legal stealing," Mackie said. The Supreme Court ruled the Agricultural Adjustment Act of 1933 was unconstitutional, and farmers buying land under the act had to turn the land back to the mortgage holders. Smiley Wooten reclaimed the land and kept the money Mackie had already paid him. Mackie wanted Odis to talk to Smiley, but without his badge Odis packed no more weight than Pug. He had closed a club in which Smiley had an interest, and Smiley was making Mackie pay for it. When Odis said he couldn't head Smiley, Mackie asked him for a loan. He didn't understand that Odis had no money and no collateral. Odis could ask Rista to take out a loan for Mackie, but if she refused he'd look like he had shucked his guts for an apron.

"The banks own the courts and most of Congress," Mackie raged. "Farmers and ranchers have to organize so we can bribe politicians the way bankers, insurance, and manufacturing companies do."

"Banking, insuring, and manufacturing are a coward's way to rustle cattle," Rista said. She returned from a day of work to find that Odis had not started supper. Angrily she chopped potatoes and onions and threw meat in the skillet.

Odis helped her with supper, not only because it was a job he had failed to do but because he wanted to talk to her out of Mackie's hearing. Rista said she would give Mackie a beef that he could sell or eat, but she dared not mortgage the ranch further. Odis pleaded with her. "Odis, when I ask for a loan, Smiley asks for a piece of ass. Is that what you want?"

Odis slammed the door and walked outside. "We can't afford a loan," he told Mackie who waited. "Take the steer or leave it."

After Mackie left with the steer, Odis walked to the corral, looking for a dog to kick, his mind filled with pictures of Smiley enjoying the wives of hard-working folks who needed a loan. He walked to the house and got his six-shooter. Rista begged him not to cause trouble with Smiley. "He cheated my brother and insulted my wife."

"You'll go to jail, and Smiley will foreclose on the ranch. The law looks after people like Smiley."

"Sometimes you have to help the law out," Odis said. "Your father would trim a cottonwood with Smiley."

"Please, Odis. For me. For Cassie."

Odis let her dissuade him, but he felt better that she had to beg.

▲▼▲

Odis and Rista worked out an agreement to take turns caring for Cassie, and Odis went back to training horses. Rista lay awake at night studying how she would repay the mortgage on the ranch. Odis sat in the dark thinking of ways to make folks like Smiley respect him.

One day while all of them worked together rounding up a pasture, they saw sea gulls flying overhead. They all stopped to watch, wondering what it was. "In Mexico folks think the end of the world will start like that," Paco said.

The next day Odis took the wagon to town for supplies, taking Cassie with him, and returned with a newspaper. A hurricane had hit the coast and blown sea gulls far inland. A front-page story said a group of believers had gathered on a hill to await the end of the world. When they saw the sea gulls some of them ran off the hill thinking they would rise and fell to their deaths. On an inside page was a story that German conscription and renunciation of the Treaty of Versailles could lead to French intervention. Odis said it might raise the price of beef. He read Rista an ad Stoddard wrote: For sale: cow gives five quarts of milk, two plows, 40 bales of hay, one shotgun. "That's the kind of cows we need," Odis said. "They give enough hay to feed themselves and have some left over."

Rista didn't hear him, her attention on a report that Will Rogers and Wiley Post had died in a plane crash. She didn't know much about Will Rogers the actor and political commentator, but she rarely talked to a cowhand who didn't have a story about or by Will Rogers the cowboy. Almost every pithy saying was ascribed to him. She went to the bunkhouse to tell Paco and Pug that he was dead. The three sat on the top rail of the corral in the dark and rode over memory trails, each of them with a favorite Will Rogers story or saying. Will Rogers was one of them, and his death was the end of the West as they knew it.

"Will was straight up and down as a cow's tail," Paco said.

"A full sixteen hands," Pug said.

"Since Shell Castlebury was old enough to use an ax," Rista said. "Look what they done to Buffalo Bill. Made him look like a fool. Putting on makeup and fancy clothes like a whore."

"I saw a picture show about Billy the Kid," Pug said. "Hell, he wasn't no hero like they made him out to be, but he could fork a horse. The man they had playing like he was Billy couldn't ride a merry-go-round."

231

"Billy didn't wear none of them shorthorn pants neither," Paco said.

"Anything they don't understand they play like it's a mirage," Rista said. "Prettier than a dirt tank but not good for anything but to look at."

"Will was as real as cowbirds before rain," Pug said.

"Hard to believe he's gone," Rista said. "It's all gone, what we believe in."

"Time to tell a joke or go home," Paco said.

"Joke's on us," Rista said.

"How much longer do you figure we got?" Pug asked. Pug was dragging his navel.

"Depends on you and Paco. And Odis."

"We'll hang and rattle as long as you can," Paco said.

"When I have to sell, I'll try to sell to someone who'll hire us. And I'll pay you what I owe you."

"Sometimes I think I want to get my money in silver dollars and put it all in my pockets, so heavy I can't pick up my feet," Paco said. "And I'll drag myself though the little village I come from and throw silver dollars to the children, and I'll get lighter and lighter and then just fly away."

Rista put her arm around Paco and put her head on his shoulder. "I want us to stay together," she said.

"I won't work for Larry Wooten," Pug said. Larry, who was grass bellied and short of hat size, managed the Three Crosses after Smiley Wooten forced Pug's mother off the ranch.

"What if whoever buys the ranch don't like cows? Likes sheep or wants to farm?" Paco asked.

"Dammit, I'll do what I can. I reckon I can hang on until the year is out," Rista said.

232

"Wind's screaming like John the Baptist out there," Pug said when he came to breakfast. A blue norther had blown in during the night.

"You better wear Odis' chaps," Rista said. "He didn't put a lot of wear on them." Her chaps looked like they had been worn by an eighteen-wheeler.

"What do I need chaps for?"

"It's 'shaps.' Don't say 'chaps' like a Yankee. If you get in the mesquite you'll be glad you got them, and they'll give you some protection from the wind and rain."

"I saddled Little Foot for you since you're used to each other," Pug said.

By the time we got to the corral the wind was driving icy drops of rain that turned to sleet as we trailered the horses to Comanche Peak. As usual I got the gaps. "We're going to have hell driving cattle into that wind," Pug said.

"If you have to, slap the cows with your rope," Rista told me. "Your horse is likely to be humped up from the cold and is not going to like facing into that wind so show him who's boss."

It was still sleeting when we unloaded the horses, and they were fidgety and hard to mount. Rista's horse bucked a couple of times so she trotted it around the trailer. "Pug, better take the

233

ginger out of Chance's horse," she said, pulling up beside us. "Then take the left. Chance, you take the right fence, and I'll take the middle. Don't leave anything behind, or we'll have to go back and get it."

Little Foot crow-hopped until Pug spurred the horse into a run then brought it back to me. I worked the balky horse as best I could and yelled at the cattle. My nose, toes, fingers, and ears were numb in a few minutes. Rain that was mixed with sleet soaked through the hat and chaps. The cattle tried to turn away from the wind but were too miserable to run. Most of the work was forcing them to face the wind. When we drove the last of them through the gap into Two-Dollar Flat, Rista rode over. "What's your count?"

I looked at her dumbly. My brain was so frozen I couldn't count my toes. I prayed that we hadn't missed any when she rode over to Pug to check his count. I watched the two of them talk, too cold to make the drive again, too lost to find the truck and trailer by myself.

"We left five," Rista said. "Let's go find them."

When we turned our backs to the wind the horses wanted to run to the trailer. Pug and Rista settled into an easy lope, and I tried to emulate them. I did okay on the straightaways but when Little Foot ducked around a tree, jumped a wash or skidded on a wet rock, I almost lost my seat. I thought I knew where the cattle were, a brushy draw that I hadn't ridden into, and I was right. It was easier with three of us to drive the balky cattle. I hunched up against the cold and let Pug and Rista do most of the yelling and chasing.

"Let's go home," Rista yelled when we drove the last of the cows into the new pasture and Pug closed the gap behind them.

It took all my strength to keep Little Foot to a manageable lope, and when he skidded to a stop at the trailer I almost lost the saddle and bruised my thigh on the horn.

The wet chaps weighed a ton as we loaded the horses, but I was too tired to take them off for the ride to the house in the truck that had no heater. Every time I stopped shivering I had to get out and open a gap. When we unsaddled the horses, I was sure we were through for the day, or at least until after lunch, but Pug and I loaded the truck with hay while Rista made cornbread to go with the pinto beans that had been simmering since breakfast. "No point in changing clothes, we're just going to get wet again," Pug said, beating the water from his hat and chaps and stamping the mud from his boots. I dropped the sodden chaps on the porch.

After lunch, Rista said, "I got chores here." Pug looked at her sharply, but she ignored him. Pug drove the truck while I opened bales of hay and fed the cattle. We made two trips, feeding by headlights on the last one, and I could feel a knot where I had bruised my thigh. "Let's go to the bunkhouse and have a drink," Pug said. "Bring a saddle with you." He took a wet saddle from the tack room and I grabbed another.

When we got to the bunkhouse, he tipped the saddle on its horn in a corner and turned on the electric heater. We shivered before it for a moment then got out of our wet hats and boots to let the warmth reach our skin. "Here," Pug said, throwing me worn jeans and a shirt. "Get into something dry."

While he got ice from the refrigerator, put it into a thick tumbler, and covered the ice with bourbon, I examined the bunkhouse. There was an overhead light and a small reading lamp on a table beside the narrow bed that had no head or footboards. On top of the table and on a shelf below were ranch and horse magazines. There were two straight-backed wooden chairs and a small, slope-shouldered refrigerator. Behind a plastic curtain was a bathroom with a shower, toilet, and washing machine. Pug's chaps hung on a nail and his clothes on a broomstick across one corner. Beneath the broomstick was a pile of worn boots. The walls were covered with pictures of horses. It was hard for me to believe Pug spent many nights in the bunkhouse when I wasn't around.

Pug raised his glass to me and took a drink. "Rista don't drink anymore," he said.

"I thought you'd have pin-ups of women on the walls," I said.

"I don't think Rista would like that." He pulled over a saddle and oiled it. "Dalhart had some pin-ups, but I made him take them down."

"Does Rista come out here often?"

"Only once since Paco died." I waited to hear the rest of the story, but that was all Pug was going to tell.

"Don't you ever get lonely out here?"

"Rista's in the house. Horses are in the trap, maybe the corral. Hell, I could go to town every night if I wanted to, but after supper I'm ready for bed. What would I do in town? Go to a movie? Have a beer and watch TV? There's nothing to convince me that this ain't where life is."

"Didn't you ever want a normal life? Wife and kids?"

Pug straddled his chair and leaned his arms on the back. "This bunkhouse suits me fine, but not many women would like it. For a long time I had to share it with Paco. 'Course there was no running water then, no electricity. If he saw this he'd think I'd gone soft. I'd like kids. I'd like a wife. It didn't happen."

I wondered if he was trying to fulfill the movie version of the lonesome cowboy. "Never had a girlfriend?"

"I wasn't no parlor ornament, never have been. I wasn't going to pretend to some decent woman that I loved her when I didn't so I went where I didn't have to pretend. I call that decent."

"You've never been in love?"

Pug emptied his glass and poured us another drink. Then he began work on the other saddle. "I guess I've always been in love," he said.

"Why didn't you marry her?"

"I didn't have nothing to offer. I wasn't going to go empty handed."

"You don't think love was enough?"

"Oh, I gave her that."

What did she give you? I was preparing to ask. A corner of her bed? The deed to the ranch? I heard Rista beating on the bottom of a metal pan. "Suppertime," Pug said, "Rista don't like to wait. I'll finish the saddles when I get back. Take your wet clothes with you."

The wind had almost stopped, and it seemed to be clearing in the north when we went to the house.

"While you boys were getting drunk I made us some love-in-disguise," Rista said, setting before us what looked like a mound of brown mashed potatoes. She cut through the potatoes, sliced through a heart stuffed with onions and bread crumbs and placed it on my plate before passing cream gravy.

▲▼▲

After Pug returned to the bunkhouse, Rista poured us coffee, and we moved to the heater in the sitting room. I rubbed the knot on my thigh. "Rista, did you know Pug was in love with you?"

"I guess Pug has always been in love with me. Him and Paco both, although with Paco it was more like a father. Pug was younger than me. That don't mean much now, but Pug was a kid when I married Odis."

"Pug worked all these years because he loves you, and you string him along so he won't leave even when you don't pay him. Probably Paco too."

"Paco loved this place. He believed it was as much his as mine because he loved it as much. He didn't want to own it in a buy-or-sell way; he just wanted to love it and live with it. If they had sent him back to Mexico, buried him over there, I'd have brought him back, legal if I could. This was his home, and he wanted to be buried here. It don't have anything to do with nationality. If you don't understand that, you don't understand anything."

That didn't answer my question. Was the ranch also Pug's, and did he want it in a buy-or-sell way?

"We were family, me and Pug and Paco and Papa. Mother too, although Mother was always at the edge of the family because this place, this land, is part of the family, and she was never a part of the land."

"Did you ever think of marrying Pug?"

"Living here and working with me is enough for Pug. If I married him he would regret the years we wasted. Pug has no regrets because he always thought anything more was impossible. He's been happy loving me the best way he knew how."

"You never wanted to remarry?"

"I thought about Stoddard after Odis died, hoping he would ask me to throw in with him. I couldn't tend cows and him too, and he didn't want filling; he wanted meringue.

"There was a man who worked for me after your mother left. He shuffled the brogue like a foreigner but he worked like a Texan. Women can tell when the heat is on a man; you can feel that look. Dalhart had a look that could drive a splinter through you. Make you leave a sick horse to be with him. Make you not care what happened to you or the horse. When my hair was up or if I rolled up my sleeves, I could feel his eyes on my neck, my arms, and my skin would bump up like I had warbles. It came a thunder gust, hell of a gully washer, rained so hard you could hardly see. Our saddles were wet and slippery, the horses skidded in the mud. They wanted to put their heads down, but we had to get the cows out of Six Mile Draw before they washed away. Eight head washed down the draw until they got their feet under them. Two never came back.

"When the cattle were safe we pulled the horses up close to a big cedar and crawled under it for a little protection. I was wet and shivering, and he put his arms around me to warm me up. And he did. We commenced kissing and found it was warmer bare skin to skin. Then the sun winds came and dried everything up.

"I never get wet or smell cedar that I don't think of him. I almost married him. He took orders from me because I was jefe, but if I had married him it would have been his ranch. He'd tell me when to change pastures and how to do it. I asked myself, which had you rather have—him or yourself the way you've always been? I fired him Christmas Day. We made love under the Christmas tree, and he packed his saddle."

"Why did you marry Odis?"

"I needed someone to help run the ranch, and the mating urge was on me. I was partial to Stoddard. I tightened my cinch, roached my hair, and pinched my cheeks for him. I thought he could fly like Jesus and ride like Booger Red. Come to find out, Stoddard couldn't ride a hay wagon, and he flew like a frog. Everything he said was a puzzle I had to cipher. I spent a lot of time listening to Stoddard when I've fired men who talked too much. When the work was done, that's when you did your talking. Here was this man who loved to talk, and I loved to hear him, but no work got done when he was talking. You needed spurs with Stoddard and blinders on his bridle.

"Odis was a blind bucker, but if you could grab the reins and keep him from running through fences until he settled down he'd be a prize stud. After we married, Odis was like a stud, choking down and not giving any slack. He always beat dark back to the barn. He wore out more tires than he did gloves. He was always looking to go to town to get something that we could have fixed or done without. A lump-jawed cow could walk by and him not notice. One time I said, 'Come here and look at this moon.' He said, 'What's the matter with it?'

"Odis didn't like working hay. He couldn't hit the ground with a rope. Paco complained about his fencing. I didn't like the way he worked cattle. He couldn't track a manure spreader. Odis wanted to be called a hand, but no one was saying it."

"Mother said he was a good father."

"I said the same about Papa. My mother didn't agree." For a moment I thought she had gone to sleep. "Odis loved your mother and he loved me, but Odis was a moon; he didn't shine unless someone shined on him, and I couldn't shine on him all the time. Frying his eggs, washing his shirts, filling his bed, giving him a daughter didn't count. He thought there was someone who could make up for what was missing in him but there wasn't. There was a part of Odis that no one could touch. He was like a dog on the highway, chasing something he never caught until it caught him."

She sat so still in the rocker that again I thought she was asleep. Then she nodded in agreement to some inner thought.

"Did you ever think of divorcing him?"

"Odis would have asked me to take him back. And I would have. We'd be getting divorced and remarried like we were different people when we weren't. Marriage is keeping and taking care of and Odis was in love with getting. Nothing I or your mother could have done would have changed him, or changed the way he felt about us.

"A woman's love is from her breast, it's always there. Some days I was mad at him, some days I didn't respect him, but I always loved him. A man's love is like his rod, sometimes it's there and sometimes it's not. It doesn't have anything to do with will and intention. I don't mean he loved me only when we were in bed. Wanting and loving are close, but they're not the same. Sometimes Odis studied me with a cold eye like I was a horse he paid too much for, but there were times his eyes filled up with me. It wasn't something I did or the way I looked; he was just filled with love for me. Maybe more than I loved him, but not so every day. When your mother was born he looked at her and he looked at me, and I knew that man would love me when he died. He loved other women too, but not for so long. That's the way he was. Maybe that's the way all men are."

"Why did you shoot him?"

"I didn't go to do it. If he had said he made a mistake. If he had said he was sorry. Odis believed that was what businessmen did, and he had reason to believe it.

241

"When I found them I was as surprised as they were. I didn't think about killing them. I thought about Pug breaking his arm, and Smiley trying to take the ranch, and the calves I had to shoot that could have been saved if I had some help, and Odis was filling his eyes with that woman and basking in her glow.

"I almost shot that barren cow he was with. She didn't give him a thought or me either, what I was going through. She just thought of herself, screaming and crying. I wanted to lay down and cry, too. I've never been able to do that my whole life.

"I heard after she and her husband divorced that she told folks I shot Odis with him begging for his life. I wished then I had shot her. People knew she lied about her and Odis, but they still went and believed her when she said that I was crazy and that Odis begged for his life."

We sat for a long time staring at the glow of the electric heater. The knot on my thigh from the saddle horn hurt but as tired as I was I didn't want to move or go to bed.

"Pug told me Outlaw was down. That was the last horse Odis trained; did a good job too. I rode out to see about him. He got up when I looked at him. His teeth were worn and grass had balled up in the corner of his jaw. I got that out with a stick and gave him some oats. He tried to eat, but he couldn't chew and everything he ate scoured him. He'd hang on for a while but one day the crows would peck out his eyes, and the varmits would start eating under his tail and I didn't want him to die like that.

"Outlaw looked at me like he knew what was going to happen but he didn't flinch. I shot him between the eyes, and his legs went out from under him. I put a rope around his neck, dragged him away from the water, stacked brush on top of him, and burned him. I didn't want the buzzards and coyotes to get him."

242

I glanced up and thought I saw tears behind her glasses. "I could have got Pug to do it, but that didn't seem true."

True to what? I wondered. Because she shot Odis she had to shoot his horse? Maybe consistency required her to shoot Stoddard too.

"Why didn't you come to see me sooner?" she asked. "I always thought when you were on your own you would come. That thought kept me going a lot of days and nights."

"I didn't know if I would be welcome," I said. Mother said Rista had never cared for anything except a horse, that she was eaten up by love of the land. I thought I hated her.

"We were close when you were small. Cassie was with you all day while I worked, but at night she let me feed you, bathe you, and put you to bed. She was gone a lot at night."

I thought I wanted to know about Mother, but I didn't want to hear that and I didn't believe that we were ever as close as Rista imagined.

"Do you remember that cotton bunny on your bed?"

"Did it belong to my mother?"

"It was your favorite toy; you slept with it every night. I gave it to you. Cassie left it on my bed. I thought at first it was to make me cry, but I think now she put it on my bed so that I would know she didn't leave it by accident. I think it was her token of forgiveness. I want to believe that way."

17

1939

Flat-heeled punchers showed up with checks to lease land for oil drilling. Not only did Rista have a fat check, there was a summer rain that brought Odis to the house to check the roof for leaks. Rista showed him the check, and they danced, stomping and whooping in the rain. Rista found a cow chip, crusty on the outside, soft on the inside. She threw it at Odis, and it exploded on his back. He grabbed a handful of mud and threw it at her. They threw mudballs and wrestled in the mud until they were exhausted and lay side by side laughing. Rista kissed his wet, muddy face. "What's the first thing you're going to buy?" Odis asked.

She could use a new coffee mug because hers was cracked and Odis took the good one. She rolled him on top of her. "The hands won't be home until dark," she whispered. "Throw Cassie a cracker."

▲▼▲

Rista and Odis bathed in the horse trough, their love so artless they used the same towel. Odis went back to work, and she went to the house, her prayers answered, to prepare supper. She could hardly wait to tell Pug and Paco the good news; the ranch had been saved. There wasn't much in the cupboard—

stale biscuits and stewed tomatoes, so she added sugar to make pooch, and for dessert, hot biscuits, butter, and molasses.

Neither Pug nor Paco showed much excitement over the meal until she told them she was giving them their back pay and when she went to town she would pay off Smiley Wooten and the ranch could be debt-free. Pug wanted her to hold his money until he had enough to buy a car. Paco wanted her to hold his money until he needed it. Odis didn't want to use all the money to pay debts.

Rista said no to the trip to Carlsbad Caverns; she couldn't be away from the ranch that long. She agreed to the truck. The oil company was putting in caliche roads to bring in drilling rigs. She could use a truck to haul horses to pastures so that she didn't have to ride half a day to get there, and to haul steers to the railroad at Claypool. She could take Cassie to school, buy groceries, and be back in time to do a day's work. But the best use she found for the truck was shutting the feed bins, closing the holes, running a hose from the truck to the bins, and killing rats.

▲▼▲

Smiley Wooten saw Odis ragged out in new clothes and driving a truck and invited him to the bank to discuss opportunity. Odis followed with one foot in the stirrup ready to jump when he sniffed a loop. He wasn't Mackie and if Smiley tried to take something that was his, he'd straighten Smiley's crook.

A group of men planned a frozen food locker in Red Rock. Smiley, who wasn't an investor, wanted Odis as an investor to protect his brother. "Some people can't or won't keep up with their business. They're distracted by Wrong-Way Corrigan, *Gone With the Wind*. No one can protect you entirely. The government won't and no one else can. I know Larry can trust you." The bank would loan Odis the money to buy in as an investor.

Odis had no collateral, and he'd have to find a way to keep Rista from saying no before she heard what the plan was. Unwilling to admit he had no hold on the ranch, he studied Smiley's bait, looking for traps. Smiley sweetened the deal.

"There'll be a slaughterhouse, and you can rent a locker that will hold a whole beef," Odis explained to Rista, who packed meat in lard to keep it from getting rancid. Odis reined in his enthusiasm knowing Rista would pick at his plan like a hen pecking and scratching at something shiny until it lost its luster. "You can take a steer to town and pick it up a steak at a time. The investors want me to supervise the operation, but I will have to be an investor."

"Why do they want you?" Rista asked.

"Because of my background in law enforcement," Odis said, telling her what was plain as a barbed-wire fence. When she wanted to know who he would be tied up with, he named Larry Wooten, Judge Gillin, and Arky Black, the grocer, who bought in to be sure that the locker didn't cut him out on fresh fruits and vegetables. "As supervisor I can sell our steers on the hoof, and the buyers can pick them up wrapped and frozen."

Rista scorned Larry who was fat in the middle and poor at both ends. Larry was a bow-tie rancher who lived in town and operated ranches the bank had seized. She took comfort that Smiley wasn't in the deal. Arky Black, who extended her credit from one steer crop to the next, was simple but as straight as a wagon tongue. Judge Gillin was no longer a judge and lost days on his notching stick but had a reputation that would carry water with renters.

"That's not many investors," she said, studying the floor plan of the locker plant. At the front Odis' office was off the lobby where renters entered to remove food from their lockers. At the rear an unloading platform opened into a receiving room with overhead tracks and track scales. There was a receiving table, cutting table, drain table, work table, trimming table, wrapping table, meat saw, meat grinder, meat block, lard-rendering kettle, a lard press, chill room, aging room, boiler room, and locker room. There was a separate room for poultry with scalding tank and plucker, a curing room for ham, and a smokehouse. Behind the locker room was the machine room with the ammonia compressors. "I'd have to mortgage both Papa's and Grandpa's ranches," Rista said.

"I'm never going to have a place on this ranch except as a hired hand," Odis said, his eyes as cold and hard as she had ever seen them. "I can run the locker; I can keep the books and supervise the workers. This will be something of my own." And there was no way she could interfere the way she had bulged into his other projects, holding back the money, telling him where he could plant watermelons and how to sell them.

The bank was selling the Three Crosses. Paco and Pug had pledged the money she owed them and most of their future wages, and with a loan from the bank she could come up with the money. She thought she owed it to Pug. But Odis wanted to buy into the locker, and she didn't know if she could keep that horse corraled. As manager of the locker he would draw a salary; they wouldn't have to wait until calves matured or they sold a horse to have money. Odis' other ventures had failed, but he had never thrown in with Arky Black or Judge Gillin.

Rista agreed to invest in the locker but only after she told

Pug and Paco and she and Odis drew up a will. The ranch would go to Cassie and any children she had. Odis had a look that would shut a barn door. Who kept Cassie? Milked for her? Pulled her around in her cart? Who taught her to count? To tie her shoes? Colors and the names of animals?

Odis went outside ready to dig a hole and throw a fit in it. Rista had rather protect her ranch than see him succeed. When he got to the corral and a horse came to the fence hoping to be fed, Odis punched it in the neck, hurting his hand. He signed the will because Rista would not invest in the locker without the agreement.

▲▼▲

Managing the locker had Odis walking spraddle legged. He drove to town every day to meet with the other investors, go over plans, or watch construction. He hired men to slaughter, hang and dress animals, to butcher, cut and wrap the meat, and one man to rent lockers, sell keys and assist those who came to get frozen packages. Odis spoke to farm groups, fraternal groups, and the PTA about the advantages of the locker.

Townspeople rented lockers, and Odis sold them steers and delivered them to the plant. Odis was elected president of the chamber of commerce, and he strode through town making waves. Every night he rubbed his balding spot with a raw onion until it turned red and then rubbed in honey. Rista expected him to get up when she did and work on the ranch when he didn't have to go to town; most Saturdays and Sundays he had to go to town.

Rista almost went with Odis to take Cassie to school the first time. She would have had to leave Odis at the locker, drive back to the ranch, and then drive back to town to pick up Cassie and then Odis, cutting her work day by half. Cassie didn't seem to mind that her mother didn't take her to school. Cassie always turned to Odis instead of her, but it was Rista who rubbed mare's milk on her gums when she was teething, parboiled poke leaves and fried them for blood builders, rode to Marcella Lucas' farm to get peach leaves for tea when Cassie had chills and fever, peeled thorns and skin from a prickly pear leaf and held it on her foot to draw a thorn, put turpentine and whiskey in a saucer, set it afire, and held Cassie over the smoke to loosen the croup. Rista cut the tail from an old wool shirt, ran a hot iron over it to sterilize it, soaked the cloth in a poultice of coal oil, turpentine, and lard, and placed it on Cassie's chest. Cassie cried that it burned and ran to Odis who removed the cloth. Rista held her up all night patting her on the back to help her breathe.

Every day Odis took Cassie to school, saw that the plant was open, the employees on time, and the machinery in running order. He looked over the books, had a leisurely lunch with friends, played dominoes in the room behind the barbershop, and picked up Cassie after school. He returned to the plant to be certain the employees worked until quitting time, put away their equipment, and left the buildings clean and locked.

Sometimes Cassie had to go home with a friend until Odis could pick her up after school. A few times she had to spend the night with friends as Odis was in meetings until too late to take her home. Rista worried on those nights, but she had no telephone and no way to get to town. When she expressed her anxiety, Odis said he made certain Cassie was with a respectable family and that he slept at the locker.

One Saturday Rista rode to town with Odis to buy groceries and clothes for herself and Cassie. Rista finished shopping, left

Cassie to play at a friend's house, and waited in the truck for Odis, fuming about the steers she needed to feed. Now that Odis was selling beef on the hoof, she fattened steers in a pen, and they had to be fed every day. She saw Lucinda Gillin and ducked her head. Lucinda wore a middy blouse, white linen skirt, and no hat. Rista didn't want Lucinda to see her in jeans and brush popper shirt.

Lucinda saw her and joined her in the truck. "I'll be back in the saddle as soon as I get home," Rista said, tugging at her worn shirt. "You always have style."

Lucinda laughed. "Style is what people say about you when they can't say you have character. Rista, I have such admiration for you. The rest of us played 'pick a fool and ride in his dust,' but you lived by your own values. Don't ever change."

Rista didn't think she could change. "Everyone loved you."

Lucinda laughed again. "I thought I wanted that so I tried to be what they wanted. Remember when I used to recite 'Curfew Must Not Ring Tonight?' And those hats. I shudder to think my only use was to give idle tongues something to wag about. When I come home they look at me strangely not to be wearing a hat. When I tell them I'm going to be a doctor, they nearly faint. Remember how silly I was as a girl? I couldn't eat an egg because it was an embryo, and when that man exposed himself I cried and didn't go riding for a year. I decided Stoddard wasn't going to be anything important so I went to college to marry an important man. One day I had to dissect a cat. I thought when I opened it, the stuffing would fly out like a pillow. I never realized it was put together in the most intricate and amazing design."

Rista didn't understand how Lucinda could be a doctor. "Who will your patients be?"

251

"Probably children at first and then a few women until ideas change. A lot of boyfriends tried to discourage me. They didn't want to marry a smart woman. But men will come if they need me."

"But a strange man, without his clothes—"

"Not much different from a bull if you dissect them. A professor tried to frighten me out of school by showing me his penis. It was hardly an inch long. When I burst out laughing, he said, 'Haven't you ever seen an erection?' I can examine a man as easily as you can castrate a horse."

"Don't you want to be married, have children?"

"I'm marrying a high-school English teacher. He's wonderful and he's very supportive of my career. He's at the house with Dad." Lucinda feared America would be dragged into the war in Europe and her fiancé would have to go. "You must worry about Odis. You married Odis Wyler?"

"Yes," Rista said, but she was worried more about Pug. She couldn't run the ranch without Pug. "We have a daughter. She's seven now."

"Give your daughter a hug for me. She has a lot to live up to."

Lucinda admired her. Rista didn't think anyone had admired her since her father died. She walked to the locker to see if Odis was ready to go home, but he wasn't there. On an impulse she stopped at the newspaper to see what Stoddard knew about the war in Europe.

The newspaper was in a false-front red rock building with a high arch over the front door and large glass windows on either side of the door. Inside, little had changed since Stoddard took over the paper, except the young woman who assisted him. It was still a two-person newspaper. Stoddard took the news off the wire and selected what his readers would see. The woman sold ads and collected birth, wedding, death, church, and social meeting announcements.

Dollie Desktop—pretty but her eyes were close together making her nose look long—talked on the telephone. Stoddard was bent over a desk. When he saw Rista, he welcomed her to his office at the back.

"I have so much to tell you," he said, closing the door. "Did you see *Gone With the Wind?* I saw it twice in Austin before it came here. *Rebecca* is coming next week. It's a wonderful movie, but *Gone With the Wind* showed what we lost. When Scarlett shot that Yankee in the face, everyone in the movie cheered. If I had been alive—"

"I don't have much time for movies. Odis runs the locker—"

"News is my business, remember? But I'm not going to be running this paper much longer. Whole armies are on the march, and when the United States gets into it the value of this newspaper will double. I'll sell it and go to England or China and report the war."

Rista left the newspaper wondering if Stoddard believed he might go to England, certainly not China. She had made the right choice. Odis was a dreamer too, but he didn't shy from work, and with the oil lease, the salary that Odis got, and the sale of beef at the locker, the ranch was recovering from the years of drought and poverty.

Larry Wooten saw her returning to the truck. Larry, whose eyes bugged out like they wanted to get ahead and see what was there, wore a shirt so new it still fit. "Smiley wants to see Odis," he said. Larry wanted his brother's approval, which he would never get because that was the spur Smiley hooked in his ribs.

Not now, Rista thought. She had work to do. "Odis is busy," she said. Larry looked puzzled, but most of Larry's horses had been left in the trap.

It was almost dark when Odis appeared; she had lost the whole day. "Larry said Smiley wanted to see you," she said, ready to fight.

Odis folded his arms across the steering wheel and stared at the street. "There's a problem at the plant. It looks like someone is taking choice cuts of meat from the lockers."

"What does that have to do with Smiley?"

"He wants me to protect Larry's investment. I may have to fire someone, maybe even file charges."

Rista didn't understand how that involved Smiley but put her hand on Odis' shoulder, sorry that she had added to his burden.

▲▼▲

Before Odis fired anyone, America was at war. The draft and defense factories drew men out of the county. Odis had to hire two elderly men to slaughter, two women to butcher, and a crippled cowboy to run the locker. Paco was too old and had never registered, but it took Odis' intervention to get Pug deferred. Those on the board knew Odis, and both he and Stoddard were deferred as essential to the community.

Stoddard's report of irregularities at the locker was buried by war news, the relocation of Japanese Americans to detention camps, Odis' formation of militia to protect Red Rock from spies and saboteurs, and stories on the movie *Sergeant York*, the death of Charlie Christian and its effect on bebop, and Jimmie Davis of Louisiana who had campaigned for commissioner of public safety with his band and whose song, "You Are My Sunshine," was the favorite song of King George VI.

▲▼▲

The Rural Electrification Administration brought electricity to the ranch and new expenses—electric cookstove, washing machine, refrigerator, lights, and heat. Rista wondered why anyone wanted to go out at night when they had lights and a warm house, but most nights Odis had to meet with renters, investors, or patrol with the militia. Sometimes he took Cassie, leaving her at Brownie or 4-H meetings or to play with children who weren't always her friends. Rista thought Cassie should stay home more but used the time to work on cow count, hay count, feed bill, heifers bred, steers sold, debts, taxes, and income. Sometimes Cassie came home crying from fights with children she had been left to play with. Rista asked her to stay home, but Cassie said her father wanted her to go with him.

Rista thought rationing would shorten his stake rope, but Odis seemed to have plenty of gas coupons. He made Rista drive on the wrong side of the road to wear the tires evenly but when he had a blow-out, she had to borrow a tire to haul calves to market. When she drove to Red Rock she saw that someone whose son had been drafted had splashed yellow paint on her mailbox, an insult directed at draft dodgers.

For Christmas Rista gave Odis an Atwater-Kent radio. She could listen to the weather and stockyard reports, and Odis could listen to the war news. Instead, he and Cassie listened to country music. When she tried to get the weather reports last thing at night and first thing in the morning, he grumbled that it was his radio.

For his birthday she gave him a Victory Bond. It cleaned out the bank account but when the war was over, they could use it on a new truck. Odis cashed the bond the next week and by the time she learned of it, the money had disappeared. "If you had a dollar in one pocket and a skunk in the other, I don't know which one you would get rid of fastest," she said.

"When you have money you have to think up an excuse to spend it," he said. "I've scratched a poor man's ass my whole life, and I'm tired of it." He accused her of controlling everything, the ranch, the money, even the presents she gave him.

Rista admitted her fear of losing the ranch. Odis told her again how lucky he considered himself to be her husband. He couldn't run the ranch without her, but she didn't need him; that was why managing the locker was so important to him. Sometimes it took more time than he wanted to give it. Sometimes he had to invest more money, but working on the ranch with her he had no freedom, no money of his own. "It's hell when a grown man has to ask his wife if he can go to town." They held each other, frightened by their anger. It was the closest she had felt to him since she had borrowed money to invest in the locker.

A hailstorm killed most of her hens and cut the hide of the horses and cattle so that they bled. While Paco treated the horses, she and Pug plucked and cleaned the hens for the locker before riding out to check the cattle. Without the locker, the hens would have been a total loss.

There was a bad outbreak of screwflies. Rista wanted to bring infected animals to the horse trap so they could be treated every day but was too short handed; the war left few cowboys in the county. She, Paco, and Pug were in the saddle from first light until they could no longer see, roping the infected animals, getting the screwworms out with a wire and treating the wound with Smear 62 to keep the flies from laying more eggs, hoping it would work because there was no time to treat them again. Odis left the locker to run itself and rode with them. She had never been so proud of him, so certain she had married the right man.

The black preacher and some of his flock from Red Rock came to help with roundup. The preacher said if white Americans lost the war, so would black Americans, and Hitler hated blacks worse than white Americans did. With their help she was able to round up, castrate, ear mark, brand, and market. It took most of a week. The old men and boys worked with Rista, the women cooked; all of them slept on the ground.

One spring a messenger waited for her when she got home. Odis' brother, Mackie, who had enlisted in the army to provide for his family, had been killed in action, leaving a widow and two half-wild boys. The messenger wanted Rista to be there when he delivered the telegram. Rista left a note for Odis and left Cassie in Pug's care. While Gertie read and reread the telegram, Rista cooked supper for her and her boys. Later she lay in bed with Gertie and stroked her hair while Gertie cried. Where would she go? What would she do?

The next morning Odis and the neighbors came. A soldier told Gertie not to send money to people who claimed her husband owed them money or said that they had something to tell her about her husband but didn't have the money to come to her. Smiley said he would wait until Gertie got Mackie's G.I. insurance to collect Mackie's debts but that Gertie had to vacate the house at the end of the month. There was a housing shortage.

▲▼▲

When men came home from the war they wanted jobs, but most of them had wives or wanted wives and didn't want to sleep in a bunkhouse. One of them, a disabled hero whose wife worked at the locker, threatened Odis. Odis said it was because

257

the soldier wanted a job but Odis couldn't fire the crippled cowboy. Rista tried to talk to Odis, but he was trapped in his mind and scarcely heard her. He kept a pistol at the locker.

Two men went to Stoddard with stories that they had counted packages when putting meat in the locker and again when taking it out and choice cuts were missing. Odis told Stoddard he would investigate. He told Rista that he suspected the two women butchers and planned to replace one of them although she had children to support.

Sheriff Wilberg, who been a deputy with Odis, warned Odis that the locker's books were going to be subpoenaed and audited. That night the locker caught fire; the building exploded, starting fires that destroyed the entire block. Odis was arrested for theft and arson.

Rista went to see Odis in jail. Before she risked the ranch for bail, she demanded to know what happened.

"There must have been an ammonia leak. All it takes is a spark."

"Why did they arrest you?"

"Some of the employees had been stealing meat. Valton Hoffman wanted a grand jury to look into it. The fire destroyed the books. They can't prove who did it but Hoffman has to blame someone."

"The other investors will come to your defense?"

"They'll do what Smiley tells them."

That did not reassure her, but Rista bailed Odis out of jail. Odis bogged his head, ready to buck. Cassie cried every day because the schoolchildren said her father was a crook. Rista worked harder than ever. Fall came late and the screwworms were bad. Rista, Paco, and Pug spent every waking hour in the

258

saddle roping and treating infected cattle. Odis drove Cassie to school and spent the rest of the day looking for a job. Rista needed Odis on the ranch, but Odis needed to regain his hat size.

Although she needed to be in the saddle, Rista rode to town with Odis and Cassie. While they ran errands, she asked Smiley for a loan to pay for Odis' defense. Smiley refused. He had a lien on her property to pay for investment in the locker. The locker was now worthless. If Odis was found guilty of arson, he could not collect on his part of the insurance, and the bank would call its lien. She would also be liable for damages to the other property owners. "You have no collateral," Smiley said. "After your property is sold you'll still be in debt."

Rista had never been thrown this hard before. The locker was going to cost her everything she had been born to, everything she had worked for? That was more cud than she could chew. "Ride over it again," she said. "Slower this time. "

"The other buildings that burned were insured, but the owners will need loans to rebuild. Sign over the ranch to me, I'll extend the loans to the investors so they can keep the insurance money, and I'll make loans to the other property owners to rebuild in Claypool. The bank is also going to relocate in Claypool. Red Rock is dead."

Red Rock was too important to the history and people of the county to die. But she couldn't think about that now. "My folks are buried on that land. I plan to be buried with them." On her own land.

"Did you know Odis had a bank account in Claypool? You don't want your daughter learning things about her father at a trial."

Rista knew a lot of men were Brigham Young drinkers—two beers turned them into polygamists. She didn't believe Odis spent all those evenings talking to investors and selling bonds, but she didn't have time to camp on his trail. You couldn't grind sausage and worry about flies. Her greatest fear was that Cassie played with some soldier's children while Odis played with his wife. If Odis spent money on women while she repaid the loan on the locker, she would find it hard to forgive.

"Valton Hoffman might be persuaded to drop the charges since the evidence was destroyed in the fire," Smiley said. "I'm not sure Odis can get a fair trial. He has a lot of enemies."

"If I sign over the ranches to you, the charges will be dropped?"

"I might could arrange that."

"And the investors and property owners won't sue for damages?"

"You'll have no assets."

Rista left Smiley's office lower than a skunk's bunkhouse, but she had no intention of hanging up her rope. Smiley had always been careless with the statutes, with no more conscience than a horse in a rodeo. She went to Judge Gillin to see if Smiley was reading the scriptures or churning dust. Gillin was no longer a judge, but he knew the law. His house—Stoddard said it was "Folk Victorian"—hadn't changed since she had visited Lucinda. The judge came to the door, his shoulders hanging over his brisket as though he was unable to stand straight. When she told him of her conversation with Smiley, he looked like he had sat on his sombrero.

"Smiley picked the investors very well," Gillin said when they were seated in the parlor. "When the war came, rationing, more money than anyone had ever seen before, the investors had everything folks needed. Odis had meat, even on meatless

Tuesday. Arky Black had sugar, coffee, cigarettes. Larry operated a filling station after Smiley foreclosed when the owner was drafted and his pregnant wife could no longer run it. We traded among ourselves. Meat for cigarettes and nylons, gas for sugar and meat, cigarettes and meat for tires. Then we began trading with others."

"What did you trade?"

He tapped her knee with a gnarled hand. "When I discovered that Smiley had tricked Rufus Brown into signing papers he should not have signed, I expressed my disapproval to Smiley. Smiley engineered my defeat in the next election with the story of pornography in my office. I went to Stoddard's father, but there wasn't time to explain before the election. When the bank foreclosed on Brown's ranch, Slash 6 cowboys planned a disturbance at the sale to alert citizens to the way Smiley operated. Smiley put up money for the newspaper to bring a movie star to Red Rock to distract people with a parade."

"You must have hated Smiley."

"Smiley brought leaders to town to sell bonds." Rista remembered pictures of the judge with generals and politicians. "I entertained them with cigarettes, veal, wine, delicious desserts. Stoddard interviewed them. Smiley talked to them about depositing government money in his bank, land the government was planning to buy for camps or airfields. I was a leading citizen again. I hoped for an appointment that would restore my reputation, Lucinda's pride in me. If it was viewed as black marketing, war profiteering we would be ruined."

"Was Smiley involved in this?" If Smiley was involved he couldn't let Odis go to trial or she would kick the lid off this can of lies.

"Smiley made it possible. First with the loans, then with Larry offering to trade tires and gasoline for what the others had. Everything went smoothly until someone complained about meat missing from the locker. If that came out it would ruin us all. You sold beef."

Whether Odis set the fire or not, he had killed Red Rock. He had ruined his name, hers, Cassie's. Smiley, Judge Gillin, even Odis could roast in hell before she would sign over her ranch.

"What are you going to do?" Judge Gillin asked.

"I'm going to go home and lick a cow's ass to get the bad taste out of my mouth." She had never wanted to work with anything more complicated than a horse. Now she faced a dozen twisting cow trails through the brush, and she had to pick the right one. Impatiently she waited for Odis, but when he returned, Cassie was with him, and Rista did not want to talk in front of Cassie. When they got home, Odis stayed in the car. "I found someone who can give me an alibi when the locker burned," he said.

Rista had so much to say it got in her way. "I need to talk to you, and it's not about arson," she said.

"Then it can wait," he said, driving away.

Rista wanted to take a rope to him for being so stupid, for risking her and Cassie's love and all they worked for in order to shine in some woman's eyes. Some woman who meant less to him than a barren cow meant to her. She was furious but she set Cassie to fixing supper, then saddled a horse to help Paco and Pug treat animals with screwworms. She saw Pug riding to the house with his arm in his bandana. A cow had broken his arm. Odis had taken the truck so Rista took Pug to the bunkhouse

262

and wrapped his arm as best she could. "I can't sit in the bunkhouse and let them cows be eaten alive," he said.

"I'll shoot the ones that can't be saved," she said. "I don't know when I'll be back so I need you here to look after Cassie. Help her with supper if you can manage it." She returned to the house to get a pistol.

She rode off looking for infected animals, studying how she was going to save Odis, her good name, the ranch, and Red Rock. There was no way she could save them all. She treated a bull, three cows and had to shoot three calves with no time to salvage the meat. At dusk she found herself riding over land that had been her first adult responsibility, where alone she had tried to help a heifer deliver a calf, past the tank where she had rescued a bogged cow, where she had roped culls out of the herd—shelly cows, barren cows, those with hollow tail; where she and Pug had pulled the rods out of a well and figured how to get the windmill pumping without grownups to help. She and Pug had been starved and exhausted when they got back to the house, but the windmill was pumping water, and she believed she could handle whatever life had to offer, even selling her grandfather's house to pay a bank loan.

She was surprised to see a dim light from candles in the old bunkhouse. She sat on her horse, studying the light, trying to imagine who might be inside. She walked quietly, not wishing to disturb her grandparents' peace, and opened the bunkhouse door. She saw Odis and a young woman she didn't know cuddled naked on a new bed. A pretty box and silver wrapper lay on a night stand. The woman wore a new necklace that glittered in the candlelight.

"I need her," Odis said.

She raised the pistol and shot him in the head.

18
Sunday, 1990

I wasn't disappointed when Pug left after breakfast to work on a windmill, leaving me behind. But I was curious.

"Windmill was squeaking. Pug went to take the head off and add oil. You don't know nothing about windmills, and I don't have time to teach you. He'll be okay if the yellow jackets don't get after him," Rista said as we bumped across the pasture to check the cattle we had moved the day before. The sun shone warm out of a blue sky and drops of water glistened in the grass and on the trees. "Pug said I worked you too hard yesterday,"

"He's older than I am," I said ruefully. My leg was stiff and sore where I had hit the saddle horn.

"Pug will work hard the day he dies. By the grace of God, so will I. You're supposed to work until you die."

"What if you fell out here when you were all alone?"

"I'd get myself home, holler until Pug came and got me, or die where I was." She stopped the truck and looked at the cows peacefully grazing. "Times like this when the air is clear, the sky's blue and the cattle shine in the sun, the world is so pretty you know that God made manure so you'd know this wasn't Heaven.

"When you're trying to help a heifer have her first calf, or you're running your horse over rocks and gopher holes that can turn your horse head over heels and you under it, God is real. In church God is pretty, but He's not real. No more than John Wayne was a cowboy. It's play-like and it only works if everybody is willing to play-like."

Mother and I went to church only when she was dating a religious man. It didn't take, but I knew if Rista belonged to a church they would try to help her, even if that meant putting her in a nursing home. "Do you ever go to church?"

"I'm not a clubber. I wouldn't go to one of them churches that don't let you speak unless you're a man and wear a robe. In the Aginers Church, I've got a right to say what I have to say, but I don't exactly have an invitation to say it. The rest of them, they don't want to say anything. The world they live in—business and radio and TV—is so ugly, they're happy to hear pretty lies about how we love each other and how God loves us so much He's going to fry our enemies. That's okay when God saves your children and favors you above all others, but what do you do when God loves your enemies?"

It was easy to imagine Rista speaking in church and driving everyone else away. "So church should be as ugly as the rest of the world?"

"It should be as true. I've seen lightning storms that looked like God was licking the earth, tornadoes that would make an Episcopalian shout, rains that would make a Baptist dance. They're real and no matter how pretty they are or scared you are, you are also in awe."

"But if you were to get sick or hurt, church members would get a doctor?" One of them must have called me.

"People who believe in doctors are sick all the time. Your mama believed in doctors."

Mother was sick a lot, although mostly I think it was unhappiness that sent her to the drug store with a headache or to the doctor with stomach cramps. "I'd want to be in a hospital where people can care for me," I said. "I'd hate to lie out here in the dark with a broken back."

"The only dark I'm afraid of is the kind of dark where you can't care for yourself. I don't mind dying. I just don't want to be reduced to arteries and bones and symptoms. I've always been more than that, and I don't want to be lessened to it when I die. When you get old you start losing things. Your glasses, your memory, your strength. The last thing you have left is dignity, and they steal that and charge you for it."

"You remember the way things used to be, Rista. There are nice—"

"If you came to talk me into living with a bunch of old folks and watching TV, you can holster it. I don't need affection that doesn't come with a willingness to work. There's been too much of that already."

"I'm going to have to go home soon."

She kicked at the ground. We had stopped so she could check the grass. "Payout is slow on cows," she said. "Two to three years. Their hooves break up the soil, water and seed penetrate, grass grows. When a plant isn't grazed it loses palatability and nutritional value. The dead tops shade out new growth."

"Before I go I'd like to know you're some place safe."

She snorted. "The only safe place I know is the Bone Yard. I'm not ready to be safe."

When she finished with these cows, she drove to other pastures to check other herds. "That's one of my favorite cows," she said, pointing at a brindle cow with one horn turned

267

down toward its eye. The end of the horn had been sawed off. "She was a pretty heifer, dropped a lot of good calves. I reckon this is her last year. She's hamburger if I can keep her in good shape. Dog food if I can't. When her usefulness is gone, so is she. I don't know about you, but it's the same way with me."

I gave my life to sales, accounts receivable, depreciation, equipment failure, human error, expensive rush orders, specialized audiences, carry-over from the previous show, ad design, amortization, labor negotiations, department budgets, consolidated budget, salary scales, benefit plans, credit extension, community relations, the National Association of Broadcasters, rights, and the ratings book. With maybe a few years of pleasurable uselessness before I died.

When we got back to the house, we ate and Rista prepared a meal to take to Pug.

"Did you get the windmill fixed?" she asked him when she took his food to him.

"Did and done." While he ate, we worked on the fence. Rista gave me a pocketful of staples and a hammer, and I put in new staples where the old had popped out.

"Dammit," Rista said. The new staples pulled out of the rotten wood when she pushed on the wire. "These posts will have to be replaced."

"Didn't you just buy new posts?"

She gave me a look that would clabber milk. "When you got this many acres under fence you always need new posts," she said. "You can't always afford them. The telephone company that owns the Three Crosses brought in a crew that put their fence posts in upside down. They just brought in another crew to pull those and put in more new ones. Their customers were paying for it." Rista dragged out the fence posts she got in Claypool and drove off before I could join her.

Pug and I took turns digging holes and setting the new posts. "Be careful with this old wire," Pug said. The wire was rusted and brittle. "Unless you want to spend tonight listening to Rista talking poor mouth and spend tomorrow stretching new wire."

"I have to go to Claypool tonight. I'll eat in town," I said.

It was dark when we finished planting the new posts and tacking down the wire. I drove the rental car to Claypool, ate at a Dairy Queen, and went to the western wear and equipment store to call Shana. I left a message at her condo and called the station. Shana wasn't there but I got the usual laundry list of problems—complaints from viewers about a severe weather bulletin during a game show, complaints from a local dance group that we didn't cover their performance, a major client was going to Los Angeles and wanted tickets to network shows, we needed a better lead-in to the five o'clock news because the network rerun wasn't holding an audience, news was over budget because of on-the-scene coverage, program had camera operators in the studio and kept them there for fifteen minutes for a dry rehearsal. And Jerry wanted me to call.

Jerry had heard rumors that Shana was being promoted because she was sleeping with me. He had seen tapes of Shana diving into a pool and posing in a bikini. That was not the image he wanted for the station. I told Jerry that Shana and I were not sleeping together but were friends. I hoped the relationship would grow, but I feared she would soon leave for a bigger market. I denied that Shana was drunk and fell into a pool.

I called Shana and this time she answered. "Rista is beginning to trust me but I'll have to hog-tie her to get her off the ranch no matter what the accomodations," I told her.

"What are you going to do?"

What I didn't want to do was go home and have to come back next month, or three or four times before things were settled. "I don't know. She's not as strong as she pretends but she can still smooth a hill."

"Smooth a hill?"

"That must be something I heard my mother say."

"I never heard your mother say that."

Shana didn't really know Mother, by my design. From the time they met, Mother talked about grandchildren. That surprised me. Rista was right about Mother not liking children. She loved me but being followed around the house by a bunch of kids wasn't her idea of fringe benefits. Why did she want grandchildren? "I'll get back as soon as I can. Do we have a good line-up tonight?"

"I have the lead story. An interview with a serial killer. The murder rate is down, but you'd never know it from watching TV. They sent me to Atlanta to get the story."

"That's a good lead. What's the rest of the line-up?"

"We promote a network sitcom and air stories about a man with five children and no job looking for a wife, a woman abducted by aliens who impregnated her although DNA showed the baby was related to her husband's best friend, and a rock singer who has been visited by an angel that gave him a message from God to the world."

"That's a good stack."

"The message is that we should love each other. If God were going to send a message wouldn't you think it would be something new? Love each other? If we haven't heard that message by now, how is one more messenger going to convince us?"

"It's still a good story."

"The other station didn't think so. They're not going to air it."

"That should improve our numbers."

"Can't it be a good program if the producer, the director, the writer, the talent who created it did a good job?"

"A program is only as good as the number of people who view it."

"Chance, the serial killer told me things that didn't check out, but Carey blew the budget to get me there and didn't have the money for me to go back and re-do it. He's going to run it knowing that it's partly false. The first to show, the last to know. We're so eager to air it first that sometimes we air it before we know what it means or get it wrong."

"Why didn't you ca—I didn't have a phone. I'm sorry."

"I couldn't call you on something like that. That's why it doesn't work for me to work at the station and see you."

Here it came, a better offer from a bigger market. "Shana, we got your image wrong." I didn't tell her we'd have to change her hairstyle again.

"I don't want an image. I know who I am. I'm losing why I am."

"Why did you do those bikini stunts?"

"Carey said the station needed me, and I wanted to help. I thought it was what you wanted me to do. I hoped it would get your attention."

"You got everyone's attention, but we want something softer, friendlier for you. We'll let Bob Blaine continue with the first segment, the grabber, the hard news. You take the second segment with the human stories and the longer features on people making a difference."

"It's not just the news, Chance. We carried a network show where a man who wears his mother's underwear after she removes them is confronted by his mother live. I don't like people I admire regarding what I do with contempt. I don't want to die knowing I spent my life showing PR films disguised as news and reporting women impregnated by aliens."

Every sweeps showed that glitz and sleazoid got a good book, even on the news. "We are on the air twenty-four hours a day, 365 days a year. There will never be that much quality. We have to have quantity to balance quality shows that only a few people watch and that are hard to sell to ad agencies." Television was for the moment, not forever, but Shana couldn't deny its impact and not even Rista could escape its dominion.

"Maybe you should take television more seriously," Shana said.

I thought the media took themselves too seriously, although they showed little respect for each other. Newspapers portrayed movie and TV celebrities as media creations made stupid by money, sex, and drugs. In movies, newspaper reporters were brash, egotistical voyeurs whose power came from snooping, meddling, and tattling. Movies showed movie and TV talent as spoiled children throwing tantrums for attention and producers and directors as sociopaths seeking to pervert the principled. Gangsters were treated with more respect, homage paid to their honesty and courage. Only newspapers and TV news showed criminals as less than romantic heroes who took the law into their own hands because of corrupt government.

"Shana, we're all in the same competition—radio, television, books, sports, religion, movies, magazines—we compete for people's time."

"Doesn't that bother you? Competing with their children, their spouses, gardens, pets, their prayers, their thoughts. I've done some bad things, but I pray I've never kept a child from looking at the moon."

"That's a choice children make. And we give them a better view of the moon than they'll get outside. I learned a lot from TV."

"Public TV. All you learned from commercial TV is what you wanted for Christmas and which breakfast cereal had the most sugar. Don't you think the information the public has on the private lives of citizens and insights into soap opera and sitcom characters is really ignorance?"

Shana was beginning to sound like Rista. "Maybe you should work in public or educational TV. Their programs are the end product. Our programs are means to an end, a product to sell a product."

"I don't want to work in TV. I thought it was a place where women had a voice. We don't have much of a voice in politics and even less in religion. But I don't want to cover trivia. I don't want to pretend grief over genuine misfortune. I don't want to be a pretty face with a sickroom smile. I don't want to be a created image—"

"What do you want?"

"I want to be your wife. I want to be the mother of your children. I want to contribute to a community, not be a celebrity for reading stories about those who do contribute. I'm sorry, Chance. I wanted to discuss this face to face but you asked. If

273

I can't be your wife and the mother of your children, then I need to look elsewhere."

"Shana, being a parent requires more time than I have right now."

"Talk honest or don't talk."

"I don't know any happy families, Shana. Kids come with a lot of pain, and I don't mean childbirth. You give up your freedom when you have children, your life."

"I am taking classes to be a child advocate. If I can speak for the station, if I can sell stories about a pop star who urinates on the city monument, why can't I do it for something I believe in?"

"That's good, Shana. You can mention the children on the show; we can tape you speaking for the children wherever you speak."

"I am not exposing the children on TV. I don't want to be something you can promote. It was fun at first, trying on different styles, different images. I'm tired of the masquerade. I know what I want. You don't have a father role model. I've thought a lot about that. I'm willing to chance that you can learn. This is not an ultimatum. But if our relationship continues, this will be the path it takes. Take as much time as you need in Texas. I'll wait until I see you to ask for an answer."

After we said goodbye, I walked outside and sat in the car. Shana had everything—intelligence, integrity, curiosity, health, judgment, looks. Everything but dedication. She didn't want wings; she wanted little feet running to trouble, little hands leaving marks on her mind. I didn't want to lose Shana, but I also didn't want to lose focus on the rest of my life because some kid was in trouble, or could be in trouble or might get into trouble if I worked late. I wouldn't be happy without Shana, and I would never be safe with her.

I was startled from my thoughts by a rap on the window. It was the lawyer I had talked to my first day in Claypool.

"I have a buyer," he said. "It's a solid offer, more than you can get from anyone else." I waited. "I'd rather not say who it is."

I had dealt with lawyers before, ad agencies, labor unions, egotistical talent. "Then I need another lawyer."

"The name of the buyer is confidential."

I started the car. He didn't move. "Is it the telephone company?" He nodded. "I don't have a power of attorney."

"They'll help you. They have very good connections at court. They think your grandmother could be provoked into actions that would get her committed for observation or for offenses."

That would work; she would kill me and some of them. She would go to jail before she would give up control of the ranch. "If they take action without my approval I will look for another buyer."

"They understand that. They want you to view them as your friends."

"You mean accomplices?"

"They said friends."

I wasn't ready to answer Shana's questions, but I needed to get back to the station. I needed to talk to Shana. I had a buyer, but I didn't have a seller. I didn't want to get in that saddle until it was on the horse.

▲▼▲

I got lost on the ranch roads before I found the road with the barricade. Then I got a flat trying to negotiate the trail around the barriers to the house. When I got to the house I looked at the tires. Only one was flat, so far. At home I would have called the auto club but here there was no telephone and if there were I couldn't tell them where I was. Rista waited past her bedtime for me.

"I wasn't sure you were coming back," she said when I went inside.

"My clothes are here."

"I'd have sent them to you if I had your address."

I'd been afraid of angering her before, of being cut out of her will as she faded to black. It didn't matter much anymore. "Rista, are you willing the ranch to me?"

"I promised your mother."

"Mother is dead."

"I'm not, and neither is my promise. You're my only heir."

Is that why Mother wanted grandchildren? Someone to saddle the ranch with? Or was it blind instinct women could do nothing about? Reproduce or be hamburger. "You don't even like me. You don't approve of the way I dress, the way I live. You don't approve of the work I do."

"You're family. I don't have to approve. I love you."

I was so startled I made an involuntary sound. Something between a gasp and a laugh. I had heard those words from two people—Mother and Shana. "What does Pug get?"

"He's on the payroll until he's paid in full, and he has a grave in the Bone Yard."

We stared at each other for a moment. "Okay, Rista, " I relented. "What do you want from me?"

"I want you to call me Grandmother. And I'd like a civil tongue when you say it."

19

1946

Her ears ringing from the shot, her nose burning from the acrid smell of gunpowder, Rista watched the screaming woman scramble off the bed and back into a corner, more afraid of Odis' body quivering on the bed than Rista's pistol. Rista told her to put on her clothes, then picked them up and threw them at her. "Get dressed. How are you going to get back to town?" The woman looked at her, as stupid as a cow in a loading chute. "Get in the truck. I'll take you to Red Rock. You can call someone."

Rista threw the saddle and bridle into the back of the truck and turned the horse loose, hoping she beat it home so she didn't cause any worry. She drove to Red Rock, let the woman out and sent the doctor to look at Pug's arm before going to Sheriff Wilberg's home. "Odis has been shot," she said.

"Don't say any more," he said. "Where will I find him?"

"My grandfather's place. In the bunkhouse."

"Alone?"

"Yes."

"You go home and stay there until I come get you. Is that the pistol he was shot with?"

"Yes."

"Better give it to me. Can you drive? Go straight home."

It was late when she got home, and she went to the

bunkhouse to see how Pug was. The doctor had put a cast on his arm. Paco was looking after him. "Odis is dead," she said. Both of them looked at her but asked no questions.

"Do you want me to tell Cassie?" Paco asked. Paco had been family elder since Claris had died.

"I'd better," Rista said. Cassie was almost twelve but emotionally dependent on her father. He had let her sit on his lap and drive the truck.

Rista sat on Cassie's bed and gently woke her. "Wake up, Cassie, there's something I have to tell you. Cassie, your father is dead."

"What? What?" Cassie said, pushing her away.

"Your father is dead."

Cassie curled away from her and began to cry. "No, he's not. I want to sleep."

Rista tried to hold Cassie, but Cassie sprang from the bed. "My father is not dead. I want to see him."

"You can't see him. Not now." She wondered if Cassie would ever be able to see him, if I. P. Rainwater could fix the hole in his face. "I'll take you to see him when Mr. Rainwater says it's okay. Do you want to talk?"

"I want to be alone. Why did you have to tell me?"

"I'll be in the sitting room," Rista said. She made a pot of coffee and took it into the sitting room, thinking how she would explain it to her daughter. She didn't want Cassie to find out from someone else. She did not want to go into the bedroom she had shared with Odis.

The next day Sheriff Wilberg and Valton Hoffman, the district attorney, came to see her. "Leland Gray didn't show up for work this morning," Wilberg said. "We think he and Myrna left town. We don't know where they went. We think she may be a witness to what happened last night, but she's not likely to want to testify. There are a lot of people who had a reason to shoot your husband, including himself, but none of them are suspects. If we dig into this we're likely to uncover a mess we don't want to get into. Red Rock is not big enough for us to let this grow."

"Red Rock has a lot of problems right now with the fire, people moving to Claypool, and talk of moving the county seat," Hoffman said. He looked like a bulldog with skin hanging all over him. "We don't need a scandal that would hurt a lot of good citizens."

"We've known you all your life. We're going to present this to the grand jury as a suicide," Wilberg said.

"Let me chew that a little finer," Hoffman said. "You walk the straight and narrow and the less folks see and hear of you, the better."

"What did they want?" Cassie asked when they left.

If Ralph and Valton said it was suicide, then it was suicide. Cassie never needed to know her mother had shot her father. "Cassie, your father shot himself."

"No. No, he didn't. My father never hurt anybody." Cassie locked herself in her room, but Rista could hear her through the wall.

▲▼▲

Rista understood horses and cows. She didn't know how to deal with Cassie who sulled and pouted and tracked guilt into every room. All mane and tail, Cassie had never broken to the bit but was bull necked, tender hided, and pail fed. She was also quick to smile and when she ducked her head and looked at her ear, she was so fetching that her father gave in to every wile. Rista had wondered if he would give her up to another man.

Cassie came home one day and said, "Mama, Peggy said Daddy killed himself so he didn't go to jail."

Rista pulled the sobbing girl into her arms. It had been a long time since Cassie had let Rista hold her, but Rista had dreaded this moment. "We don't know exactly what happened. Some bad people wanted him to take the blame for some bad things, but your father wasn't going to jail. I wouldn't have let that happen. Try to remember him the way he was. Remember the time you told Daddy you had an imaginary friend and he asked her name, and you said, 'She doesn't have a name; she's imaginary'?"

Cassie laughed a little and then cried some more. "I want my daddy. Not the one with the pistol. I want the one in the picture with me. No one will ever love me like Daddy did."

"You're going to marry a man who loves you and wants to spend all his time looking at you and making you laugh," Rista promised.

Cassie did not like ranch work and had a talent for incompetence. Her father did not make her gather eggs because she was afraid of the hens or milk because she was afraid the cow would kick her. She didn't have to work horseback because she never learned to ride well. Rista made her help with meals, but she didn't have to cook by herself because she never learned to plan meals. When Rista made her wash dishes, mugs were broken. When Rista told of working from sun-is to sun-ain't for fifty cents, Cassie said, "You were poor. I'm not poor and I'm not going to work like that."

Smiley kept Odis' share of the insurance as payment for the locker loan. Stoddard used the insurance money from the Red

Rock newspaper to buy the Claypool newspaper. He wrote great obituaries. It made Claypool a good place to die, but he did it because the radio could only announce the funeral giving folks nothing they could clip and frame. The fire was no longer news except to Red Rock denizens who kept grudges like others kept Sabbath. Suicide disgraced the whole caboodle, especially when committed to escape punishment. Because Odis had ridden death out of town, that left no one to punish but his family.

Rista steered clear of Red Rock, which was being deserted by those who had escaped the fire. She sent Cassie to school on the bus. Most of Cassie's friends had moved to Claypool. The other students fulfilled their parents' wishes by shaming and jeering her. "What kinds of birds are there?" "Redbirds, black-birds, and jailbirds." "How many sides does life have?" "The right side, the wrong side, and suicide." Cassie hated school and wanted to quit, but Rista would not let her. Cassie hid in her room, reading a mail-order catalog, dreaming of what she would have—pretty dresses, rings and bracelets, a real bathtub with a mirror.

▲▼▲

Rista checked fences in a new pickup dragging a gooseneck trailer. She had trailered Pug and Paco and their horses to Comanche Peak. In Fort Hoggard, she saw a horse with poll evil, roped and loaded it, and took it to the corral to pen up and treat. Stoddard's car was in front of the house.

Stoddard had come to tell her that Truman had beaten Dewey to everyone's surprise. Cassie entertained Stoddard who was charmed by her. Cassie was willowy like her mother but not so tall. Stoddard told Cassie of the entertainers he had met—Tex Ritter, Jimmy Wakely, Ernest Tubb—before taking Rista for a

281

drive. "Your daughter is going to be a beauty like you," he said. "I never found anyone I loved as much as you. I hope you'll give me another chance, Rista."

It had been two years since Odis' death, and Stoddard's hands felt so good, his kisses were so wild, so precipitate that she made love to him in the car. "Don't take me home right away," she said. "I don't want Cassie to see me like this, all flushed and happy."

"I love to see you like that. Looking at me the way you are now."

"Let's walk for a little," she said. They walked arm and arm over her land, and she had in her grasp everything she wanted.

Stoddard came to see her often. He took her to a jazz concert. The music was all right for a while and then the musicians got in a race to see who could finish first. The man playing the horn finished before the others and stood to the side smiling, pleased with himself while everyone applauded. Everyone but Rista.

Stoddard invited her to parties. She met politicians and the horses they hoped to ride—women who wore their worth on their fingers and necks and men who talked of oil, insurance companies, and veterans' landholdings. Rista watched Stoddard swell with their importance.

Stoddard wanted her to drop her work and go with him to photograph a flooding river, an oil-well fire, the world's largest hog, to listen to a speech by Judge Sarah Hughes who could not serve on a jury because she was a woman. "Why would a woman want to serve on a jury?" Stoddard asked her. "Men don't want to."

Rista would not make love to him in her house because of Cassie. He did not like making love under a tree, in his car, or in the back of her truck. For a few hours with Stoddard, Rista had to miss half a day's work driving to Claypool.

Stoddard lived in a large, two-story white house with columns, stained glass windows, and upstairs and downstairs galleries. Rista always drove to the back of the house, out of the sight of neighbors, and entered a back door into the kitchen. On her first visit, Stoddard showed her his autograph collection—Ma Ferguson, Governor W. Lee O'Daniel, Billy Sunday, former Miss America Jo-Carroll Dennison from Tyler, Ranger Frank Hamer, All-America footballer Dick Todd, and his proudest possession, a signed photograph of Clyde Barrow and Bonnie Parker.

Stoddard led her across the parquet floors of the large parlor and dining room that were sparsely but elegantly furnished for entertaining. Stoddard entertained her in the large upstairs bedroom with the bay window and four-poster bed.

One afternoon as they lay indolently against his pillows, she said, "A telephone company bought the Three Crosses."

"They've owned it for three years," Stoddard said smugly. He liked people to believe he knew everything.

"Why didn't you report it?"

"News is what will sell an ad."

"Stoddard, they bought the ranch as a tax dodge. They use it to entertain politicians who protect their monopoly and regulators who set their rates. They bring in women to entertain judges and legislators. They buy exotic animals for them to shoot—buffalo, elk, an old circus bear so tame they fed him by hand, just so the governor could shoot him and hang his hide in the governor's mansion. Doesn't any of that bother you?"

"It bothers me but it's legal."

"They want to put telephone poles across my ranch although

they are there only on the weekend. Every time the line goes down they want to come on my property and repair it."

"That's great," Stoddard said. "You can have a telephone at a fraction of what you would have to pay for a line out to your ranch."

"I'm going to court to stop them."

"Take whatever they pay for the right of way across your property and be glad you got it. There is no way you can win in court. If you did, they would appeal until you ran out of money, and they'd own your ranch."

A lawyer had told her the same thing. "Where do poor people get justice?"

"When poor people run the country, poor people will get justice. Then they'll be the only ones who do."

"They have a swimming pool, fountains, a greenhouse, tropical trees—Six Mile Draw has gone dry. They waste more water than I use. They have an airstrip, paved roads that funnel water into the draw so that when it rains, my pasture floods."

"Have you been to the Three Crosses?"

"Someone shot one of my cows across the fence; I went over there to find out who it was. Stoddard, because it's legal doesn't mean it's right."

"It's the way business is done."

"You could expose the way they do business. You could take a stand for farmers and ranchers and citizens who don't have a voice."

"Farmers and ranchers are moving to town. Red Rock is a vacant lot. The future is business. The newspaper is a business like any other, and if I don't support them, they won't support me."

With the insurance money from the fire, he could have gone where he wanted, written what he wanted. He bought the Claypool newspaper.

"Stoddard, did you know that Rufus Brown thought he was paying off his loan on the Slash 6 when he was buying into Smiley's gambling club that Odis shut down?"

"I was going to look into it, but there were so many other things—"

"Like a movie star coming to town."

"That was something, wasn't it? Smiley and I did that. The only movie star that ever came to Red Rock."

Rista could feel her saddle slipping. She disentangled herself from Stoddard. Every time she stuck out her neck for him to smear a loop on, he threw the rope in her face. "Did you know that Odis was taking food from the lockers?"

"I knew that whole locker bunch was involved in some shady stuff."

"But you didn't report it."

"Do you know how much investigation that would require? If it were official corruption I would have editorialized about it, but you can't do that with business. I'd have been sued and even if I won, the lawsuit would have cost me a lot of money. Other businesses would move their ad dollars to the radio station, and that would be the death of the newspaper."

She had used all her kindling and still didn't have his fire going. "Stoddard, you don't have enough grit for an egg sandwich."

"If they tried to interfere with freedom of the press—"

"Why would they interfere when you write what they want you to write? You don't have the guts of a pissant."

"Is that the kind of newspaper you want me to print? Expose everyone? Report that you killed your husband?"

Rista faltered like a buffalo, not knowing whether to run or fight. Stoddard pulled her back beside him. "Rista, I'm glad he's dead. I would never betray you. If you don't see that as courage, I'm sorry."

She always parted from Stoddard with question marks while he believed sex was the only punctuation needed. News was whatever sold ads? What business allowed? If she couldn't trust the information she received, what could she trust? Outsiders had bought the Three Crosses and turned off the water supply for her cows, and Stoddard said it was none of her business. A lawyer in Claypool told her the same.

Stoddard knew she shot Odis, and he could have turned Red Rock into a lynch mob. She wondered what else Stoddard knew and why he didn't tell. He seemed as shallow as a coyote's grave, but he was a powerful and dangerous man. Almost as powerful and dangerous as Smiley Wooten.

A few days later, Rista received a check from the telephone company paying her more than market value for the cow a judge shot. They also sent a warning that they would prosecute if she trespassed on their property or tampered with the game-proof fence they were erecting. Rista swore she would never own a telephone.

▲▼▲

Stoddard invited her to Dallas where he was to attend the state fair, interview a young actor named Dana Andrews, and attend a party with the governor and perhaps a congressman. They would eat in fine restaurants, stay in the best hotel, have a week to themselves. She deserved to have some fun, he said.

The day she was to meet Stoddard, Paco was unable to leave the bunkhouse. Paco rarely rode anymore, but he checked pastures, cattle, and water from the truck, picked up eggs, repaired the corral, fixed the screen door. Rista enjoyed seeing him sitting in the sun mending tack and oiling the saddles.

Rista went to the bunkhouse. Paco had a hard time breathing. He did not want to go to the hospital; he wanted to die at home. He wanted Pug to receive any money she owed him.

Angry that she had not met him at the train station, Stoddard drove out to get her. She told him she could not leave Paco. "Take him to the hospital. They can take care of him and we can go."

"He doesn't want to go to the hospital."

"Are you going with me or not?"

Rista looked at him in his slicked-up clothes and California shoes, looking like a pink pretty the way Brownfield used to dress him. She was ashamed at what he had become. When he drove away she didn't know if she would ever see him again. Or cared.

Pug put Paco in a chair and dragged it outside because Paco wanted to sit in the sun. "I'll take your money to your village, just the way you said," Pug said.

"I want you to have it," Paco said. "Buy a pickup. Paint it purple. Every time you pass my grave, honk. Say, 'Get up, Paco. Time to shake a bush.'"

When Paco could no longer talk, Rista held his hand, and Pug sang his favorite songs until he no longer heard and his fingers slipped from her grasp.

▲▼▲

Rista needed a hand to replace Paco, but there were few cowboys left and most of them were married and wanted a house for

287

their family. That would leave Pug alone in the bunkhouse. Pug met a high-school dropout who needed a job.

Shad Carter had no experience with cattle, but he could ride; he had no horse but had a pickup. Pug was thirty-five and willing to train a younger man to do the running, chasing, climbing, picking up, throwing, and shoveling. Shad moved into the bunkhouse, parking his old pickup beside Pug's new purple one. Rista shook her head at the three trucks in her yard. She had been reduced to nursemaiding cows and storing horses.

Shad got along well with Pug, and he didn't mind chores and errands. He drove his own truck to town to get the mail, groceries, human and stock remedies, and returned with news of Axis Sally and Tokyo Rose going to prison, the Nationalist Chinese government fleeing to Formosa, the Soviet Union exploding an atomic bomb. Cassie had turned fourteen, had a driver's license, and drove Rista's truck to school.

Mackie's body was sent home six years after the end of the war. His widow had remarried; his children were grown. Rista was the only family left to meet the train in Claypool. Stoddard was there with a camera to report the burial. The train was two hours late, and, as it was a rainy day, they sat in his car. "They say it rains when a good man dies," Rista said. It had rained when Odis was buried, a frog strangler of a rain that ended a drought and set the Aginers to shouting and praising God.

"There must not be many good men in Texas," Stoddard said. He talked of *All About Eve* and *Born Yesterday*.

Stoddard was in his early forties, and Rista thought him more mature. He still looked like the mercantile dressed him, only now every issue of Stoddard's paper carried a two-page ad of Claypool fashions. Stoddard looked at her church dress, the blue dotted Swiss she bought for the pioneers' reunion and wore to weddings and funerals, but said nothing.

Stoddard agreed with Senator McCarthy that communists had infiltrated the government. He believed that without McCarthy Truman would not have sent troops to Korea and military advisors to Vietnam. Rista didn't know where Korea or Vietnam were, but she hoped Shad wasn't drafted; she needed him. She was surprised by Stoddard's belligerence.

"It's the radio station," he said. A preacher on a popular radio show denied Hitler killed Jews, declared that God intended blacks to be servants, and threatened to expose communist teachers in public schools. "If I exposed him I'd look like a communist myself. Judge Gillin called him on the air to rebuke him, and the preacher called him a fellow traveler. The judge got so confused he began talking about someone named Izzie."

"Izzie was a black man who was hanged because a mob wanted to lynch someone."

"Oh, yeah. He was found hiding in the women's bath at the hotel and had raped several white women."

"Stoddard, that was the story they made up to escape the law."

"I'm pretty sure I read that in the newspaper files."

Rista and Stoddard followed the hearse to the Red Rock cemetery in Stoddard's car. Stoddard took photographs and the American Legion did its job although she jumped every time they fired. On the drive back to Claypool, Stoddard confessed that he had sworn he would never see her again after the state fair. "I tried, Rista. I can't stay away from you. I can't be happy with anyone else."

Rista wondered how she could love a dime-bucker who

reared, pawed, twisted his tail, swapped ends, and never went anywhere. She went home with Stoddard although she had to leave early to pick up Cassie from school.

▲▼▲

"Hold your hat," Stoddard said. "*Desperate* is coming to Claypool and so is Lachelle Tremayne."

"Who is Lachelle Tremayne?"

Stoddard indulged her with a smile.

The story of the movie was more interesting than the picture. Velma Mayfield had been an alcoholic at fourteen, a prostitute at fifteen, a drug addict and pornographic film star at sixteen. The producer of *Desperate* discovered Velma when she came to his house as a call girl, married her, changed her name to Lachelle Tremayne and cast her in his next film. Lachelle fell in love with the leading man and left the director to live with the actor. The actor was arrested after Lachelle was hospitalized with stab wounds. Lachelle went back to the producer who saw potential in casting her and the actor as lovers in the film version of a hot new book his studio had acquired.

"They wanted the character to be bouncy, breezy, and beautiful like me. It was easy. I've been me for a long time," Stoddard had quoted Lachelle as saying.

"She's famous for playing a whore when she is a whore?" Rista asked.

After the movie, Stoddard took Rista to a party at Smiley Wooten's bank to meet Lachelle, who was tough enough to hunt rattlesnakes with her nose. Stoddard tried to interview her, but she shunned him like a polecat in the privy.

Rista missed the next party because she had to scatter hay to dry it after a rain and then restack it. After promising to spend the night with him, she left a party early because of a torrential rain. She knew the water gaps would be washed out and needed to be replaced or the stock would scatter. That meant she and the hands had to be in the trucks with fencing equipment, and saddled horses in the trailer, before daylight.

Stoddard was frustrated but patient. Rista slipped into his house through the back door when she could, but she liked it best when he came to the ranch and they rode together or drove around in the truck checking the pastures. He rarely had time for that. He had a newspaper to run.

Stoddard asked her to marry him. They were in his car parked in the shade of an oak motte. "Cassie is almost grown. She doesn't like living on the ranch; she never has. You don't want to live out here by yourself."

Rista was surrounded by the things that made life precious to her—horses, cattle, the land, the water, the sky, the graves. "Stoddard, I could never live any place but here. I would be miserable. I would make you miserable."

Stoddard was silent a long time before conceding. "You can live on the ranch, and I'll drive to Claypool every day. I'll have to have a telephone. I'll have to stay in town some. There are people I'll need to entertain. Maybe we could fix your place up, and we could bring them out here."

"Stoddard, I don't fit in. I don't want to hear about movies and fashions. They don't want to hear that I had a sick horse and drenched it with Harlem Oil and Watkins colic dope. That I found a cow with bloat, roped her, tied a stick in her mouth, left her for an hour and she got okay. That the cure for milk fever is to take a tire pump and fill the cow's bag with wind. That's all I know."

"You ask me to give up everything for you, and you give up nothing."

"I can't fold into your dream. I wish I could. I love you, but I can't be your play pretty. This may be all we ever have."

"I need someone to entertain people I invite to my house— the mayor, the governor, entertainers. Have you ever used the album I gave you?"

"You make idols of those people. Think who you're celebrating."

"People make them idols," Stoddard said. "I help them worship what they idolize. I guess in that sense I'm a priest."

"You're not a priest; you're a pimp. Folks don't idolize them, no more than a cow idolizes its cud. It's something God gave a cow instead of a dream box. He must've done the same with some people."

"I'm sorry I didn't know your opinion of me sooner. I wouldn't have kept you from your cows." Stoddard wore the magisterial look that she disliked, the look he never wore for politicians, entertainers, or advertisers but reserved for readers and for her. "I didn't realize murderers were so idealistic."

Rista got out of the car and walked to the house. Stoddard drove around her without looking back.

▲▼▲

Rista found a horse with the strangles and came to the house to ask Cassie to get the vet. Cassie was in bed with Shad. "Pick up your bedroll," Rista ordered Shad.

"You can't order him off the ranch; he's my husband."

"Cassie, you're sixteen years old."

"We got married in Mexico," Cassie said, proud of her deceit. Rista had sent Shad to deliver a horse; Cassie had played hookey from school.

"I'm sorry, Mrs. Wyler," Shad said, clutching the sheet about him. "We . . . I got carried away. I thought it was the right thing to do."

"What do you plan to do now?" Rista asked.

"I'd like to work for you," Shad said. "And move into the house with Cassie if that's agreeable."

"You can move into the house if Cassie agrees to finish school and if she gets up and fixes breakfast," Rista said.

Cassie cut her a look that took the nap off her Stetson but Shad agreed.

Shad moved into the house leaving Pug alone in the bunkhouse. Rista asked him if he wanted to move into the house also; there was a spare bedroom. "Cassie and her husband would always be there."

"I wouldn't feel right sleeping in the big house," Pug said. "I'd be as out of place as a politician in the poorhouse."

Cassie fixed breakfast before going to school, but Shad helped with supper because Cassie had something at school almost every night. Rista was pleased that Cassie had friends after her rejection in Red Rock, but it troubled her that Cassie was so like her father, shunning life on the ranch for the lights and noise of town.

"You're married now," Rista said. "You need to stay home with your husband."

"I hate it here," Cassie said. "When I finish high school I'm leaving."

Rista thought otherwise. She recognized that look in Shad's eyes. He was at home with the horses and cattle, and he dreamed of the day the ranch would belong to him and Cassie. Watching him, Rista felt content. The land would belong to her

293

grandchildren. If Cassie got pregnant she would feel the same ties that Rista and Shad felt.

20
Monday, 1990

"I changed your tire," Pug said when he came to breakfast. He had also gassed up both pickups from the storage tank. "I'll fix the flat later."

"It's a rental car. Let them fix it," I said.

"I can fix flats," Pug said, as though I doubted it. "Hell, I spend more time fixing flats than I do branding cows."

"Tell him about the time you had a flat," Rista said.

Pug looked up sheepishly, and they smiled at each other. "I got drunk, had a flat on the way home. Changed it. Got back in the car and started off again. I had changed the wrong tire."

After breakfast, Pug climbed on the barn roof to replace shingles that had blown off. "I think we better work around the barn while he's up there," Rista said. She got a bucket and tossed me a coiled rope. "Practice your roping while I call in the horses."

"I'm not going to have to rope anything am I?" I asked. I had learned all the cowboy skills I wanted.

"You used to be a good roper," she said. She put feed in the horse stalls and whistled, called, and banged on the bucket. While the horses came in, Rista told me she had bought me my first boots, taught me to ride, had given me a rope to practice with. "You chased a calf around the corral most of a morning to get your rope on it and when you did, the calf dragged you

295

around but you wouldn't let go because it was the first one you had roped. Get those burrs out of the horses' tails," she said. "Work them out, don't cut them."

While I pulled cockleburs from the horses' tails, she lifted their feet and inspected their hooves. "These shoes need to be reset. It gets harder every time." I thought she was going to ask me to do it. "I'll do a couple. Maybe Pug can do the rest when he gets done with the roof. You don't remember roping and riding?"

Mother didn't reinforce those memories, but something stirred. "I think I remember. Kind of. A cow was mad but you said you'd watch it."

She got a pair of nippers and a rasp and, holding the horse's foot between her knees, cut and filed the hoof, then fitted and nailed a shoe to it. When she finished she grimaced as she straightened her back and stretched her knees. "The calf's mother was wall-eyed outside the fence. You were scared until I told you I'd get inside the corral with you. You forgot about the cow after that, no matter how much it pawed and shook its horns."

When she finished shoeing the second horse, Rista took the rope I had hung on the fence, formed a loop and tossed it over the snubbing post in the center of the corral. "Houliann," she said. "This is an ocean wave." She flipped the rope so that the loop undulated. She showed me a "butterfly," with the loop spinning on first one side and then the other, a "wedding ring" with the loop spinning around herself and "star gazing," spinning the rope around her body, slowly sitting, then lying on her back and still spinning. It didn't look difficult to me. I was embarrassed at her efforts to impress me; I was more concerned with the bruise on my thigh. Would it lead to cancer?

"I could have been a champion roper," she said. "Papa said,

296

'Ranch first, rodeo second.' There was never time for second. I could have won money during the war. That's when women got to rodeoing, but Odis wouldn't hear of it, and I couldn't leave Cassie alone. I did enter some jackpot roping contests. The men liked me putting money in the pot, but after I took the pot a couple of times they refused to compete with me. Odis said it embarrassed him, so I gave it up."

"Did you ever wish you were a man?"

"Only time I wished I was a man was when my horse cut its leg. We used urine to stop the bleeding. That was no problem for the cowboys, but I had to pee in my hat and pour it on the wound."

"Do you regret that you were never given a chance at the rodeo?"

"Most of the regrets I have are for things I prayed for. I thought that oil money was the answer to my prayers. We paid off the note on the ranch and bought a pickup. Odis might have been different if it hadn't been so easy to get to town—the pickup and the lease money and the roads all coming together."

If she could have kept Mother and Odis on the ranch she would have been queen of the rodeo. "That's all you regret?"

She flipped the rope off the snubbing post and recoiled it. "I regret what shooting Odis did to your mother. When she found out, she lost who she was. She didn't know whether she was supposed to drag her rope like her daddy, shoot anyone who dallied with her like her mother or be a misfortunate that folks should feel sorry for."

Mother was all three, and maybe some more people besides.

"Folks were so sure she was tangle footed that they convinced her. When I was a kid, everybody knew windmills, fences, screwworms and told other folks how to fix it. When you

297

were a kid, everybody knew psychology and what was wrong with everybody else. Folks didn't study nature or themselves, they read magazines that told them what they were supposed to be like, and anyone who wasn't a black baldy wasn't a cow. What was wrong with you was what was wrong with America, and newspapers said America was no longer liked. What was missing in your home was what was missing in American homes, and the TV said it was commotion, and they gave you plenty of that. Kids were all cut from the same leather and folks were to punch the holes all the same. Spend a day with cows and you know it took a lot of money to sell that lie."

Rista blamed everything on the media because only the media punished her for murder, and the media didn't recognize double jeopardy, clemency, or pardon.

"You ruined my mother's life."

"I reckon I ruined a lot of lives. And a lot of folks ruined mine if I want to think of it that way. Cassie, Odis, Stoddard, you, Rusty, the oil company, the telephone company. Or maybe I chose my own trail and rode it into a corner. Cassie made her choices. I know you don't like me talking about your mother, but you got a right to know what she was like, and I got a right to love her no matter what she did."

"Love her for what she did? What about what you did?"

"I'd rather had my daughter than all this land and everything on it. But she was never mine. Holding her was like trying to catch a minnow with a hay hook. Land you own. Children are on loan from God." She swung the rope over her head and dropped a big loop that seemed to turn over the snubbing post. "Blocker loop. You'll understand this when you have kids of your own—children are cannibals. They eat your days and return them to

298

you as a life, or they don't return them at all." She built another loop and again roped the snubbing post.

"Cassie burned the wagon when she left. I didn't know who she left with or where she had gone. I asked around Claypool, although it shamed me. I hired private detectives. They told me where you were. They didn't tell me Cassie was dying." She flipped the rope off the snubbing post and coiled it. "I admired Cassie's daring in going so far from home, but I always thought she would come back."

"You killed her father."

"And it cost me more than I could afford. I'm still paying on it. I can't abide you blaming me for what happened to your mother."

"Was the second killing easier than the first?"

"I knew about the nights I would wake up reliving that scene. The times I would be alone in the pasture and hear Odis' voice. I knew about packing silence when I wanted to yell. Hearing Cassie crying herself to sleep. I always thought I would have a chance to tell her."

"You shot Stoddard anyway."

"Brother Bob was working roundup when the O-Bar and the Slash 6 both claimed a young bull. Dan Beasley and Rufus Brown exchanged words over it, their cowboys sided up, and Dan and Rufus looked for guns. Brother Bob got the two to pray with him, and while they were praying he sent a cowboy after whiskey. He gave the whiskey to Beasley and while Dan was cooling his saddle under a shade tree, Brother Bob bought the calf from Rufus, put it with the O-Bar herd and everyone went back to work. He didn't like buying whiskey, but he said it was the Christian thing to do."

"We're not talking about buying whiskey; we're talking about killing a man. Two men. Do you think you were right?"

"I was true," she said. She tossed the rope to me and went to the house.

True to what? I shook out a loop, tossed it at the snubbing post, and missed. She wasn't leaving the ranch and she wasn't going to let me punish her. Pug called to me to bring him more nails. I put the rope up, carried a bucket of nails to Pug, and steadied the ladder. After dinner, Pug carried the ladder to the house to nail down loose shingles and replace missing ones. I helped, which meant watching, fetching a shingle, or helping him move the ladder.

When he was satisfied that the house roof would turn one more rain, he went to the corral to finish the job Rista had started. I wondered what she was doing, but I didn't want to hear any more of her excuses. Pug shod while I held the horse he worked on. Pug's hands were thick, calloused, with broken nails, his fingers misshapen like they had been caught in a rope.

When he finished with the shoes, Pug examined the horses. "Better worm them while we got them up," he said. While Pug held the horses' mouths open, I squeezed medicine from a tube on to the back of their tongues. "In the old days me and Paco used to chew tobacco, spit it in a bucket when we were done with it, and poke it up the horse's ass to worm it. When things got a little better we'd hold the horse's head up and pour a quart of sorghum molasses down its throat. Do that for three or four days and he'd get to like it. Then we'd pour a quart of mineral oil down his throat, and he'd gulp it down before he knew what it was. The worms'd come out to play and have a good time in that oil and they'd slide right out. This stuff Rista uses gives them a bellyache, and they don't like it."

"Did you ever tell her that?"

"Lots of times."

"Pug, you knew Rista killed Odis. And Stoddard. You never said anything to anyone. Didn't the sheriff ever talk to you?"

"Ralph knew I would lie to protect Rista if I had to."

"Why?"

"Because I ride for the brand. You have your country; I have mine."

▲▼▲

After a supper of bean dumplings, I followed Rista into the sitting room. "Why did Dalhart paint his name on the water tower in Red Rock?"

"A man likes to leave his mark on something. Dad, Bamanitious, Knock, Paco, Pug, all left their mark on this place and on each other. Stoddard, Smiley, Odis left their mark on the whole county. I left my mark on Cassie, and I reckon on you."

How would I get it off? Did I want to pass that mark to children?

Rista showed me Odis' safe where he had kept his good hat, spurs, and boots. "That was your grandfather's. I reckon he would want you to have it."

I carried it to the bedroom. It wasn't as heavy as I expected or as safe—a metal cabinet with a combination lock. The combination was painted on the side. Inside the safe were letters Rista had written to me and Mother that were returned unopened. Did Rista forget the letters were in the safe?

The letters were from a grandmother to a grandchild about horses, calves, fawns, coyotes, an armadillo she had seen taking a mud bath, a cottontail she rescued from a bull snake. In some letters she wondered if I had gotten the birthday or Christmas present she sent. All of the letters mentioned her love for me and Mother and the hope that we would soon be reunited.

I remembered cowboy clothes, boots, chaps that bore a brand I now recognized as Rista's brand. Long after I was too old to believe in the jolly man in the red suit I believed in a Santa Claus, because there were times Mother could scarcely feed us and yet on Christmas morning there were presents—watches, savings bonds, clothes. When times got better, the presents stopped. I suppose Mother sent them back or gave them away, but she never told me that Santa Claus was Rista.

Mother's stories about Rista, while true, weren't accurate. She had killed two men, but she wasn't ruled by hate. She loved me; at least she loved the boy who left when he was five. She loved my mother. She may have loved Odis and Stoddard. How could she have wrecked so many lives?

I loved Shana and couldn't bear losing her, but Shana was going to walk away if I couldn't agree that we were a family. She had no idea of the family I came from and the things we did to each other. I didn't know if I could forgive Rista for what she had done to Mother. I didn't know if I could forgive Mother for what she had done to me.

The last week of her life Mother said, "I wanted you to have a father, a normal life."

"You wanted someone to make your life worthwhile," I said.

When she said, "You did. You always did," I didn't know she was asking forgiveness.

21
1952

"There's nothing to trouble over," Rista assured Cassie who suspected she was pregnant. "I could deliver the baby myself. I've delivered plenty of calves."

"It's not a calf. And it's not delivery I'm worried about. I don't want to be trapped out here by a husband and child." Cassie looked prettier than Rista had ever seen her, and more distraught.

"Cassie, Shad is your husband. Your place is with him."

"That's not what you told my father. He could have been sheriff. He could have been someone important, but you said his place was with you."

"Who told you that?"

"He did, and if Shad's place is with me then he'll leave with me."

"Shad loves this place. He doesn't want to leave."

"I was too young to know what I was doing when I married Shad. You said he would make me laugh. Shad never made anyone laugh."

"Cassie, you're pregnant; you're not thinking straight." She tried to put her arms around Cassie. Cassie pushed her away.

"I'm old enough now to know what love is and it's not Shad."

"Cassie, Shad is the father of your child."

"Don't be too sure about that."

"Cassie. I can't bear you talking that way."

"I wanted to get pregnant to get away from here. Shad is never going to leave this place. He's happy smelling like a horse and bringing cowshit in the house. I'm not."

"Where will you go?"

"Wherever the man I love wants to take me."

Rista wanted to believe Cassie was talking heifer dust. "Have you been seeing someone else?"

Cassie bit her lips. "Long enough for him to be the father."

Rista sat down in a chair as hard as her thoughts. "I was always faithful to your father."

"That's easy for you. You don't need love. You don't need anyone."

"Cassie, you have your whole life before you."

"You don't care about my life. All you care about is Shad. You can have him. Sleep with him for all I care. I want to live."

"This is living. Seeing the sun come up and having the whole day in your hand. Seeing horses running for joy, cows standing, enjoying the sun. Doing something useful. I was younger than you and by myself when I saw a heifer trying to have a calf—"

"I've heard that story until I'm sick of it. I'm sick of you and your cows. Sick of this ranch. Living is going to Dallas, Houston, New York on your lover's arm. Going to parties with him, seeing him talking to important people and knowing that everyone loves him but he loves you."

Rista felt a sickness in her stomach that threatened to escape through her mouth. "You've never been to Dallas."

"I have seen the way people look up to him, and it makes me important too because he loves me."

"Who? Who is he?"

"It doesn't matter who he is. He loves me. He had me put on his shirts so that whenever he wore one he would think of me."

Rista forced herself to look at Cassie. Cassie was trying to punish her with a cruel joke. When Cassie turned away from her gaze, she saw again the thin chain under Cassie's shirt. "Where did you get this?" Rista asked, catching the chain.

"Shad gave it to me."

"Shad didn't give you this," Rista said, examing the thin gold ring with a tiny diamond.

"It's just a cheap ring."

"Cassie, Stoddard is forty-four years old. He's older than I am."

"I don't care how old he is," Cassie said, snapping her eyes. "I love him. You had your chance. If you had loved him he would have married you. But you're too selfish to marry anyone. You want everything for yourself. Anything Daddy did you drove him to it because you wanted it all for yourself. And now you're trying to do the same with me. You can't run my life, and you can't ruin it."

"Cassie, Stoddard is a talker. He says pretty things."

"I want to go to sleep every night listening to him. He writes poems to me. 'Special flowers show their beauty after hours.' 'Why is the moon your friend? Is it because you are the brightest reflection of its rays?'"

"Cassie . . ." Rista could not humiliate Cassie by telling her that Stoddard had written those poems to her. And to how many others? "What do you think Shad will do when he finds out?"

305

"I'll be gone. Stoddard is going to sell the newspaper, and we're going to Hollywood so he can be a movie reviewer."

"Cassie, you are not to see Stoddard again."

"I will and you can't stop me."

"Stoddard will never marry you."

"If I tell Stoddard I'm carrying his child he'll have to."

▲▼▲

Unable to think, Rista left the house, saddled a horse, and rode trying to get a rope around her thoughts. Stoddard took confusion wherever he went. She was disappointed in Cassie, yes. Concerned for Cassie's future. Afraid she would lose her daughter and grandchild. Was she jealous? She envied the freedom of Cassie who could abandon her husband, her home, her heritage without qualm. If Stoddard had gotten Rista pregnant what would have happened? She wouldn't have given up the ranch, but Stoddard might have felt required to leave the county and perhaps he would have done some of the things he said he wanted to do.

It wasn't jealousy she felt, or love, as much as outrage. Stoddard had seduced her daughter, given Cassie the poems, the ring he had given to her. He had sold Cassie his dreams of glory, his need of people brighter and gayer than himself, his desire for someone to show as his worshiper.

The images of Cassie modeling shirts for Stoddard, responding to Stoddard's touch the way she had was more than she could abide. She spurred the horse trying to outrun the pictures in her mind, then pulled up to let the horse blow. She had never run from anything.

▲▼▲

Stoddard seemed surprised to see her but invited her into his office. "This has nothing to do with you," he said when he had closed the door.

"Cassie is my daughter. She is married and she is pregnant. This has to do with a lot of people, and Shad may be dangerous if he finds out."

"Rista, I loved you but you would never—" Stoddard sat down and reared back in his chair, spread out like a loose herd. "Cassie loves me. She loves to be with me. I like to take her places—"

"Where are you going to take her when her husband finds out?"

Stoddard refused to look at her.

"Is the newspaper for sale?"

Stoddard half nodded. "I'm thinking about it."

"Stoddard, don't ever try to see Cassie again."

"You can't stop us," he said, standing up. He turned from her glare and looked through the window at the working part of the newspaper. He turned back. "Rista, let's try to be friends."

"How can you imagine . . . . If you see Cassie again I'll . . . . Maybe the law can't do anything, but your subscribers can. Your advertisers can. It will ruin you, Stoddard."

"If you try to stop us, I'll tell Cassie you killed her father."

Rista had not been a piker since she had tried to help a heifer deliver her first calf, but her spit left her. She tried to swallow. She had to prevent Cassie from ruining her life, but if she stopped her, Stoddard would tell Cassie she had killed Odis. Cassie would never forgive her.

Stoddard reached out to steady her. "Rista, it'll be all right if you give your blessing. We can be a family."

Summoning her strength, Rista hit him, knocking him

against the wall. He did not defend himself, and she turned and left the building, stopping at the door to give him a last warning look, but Stoddard was nowhere in sight.

▲▼▲

Rista spent her days outside and when she was in the house she and Cassie shied from each other. Shad thought Cassie was dragging her tail because Rista was bowed up that Cassie was pregnant so young.

All Cassie had read about love between two people, one of whom was married, contained words like cheat, sneak, shame—none of which she felt. She felt love for the first time since her father had abandoned her by killing himself, happiness for the first time since Rista told her he was dead. She didn't want to be owned by land and horses; she wanted to be possessed by a man who filled his eyes, filled his heart with her. Shad cared too much what Rista thought; Shad wanted the land as much as he wanted her. Stoddard was willing to give up the newspaper to have her.

Cassie had fallen in love with Stoddard when he came to see Rista. He treated her like an adult. He liked the way she looked and the way she looked at him. He liked to make her laugh, and she laughed whenever she could. When she didn't see him she read his stories in the newspaper, saving them to read again. The Kinsey Report, the Daughters of the American Revolution turning away a Negro singer, the Brink's robbery, the Texas City explosion, the assassinations of Count Bernadotte and Mohandas Gandhi. But she liked best his stories of Judy Holliday, Bess Myerson, Danny Kaye, Loretta Young.

Cassie didn't know what Shad would do if the baby were not his. She didn't know what Stoddard would do either, but she knew she had to leave before the baby came, and she had to leave when Shad was gone or when Rista was there.

Rista, Pug, and Shad came in from work to find there was no supper; Cassie was in town. Rista prepared supper; Shad made a joke about his child being marked by bright lights. Shad was asleep when Cassie came home; Rista was unable to sleep until she heard Cassie in the house. She and Cassie fixed breakfast the next morning, but Rista said nothing until Shad left for the Big Rock pasture in the truck. "Where were you last night?" she asked.

"How dare you talk to Stoddard. You have no right to interfere in my life."

"Cassie, you are going to get someone killed."

"Stoddard is going to take me away."

"When?"

"When he's ready."

"Cassie, he hasn't even offered the newspaper for sale."

"Leave me alone. Shut up." Cassie ran outside, got in the truck, and left. She did not get home until late, and she was crying. Shad said it was her hormones and told her he would see that she mothered up. Cassie packed her clothes.

"What are you doing?" Shad asked.

"I'm leaving. I don't want to be married to you."

"What about our baby?"

"It isn't your baby," Cassie said. She picked up the suitcase and the lamp she had gotten with S&H Green Stamps and started outside.

Shad caught her by the arm. Rista stepped between them, her arm on Shad's arm. "Let me handle this," she said. She followed Cassie to the truck. "Cassie, don't leave like this. Give Shad a chance to talk it over."

"Stoddard is going to Dallas to see *The Greatest Show on Earth*. There's going to be a party afterward. Linda Darnell will be there, maybe some of the stars from the movie. I'm going with him."

"Cassie, please, let's talk about this."

"If you had gone with Stoddard you'd be married to him, but you want me to end up like you, alone."

"I'll talk to Shad. I'll fire him if you want me to. Come back after Dallas."

"I'm going to stay in Dallas until Stoddard can take me to Hollywood. I'm never coming back."

"What about your baby?"

"You're not getting your hands on this child." Cassie slammed the door of the truck and drove away. Rista watched the tail lights bouncing down the road, reluctant to go inside. When she turned to the house she saw Shad waiting beside the door.

"She's coming back, isn't she?" Shad asked.

"I don't know," Rista told him.

"I don't get it. What did I do? What is it? Someone else?"

"Cassie was so young when she married. She didn't know what she wanted. She's changed."

"Then she can change back. I'm not letting someone else have her. And I'm not letting them take our baby." He jerked free of Rista and abruptly left the house. A short time later she heard him drive off in his truck, throwing gravel.

Pug knocked on the door. "I saw your light on," he apologized. "Shad came to the bunkhouse. He wanted to borrow my pistol, but I told him I lost it. I thought you should know."

"Pug, Cassie left. I don't know what to do."

"Shad's going to look for her. I took the rifle out of his truck."

"Do you think he will shoot Cassie?"

"If he finds her with someone else he won't shoot her first."

Rista nodded. If Shad got his hands on a gun and found Cassie and Stoddard together he would shoot Stoddard. Maybe both of them. And go to prison. In one night she could lose her daughter, son-in-law, and grandchild. "Pug, I need to borrow your truck."

▲▼▲

Rista drove to Stoddard's house, parking in the back where she always parked, parking Pug's truck beside her own. Stoddard sat on the back porch. "Where is Cassie?" she asked, stepping up on the porch.

"She's in the bathroom, crying. It's not what you think, Rista. I can't take her to Dallas pregnant."

"What are you going to do?"

"She can stay here while I'm in Dallas. She'll be okay. I have a housekeeper."

"Stoddard, if I can find her, Shad can find her."

"He's not going to hurt her; she's carrying his child. It'll give them a chance to talk, see if both want a divorce."

Rista pulled the pistol from her belt.

Stoddard slowly stood. "I always loved you, Rista, but I—" He fell back into the chair, slumped forward, and slowly slid to the floor.

Rista stared at him, hardly aware she had pulled the trigger. When she heard Cassie call Stoddard's name, she hurried to Pug's truck before Cassie saw her, before Cassie saw what she had done. This time she did not go to the sheriff but went home and put the pistol where she kept it beside her bed. She did not know what she would do when Wilberg came.

Shad skidded to a stop outside, punishing his pickup in his anger, then her house, his boot heels thundering on the floor. "Has Cassie come back?"

"No."

"She has been seeing that bastard Stoddard Keating. Everyone in the county knows it and has been laughing behind my back. Did you know it?"

"I tried to tell her what a foolish thing she was doing. She loves you, Shad. I know she does. She's just confused. She's so young—"

Shad picked up the pistol where she had placed it beside the bed. "It's time for her to grow up," he said as he left.

"Shad, don't—" she called after him as he drove away in a spray of gravel. She feared Shad would find Cassie, that Cassie would refuse to return. If Cassie came back, Rista would protect her no matter who she had to shoot. She got out the shotgun and rifle she kept in the house.

Cassie came home first. She was crying, and her eyes rolled in fear. "Did you see Shad?" Rista asked her.

"I thought I passed him, but I was afraid to stop."

"Did he follow you?"

"I don't think so."

"If he comes back, I want you to go into my room and stay there until I tell you to come out."

"Mama," Cassie said, falling to her knees and putting her head in Rista's lap. "Someone killed Stoddard. He was going to marry me, Mama. He was. We would have been so happy. He did love me, didn't he?"

"Yes. Yes, he did."

"He said he always loved you, but he was afraid of you. Do you think he was going to marry me to punish you? Or because I reminded him of you when you were younger?"

Rista had pondered those questions, and she did not want to hear them now. "Stoddard loved you. He was going to marry you. Remember that."

Rista stroked Cassie's hair and tried to comfort her until she heard a car. "Take this with you," Rista said, handing Cassie the shotgun. "If someone tries to break down your door, pull both triggers. Don't come out until you hear me or Pug."

It was Sheriff Wilberg who slowly walked across the porch and knocked on her door. She opened the door with the rifle in her hand. "Armed and dangerous," Wilberg said. "You look like you been expecting company."

"Come in and sit," she said.

"This is official business, Rista. Stoddard Keating was killed tonight in Claypool. We're looking for his killer. Where's Cassie?"

"In her bedroom."

"I need to talk to her. We found a suitcase of clothes we think may be Cassie's in Stoddard's bedroom."

Rista got Cassie and sat with her arm around her while Cassie told Wilberg that she had heard a shot, found Stoddard dead, and saw a pickup driving away with its lights off. Cassie returned to her bedroom.

"Where's Shad?" Wilberg asked Rista.

"He's out."

"Where's that pistol that killed Odis?"

"Shad took it."

"If Shad shows up here, tell him we're looking for him. Tell him it'll go a whole lot easier for him if he turns himself in."

▲▼▲

Shad raced the sun out of Texas. Rista and Cassie holed up also. Neither was welcome in Claypool. A newspaper syndicate took over Stoddard's paper and printed stories of Odis' suicide after rumors of theft and arson. Rista advertised for a cowboy; none showed up. Cassie helped, checking the pastures from the pickup because she was too pregnant to ride.

Pug went for the doctor when Cassie went into labor, and Rista assisted the delivery. "I don't make house calls," the doctor told Rista, "and I like to see my patients in the hospital. But I figured it would be useless to ask you to bring your daughter to Claypool, and it might be dangerous. A lot of folks liked Stoddard."

Cassie named her baby Chance because she didn't want him to have a dumb cowboy name. Rista bathed Chance, cared for him while Cassie recovered. She gave him a sugar titty, watched the changing expressions on his face, touched his lips, or tickled his cheeks to see him laugh. She took him to see the cows, to pet the horses, and held him in the saddle when she rode. She wanted to introduce him to the wonders of the world. Claypool would come soon enough.

22
Tuesday, 1990

Pug took me with him in his truck to check the pastures. In Fort Hoggard, water ran over the trough. Pug cut washers from an inner tube he carried in the truck and replaced the leather gaskets. He pushed down the float a couple of times to assure himself that it cut off properly before leaving. In The Burn, he studied one cow for a long time. "I don't like the looks of her," he said. "I'll check her again tomorrow."

In Two Dollar Flat when he checked the water trough he found the wooden cover on a float had been knocked off by cows rubbing against it. "Got here just in time," he said, putting the cover back in place. "They didn't damage the float or rod. That would have been trouble."

Without a word, he stopped at a cattle guard, got out of the truck and unloaded two shovels. "Them other two can wait," he said. "This one can't."

The cattle guards were metal pipes placed over holes where a gate would have been. Trucks could drive over the pipes, but horses and cattle stepped through them if the holes were kept clean. Rain, weeds, mud from truck traffic slowly filled the holes under the guards until they were no longer effective. Using the winch on the front of the truck, Pug pulled up the frame the pipes were attached to, and he and I dug out the hole. When the work met Pug's satisfaction, he replaced the guard.

When we got back to the house, Rista had dinner waiting. Fried potatoes, fried onions, chicken fried steak, and gravy to pour over everything. After eating, Pug left to work on a windmill in Big Rock pasture. It was pumping when we checked it, but Pug thought it was straining.

"I worry about him up there on those towers, but I can't climb them anymore," Rista said. "If the wind shifts, the fan will knock you off."

"What happens if he falls?"

"I reckon it would kill him. Cripple him for sure. I wouldn't go look until I was sure he was dead. I'd want him to do the same."

Rista and I were nailing another plank on the corral when Pug returned. He had seen cows on Comanche Peak that couldn't get down. "I don't know how long they been up there."

Rista called up the horses, and Pug and I saddled them. "Saddle Bullet for me and Charro for Chance," Rista said.

Pug gave me a thin-tailed sorrel. "Charro's rat tailed and rough gaited, but he's sure footed on rocks."

We loaded the horses and trailered them to Comanche Peak. Rista said it was the highest elevation in the county, used by the Rangers to scout for marauding Indians, and used by the Indians to scout for buffalo and horses. The Indians considered cattle a sorry substitute for buffalo. Despite the name the hill was more a small plateau than a peak.

"Give Charro his head and let him find a way up," Rista said. I fell in behind her and discovered why she chose Bullet. Charro was a rough ride and tossed his head as he climbed through the sparse vegetation. Pug's horse was heavy footed and looked kind of droopy, but he was steady. Riding Bullet was like swinging on a gate.

Half-way up the hill we ran into rock, and Charro groaned as his shoes slipped and skidded. Sometimes he paused to regain his balance, sometimes having to hop, moving both front feet at the same time. I gripped the saddle horn and dug my boots into the stirrups.

"Back out of them stirrups," Rista yelled back at me. "Hold his head up and be ready to jump if he falls. You don't want to be under him."

We stopped before a wall of rock rimming the top to let the horses blow. The wall was broken and splintered in places, but I saw no footholds for a horse. I didn't know how the cows got on top, but I could see why they couldn't get down. Rista and Pug seemed to enjoy the view. I didn't turn to look. I vowed if I survived this ride, I'd never get on a horse again. "What do you see?" I asked Rista.

"My life. Try to work back to your left. There's kind of a trail."

"We call it Kamikaze Trail," Pug said without humor.

I let them pass in front of me. If they fell and died or broke something, I'd forget the cattle and go back to the truck. Without any hint from me, Charro followed up the trail, skidding, stumbling, jumping from one footing to the next. When we reached the top, I got off and stood beside Charro. His muscles quivered and jerked. So did mine. Rista and Pug went after the cattle without pause. I had to remount and get out of their way as they herded the cows down the trail we had just climbed.

It took a lot of yelling and popping with ropes to get the first cow to take to the trail and then the rest followed. "Don't push them," Rista said, "let them go down easy."

From the safety of the top, I did survey the country. You could see a long way. Rista pointed out her house and the different pastures. "I reckon the Indians spotted Grandma and Aunt Jack from up here. That's how they found Aunt Jack although Grandma hid her. I come up here sometimes and try to imagine where Grandma hid her and where she was buried." She leaned over the saddle horn, almost touching the horse's neck with her nose.

"I guess you hate Indians?" Almost as much as she hated banks.

"Hell, Paco was Indian and proud of it. He's the only one I knew. Papa was afraid of them, but he admired their kind of life. I think if he could he would have kept this country the way it was when he was a boy. Horses and cattle were wild, cowboys near as wild as Indians, every day was dear. Those kinds of adventures are gone," she said, turning her horse to the trail. "Still got adventures of the heart but this old heart is about adventured out." She spurred her horse over the rim rock and down the treacherous trail after the cattle.

Did that mean she was considering a nursing home? I abandoned all thought of it when I looked down the trail that was scarier from above than from below. When Charro slid, skidded, and stumbled to a stop I got off and led him the rest of the way; let them sneer. Leading Charro was scary enough with me stumbling and a thousand pounds of skidding horse behind me. The cows headed toward water at a trot, and Rista and Pug raced after them to prevent them from drinking so fast that they bloated and died. I led Charro to the trailer and waited for Rista and Pug to criticize the cowardly way I had walked down Comanche Peak.

"You boys'll have to look after yourselves tonight," Rista said as we unloaded the horses and returned to the house. "I'm a bit off my feed." Pug studied her like he was checking her for lumpy jaw but said nothing.

I helped Pug fix a supper of bacon, eggs, biscuits, and molasses fried in the bacon drippings. "That's Rista's favorite," Pug assured me but Rista had no appetite and went to bed without supper.

Pug and I ate in silence and while we washed the dishes I asked, "Did it take three riders to get those cows down?"

"Rista's done it by herself, but it takes a hell of a cowboy."

"I wasn't much help."

"You pretty much stayed out of the way."

"I could have been killed or seriously injured."

"She put you on Charro, the best horse we got for rock. I hoped Rista would take him, but I knew she wouldn't. Bullet's a good roper but crock headed when it comes to hills. You didn't see him rear and try to turn back when she made him climb the rim rock?" I was hanging on to my horse and looking for places to fall; I didn't have time to look uphill. "I thought he was going to go over backwards on top of her."

"What did you do?"

"Nothing I could do but get out of the way so I could ride for help."

"Why didn't you ride Bullet?"

"She's jefe. I'd ride a bronc off Comanche Peak if she told me to."

"How much are those cows worth?"

"Markets kind of down right now. Those would be discounted."

"Then why take the risk?"

Pug looked at me like I was beyond learning. "They would have died up there without water."

"Why did she take Bullet?"

"He needed the work. There's a lot of things he doesn't know. She'll teach as long as she has a horse."

"Why did she want me to ride up Comanche Peak?" They were always giving me tests when I didn't know I was being tested, and they never told me what my grade was.

Pug placed a wad of tobacco in his mouth and worked on it for a moment. "I think she wanted you to see what Doss and Claris and them Indians and cowboys saw."

"What?" I hated that corny cryptic western palaver. I liked sound bites—simple, neat, clear.

"I reckon whatever you saw. Or didn't see."

On television we reached a conclusion every thirty minutes. More often than that on the news. "I'm never going to ride Kamikaze Trail again. I'll probably never ride another horse."

"Hell, Chance, you're all the time worrying about getting the brand straight when your iron ain't hot."

What that meant was going to be on the final exam, but I didn't have time for it now. "Pug, Rista can't work like this. What will happen when she can no longer ride?"

Pug took his time with the answer although I think it was not the first time he had heard the question. "She'll ask me to take her out in the pasture and leave her."

The fool would do it too.

23
1954

Rista found that an oilie checking pipelines that ran across her property left a gate open, allowing bulls to get into a pasture with young heifers. Cassie drove the truck and she, Pug, and Rista chased the reluctant bulls out of the pasture. By the time they separated them several heifers had been stuck, and one bull broke its rod, reducing its worth to hamburger.

When the heifers were ready to domino, Pug and Rista penned them in the horse trap to help them drop their calves. Even Cassie helped, letting Rista pull Chance in the cart that Odis had built for her. One day while assisting a heifer, Rista heard Chance screaming and found him digging in an ant bed. Rista removed the ants, washed the bites with coal oil, and rubbed them with aloe vera. "That's what happens when you ride through someone else's gather," Rista told Chance. "Don't stir up an anthill if you can't stand a little pain."

Despite Pug's, Rista's and Cassie's help, two of the heifers died trying to deliver. Rista wrote a ring-tailed letter to the oil company. A representative of the company came out to apologize for leaving the gate open and to negotitate the damages. Rusty McGinty found Cassie checking a pasture in the pickup with her son, in boots and hat, sitting beside her.

Rusty had graduated from high school, fought in Korea,

attended a community college on the G.I. Bill and had a job as a troubleshooter with an oil company. He hurrahed Cassie about the heifers—wondered if maybe they didn't end up on the table—making Cassie laugh. He played patty cake with Chance and offered better than market price for the bull, the heifers, and the calves they would have borne. Then he asked Cassie for a date.

Rusty looked like he knew his way around an oil patch, a pool hall, or a dance floor. Cassie was lonely and confused. She cried herself to sleep over Stoddard's death, but sometimes she cried for Shad. Once she dreamed that Shad returned, and they were happy in their own home. When she awoke she hated Shad for killing Stoddard and wanted him in jail. Her situation was too complicated to explain to Rusty, so she said no.

"There's a big dance in Claypool in a couple of weeks. What if I took you to that?" Did she dare show her face in Claypool? Again she said no.

"A dance or a movie is about all I can offer you around here," he said, "but I don't plan to be here forever." He winked at her as he left.

▲▼▲

Shad did return, not to Cassie but to jail. Cassie visited him only once. She did not take Chance who was almost five. She wasn't sure she wanted Chance to remember Shad. She didn't want him to remember Shad in jail. Shad told her that he had planned to make Stoddard crawl and might have shot him if he had not found him dead. "Would you have killed me?" Cassie asked.

"I was crazy, out of my head with what you had done and what people were saying. I don't know what I would have done."

322

At the trial, Valton Hoffman charged that Shad Carter killed Stoddard Keating because his wife was having an affair with Stoddard, and that he fled the state to avoid prosecution. Sheriff Wilberg testified that someone had driven to the back of Stoddard's house. Stoddard had gone outside to confront that person and had been shot dead with a pistol that belonged to Clarista Wyler, Shad's mother-in-law. Shad Carter had the pistol in his possession when he was arrested.

Neighbors testified that there was a lot of coming and going at Stoddard's house that night. At least two or three pick-ups had driven to the back of Stoddard's house, but no one could positively identify Shad's pickup as being one of them.

Cassie testified that she was in Stoddard's house when he was murdered, that she was planning to divorce Shad and marry Stoddard, and that she did not see who shot him. She thought she saw Shad leaving the ranch as she returned, after Stoddard had been shot.

Rista testified that Shad took her pistol after Pug Caldwell refused to loan Shad his pistol. It was a truth as good as a lie.

"I took Rista's pistol when I was unable to find my wife," Shad said.

"Did anyone tell you where she was?"

"I was told she was with Stoddard Keating. I went to his house, but he was already dead."

"Why did you leave the county?"

"Because my wife was having Stoddard's baby."

No witnesses could place Shad at the scene of the crime. The jury was unable to reach a verdict but Shad was advised to leave the county and preferably the state. He did not ask Cassie to go with him.

The radio station and the newspaper syndicate that had taken over Stoddard's paper had a reporter in court every day following the progress of the trial. After the trial, the stories continued. Cassie and Rista were usually refered to as scandal-ridden, Odis' alleged crimes were repeated, and Cassie was described by anonymous sources as "slut," "chippie," and "hooker." The radio reported rumors of sexual depravity that included Rista, Cassie and Stoddard, and sometimes Shad.

Rista was in the truck with a pistol when Pug got in beside her. "Get out, Pug. I'm going to Claypool to talk to the editor." Pug didn't get out. "I won't shoot him, but he won't listen if I don't pack a gun."

"You'll go to jail, there will be more stories in the paper, and what will that do to Cassie and Chance?"

"What am I going to do, Pug? Everyone in the county is hearing awful things about Cassie. Chance may read them some day."

"Remember that black blizzard where you holed up against a horse and hung on until it blew over? Then you got up and started cleaning up the mess. That's all you can do. Talking to the editor is whistling in a high wind. It might make you feel better, but the wind won't notice, and neither will anyone else."

What Rista remembered most about the blizzard wasn't the sand or the cold; that was endurance. She remembered how long it took to clean up—replacing broken windows, sweeping and shoveling out dirt, beating dust out of clothes and bedding before washing them. "It's so unfair, Pug."

"Life is unfair."

"It's fairer than the newspaper," Rista said. "Life is unfair to everyone."

Cassie and Rista returned to self-imposed exile. Not even

friends offered sympathy to Cassie who had lost her lover and her husband. Neither Rista nor Cassie read the newspaper. Rista listened only to the weather and market news on the radio. Cassie listened to music until a deejay dedicated "Your Cheating Heart" to her, "She's a Hum Dum Dinger From Dingersville" to Rista, and "Nobody's Darling But Mine," to Shad.

▲▼▲

Rusty McGinty came to see them when he had business nearby, and he seemed to have a lot of business nearby. He brought magazines for Cassie and candy and toys for Chance—a yo-yo, a wooden man who danced when his strings were jerked, a ball attached to a wooden paddle with a rubber band. Rista kept Chance while Rusty and Cassie drove around the ranch.

Chance played for a while with the new toy and then returned to the toys that Rista had made him—tin-can stilts, a stick horse made from a pitchfork handle, chaps cut from inner tubes with bottle-cap conchos.

While Chance rode his stick horse and shot his cap pistol, Rista read of sit-ins at soda fountains. Publicity about Nanette Fabray. The assassination of Anastasio Somoza. The collision of two ships off Nantucket. Photographs of Elvis Presley, gossip about Martin Luther King, publicity about Dorothy Malone, photographs of Jim Brown. Hungarians revolting against Communism. The kidnapping of Peter Weinberger. An earthquake in Iran, a blizzard in Western Europe, an explosion in Colombia. The United States training the army of South Vietnam. The assassination of Carlos Armas, the kidnapping of Cynthia Ruotolo. A fire in a home for the aged, the collision of two airliners over the Grand Canyon. A governor calling on the

National Guard to prevent nine black children from going to school.

Was she supposed to rejoice that a dictator died? That Britain exploded a hydrogen bomb? That citizens died fighting tanks? That Nanette Fabray negotiated a new contract? Was she supposed to send books to children who weren't allowed to go to school? Blankets to survivors of sinking ships? Condolences to parents of kidnapped children? She dropped a magazine and called Chance to her side where he was safe, wishing she knew nothing about things she could do nothing about.

"Hell of a world, ain't it?" Rusty said, seeing the magazines at her feet when he and Cassie returned. Rusty seemed bigger, Cassie quieter.

It didn't seem like a world to Rista; it seemed like folly. Like scattering a herd and calling it a roundup. Like calling every calf a herd bull when half were heifers and most of the others would become steers. She felt a fool for looking at magazines when she could have been watching Chance play, cattle graze, or buzzards soar.

▲▼▲

Ralph Wilberg came to see Rista, "to clear up a few things. We found the gun that killed Stoddard, we found Shad's fingerprints on the gun, Shad had every reason to kill Stoddard, what more did a jury need?"

Rista answered only direct questions. Cassie crept from her bedroom to hear Stoddard's name. She and her mother never spoke of him, although each, in the solitude of their own beds, sometimes whispered his name. "Stoddard. Stoddard." Only the inflection was different.

"I can't think of but one other possibility," Wilberg said.

"The gun that killed Odis killed Stoddard. Maybe the same person pulled the trigger."

Cassie was puzzled. Her father had shot himself; how could he have shot Stoddard?

"Do you have anything you want to say?" Wilberg asked. "I stretched my neck pretty far when Odis was killed. Valton didn't chop it off. But this new D.A.—" He turned his hat in his hands. "I've known you a long time. I know you don't belong in jail. This new D.A. is from Claypool. He owes me nothing, and he owes you even less. I think he would go for the chair unless you and me could make it look like an accident or self-defense."

"Do I need to see a lawyer?" Rista asked.

"You need to get straight with me," Wilberg said. He and Rista looked at each other for a long time then he slowly got to his feet, put his hat on his head, and walked out without saying goodbye.

When Rista looked up she saw Cassie standing in the doorway. "I thought you were asleep," she said.

"You killed my father. You killed Stoddard."

"You don't understand," Rista said.

"Why didn't you shoot me too, Mother?" Cassie said. "You were jealous of me and Stoddard. You couldn't bear to see me marry the man you loved so you shot him. Why didn't you shoot me too?"

"Shad would have killed Stoddard, maybe both of you."

"But he didn't. You did."

"I did it for you."

"Don't you ever say that to me. Don't you dare. Did you kill Daddy for me too? Or did you kill my father so that you could have Stoddard? Only he didn't want you. I was the one he wanted."

327

"Cassie, we have to trust each other."

"I'll never trust you. And you better not trust me either. You killed Stoddard because he loved me instead of you, and you couldn't bear for me to have him. If I tell the district attorney, he'll put you away where you can never harm anyone else."

Rista knew that if Cassie talked, she might never again see her land, her horses and cattle gleaming after a rain. "Cassie, some day all this will be yours."

"I don't want it. I hate this place. I can't stand to look at you."

"Cassie, please don't take Chance away from me."

Cassie smiled scornfully at her mother. "You must think he looks like Stoddard."

"He looks like you."

"I don't want him to have anything to do with you. You'll ruin his life the way you ruined mine."

"I never meant to hurt you. I did what I thought—"

"Don't you dare say you did it for me. I want this ranch to go to Chance. Write it. Write it now, or I'll go to the law."

"I'll write a promise to leave the ranch to Chance, and I'll have a lawyer make a will when I get to Claypool."

"And I want the oil lease money."

"Cassie—" She needed the money to buy Red Rock. Through a Claypool lawyer she had been quietly buying the town a lot at a time.

"Rusty told me you got a check for a new oil lease. I want it."

Rista endorsed the check. "Cassie, you can live in Red Rock. You always wanted—"

"I wish I could tell you how much I hate you and everything about you. If I thought you would get the electric chair and they'd leave me out of it I'd talk to the law right now. I don't ever want to sit in the witness chair again, not even to see you dead."

Cassie went to her room. Rista sat in the sitting room thinking how, when Cassie calmed down, she would explain what she had done. If Cassie understood she could forgive her some day. Rista wondered if she could ever forgive herself.

Two days later when Rista returned to the house at dusk she found Cassie and Chance gone, their clothes and Chance's toys missing. Cassie had left a note. "If you try to find me or Chance I will tell everything I know." On Rista's bed lay a limp-necked stuffed rabbit. Chance had left his favorite toy.

Pug and I spent the morning cleaning out the water troughs. Pug pointed out armadillos, jackrabbits, deer, but I wasn't listening. Shana ran through my mind like a bad jingle. I was miserable without her. Would we make each other happy if I married her? Would we make happy children? Or would we pile up hurts that we could not forgive? "Pug, do you ever see your family?"

"They drifted away. Depression. Drought. Debt. Me and my brothers had to leave because Mama couldn't feed us. My sisters married soon as they could. After the bank foreclosed, Mom lived with one daughter then the other. I sent her money when Rista could pay me."

Pug was so rooted that I had forgotten he didn't have much of a family either. "You don't have any family left?"

"This place is my family." Was he asking me for a job or was he claiming kinship?

"Pug—" I stammered.

"We're not friends," Pug said. "I don't particularly like you. But you don't have to like family. You just have to belong."

That was the problem. How did you learn to belong?

▲▼▲

After dinner, Rista and I went to look for Aunt Jack. While I

331

walked around looking for depressions or places where the earth had been disturbed, Rista told again how her grandmother had hidden JackieLou and run for the house to warn her husband and son and to draw the Indians from JackieLou's hiding place. The neighbors who buried Aunt Jack had returned to Tennessee and neither Doss nor Claris had been able to find her grave.

"Dad was six years old and scared. All he remembered was that the Indians had scalped Aunt Jack and that the neighbors buried her in the trees where they found her. Hell, she could have been a mile from the house. I started with the tallest trees closest to the house."

"Maybe her mother hid her in bushes," I said. "They'd be trees now."

"That's what I been thinking."

"How long have you been looking?" I asked, digging at the hard ground. When I broke the surface with the pickaxe and reached a hard crust that had never been disturbed, I looked for another site.

Rista followed, driving a piece of sucker rod in the ground at each spot. "One of my first memories is riding behind Dad on a horse looking for Aunt Jack. I think they buried her deep so the wolves wouldn't dig her up. Still, the ground would have settled over the years."

"Why is it so important that you find her?"

"We're family," she said, stumbling over the rough ground. She seemed older, stiffer today, leaning over the rods she carried. She didn't put them down so she didn't have to bend over to pick them up. She had seemed stronger the first time I saw her. Had that been a pose? Had she realized she had nothing to fear from me? "We belong together."

That was the lead I waited for. "When I go home, I'd like to know someone was looking after you," I said.

"I've always taken care of myself. I intend to continue."

"You old hypocrite. You've depended on Pug most of his life and Paco before him."

She nodded. "Hypocrite just means you want more than one thing. Like wanting to own land and honor your parents. Doing right by saving the ranch meant doing wrong by raising baldies that can't walk to water but that you don't have to chew. There's something unnatural about a cow without horns, like a stag steer that's not completely castrated. We'll all be baldies soon enough."

"Was Odis a hypocrite?"

"Odis was your grandfather. You might try calling him that." She studied the horizon for a moment. "Smiley Wooten wasn't complex enough to be a hypocrite. He was the same in the bank or courthouse as he was in church. They were just tools to get what he wanted. Odis wanted to decide what was right and wrong for everybody, including himself, but he didn't have a bank or courthouse or church to back him. When Odis felt the cinch tighten he'd buck into a bog. He bucked through a barbed-wire fence, caught his guts on the wire and ended up nothing but hide."

"You wanted to decide what was right and wrong for Pug, for Odis, for Stoddard."

"Odis covered up his messes like a cat. I couldn't have helped him, if he had let me. I always felt bad about Stoddard. I might could have done something with him but I would have had to put a twitch on his nose to do it. You put work horses in the horse trap, throw them some corn now and then. Show horses you have to keep in the barn, feed them special oats

333

measured out by hand, pamper them so the vet only has to look at them once a week. Stoddard wanted to be a show horse, but he didn't have the show so he swatted flies in the show barn with the cloud watchers."

"What are cloud watchers?" I hit crust and tried another place. Rista tottered after me.

"Horse that holds its head too high to watch cattle. I should have put a martingale on him. If a horse can't see cows, what's it good for?"

"Show."

"You got it, cowboy. And a parade horse always follows the clowns."

"Did Stoddard love my mother?"

"Stoddard loved excitement and she was part of that. I wasn't made for excitement; I was made to be useful."

"Did you love Stoddard?"

"He was the only foolish thing I ever allowed in my life. A puppy would have been smarter."

"Why didn't you marry him?"

"Papa told me not to marry a man with small hands, and Stoddard had small hands." I waited for a reasonable answer. "I've never trusted coat-and-tie men and Stoddard was high stocking. His shoes were always shined, but I had to brush the hair out of his eyes. I couldn't abide the me he would have turned me into—slick hands, lady nails, hair in a pile. I near cried when you came in here looking like a banker."

"You didn't like the way he wanted you to look?"

"It was who he wanted me to look like. He was in awe of sparklies. He would have invited folks like that into our house

334

for our friends and children to stare at—trinkets, good for nothing except to be ogled."

Being ogled was the point. If you opened a business, celebrated an anniversary, honored someone for sacrifice or achievement, you hired "trinkets" to draw attention to the event. At the station's last anniversary we had a port-a-princess best known for her divorce and an actress best known for her affair with a politician.

"Pug's sister starved to death, she and her baby, and Stoddard wrote a headline about the Prince of Wales letting someone else be king. Did anyone starve because the prince didn't become king? An honest man stole one of my calves to feed his family, and Stoddard had a whole page of pictures and stories about the Dionne quintuplets. Germany occupied the Rhineland and Stoddard gave more space to The Great Ziegfeld. Stoddard threw about as much dust as he did light."

If Stoddard had to choose between winning a Pulitzer and keeping his newspaper in the black, I knew which he would choose. So would I. It would be wonderful if he could do both, but perhaps Stoddard didn't have that kind of talent, or courage. Few people did. "You could have turned this ranch into a museum for Longhorns and cowboys like Paco and your father. You chose to provide what the market wanted."

Rista wasn't a willing target. "If I hadn't improved the cattle, not even an oil well could have saved the ranch. Stoddard wasn't trying to save the newspaper; he used the paper to buy favor with people."

Rista led me around all day, telling me where to dig, sometimes attacking the ground herself. I stopped digging and leaned on the shovel to catch my breath. "Did you ever subscribe to a paper? You don't own a TV."

"I'd rather sit on the top rail of the corral and watch the moon rise or sit on a horse and look at Six Mile Draw when it used to run all the time."

Rista could hardly imagine life outside the county; when I was a child on TV I had seen Kenya, the Congo, the Suez Canal, Algeria, Vietnam, Cambodia and places she had never heard of. "I saw a man walk on the moon."

"Paco spent a lot of nights lying on the ground or sitting on the corral and looking at the moon. I reckon he knew more about the moon than anybody I know. Maybe more than the man who walked on it."

"Did he know how far he could hit a golf ball on the moon?"

"Paco knew you planted potatoes in the dark of the moon, cut hair or mane in the full of the moon. If you saw your shadow in the moonlight you'd see a clear sky when the sun rose. If you conceived a child in the full of the moon she'd have four faces. I know Cassie had more than one."

"There are children in the world whose only knowledge of horses is what they've seen on TV."

"Then they know about as much about horses as Stoddard did. When he found a horse hard to ride he called it a dragon."

I had ridden a few horses into dragons myself. The army shipped old ammo across the state to be destroyed. We knew it wasn't hazardous and stated that, but we reported the progress of the convoy every day. We also produced storm warnings that saved lives, special reports that served justice, news programs that called attention to abuses of power. "You have no idea how scary it can be on a slow news day, fearing the competition might have a big story."

"I've been scared my whole life. Scared I'd lose this place. That I wouldn't measure up to the folks who gave it to me. The only difference between me and my mother is that I slapped a saddle on it. You either ride fear or it rides you."

It was easy for Rista to talk. She had the ranch, she had Pug, she had a mother and father and grandparents. I had tried to hang on to Rusty and a half-dozen other potential fathers, but they had all left. Then Mother left, and I was alone, or would be when Shana left. Shad wouldn't claim me. Rista would but I was afraid of her embrace. Nobody left her; she shot them. "Was Stoddard my father?" Did I want Stoddard to be my father?

"I don't know, Chance. I wish I did. In some ways you're like him, trying to turn a cow pie into a carnival."

"Do I look like him?"

"You look like your mother. You act like Stoddard."

How was I to know how to act? She had killed my grandfather and killed or driven away my father. "If you don't know your own father, what can you count on?"

"I'll tell you what you can count on, like Papa told me. You can always count on your ribs." She poked me. "There's one, two, three . . . ."

25
1959

When Cassie took to the tules, Sheriff Wilberg came to see Rista again. Folks said Rista and Cassie had lied to keep Shad out of jail, that Cassie had rejoined Shad, that the two of them were singing with their tails up and wagging their chins at the law. The rumors damaged Wilberg's and the D.A.'s chances for reelection. Ralph wanted to know where Cassie was, threatening to charge Rista with Odis' murder if she didn't tell. "I'll tell the court that I told you I shot Odis and gave you the pistol I shot him with and you kept it a secret," she said. Wilberg and the D.A. lost the election.

When Rista signed the oil lease check to Cassie, she threw herself on the mercy of the calf crop. She had to go to Claypool to borrow money to hire detectives and to send gifts to Chance when Rusty located long enough for a mailing address. Claypool was waspy. Women went around her like she was a mudpuddle. Men refused to step out of her way. Larry Wooten, who managed the O-Bar owned by lawyers, and Ralph Wilberg, who provided security for the Three Crosses owned by the telephone company, put their heads together. Rista refused to be ignored. "Hey, Ralph, Larry, how do you boys like being pimps?" she said in a voice that put folks into stores they hadn't planned to go in.

A lawyer helped her make arrangements with a detective agency. At the bank, Smiley was distracted and provided the loan without asking for favors. Rista wondered if he had lost his appetite for her or if her ranch was no longer worth his interest. Before leaving town, she bought gifts for Cassie and Chance. She did not want Chance to forget her. As she walked to her truck, someone yelled "whore" at her back, but when she turned, they all looked guilty, avoiding her eyes.

To spare Rista, Pug bought supplies when he went to Claypool to paint his nose with his pals. He soon tired of questions about Shad, and comments about Rista brought a quick response. After he was twice arrested for fighting, Rista resumed the buying trips and when Pug's hair got curly, he went outside the county.

At Christmas, Rista went to the post office to mail presents to Cassie and Chance. She heard two women complaining that their husbands wouldn't let them write checks. Rista said, "Shoot the sons of bitches and they'll treat you equal." A city man was scandalized, as much by Rista's language as by her philosophy, and threatened to call the police. "When women shoot like men they'll be treated like men," Rista said, pushing past him.

That story was coyoted around the county and the next time Rista was in Claypool, a woman not only spoke to her in the grocery store, she followed her outside. "I got some eggs here if you can use them. They're yard eggs and the store wants cage eggs. The last time I was here they counted me out of four eggs. Arky Black always gave me an honest count. I hate seeing these chain stores put honest folks out of business."

Rista thanked her, more for the kindness than for the eggs.

"You don't remember me. Roy and me owned the picture

show in Red Rock. When it burned, the marquee fell on me. Everyone thought I was trying to save my husband but I wasn't. I knew Roy was with another woman and I was going to lock them inside. The marquee not only saved my life, it saved my soul. Roy straightened up and his last years were good for both of us. The kids turned out well. I took Roy's life insurance and bought a place in the country, got some chickens, and I've been at peace. I don't know whether your husband started that fire or not, but I figure you and me got more in common than we do with folks in Claypool."

Another time a woman said, "I got a truckload of carrots if your horses or cows will eat them. Name's Marcella Lucas." She extended a big, rough hand. "You'll have to load the carrots yourself."

Odis had made fun of Marcella because she was sturdy, farmed with another woman, and complained that the locker, the grocer, the bank, the garage tried to cheat her because she was a woman.

Rista followed Marcella to an irrigated farm on part of the old Slash 6. The woman pointed her at a pile of carrots, handed her a shovel, and went into the house. Rista shoveled carrots and after a while the woman came out and took her place to give her a breather. "They contracted for carrots and then culled these because they're not uniform in size. I figure you and me, we're like these carrots. We don't package well, and they'll cull us when they can." She handed the shovel to Rista and went back in the house. She didn't come out when Rista left.

▲▼▲

Rista couldn't afford to replace Shad and couldn't have found a hand if she could have afforded one. She hired day help when she could—men who drove to the ranch after daylight and returned to their air conditioners in time to watch westerns on TV.

One day a stranger showed up looking for work. After the war he had cowboyed some, rodeoed some and now he wanted to cowboy again. He was a blazer with a pickup so new the windshield wasn't cracked, a blooded Quarter Horse trained for roping, a saddle flowered with stamping, silver conchos and mohair saddle blankets.

"Folks call me Dalhart," he said, pushing back his Stetson. He had a tanned, open, pleasant face, and a lean, muscular body capable of moving hay or cattle.

"Is that where you're from?" Rista asked.

"It's what folks call me."

Rista said she couldn't afford to hire him. He lighted a cigarette and leaned against his truck, surveying the ranch. "Don't look like you can afford not to," he said.

Rista agreed to take him on for a month and if she couldn't afford him after that, she'd give him his wages and a reference. He moved his things into the bunkhouse, worked his own horse when he could, worked Rista's horses when he had to, and did what Pug told him.

"What do you think?" Rista asked Pug, who hadn't been paid full wages since Cassie took the oil lease check.

They inspected a fence Dalhart had repaired and a water gap he had replaced. Pug checked the wire—wrapped tight but not weakened by kinking. "He's a hand," Pug said. "Works hard, doesn't have to be told twice what to do or how to do it."

"He's not Paco. What else you got against him?"

"He's got a better truck, better saddle, better horse than we got. What's he doing here?"

342

"What do you think he's doing besides working?"

"Planning."

Dalhart and Pug worked together, were sociable at the table, but they didn't sit on the top rail of the corral and palaver, and when Dalhart complained about the sparseness of the bunkhouse, Pug said, "Better cowboys than you had it worse."

Dalhart read each night before going to sleep but kept the books locked in a surplus army footlocker under his bed. "You ever ride the boss lady?" he asked Pug one night.

"No," Pug said in a voice to discourage further conversation.

"Faint heart never filled fair lady," Dalhart chided. "She's a straightaway bucker, no sunfishing, no ducking and dodging."

"Shut up or I'll shut you up," Pug said, rolling over to face Dalhart.

"Okay, go to sleep. Hell, I'll talk to myself."

The next day Pug followed Dalhart to the Big Rock pasture. "I thought you were working Fort Hoggard," Dalhart said.

"I'm going to after I stomp your ass," Pug said getting off his horse.

"What for?"

"For what you said about the jefe."

"That was last night," Dalhart said.

"Rista don't allow fighting in the bunkhouse."

"I haven't done anything you haven't thought about."

"Get off the horse before I drag you off," Pug said.

Dalhart got off the horse and landed the first punch. He was tough but no match for Pug and Pug pommeled him until Dalhart said "calf rope" and promised he wouldn't speak Rista's name again. That night at supper Rista asked what had happened as both had bruised faces and scraped knuckles. Both reported a run-in with a waspy cow.

When she caught Pug alone, Rista asked him again what happened. "We don't see things eye to eye," Pug said.

"What things?"

"Men things."

"Have you got anything against me keeping him on?" Rista asked.

Pug took off his hat and rubbed the scar where Rista had patched his scalp. "I don't hold the jerk line and I've never complained about anyone I've worked with, not even Odis."

"You complain," Rista said. "You just don't say anything."

After the fight Dalhart sat on his bunk watching Pug through his eyebrows. His face told stories he didn't intend to tell. Pug made a show of placing his pistol under his pillow. He placed his boots, saddles he pretended to work on, bottles of linament and neat's-foot oil around his bunk to warn him if Dalhart came with a knife or club. And he slept on his side with his face toward Dalhart.

On Christmas Day when Dalhart loaded his saddle and footlocker into his truck and drove away, Pug went to the house and asked Rista if he could have the rest of the day off.

"What are you going to do?" she asked.

"Get drunk," Pug said.

"Can I come to the bunkhouse and get drunk with you?" Rista asked.

"Do we have to talk about Dalhart?"

"I plan to talk about where I think Aunt Jack is buried and how bankers are the ruination of the country. Pug," she said as he started out the door, "you're the best friend I have. I couldn't bear it if you left me."

"Then neither of us is getting drunk," Pug said. "Bring a clean glass if you want one."

▲▼▲

When Rista got another oil lease and went to the bank to pay off the loan, she discovered that a national banking firm had taken over the bank. Smiley had lost bank money in Billie Sol Estes' schemes. The banking firm fired Smiley by paying him a large sum of money and Smiley was hired as business manager of the Three Crosses Ranch.

Sometimes Rista saw Smiley on the fence line. She checked one side of the fence in a truck or on horseback; Smiley rode the other side in an air-conditioned Cadillac with a governor, legislator or utility regulator beside him and a wet bar in the back seat. Sometimes the passenger and a woman were in the back seat, and Smiley served them drinks from a cooler.

Once Smiley came to see her. He was twenty pounds older than she had last seen him, with jowls and a saddle blanket around his middle. The telephone company wanted to buy her ranch or any part of it. "They need another headquarters," Smiley told her. "During hunting season they have a lot of people who want to come out here—politicians, judges, media people. The politicians don't want a bunch of dirt daubers looking over their shoulder, and the nosy newsies don't want the pols to know they get the same favors. We have enough lobbyists to entertain both groups, but we need a separate place so they don't have to mix except for business."

"You know me better than that, Smiley."

345

"They're going to own this place sooner or later. They can pay any amount you ask for."

"I'm not asking for anything except for you to stay off my land."

"They know where Cassie is. They think Cassie will sell, and they can wait. Why work like this when you could afford to do anything you like?"

"I do what I like," Rista said. "And I don't like talking to you and that bunch of crooks you work for. Now git."

"There are people who think you're the criminal, Rista, and they're powerful people. They can force you off this land, but they don't want to do that. Sell them your grandfather's ranch, and they'll leave you alone."

"If they try to force me off any part of my land I can't get them all, but I can damn sure get you, and you won't be the last."

Rista plowed up the road to her house and placed boulders and No Trespassing signs across it. She drove to the employment office in Claypool, hired every able-bodied man available, gave them picks and shovels and set them looking for Aunt Jack's grave. They found nothing, but Rista swore she would die on her land and would lie in the Bone Yard and so would Aunt Jack.

26
Thursday, 1990

I was awakened in the night by a sound. I listened for a while and then investigated. I listened outside Rista's door. Labored breathing. I knocked on the door and called. There was no answer. I opened the door and looked inside. I could hear her gasping for breath but could not see her in the darkness.

I went to the kitchen and turned on the light to look for the keys to the car. They were missing from their nail. So were the keys to Rista's truck. Using the light from my bedroom and the kitchen I returned to her room. In the dimness I could see her eyes. She was awake. "Rista, I need the keys to my car." She didn't speak but shook her head no. "I'm going to take you to the hospital."

"No," she gasped.

I looked on the surfaces around her bed for the keys, then checked the nails in the wall. "I'm going to town to call an ambulance."

This "no" was louder, but I didn't take heart from it.

I'd have to take Pug's truck. I ran to the bunkhouse, opened the door, and flipped on the light. Pug was instantly awake. "I need the keys to your truck. I need to take Rista to the hospital."

Pug slipped on his hat, shirt, jeans, boots. "Does Rista want me to take her to the hospital?"

I groaned. "We don't have much time. Give me your keys."

Pug slipped into his jacket, put his keys in his pocket, and started to the house. I followed. Pug opened the door and went inside but stopped in the kitchen where he had eaten every day of his adult life. "Rista, do you want me to take you to the hospital?" he asked softly.

I caught him by the arm and tried to drag him into her bedroom. He brushed off my arm. I caught him again, determined that he would see her. When I dragged him into the bedroom I thought he would take charge. Instead he kneeled beside her bed. "Do you want to go to the hospital, Rista?" She shook her head no.

"She's dying," I said, furious at both of them playing master and servant. "Give me your keys. I have to get her to the hospital."

Pug slowly stood. "She's jefe. You're a greenhorn, button."

Angrily I looked around the room. No keys, no telephone, no 911, no neighbors. I was captive to Rista's stubbornness. I looked at Rista—immune to reason. I turned to Pug to make another appeal—deaf to entreaty. I leaned against the wall and stared at her.

With one hand she motioned me closer. I kneeled beside Pug. She gasped to catch her breath. "Outside," she croaked.

"She wants to go outside," Pug said. "Get a quilt."

I jerked the quilt off my bed and by the time I returned to her bedroom, Pug had placed her in a chair and picked her up, chair and all.

"It's freezing out there," I protested.

"Throw the quilt over her," Pug said.

I threw the quilt over her, then took one side of the chair, and

348

we carried her into the yard, our breaths drowning out hers. The moon was big and so bright Rista made a shadow on the ground. The barn gleamed under the light and the ranch shimmered. Two horses had come to the corral for water, and they snuffed and blew and noisily drank, then stood watching over us. Pug tipped the ladderback chair so that Rista could breathe more easily.

When Rista could no longer hold herself erect, Pug sat in the chair and held her. We both knew she had been dead a long time when Pug carried her in the house and laid her on her bed. I spread the quilt over her. This was what I wanted, wasn't it? Rista dead and the ranch mine? What the hell was I going to do now?

Pug handed me the keys to both trucks. "Take Rista's truck," he said. "It's licensed."

Anger boiled in my throat at their collusion, then quickly subsided. "Might as well wait for morning," I said.

"She'll want to be buried here. It's not as easy as it used to be. Legally."

"I'll take care of it."

"I'll make coffee," Pug said. "When my time comes I hope to die by surprise. I want the expression on my face to be, do what? Me?"

"Did you know how sick she was?" I asked.

"I saw it a couple of times. I don't know how many times I didn't see it," Pug said. "That's why I called you."

"You called me?"

"Rista has been hanging on waiting for you."

"Did she know you called me?"

"I wanted her to think coming to see her was your idea.

Seeing you on this ranch has been tonic. I hadn't see her this spry in years."

"And it killed her."

"She lived the way she wanted to live and died the way she wanted to die. How many people can say that?"

"I never called her Grandmother."

"She forgave you. She'd forgive you anything."

"She didn't forgive Odis." Or Stoddard, I thought.

"Sure she did." I gave him a doubtful look. "She shot him; it didn't mean she didn't forgive him. Every year on their anniversary she goes to the Bone Yard, pours whiskey on his grave, and leaves a cracker."

"A cracker?" I asked. Pug shrugged.

"She wouldn't die until you got here. Then she realized she was going to have to live a little longer because you were going to sell the ranch and that telephone bunch wanted it."

There was an appeal to her world—the certainty of the land that endured, the solid reality of horses and cows. Days that stretched into years. My days were measured in thirty-minute segments with commercial breaks. In my world, a morning without being the bad guy was a good morning. My beeper or telephone rang constantly calling me to placate clients, pamper talent, mediate disputes. I didn't remember the last time I had enjoyed the moon. There was also reality. Rista had left us short handed and afoot. "Pug, I can't run this place. This is the past. Television is the future. It's where things happen. It's where I belong."

"Rista wanted you to know the place before you sold it. To know what you were selling. She never intended to saddle you with it."

Pug poured coffee and we stared into our cups, sipping and staring for a long time. "Didn't you ever want to come over here and break down her door?" I asked.

"I figure I was what she needed me to be," Pug said.

"It doesn't bother you that Odis, Stoddard, Dalhart—"

"I'd've killed Dalhart for the way he talked, before Rista shot him for trying to take over her place."

I looked out the window at the moon and wondered why the coyotes weren't wailing. Where were the special effects?

"I was the one with her at the end. I was with her most of her life."

I was startled at how close Pug was to breaking down or breaking the furniture.

"Rista was my life. I've lived on this ranch since I was thirteen. And I loved her just as long. I've always done the work I loved to do, and I've done it with people I wanted to be with. What more could she give me? If I'd had the money, I'd've paid her to work here."

Pug got a cup of coffee and stood staring at the darkness inside the room where Rista lay. "Mother had kind of a school at the Three Crosses. The first time I went to school in Red Rock I didn't have a tablet or pencils. I didn't know you were supposed to stand up when the teacher rang the bell once and go outside for recess when she rang it twice. The other kids made fun of me because I was so dumb. Rista told them if they didn't leave me alone, she'd crawl their hump. She would have tried it too. When Stoddard yelled that my dad was a saddle tramp and ran for his house, she roped him and dragged him back to apologize."

"Pug, I'd have been proud to have you for a grandfather."

"You're jefe now and I'll do what you tell me."

It was a strange kind of belonging, being owned by what you possessed and all twisted up with love and true and—I waited for the bonds to constrict. For now they felt comfortable.

"I have to go back to Florida. I can't live here." I didn't know anything about ranching, and I couldn't count on Pug for long. I could hang on to the ranch until it cost me something important. Move Mother here. I might like to be buried here some day, Shana beside me.

"With a bull, it's not the amount of time he spends, it's the amount of good he does."

I ground my teeth to keep from screaming. I wanted more than western wit. "Have they ever found oil on this place?"

"A couple of dry holes is all, but there's money in leasing it."

"How much money is there in the bank?"

"Maybe enough to get by until the next calf crop. There'll be some inheritance taxes."

"I have money in savings, but I can't pay you what Rista owes you."

"I don't have anything to spend it on. I'm too old to get drunk anymore. I'd like to be buried here."

"It's in the will. I could lease the ranch to you while I decide what to do with it. Can you hang on to it that long?"

"I'll hang as long as I can get a walker across a cattle guard. I'll have to hire day help. Hell, I spent half my time worrying about Rista, anyway. Now I can get some work done." He rubbed the scar on his head. "There's money in hunting. I can pick up after them if you need me to."

"Let's try it for a while. I'll have a phone put in."

"I don't want a phone. I don't want the bother."

"How will I reach you?" I asked.

"Can't you write a letter?" I had three telephones in the condo, a cell phone, a computer with fax and e-mail, and a TV station at my disposal. It would take a week to get a letter to Pug and get his response if he checked the mail every day. "I deposit checks in Rista's account at the bank," he said. "They send you a statement. What else do you want to know?"

"I'd like to know how you are," I said. "Move into the big house."

"I wouldn't feel right. I'll make sure vandals or rats don't get in it. In case you ever want to come back."

Come back and look for Aunt Jack? Shana might like that. "What will I do about Red Rock?"

"I reckon I can keep folks from moving in."

"Squatters," I said, surprised to find myself in Claris' position. I was beginning to feel like family. "Did Claris force people out to take their land?"

"Way I see it, Claris saved it from vandals. The land wouldn't support farming but they'd've kept plowing it up until they turned it into desert and it blew away."

"Do you think the telephone company would buy Red Rock? Use it as a ghost town or tax write-off or something?" That would save the ranch for a while. Then I could start selling off her grandfather's place, a few acres at a time as necessary.

"They could use the courthouse to entertain. I'll get Rista's things out of it."

I needed to call Shana and ask her to come for the funeral. I wanted her to see Red Rock, to see Rista's stories and photographs in Ziploc bags, to see the ranch, if for the last time. Her introduction to my family. "I'd like you to meet my fiancée."

Pug nodded, walked to the door, and spat outside. "What will you tell your children about your grandmother?"

I didn't know who my father was; I was still discovering my mother. Shad was right, I couldn't ride with Rista, and I didn't want to. She rode true but it caused too much pain. Her way of life was gone, and that was a good thing. I wouldn't sentimentalize its excesses. I would demand more of life than Mother demanded but not as much as Rista. And I would learn to count on my own ribs. "My grandmother was a briar breaker," I said.

Pug looked at me and nodded his blessing. "You'll do," he said.